JESSICA JUDE

Queen of Vengeance

First edition

ISBN: 979-8-9906231-4-9

Cover art by Haya in Designs

This book was professionally typeset on Reedsy. Find out more at reedsy.com

*To everyone who's ever felt they were too much or not enough,
you're the perfect amount.*

Contents

Author's Note

Wesbourne is a fictional island country set in the middle of the Atlantic Ocean between North America and Europe. It is ruled by a queen, and you can read about her story in *Queen of Wesbourne*, my debut trilogy. While the country is a fantasy concocted in the playground of my mind, all of my books are contemporary and take place in the modern world.

This book is the second in a series, and while they can be read alone, the reading experience will be enhanced by reading them in order. Book 1, *Ace of Betrayal*, takes place before the majority of events in this book. However, there is a slight overlapping of timelines. The last scene in *Ace* is repeated through a different POV in chapter 10, and all following events are subsequent.

The following book contains mature content and potential triggers, including: sexual abuse / dubious consent (not between MCs), physical abuse, assault, eating disorder, substance abuse, overdose (off-page), death (off-page), grief, chronic illness, language, and explicit sexual content. It is not intended for readers under 18. If you prefer to keep the door closed, you may want to skip chapters 7, 8, 22, the very end of 28, 29, 30, 34, and 46.

I chose to include mixed connective tissue disease in my story, a rare autoimmune disease that attacks the framework of the body and can cause severe pain. I am fortunate to not have struggled with this disease myself, but I do believe more awareness should be brought to the fact that many people suffer from autoimmune diseases, including friends of mine. Unfortunately, at this time, there is no cure for MCTD, and creative liberties were taken here.

Each chapter is named after a song that fits its vibe. Listen if you'd like or chalk it up to me being extra. The choice is yours. Access the entire playlist by going to JessicaJude.com/Queen-Playlist. And finally, I am not responsible for any therapy bills incurred by this book.

xoxo Jess

1

"Bad Blood" - Taylor Swift

Lux

I should have ordered a car service. The traffic on Twenty-Fifth is horrendous this morning. The Wesbourne Traveling Art Exhibition has brought thousands of visitors into the city.

To make matters worse, I'm terrible at parallel parking. Blame that one on my too-busy-with-his-new-wife-and-kids dad. I can never get close enough to the curb, so I have to pull back into traffic like a fool or risk getting sideswiped. It looks like that will be the least of my concerns today, though, since no one is letting me back up in the first place.

A roar grows louder behind me, and I catch a glimpse of an old motorcycle in the rearview mirror. Instead of merging into the next lane to avoid hitting me, he whips his bike into the parking space I've been trying to get into for the past five minutes.

He. Steals. My. Spot.

I blink into the mirror, thinking maybe my eyes have tricked me, but nope. The man is straddling the bike, looking quite pleased with himself, and wearing way too much leather, even if he is trying to throw off "cool biker guy" vibes. It's literally eighty-five degrees outside.

"You prick," I yell at him. My car top is down—you don't cover a car like this with a roof—so I know he can hear me. "That spot is mine!"

He tugs the helmet from his head, and a mane of thick brown hair spills out from beneath it, way too long to be decent. It reaches all the way down to his shoulders. A slow smile spreads across his face as he swings a leg over the bike. Then—eyes locked on mine in the mirror—he flips me off. Just tosses that bird into the air and saunters away, like this is all over now that he got what he wanted.

That's where he's wrong, the bastard.

My hands tighten around the steering wheel. I briefly consider backing into his bike. The vision of its crushed shape beneath my wheels holds a special appeal, but I really don't want to scratch the paint on my car.

Horns blare at me now that I am no longer trying to park on what is clearly a full street, but am instead holding up traffic by sitting in the middle of the lane. I shift back into drive and head for the parking garage several blocks away.

Pedestrians clog the sidewalks as I exit the garage. The salon is six blocks away, and I'm in five-inch Jimmy Choos. I mentally curse that biker my entire walk. I haven't managed to get a spot in front of the shop even once in the past two years, and when the opportunity finally presents itself, some asshole has to steal it from me.

I glare at the bike as I round the corner. Sitting there innocently, waiting for its owner to come back. It's older than I am and doesn't look expensive. What would it take to shove it into traffic, let some other wanker run it over? It's not like *they'd* have a Ferrari with a paint job to protect.

But as I approach the bike, an even better idea presents itself.

I snap a picture of the license plate and head into the salon. I'm led to the VIP area, where Taleah is waiting for me. She listens to my sob story and makes the appropriate sympathetic noises, then fills me in on the latest gossip while massaging her secret regenerative serum into my scalp. I have a reputation for knowing everything about everyone, thanks to Taleah collecting juicy morsels between my weekly visits.

When she's done and her assistant starts on my blowout, I open the ALPR app on my phone. It has come in handy more than once since Hans hooked me up. It's arguably the only good thing to come out of that relationship, but it's more than most guys leave me with.

You never know when you might need to run someone's plates.

I enter the number from the bike. It's registered to Jonathan E. Lawson. I don't know the name, of course. There's no way that guy has ever set foot in the Hills unless it was to make a pizza delivery. And judging from the hair, I doubt he's been inside a decent salon in a long time either.

The ALPR gives me his address, and my GPS tells me it's in the Junction. Not that I expected anything different, but it does complicate things. For starters, I've never actually been there before. I've driven past it, of course, and heard all of the horror stories. Houses that are nothing more than shacks. Children running around like diseases. Crime that even the police are too scared to fight.

A movement outside the window draws my attention. It's the prick strolling to his bike holding a brown paper bag marked "Cafe de Olla." He swings a thick, jean-clad leg over the bike. My own thighs clench in response, startling me into dropping my phone.

By the time the assistant retrieves it from the floor, Jonathan Lawson has disappeared, leaving nothing but a cloud of black smoke and the roar of his engine behind. What the heck was *that*? The man is repulsive and the furthest thing from my type.

That makes revenge a necessity. I can't afford to have that man haunting my dreams, taunting me to get back at him.

The Junction be damned.

I'm supposed to meet several girlfriends for lunch. I use both terms loosely, because while we are friendly, I would never call them during a crisis, and while it may be noon, the most food that will be consumed at our table is three blackberries and several lettuce leaves, sans dressing.

Hardly girlfriends and hardly lunch, but I text them all the same to let them know I won't be able to make it. They're nothing but ladder climbers anyway. Now they can enjoy their salads and bitch about me all they want, all while plotting how to use their connection to me to score one of Wesbourne's wealthiest bachelors or a position chairing the next society event.

I ask Taleah's assistant to snap several photos of my new hair. She does not have an eye for these things, and I have to keep asking her to change the angle or move to a new position. Finally, she produces several that will do. She asks if I took a before photo so I can post them side by side.

I shoot her a look out of the corner of my eye. "Don't be ridiculous. Before-and-afters aren't on brand for me." God, what a pedestrian idea.

She skedaddles soon after that, and after uploading the new pics to Instagram, I prepare for my new mission. It's time for a little reconnaissance.

I direct my car toward the seedy side of the city, following the GPS's instructions. It glitches out several times, as if it's giving me time to change my mind.

The Junction is pretty much what I imagined. The houses are no bigger than my bedroom, and they could all use an architect and a landscape artist. Rusted-out cars sit in driveways that used to be gravel but are now nothing more than weeds. The worst one has grass higher than the porch and a blue tarp where a window should be. I shudder.

There are no children running around, which I suspect is due to school being in session. I expect to see drug deals going down on every corner, maybe a prostitute or two, but aside from several people sitting on their steps, I observe no suspicious behavior.

I find the Lawson house easily enough. It's a yellow rectangular box, with a dingy white door in the center. Someone has taken the time to plant flowers in the tiny window boxes, although I'd bet my $2,000 shoes it wasn't the biker himself. The whole scene looks cheap and old, but at least it's not falling apart like some of the others I've passed. I'm not sure how I'd feel about getting revenge on someone who lives in a hovel. I could maybe convince myself they are a disgrace to humanity, living that way, and need to be taught a lesson, but it would definitely make my mission harder.

But now that I've assured myself he is fully deserving of my revenge, Mr. Lawson is going down.

2

"I Did Something Bad" - Taylor Swift

Lux

The cocktail tastes the way my housekeeper's floor wax smells—sharp and lemony. I dutifully smile at Pierce as he returns to the kitchen to retrieve some for the guys. Maeve and I share a look across the table before scurrying to the bathroom to dump our drinks into the sink.

I thought we were going for stealth, but after we're back with the guys in the red glow of the game room, Maeve announces, "I wouldn't drink those if you ever want to produce children." She flicks her onyx-colored hair over her shoulder and sits down.

Heath slowly lowers his glass, but Rhett tosses his back with a flourish. "Easier than a condom," he says with a grin. His gold bracelet glints in the light of the chandelier as he swipes the back of his hand over his mouth.

Pierce cuts Maeve a glance before taking a cautious sip of his own drink. He spits it back into the tumbler. His cocktail-making record has been anything but stellar recently. "Who's ready to play?" He pushes the glass aside and shuffles the deck of cards.

Tuesday nights are for poker, and poker is for plotting revenge.

6

We've carried on the tradition for years. The only thing that's changed is Walker deserting us for a boring life in an Oxford library.

Pierce loosens his tie and deals us in. We submit our antes—the grudges we've collected over the week—catcalling, negative comments on socials, getting snubbed, the usual. The winner chooses the revenge plot of the week.

I squirm in my chair as we play. I haven't been this excited by a victim in a while, not since submitting Pippa Berstein for blowing my then-boyfriend.

Was it the sadistic grin on the guy's face when he flipped me off? Or the way my body recoiled from the sheer masculinity of him? It doesn't matter, because I can't wait to take him down.

By the third round of betting, the stakes are high enough. Rhett proposes a YouTuber who did a critical piece on him, and Heath submits a girl who has been following him around town. "I think she's harmless, but it's still creepy." He runs a hand through his saltwater waves.

"She's actually following you?" Maeve twists her pearls between her fingers.

"She's in the surf shop like every day."

"What the fuck," Pierce says.

"Why does this guy get a stalker?" Rhett slaps Heath's chest. "Of the two of us, I obviously have much more to offer."

"You can have her." Heath tilts his cup to his mouth before remembering the contents. He sets it back down and looks at me.

My muscles vibrate as I throw my chips into the center of the baize-covered table. "Jonathan Lawson stole my parking spot downtown today."

"He stole your spot," Maeve deadpans. She releases her pearls, and they drop against her collarbone with a dull clunk.

"Yes," I say emphatically.

"That's an opening bid, not high stakes."

"It was on Twenty-Fifth!"

"Okay, but—"

"I had to walk six blocks in heels!"

"You really think that's equal to Heath being *stalked*?" she says.

"Or Rhett being publicly shamed?" Rhett adds.

"He also flipped me off!"

Maeve sighs and turns to Pierce. "Dealer decides."

Pierce looks at me and quirks the corner of his mouth. "All good."

I let out a tiny breath of relief. I'm not opposed to taking that wanker down myself, but it will be loads more fun with my friends' help.

As luck would have it, Maeve has the winning hand—a royal flush—which she lays down with exaggerated finesse. She looks at Heath with a feline smile. "Let's take that bitch down."

Looks like I'm on my own after all.

The problem with Heath's stalker is that she got caught. I have no intention of making that rookie mistake.

* * *

On my schedule the next morning, I have Pilates class, lunch with the prime minister's wife, and a photo shoot at the new Prada store. None of that keeps me from heading straight to my bank of computers with my coffee.

It takes less than an hour to uncover more than enough dirt on my target. It seems our arrogant biker has a sister with an autoimmune disease. He also sells drugs on the side. Couldn't he have been a *little* more creative?

The next order of business requires sitting outside the Lawson house. If I'm to learn his weaknesses, I need to know his habits. It will have to wait until tomorrow though, after my assistant, Hazel, cancels all non-important meetings and events.

Priorities, people.

The next morning, I expect Mr. Lawson to go to work. I do not expect that to be before eight o'clock. After sitting across the street for three hours, I give up. Even replying to comments on Instagram gets old after that long.

It takes three days of showing up earlier and earlier to catch him before he leaves.

He's taking the corner on his bike when I pull up. "Gotcha." I do a quick U-turn and follow him down the street in my rental car, since he might recognize my Ferrari.

I'm not sure what I thought his place of employment would be—a factory, maybe—but I wasn't expecting to follow him back across town to a small garage on the outskirts of the downtown district. "Rebel Wrench" is splayed across a sign mounted to the front of the old building in a retro black font. Several glass garage doors span its width. I haven't been here myself, but I've heard the name.

Mr. Lawson dismounts the bike and walks to the door. I do my best not to notice the way he saunters over, like he literally owns the world. He's cocky, and I'm annoyed, I remind myself. Nothing about that man is attractive.

Instead of opening the door, he presses his palm to a scanner. The door unlocks, and he disappears inside.

I let a slow smile spread across my lips. Mr. Lawson not only works as a mechanic, he *owns* the shop. He really is making this too easy. There are too many choices. The hardest part won't be getting revenge. It will be deciding where to strike first.

A quick Google search confirms why I've heard of this shop before. The Rebel Wrench specializes in luxury cars. According to their reviews, they come highly recommended.

That's all about to change.

It only takes me forty-five minutes, sitting across the street. I'm done before his employees even show up for work. A few bad reviews from fake email accounts reserved for these sorts of things, several texts to the loudest mouths in the Hills, and an Instagram post I pretend to share on behalf of someone who wants to remain anonymous.

The number one key to getting revenge on someone is finding their weakness. The second one is just as important—leave no trace.

By the time I leave my illegal parking spot, I've set in motion the wrecking ball that will crumble Mr. Lawson's world.

He won't know what hit him.

3

"Silver Spoon" - KISS

Slate

"Dude, I think my balls melted together." Tyler stops hammering shingles to wipe the sweat from his eyes.

"Nah, that's from underuse," Chris says with a smirk.

"You're just jealous I've got some. Yours are tied up in a neat bow in Mary Louise's purse," Tyler says.

Chris launches at him, but I grab the collar of his shirt. "I do not need to scrape either of you jackasses off the pavement. Get back to work."

It's close to ninety degrees and the beginning of October. I don't blame Tyler for stripping down, but— "Put your shirt back on, Ty. You're attracting attention."

He looks from me down to the street, where Mia Thorne is waving up at us. Tyler's brown chest inflates several inches as he grins at her. "I can't help it if she wants more than a new roof."

"I don't want her thinking she owes us anything." I cut open another bundle of shingles.

Mia is a single mum whose worthless husband left her with three kids and no money, to run off with a twenty-two-year-old bartender.

11

The roof on her double-wide was a piece of shit ten years ago. This spring, it let in more water than it kept out.

"If the fine lady wants to thank me for services rendered, I will not deprive her of the pleasure." Tyler widens his blinding grin.

I sling a pair of gloves at his bare chest. "This is about being neighborly."

He throws his head back and laughs. "If you want first dibs, mate, just say so."

"You're a fucking prat." I swing my hammer down harder than necessary and narrowly miss hitting my thumb.

Tyler and Chris both hoot.

"Dude, when's the last time you got laid?" Chris says.

"Maybe you should go see Laney tonight," Ty says at the same time.

I shoot them both glares. "What I need is for the two of you to shut your fucking mouths for once in your life and get this roof finished."

This quiets them for approximately two minutes, but the second a V12 engine starts purring a few blocks over, both of them start drooling again like fucking morons.

Chris whistles. "Damn, I think I just found my balls again."

We all stop to watch a 1962 pearly white Ferrari California Spyder pass by, top down like this is Malibu and not the Junction.

Ty sucks air between his teeth. "I would give up sex for a year to drive that baby."

"But then how would you pay the bills?" Chris asks in a high-pitched voice.

Ty punches him in his ample gut, causing him to double over. I grab him before he can career off the roof. "You're both idiots," I mutter, and return to hammering.

"Come on, mate. Tell me that car didn't make your dick hard as a motherfucker," Ty says.

I've seen the Ferrari before, but I can't remember where. I've never worked on it. A guy doesn't forget putting his hands on art like that.

"Maybe he was too busy looking at the driver," Chris says when I don't answer.

"She was almost as fine as her car," Ty agrees. "I'd like to wrap that long, blonde hair around my wrist and show her what she's been missing out on."

Chris makes a vulgar gesture. It's a miracle the guy is married.

"What was she doing here?" Ty nails down the next set of shingles.

"Definitely not looking to get laid," I say. No woman with hair and a car like that looks twice at a guy with dirt under his fingernails.

"How do you know, mate? Maybe a set of calloused hands is just what she needs."

"There is only one reason someone like that comes to the Junction." I slice open the last bundle. "It sure isn't for sex."

They both look at me like they're waiting for an explanation.

I stick the knife back into my pocket and shrug. "Money." They watch as I start nailing again.

Ty guffaws. "You must've hit your head with that hammer, bro, if you think anyone's coming to the Junction for money. Look around you."

We're surrounded by houses with cracked and peeling siding, dirty fifty-year-old windows, and porches that were converted into living space when eight hundred square feet wasn't enough for a family of five.

"She's probably scoping out the perfect site for a bunch of condominiums," I say.

Any business that opens in the Junction usually closes its doors within months. A car worth more than a few thousand gets pinched within days. An innocent kid who sticks around is looking at jail time within a few years.

There's nothing around here for a Silver Spoon. Nothing except cheap land.

***

One Week Later

Pop's Value Shop is packed. It seems everyone decided to do their grocery shopping on the same Saturday afternoon. While it's nice to see so many people supporting one of the only Junction businesses still alive, Pop's is a small hole-in-the-wall that never has more than ten gallons of milk in the fridge and only carries three varieties of crisps, all generic brands.

It works for my family, but we've never been picky about the food we eat. And it's not like I'd spend a single cent outside of the Junction if I could help it, not when it can do more good here. What makes no sense is why all of these people are suddenly shopping here instead of at the supermarket fifteen minutes away.

"What are we doing here, Ty?" I hiss. "It's too crowded." We're standing in an aisle that holds everything from breakfast cereal to torch batteries. There are people brushing past us on both sides.

Tyler elbows me in the ribs. "I told you. I want to ask her out."

I roll my eyes. He could bang any woman he wants, but for some reason he's set his sights on the brunette behind the counter at Pop's, with her high ponytail and perky tits, and who is currently ringing up orders for a parade of customers that reaches the door. "The line is way too long, man."

"No pain, no gain."

Fuck on a cracker. I pinch the bridge of my nose. "Then get her bloody number so we can get out of here."

"Give me a second." He glances down the aisle. "I don't want to rush."

I cough the word *wanker* into my palm. His elbow reconnects with my ribs. I chuckle and move out of his way. He follows me, eyes trained on the crowd of people in front of us.

"Dude, isn't that the Ferrari girl?" Tyler's elbow searches blindly for my side again, trying to get my attention. "The one driving down Church Street last week?"

I follow his line of sight. Standing out like chalk on a blackboard is a woman in a tiny white dress, buttons parading down the front. Her shoulders are bare, covered only by the long blonde—almost white—hair that surrounds her like a fucking halo. Her legs go on forever, ending in a pair of heels that look like they could be used as a lethal weapon if necessary. Her exquisite face is scrunched in confusion at the box of protein bars she's holding.

"No fucking way." Tyler's voice has gone breathy as he ogles her over the cereal boxes. "That's Lux Colombia-Clarke. You know, the socialite—"

I know who Lux is. I doubt there's a single person below the age of thirty-five who doesn't. And I'm far from the only straight dude who's fantasized about making that pretty little mouth pucker around my dick.

What I don't know is why she's in the Junction for the second time in a week. Because that was definitely her driving the California Spyder the other day.

Everyone is giving her a wide berth, watching her every move. It's like the lion cage at the zoo.

"God, what I wouldn't give to fuck one of those high-and-mighty princesses," Ty muses. "Show them what a real man can do in bed." He shields his mouth with his hand and lets out a low laugh.

I move aside to let the Reyeses pass in front of us. When Mrs. Reyes strains to reach the box of corn flakes on the top shelf, I grab it for her. She smiles at me, no less beautiful for her missing teeth or snow-white hair.

"Bless you, Slate." She pats my arm before following her husband down the aisle.

"Do you think their moans are high-pitched? Or more guttural?" Ty's voice snaps me back. It takes me a minute to realize he's still talking about the "high-and-mighty princesses" of Wesbourne's upper crust and *not* the Reyeses. Thank fuck.

All the same, I do not want to visualize any sounds coming out of Lux's soft mouth while standing in the middle of a busy grocery store. Or anywhere other than my shower, soap on my palm.

I close my eyes and shake my head. "Can we go now?"

"Dude, I need a date tonight."

"Then go get the fucking number, and let's get out of here. Because I am this close to leaving your ass in this store."

Tyler turns to me, eyes wide. "A guy can't just walk up to *that* and ask for her number."

It's a good thing the store is buzzing with noise, or everyone would be able to hear him. As it is, a mom with several young kids gives us an irritated look before retreating to a different aisle.

I clap a hand on his shoulder. "Mate, you're a fit bastard. She's going to shit herself that you're talking to her at all."

His brows knit together. "Not Hannah. *Lux.*" At least this time he whispers it.

"You've got to be shitting me."

"Come on, man. When else will I get the chance?"

I close my eyes. "Fuck me now. You're not going anywhere near her."

"Dude, why you always got to cock-block me? You going after her yourself or something?"

Lux has moved over several aisles and is glaring at a bottle of juice. I'm guessing the Junction doesn't carry the ten-dollar brand she's used to buying.

Her cheekbones are high and perfectly arched, the skin over them soft and dewy, like an AI image brought to life. Her lips are bow-shaped, like my sister's Barbies'. Her tits are also impressive, even if they're fake. She's so thin, I could probably fit her whole waist in my hands. And those legs. I imagine what it would take to soak her silk panties, to make her moan my name—

As if she can read my thoughts, her eyes lift from the bottle in her hand and zero in on me. It happens so naturally, making me wonder if she's done it before. Like she knows exactly where I'm standing. Like she's been watching me.

Our eyes meet with an intensity I've never felt with anyone before. Hers are a deep chocolate brown, such a striking contrast to her pearly hair and skin. There's a spark of something in them, visible even across the distance between us.

My cock stirs inside my jeans as the seconds tick by. I expect her to drop her gaze, to huff about being stared at by strangers, to—at the very least—snap at the kid who bumps into her from behind, but she doesn't. She stands there like a statue of a Greek goddess, looking at me.

Keeping my eyes locked on hers, I say to Tyler, "I'd rather be dead than fuck a Silver Spoon."

4

"Dollhouse" - Melanie Martinez

One Year Later

   Lux

My mum's mansion was chosen with the utmost care. While most people consider the floor plan or whether there are enough bathrooms when house shopping, my mother only cared about two things—that it was one of the biggest and most ostentatious homes in the Hills, and that it was visible from all angles.

Most residents of the Hills prefer their privacy: gates, trees, long driveways. Sarah Beth Colombia cares about visibility. "What's the point of having all of this if no one can see it?"

This is why she never moved out of this ostentatious mansion, with its walls of windows and sharp angles, even after my father divorced her. She's been through more husbands than I can count since then, but after every wedding—which she titles "the event of the year!"—her new husband is forced to move into *her* home, regardless of the perks of his previous address.

As far as I've been able to tell, none of them care, not when they get the privilege of banging a woman who looks as though she's still in her twenties. If they weren't scared off by someone who literally named

18

her house Colombia Castle, I'm not sure they deserve any further warnings.

The butler answers the door in his penguin suit. Yes, Mum has a fucking butler. I'm not sure what the guy does all day, because it's not like she hosts that many guests or dinner parties. She prefers to go out. It means more eyes. But she's trained him well, because even though I've spent more time with the man than my own father, he doesn't smile or show any hint of recognition when he sees me.

He does open the door for me, however, and I step inside. "Nice to see you too, Hemsley," I say.

The parquet floor in the foyer gleams with fresh wax. I have vivid memories of racing my brother across it in socks while the housekeeper chased us. We stopped playing after she slipped and twisted her ankle.

"Is Alex here?" I didn't see his Range Rover in the driveway, but sometimes he parks it in the five-car garage.

Hemsley shakes his head but doesn't say anything.

"Mum," I call. "Where's Alex?" She must be home, or Hemsley would never have let me inside. When there's no answer, I move to the stairs and call again. "Mum!"

The butler comes over to block my way up the floating staircase. "I will let her know you wish to see her."

I roll my eyes and back away. If he doesn't want me going upstairs, it can only mean one thing—she has a new lover up there.

As Hemsley takes his tired old body up the stairs it would have taken me a fraction of the time to climb, I head to the living room off the foyer. It's been redecorated since I was here two weeks ago, but that's not surprising. Sarah Beth goes through rooms the way she goes through husbands.

The walls are painted white, several shades lighter than the ivory they were last time. All of the furniture is white as well, and to a girl who swears by all things white, it still feels like a mausoleum. There are no family portraits anywhere in the house that I'm aware of, because Sarah Beth is not the sentimental type, nor does she condone the display of anything that might convey her age.

"Lux?" she calls from the stairs.

"I'm in here, Mum."

She stops at the entrance to the living room, hands perched on tiny hips. "How many times do I need to tell you not to call me that?" She's wearing a pleated white skirt much like mine and a cropped beige top that shows off a slice of her tanned stomach.

I take a deep breath before approaching to plant a kiss on her cheek. "Only a few more, I promise."

She holds me away from her before I can do anything else that reveals she gave birth to me. "You're looking a teeny bit puffy, love. Let me send you the link to this diet I found on TikTok. You'll love it."

Before I can object, she pulls her phone out. Seconds later, a chime sounds from my purse.

"There." She smiles as she slides her phone back into her pocket. "It did wonders for me." She pinches her hollow cheeks.

I force my face to remain neutral. It's as if she doesn't even remember the years of doctor's visits and being told I was "severely malnourished." The years I spent hunched over the toilet in preparation for another pageant or society event, believing my size was a representation of my value. Okay, that last one will probably never fully go away.

"Thanks, Mum. I'll check it out." I give her one of my practiced smiles, the only ones she's willing to accept from me. "Where's Alex?"

I imagine her eyebrows would flutter upward if they could, but her face is frozen in time with so much Botox she should come with a warning label. *This woman cannot move her face.* "I have no idea. But I'm glad you're here, because there's something I want to show you."

She grabs my hand and pulls me from the room.

Hemsley is no longer in the foyer when we move to the staircase. Whatever or whomever Sarah Beth was doing upstairs must be tucked out of sight if I'm being allowed into her precious upper chamber.

The master bedroom takes up half of the second floor, but that's not where she leads me. Instead, we turn toward the gift-wrapping room. Or what used to be the gift-wrapping room. Once she flips on the light, I see that the entire space is now lined with shelves glowing with back lighting.

"What do you think?" She moves so I can get a better view.

My mouth hangs open as I survey the purses showcased on the shelves. It's like a museum of handbags. But not just any handbags. *Hermes* handbags. *Vintage* Hermes handbags.

"Victor bought them for me at the PCC gala's silent auction. He's such a sweetheart. You were there, weren't you?" Her voice is pure innocence.

Chilled blood now flows through my veins. I was there all right. "They're . . . exquisite," I manage to get out.

I step into the room, closer to the HSS Birkin 35 in Poussiere porosus crocodile. One of the stitches around the dewdrop roses is still loose, exactly the way it was the last time I carried it. The feature in *Vogue Wesbourne* has a shot of me holding it above my head because I told them it was my favorite.

I spent five years on this collection, starting when I found a rare Hermes at a vintage shop downtown. I know each bag in this room like the back of my hand.

Sarah Beth is still standing in the doorway, watching my face intently. She knows that I know that she knows, but that doesn't stop me from giving her what she wants.

"It's incredible. Truly," I say. "Victor has a good eye."

She beams. I've said the right thing. "I had some friends over for a garden party yesterday, and of course they were all *dying* to see them. Gisele Collingsworth was green with envy!"

I smile and nod, encouraging her to go on. She tells me about the nasty Pembroke divorce, which I pretend to not have already heard about from Taleah. Austin Pembroke took his mistress along on their family trip to Necker Island, and his wife had finally had enough.

"I *told* Natalia she should see someone about her under-eye bags, but she wouldn't listen to me. I'll bet she booked an appointment with Dr. Dunne on the flight home," Sarah Beth says. "Right after calling the divorce lawyer."

She continues giving me the run-down on her friends—all of whom are closer to my age than her own—but I block her out and think about the things I'd like to do to Walker for putting these bags up for auction. Sure, we nearly sabotaged her precious college paper, but I'd like her head on a platter at the moment.

"—so I told John to guess, and he said twenty-five!" She claps her hand onto my arm as she laughs. "I told him he was only trying to flatter me, but he insisted I don't look a day older. Do you think it's the hair?" She runs her hand through her blonde tresses. "Javier took off half a centimeter last week."

"It's everything, Mum. You look amazing." She does. No one would believe that she's forty-nine. Well, except for me, because I've known her all twenty-four years of my life.

She tuts, like I've just said something ridiculous, and adjusts her hair in the mirror on the wall. "I lost one pound last week. Rita saw the change in my face immediately." She turns toward me. "Your father must have so many regrets."

I inflate my lungs before responding. "I'm sure he does. But we're better off without him, right?"

She goes on like she hasn't even heard me. "I saw them the other day, eating at Nicholson's. She had crow's feet—can you believe it?

Crow's feet!" She throws her head back and laughs. "He traded me in for a younger model, and look where that got him. He may be a doctor, but he sure isn't very smart, is he?"

"Right." I clap my hands together. "So anyway, could you tell me where Alex is?"

"I don't keep track of your brother." She waves her hand in dismissal.

"He *lives* here, Mum." When her eyes throw daggers at me, I add, "Sarah Beth."

"Not anymore he doesn't."

"What do you mean?"

She flips off the light switch and heads for the stairs. "He moved out."

"To where?"

"How should I know?"

"He's your son!" She may not want to admit to the world that she has two children, but I will remind her every chance I get if she's not going to be more helpful than this.

"Really, Lux. I don't have time for this. If you only came here to yell at me, you can see yourself to the door." She turns at the bottom of the staircase and gestures toward the front entrance.

"Why did no one tell me?"

"Oh, love. It's time you realize the world doesn't revolve around you." She grasps both of my shoulders with her thin hands. "We didn't tell you because we simply didn't think about it."

I clench my jaws and refrain from shaking her. "The last time I talked to him, he'd been holed up in the game room for six days straight playing video games. How did he go from that to moving out on his own?"

"Relax, Lux. He's twenty-six years old. He can take care of himself." She moves in the direction of the kitchen.

I'm not leaving until I get some answers, so I follow her down the hall. Alex has been declining in the past year, and I am sometimes the only reason he takes a shower. "He never said anything to me about wanting to move out." In fact, I've been worried he is going to mold on the sofa. I planned to try to talk him into a game of tennis—anything to get him out of this house.

Sarah Beth snaps her fingers at Mrs. Uebele. "I need a tea." Only after the housekeeper hands her a glass of iced tea and a napkin does she turn back to me. "Maybe he doesn't tell you everything." Her tone carries a definite note of mockery, like we're on a primary school playground.

I cross my arms over my chest. "So you don't have a clue where he went?"

She takes a long drink before answering. "I think he moved in with some friends."

"Friends? What friends?" I snap. People like us don't *do* roommates.

Her glass hits the counter with a sharp crack but doesn't break. "Really, Lux. You are stressing me out." She flutters a hand in front of her face in the weakest display of affectation I've ever seen.

I drop my arms to show her I'm not a threat. "I'm just trying to figure out where he might have gone."

"Like I already told you, I don't know. He just gathered his things and left." She leans against the counter with both hands. I wonder if it's affecting her more than she's letting on.

"Thanks for nothing." I head toward the front door. Clearly there is no more intel to be gained here.

"Lux, wait." Mum follows me into the foyer.

I turn, my fingers resting on the door handle. Hemsley hasn't appeared to show me out.

"How is Carter?" she says, her face as earnest as the Botox will allow.

"He's fine. Why?" I'm too tired of her games to even keep the edge from my voice.

"I was just wondering if he . . ." She casts an obvious glance at my left hand.

I hold it up to show her that it's still empty and flash her a tight smile.

"What are you doing to encourage him?" she asks.

My molars grind against each other as I count to ten. "I'm twenty-four, Mum. There's no rush."

"I had a diamond on my hand by the time I was twenty-one," she reminds me for the four thousandth time, then takes another sip of tea.

"I know, Mum." *And divorced six years later.*

"You're not getting any younger."

"Aware of that too."

"Some men need confidence that they won't be turned down. Maybe if you try—"

"Or maybe if I wait longer, I won't have to go through so many husbands to find happiness." I'm through the door before she has a chance to say anything else.

I can normally keep a better handle on my emotions. But finding out Alex is gone has tipped me over the edge.

I call him as soon as I get back to my car, but it only rings through to his voicemail. I send a text but don't expect a reply. He's not big on communication in any form, and he abhors texting. I call once more, but it disconnects before I'm even out of my mum's driveway.

Where the fuck is he?

5

"Demons" - Imagine Dragons

Slate

I toss the paper aside and grunt. It doesn't make any sense. We were doing fine—more than fine—until last year. Then out of the blue, sales started dropping.

We used to be booked up a month in advance. Now we can fit someone in with thirty minutes' notice. I had been planning to add three more bays and six more mechanics, but when profits tanked, I had to put them on hold. I thought sales would even out again within a month or two, but they've been hovering in the same range ever since. We got some bad reviews a year ago, but I didn't think that would be enough to scare our regular customers away.

Maybe it's time to hire a marketing expert.

I lean back in my chair and stretch. I need to get out of this office. The room was white at one point, but over the years, it's turned a dingy gray. As the Rebel Wrench has grown, I've found myself behind the computer more and more. If I could afford it, I'd hire a bookkeeper to do this kind of shit for me.

My phone rings.

"Are you able to meet me?" Tyler says. "I'm trying to work through the logistics for tonight."

"I'll be there in thirty minutes." I end the call and grab my jacket from the back of my chair. This is the escape I need.

As I walk through the waiting area, the tension in the room tells me I won't be leaving yet. Chris is behind the counter, red blotches climbing their way up his neck and onto his swollen face. The customer in front of him is yelling obscenities about his bill, about Chris, and even about Chris's wife, whom there's no way in hell he knows.

The waiting area has received more attention than my office, but it's still stark in comparison to what the Silver Spoons are used to. Chrome and leather chairs line the gray walls, a vintage vending machine sits in one corner, and 80s rock emanates from the speakers at a low volume.

I clap a hand on my mechanic's shoulder. "I'll handle this, Chris."

He darts an appreciative look my way before slipping through the door leading to the bays.

"What can I do for you"—I scan the order form on the counter—"Mr. Baldwin?"

Baldwin is here to pick up his Jaguar E 350, and I'm confident this is the first time we've done work for him. His face is flushed with anger. He props both hands on the counter. "I'm being overcharged." A fist pounds onto the customer order like that will correct it.

I cross my arms over my chest and blink at him. Then I do him the courtesy of reviewing his charges. "Everything checks out, Mr. Baldwin." I repeat his total out loud.

He blusters some more. "If you think for one second that you can take me to the cleaners like this, you're about to find out differently." He thrusts a meaty finger in my face.

I stare at it before slowly pushing it aside. "Here's the thing, Mr. Baldwin. You brought your car in to have work done on it. We quoted you the cost, and you agreed to it. It looks to me like you don't have much choice here."

"Unlike you, I have a PhD. So don't think you can fleece me with your Junction tactics." Spittle flies from his mouth and lands on the counter. "That may be the way they do it down there, but that kind of shit doesn't fly around here." He doesn't need to add the rest of his thought: *Where you don't belong.*

"I may not have a PhD," I say. "But I can tell you one thing. If you wish to get your car keys back, you'll pay that bill."

Whether it's something in my voice or the expression he reads on my face, he decides to back down. He yanks his wallet from his pocket and slaps a black card onto the counter. As he walks out the door, keys in hand, he calls over his shoulder, "Don't expect me to come back."

I roll my eyes as the door shuts behind him. Business would have to be in the fucking gutter before I'd want him crossing this threshold again.

Before I can make it to the front door, a figure rises from one of the chairs against the wall. It's a woman, early forties, with the kind of hair and breasts that come with significant price tags.

"That was impressive." Her voice is low and husky. God only knows if that's her normal voice or the one she uses when she's on the prowl for fresh meat.

"I didn't realize anyone else was in here," I say.

Her laugh is as gravelly as her voice. "Ethan Baldwin is as broke as my car's windshield. He thinks he's special because of his last name."

"I gathered as much."

She places a manicured hand on my arm. "I've heard things about you, you know." Her long red nails trail up my arm. I'm not wearing my jacket yet, so they skate along my tattoos, tracing them and causing goosebumps to break out on my neck. "All the women in my book club are talking about the hot guy over at the Rebel Wrench. So when my windshield broke, I had to come see for myself."

There's a good chance she broke it herself. It wouldn't be the first time it happened. I refrain from glancing at my phone for the time. "They were probably referring to one of the other guys, ma'am."

Her smile only grows wider, red lips straining over snow-white teeth. "I don't think so," she purrs. "No way there are two of you this delicious here."

I swallow my sigh. "You really are too flattering, but I need to be on my way. I'll have someone come out to take care of your order."

The woman's fingers clamp onto my arm before I can retreat. "Surely you have time to take care of me yourself? After all, I canceled my hair appointment to come pick up my car." She fluffs her red mane, and it's obvious she did nothing of the sort.

"I really don't—" I freeze when she rubs her body against mine. If the breasts displayed by her low-cut top are fake, as I suspect, they are at least well-made.

"Surely there's a closet back there we can use. Trust me, I'm wound tightly enough it won't take long."

"That's not happening."

Her hand moves from my stomach across my chest before wrapping around my neck and tugging me down. "I promise it will be worth your while," she whispers in my ear.

She's drenched in perfume that probably cost more than my mortgage. I fight the urge to gag. I pull back gently enough that she can't sue me for assault.

Her hand travels back down until she reaches my belt. "When are you ever going to get an opportunity like this again?" Her fingers skim over the bulge in my pants that, despite my best efforts, has grown since she began her advances.

I clamp my fingers around her wrist and pull it away. When there is over a foot of space between us, I say, "I need to go."

Her lower lip protrudes in a pout. "I will be the best lay you ever had."

"I highly doubt that."

Anger finds its way into her eyes, aging her instantly. "I know things you could only ever dream about."

This time I can't hide my smirk. "All the same, the answer is no."

She's still huffing around the waiting area in her sky-high heels when I reach the car park.

My phone rings as I'm firing the engine on my bike, and I answer immediately. "Briar?"

"Hey." Her voice sounds weak. "You still at work?"

"I'm just leaving. You okay? What's wrong?"

She lets out a soft laugh. "I'm fine."

"You never call when you're fine." My brow furrows as I wait for her to tell the truth.

"Okay." She drags out the word. "I'm not feeling the best. I was wondering if you could bring home a croissant?"

"Of course." She loves the croissants from Cafe de Olla, and I usually pick one up at least once a week. "Anything else?"

"That's all. Thank you."

"I'll be home soon," I say and hang up. I send a quick text to Tyler to let him know I can't meet him after all and head downtown.

Briar's on the sofa when I get home, wrapped in the same colorful afghan Mum used to use when she'd get her terrible migraines. Her face is pale, but her lips curl into a smile when she sees me. She turns down the volume with the TV remote and moves her feet so I can join her on the sofa.

Instead of sitting down, I lean over to feel her forehead. It's warm but not alarming.

She swats at me, straining to see the TV. "Move. You're blocking the screen."

"I want to make sure you're okay," I say.

She gives me that irritated look she mastered by age four. "I told you, I'm fine."

"And yet you called me for a croissant."

She pulls the pastry from the bag and tears off a huge bite with her teeth. "Yeah, because I'm hungry," she says with her mouth full.

I sink onto the sofa beside her. She hates when I hover, but what the fuck else am I supposed to do? The images of her curled in a ball of pain on the floor still haunt me every time I close my eyes.

I am responsible for her. I may fuck up at everything else, but I will not let her down.

When I'm convinced that she's not secretly hiding her pain from me, I relax and rest my head against the back of the sofa. Some plant with long tendrils tickles my neck. I brush it aside. "We live in a fucking jungle." There is something green on every surface in this room.

"It's called atmosphere." She takes another bite of croissant, eyes glued to the TV, where a bunch of rich kids are arguing about which restaurant serves better caviar.

"What kind of garbage is this?" I ask.

She nudges my thigh with her feet. "Be nice. I like it."

My phone buzzes in my pocket. Tyler again. I forgot about his dilemma at the warehouse. We work it out over text for the next few minutes while Briar quietly watches her show and munches her croissant.

"Who are you texting?" she says after a bit.

"Mind your own business."

She clambers over to look over my shoulder. "Is it a girl?" She drags out the word.

I push her away, and she falls against the pillows.

She squeals. "I knew it!"

"You're a moron."

This only makes her laugh again. "My big brother, settling down at last."

I shake my head at her idiocy, but I don't have the heart to burst her little balloon, not when she's already been dealt the shittiest hand by fate. If she wants to think my best mate is a girl I'm gonna propose to someday, fine by me. If it's putting a smile on her face, it's more than welcome.

"Does she know?" Briar's toes burrow under my leg.

I finish typing my text. "Does who know what?"

"Your girlfriend." She says it in a sing-song voice.

I glower at her. "Know what?"

She bites her lip. "About your side . . . hustle."

I snort out a laugh. "What are you talking about?"

"I know how you pay for all of my bills, Slate. I'm not stupid."

My eyes settle on her—that ratty old sweatshirt, her brown hair in an unraveling braid from spending all day on the couch, too scared to tell me how much it hurts. I'm an idiot if I thought she didn't know.

I didn't want her to find out, but she's seventeen now, practically an adult. I've tried to shelter her from this life, but growing up in the Junction doesn't afford a lot of places to hide.

"How long have you known?" I say quietly.

She scoffs, as if she's offended I had to ask. "Do you think I don't hear you sneaking out at all hours of the night? Or know that we don't have insurance and that the shop isn't doing well, but somehow the hospital bills never end up in collections?"

I lace my fingers together between my knees. "I had hoped."

"Why?"

"Because I want to protect you from this, Briar. You're not like the rest of us. You're . . . good."

Her dainty brows crinkle. "You're good too. Even if you don't see it."

My entitled clients at the shop wouldn't agree, nor would the guys I've beat to a pulp over deals gone wrong. In fact, there aren't many people who would.

I rest my hand on her ankle. "Not everyone belongs in one of your fairy tales."

6

"Drugs" - Falling in Reverse

Lux

I still haven't heard from Alex by the time I get home. It's only a ten-minute drive from my mum's, but that's plenty of time to answer the phone for a frantic sister.

While sitting in traffic, I call Michael Teague, the only one of Alex's friends in my contacts, but he hasn't heard from him either. In fact, he tells me he hasn't spoken to my brother in over a year.

"A *year*?" I repeat.

"It's been at least that long. He kind of dove off the deep end."

"What's that supposed to mean?" I snap.

"Nothing. But the people he was hanging out with, the things they were doing . . . That's not really my scene."

We end the call, and a chill creeps through my veins. If Alex hasn't been hanging out with guys from the Hills, who has he been spending time with this past year? And who the hell are these so-called friends he moved in with?

From my driveway, I call him one last time but am no longer surprised when he doesn't pick up. I pull up my location-sharing app and let out a sigh of relief when the red dot pops up on the screen.

At least his phone's not turned off. But while it's a relief to know I can track him, my breath hitches when I zoom in to see where he's at.

The Junction.

It's been close to a year since I last set foot in that part of the city, and I haven't missed it. Taking down Jonathan Lawson was worth the unease I got from being there, but that is definitely dread gurgling in my stomach now. Still, anything is worth getting my brother back.

Instead of going inside and wasting any more time, I back out of my driveway and head south. Dread plagues me the entire way. I have no idea what state I'll find Alex in when I get there, and even less of an idea how I'll convince him to leave. He can't go back to Sarah Beth's, which means I'll have to convince him to move in with his little sister.

I know I'm getting close to the Junction by the smell. A scent I can't identify is seeping into my car. Something fried, maybe, and diesel fumes?

Two-story blocks of flats line the streets. Many of the windows sport brightly colored curtains, mismatched and hanging crookedly. Tall weeds hug the brick walls, as if the lawn guy got high and forgot to finish his job.

The app shows that Alex is on the next block, and I pray to whatever gods may be listening that the neighborhood will magically clean itself up on the other side of the street. They either don't hear me, don't care, or enjoy laughing at my expense because—and I didn't think this was possible—it gets even worse.

Instead of curtains, the windows are boarded up. What are they hiding behind that plywood? A shudder ripples down my back.

I approach the location of Alex's red dot. I beg it to move a little further. "Not here," I plead. "Please not here."

It doesn't listen. I come to a stop in front of a three-story building made of sandstone brick, which has yellowed with age. The metal-framed windows look older than my grandfather, and he's ancient.

Everything is covered in a greasy grime.

Can I really go in there? I zoom in as far as the map will let me, but I can only see that he's somewhere in the building. No indication of what floor or section.

I glance down at my outfit. At the very least, I should have changed. My tennis skirt and pink top are going to draw attention. What I wouldn't give for a pair of jeans right now, not that I own any.

I take a deep breath and remind myself why I'm here. I need to get Alex out of this place, even if it kills me. But that doesn't mean I can't take precautions.

I drop a pin in the group chat. *If I don't check in within thirty minutes, send help because I've probably been raped and/or killed xx*

Then I wipe my palms on my skirt and get out of the car.

A guy is lounging on the cement steps leading up to the building, smoking a cigarette. I paste my publicity smile on my face and approach him.

"Hi there," I say. "I was wondering if you've seen this man." I unlock my phone to show him a picture of Alex.

He narrows his eyes as he takes another puff on his cigarette, not bothering to direct his smoke away from me. "Never seen 'im."

My disappointment skitters like a beetle, but I couldn't have expected to get lucky my first try. "Okay, thanks," I say.

Before I can take more than two steps toward the building, the man calls out. "I can help you with something else though."

I pull my brows together in confusion as I turn back to him. "What's that?"

A lewd smile stretches across his face. "Why don't we go inside, and I'll show you?"

"Ew." It comes out before I can think better of it. The disgust must be visible on my face. It's so thick I can taste it. This guy could easily overpower me, and I'm having serious regrets about venturing out of my car. "Thank you for the offer, but I'm in a hurry." Like I'd give him the time of day if I wasn't.

I move to the flat as quickly as my heels allow. He doesn't try to follow, but his laughter echoes through the eerily quiet neighborhood.

The building has a shared foyer, although there's no doorman. Not even a security guard. Just a bank of mailboxes on the right and a set of stairs on the left. Further down the hall are the doors leading to the first-floor flats. I might as well start there.

There's no answer at the first three doors. The fourth is opened by an old woman in a ratty bathrobe and slippers. She barks at me for interrupting her daytime TV. I want to ask her if she's ever heard of Netflix, but the rage behind those coke bottle glasses stops me.

That's it for the lower-level flats. My heels clink against the metal steps as I head upstairs. I don't trust the pipe railing—god, the amount of germs—so I do my best to keep my balance without touching anything.

A man in his midthirties answers the second door. The scent of spicy aftershave wafts out from inside.

I hold up my phone with Alex's picture. "Have you seen this man?"

"That's the guy that sold me his phone." The man scratches at his freshly shaved chin. "You the person that's been calling?"

My heart careens off a cliff.

He must read the disappointment on my face, because he says, "You trying to find him?"

I should think that would be obvious by now, but I nod. "Do you know where he is?"

He shakes his head. "I don't have a goddamn clue, lady. Sorry."

"Thanks for nothing," I mutter. I turn from the door as another voice yells from inside.

"Malcolm! Wasn't he hanging around AJ?" A woman with tight black curls tied up in a neon-yellow headband sticks her head out the door. "Yo, wait a second."

Between the two of them, they manage to give me a set of disjointed directions to "AJ's place," where my brother may or may not be. I ask for the address for my GPS, but they look at me blankly.

"Just follow the directions and you'll find it. Big two-story house. Has a purple octopus painted on the garage door," the woman assures me.

I thank them both and head back to my car. Fortunately, the loafer on the steps has disappeared.

I drive to the street they indicated. It takes fifteen minutes, but I finally find the sketchy house, which has the world's creepiest mural of an octopus painted on the attached garage. God help us all if my brother is in there.

A girl whose top barely covers her boobs answers the door when I knock. Her gaze travels me from head to toe, taking in my designer labels and heels, no doubt, and calculating how much they'd fetch on the black market. Possibly my organs too, based on the way her nostrils flare.

"I need to see Alex." I force as much confidence into my voice as I can.

She crosses her arms over her perky chest. "Don't know anyone named Alex."

"Please." I dig my phone out of my purse and show it to her. "He's my brother."

She couldn't look more bored if she tried, but she calls over her shoulder, "We got anyone here named Alex?"

Someone hollers something from inside. She looks me over once more before swinging the door open. "He's upstairs," she says.

Without waiting for further invitation, I step in past her. The whole place is dim, even though it's the middle of the afternoon. Once my eyes adjust, I see why. There are thick blankets covering the windows, blocking all light. Sunshine couldn't get in if it tried. And looking around, I'm not sure it would want to.

People are scattered around like flies on a carcass. The first floor consists of three rooms that open into each other, and there must be at least a dozen bodies in each one, all in various states of undress, intoxication, and debauchery. The smell of marijuana and body odor hangs heavy in the air.

I desperately want to cover my nose, but all of the hungry glares directed my way force my hand to stay at my side.

Catcalls ring out as I pick my way across piles of clothing to the staircase. When I get to the top, I see several open doors lining a hallway. I peek inside the first one. A half-dressed couple is on the bed making out. I quickly move on. In the next, several people are doing lines of coke off a cardboard box.

The last open door reveals a group of people lounging on an old mattress on the floor. I'm about to move on when I hear it. I would know that laugh anywhere.

"Alex?" I step into the doorway. "Are you in here?"

No one answers, but the laughter stops. It's too dark to make out his face, but I know he's here. He has to be. I heard him laughing.

"Alex," I say again. "It's Lux."

"Hey, Alex," a voice says. "I think someone's looking for fucks."

Laughter shrieks. I study each face, trying to find my brother. I can't decide if I'm glad he's here or disappointed. I think I've been hoping that this was all a mistake, that he was at the store on an errand. Not living in this . . . hovel.

"Take your clothes off!"

I freeze. The voice comes from the center of the room, in the midst of the bodies on the moldy mattress.

"Don't be shy!" he says.

"Alex?" There's no way to mask the devastation in my voice. It coats every syllable.

There are no lights on in here, and like downstairs, there are blankets covering the windows, but he should be able to recognize his own sister.

"Give us a show," he says.

The others echo the cry.

"Alex, what is wrong with you?" I shriek. "It's me! It's Lux!" I lurch toward him, reaching for his face so he can see me.

He laughs again as I touch him. Even in the darkness, I can tell that his pupils are dilated. He is so fucking high. Whatever he's tripping on is nothing I'm familiar with.

"Alex." I slap his cheeks, but he just lolls his head back and cackles.

"Don't bother," someone says. "It'll take twelve hours for him to come down from it."

I turn in the direction of the voice. "What's he on?"

"Insidion." It's a guy talking, his words slurred and edged with hysteria. "Want a hit?"

"No, thank you." I try slapping Alex again, but he slumps backward on the mattress, out of my grip. "Where did he get it?"

Another laugh, this one more hysterical than the last. "Same place we all do."

I stand up and brush my skirt off. "And where is that?"

"You're not from around here, are you?"

"Just tell me who's supplying him."

I count three beats of silence before a different voice, female this time, says, "The Wolf."

I blink at her in the dark. "You expect me to believe a wolf is supplying him?"

They find this uproariously funny. "Not *a* wolf, lady. *The* Wolf."

"Okay." I drag out the word. "And who is the Wolf?"

They titter again. I'm tired of being their entertainment. Alex is passed out cold now, completely oblivious to the fact that my world is crumbling while he snores.

"Look, I need to know how I can find him," I say.

"No one knows who he is." It's the guy again.

I perch my hands on my hips. "How can you buy drugs from someone if you don't even know who they are?"

The girl who spoke earlier stands up. I take a step toward the door, but then I realize she barely reaches my shoulder and is tiny enough even I could snap her in half. Thick black hair frames her pixie face.

"It's obvious you don't belong here," she says. "You should go before this turns ugly."

I'm not sure if she's threatening me or warning me. "I need to help him." I gesture toward my brother.

She looks back at Alex, still sprawled out like a corpse. "He's fine. You need to leave."

"I'm not leaving without him."

Someone laughs. "You stay, you party."

"Tell me where I can find the Wolf, and I'll go." I don't know what I'll do to him, but that's a bridge I can cross later. I have to cut off Alex's supply.

The girl's smile is haunting. "Even if I knew who the Wolf was, I wouldn't tell you. Give up the witch hunt and go back to where you came from."

"I just need him to quit selling to my brother. That's all."

"You won't find him," she says quietly. "And if you somehow manage to, you'll regret it."

7

"Face Down" - The Red Jumpsuit Apparatus

Lux

You won't find him. And if you somehow manage to, you'll regret it.

The girl's words haunt me the entire way back to my car, which is being petted by several suspicious-looking men.

"I wouldn't bother," I say. "I'm friends with the police commissioner."

They look at me, and then at each other, before sauntering off, smirks on their faces.

The police commissioner and I don't exactly invite each other to dinner parties, but he knows who I am and would gladly throw a group of hoodlums behind bars if I promised to help with his next campaign.

The trembling starts as I put the car into drive and head down the street, back toward safety. By the time I'm out of the Junction, I'm shaking so hard I find the nearest car park and pull in. I rest my head against the steering wheel until I'm calm again. It all washes over me as I sit there—what I saw in that place, my brother not recognizing me, the fear that tasted like tar. It's all seared into my brain, and no amount of therapy or meditation will ever be able to scrub it out.

I have to accept the fact that I wasn't strong enough to drag my brother from that place. That I just left him there.

I knew Alex used, but I thought it was the normal stuff. Weed, of course. Some prescription meds. Oxy. The occasional line of coke. But insidion? That stuff is hardcore. The overdose rate is ridiculously high.

I'll never be able to forget the way he looked straight through me, like I meant absolutely nothing to him. And maybe I don't. He left without a word, didn't even bother to let me know he was selling his phone, before sequestering himself in that place like an addict.

I guess that's what he is now.

My phone chimes from my handbag on the seat beside me. I tug it out and realize my mistake. It's been over an hour since I sent that message to my friends, and they've alerted the bloodhounds.

I type out a text as quickly as I can.

Me: *I'm here. I'm fine. Sorry, forgot to text xxx*

Maeve is the first to reply as usual.

Maeve: *WTF?*

Rhett: *I'm gonna kick your ass*

Walker: *So glad you're okay! A little heads up would be nice next time. xx*

I'm still a little miffed at her for selling my Hermes collection, but it is the best thing ever that the six of us are back together.

Pierce: *Prove this is Lux.*

It's a good point. If something did happen to me, the first thing the kidnapper/killer should do is let everyone know I'm fine. I snap a selfie, forcing a smile, and attach it to my message.

Me: *I'd tell you all to go fuck yourselves but that wouldn't be on brand for me so I'll just remind you about my party next weekend. Better have those costumes readyyy!!! xx*

Heath: *Yep definitely her*

A tiny smile lifts the corners of my mouth, a gentle reprieve from the weight that has settled across my shoulders. But it doesn't last long. It's already after six, and I'm supposed to meet Carter for dinner tonight.

I send him a quick text too. *Any chance we can do dinner tomorrow night instead? I got caught up with something and am going to be late xx*

I don't wait for his reply before turning the car toward home.

When I get there, the house smells like sunshine and roses, courtesy of Ms. Griffin's lemon cleaner and the fresh bouquets she replaces every Friday. The muscles in my shoulders relax as I walk through the spotless rooms—the white kitchen with its pink cupboards; the living room, where the sunset is glowing through the arched windows framed by blush-colored drapes; my bedroom with the king bed bedecked in a myriad of beige and pink pillows.

I long to flop onto those pillows and succumb to the sleep of the dead, but another check of my phone shows that Carter hasn't texted back, which means our dinner is still on. And if I don't want him to be in a pissy mood about it, I'd better hurry up.

The lights in my closet blink on when I walk in. I scan the unopened garment bags on the left side. Carter remembers everything I wear, so I need something new for tonight. The Gucci bag holds a long-sleeve beige netted dress dripping with teardrop-shaped pearls. I was going to save it for the Bunsens' engagement party in two weeks, but it's stunning enough that Carter will hopefully overlook my tardiness.

* * *

Carter has booked a table for us at Sora, a Japanese restaurant that has literally the best sukiyaki I've ever tasted, and I've been to Japan plenty of times. The host leads me to our table, which is located near the waterfall cascading down the rock wall but far enough away to avoid the fine mist spraying from it.

My boyfriend is classically handsome, the kind that ages exceptionally well. His light brown hair is the perfect length and texture to stay styled all day long. He's tall, but not too tall, and has the body of someone who plays tennis and golf for show, then sweats for an hour in the gym every day. He's already sitting, but he stands when I approach and gives me a quick peck on the cheek.

Shit. I'm in trouble.

I take a seat, and the host scoots in my chair and lays a napkin across my lap. I wait until he leaves before speaking. "I'm so sorry I'm late."

Carter keeps his eyes on his menu. "I suppose you have a million things more important than dinner with your boyfriend."

I reach for his hand across the table, but he lays the menu down and folds his arms across his chest.

"It's not that, I swear. Didn't you get my text?"

He snorts and glances to the side, where other patrons are happily slurping away at their miso soup and fugu. "I got it."

I blink down at my napkin, ignoring the lump in my throat. "I saw Alex today."

Silence.

"He was in the Junction."

This gets Carter's attention, but he still doesn't say anything.

"He was tripped out on insidion. It took me forever to find him, and when I did—" My voice breaks, and I swallow. "He didn't even recognize me."

Carter's nostrils flare as he inhales. "That's not the kind of place for a girl like you."

I can still smell that house, that dank musk, as if it has permeated my skin and is hanging out in my pores. I need to get a detox scheduled ASAP. "Obviously. It's not like I would have gone if I'd had a choice." I take a drink of water, then smile at the waiter as he approaches to take our order.

After he leaves, Carter says, "Have you given it any more thought?"

I search my brain for what he's talking about, but I come up blank.

When I don't answer, he snaps, "Moving in with me."

Oh, *that*. My lips part, and he reads the hesitation there.

A cord in his neck twangs. "So that's a no."

"It's not a no. I've just—" I pause, searching for the right words. "I just haven't given it enough thought yet."

"Too busy rescuing your brother from the slumlords?"

My gaze darkens, and he relents.

"I'm sorry, babe." He uncrosses his arms and leans across the table. "I'm just worried."

"About what?"

He fiddles with the bracelet on my wrist, the one he gave me on our one-year anniversary. It's a delicate 18-karat gold chain, studded with pearls. "Worried that you're going to end this whole thing on a whim."

"Why would you worry about that?"

Before he can answer, the waiter arrives with our food and arranges the plates on the table. I dutifully take several pictures for my Instagram followers, but the appetite I walked in here with has vanished.

Once the server is out of earshot, I say, "You don't need to worry."

Carter's eyes flick up from his Matsusaka beef. "I don't? Prove it."

"How?" Dread coats the inside of my mouth.

He pops a piece of steak in his mouth and chews. "Move in with me."

"Carter . . ."

"What?"

"It's not that simple."

"What's not simple about it? You love me, I love you. We should be together."

I lift a piece of sashimi with my chopsticks but can't bring myself to eat it. "I love my house. I—"

He slams his fists onto the table, causing the dishes to rattle. My fish falls onto the plate. Several other patrons are giving us curious looks.

"That's not what it is, and you know it. You're unsure about *me*."

"Of course not." I lay a hand over his wrist. It's warm beneath his suit jacket. "I'm just not sure I'm ready for that. It's a big step." The biggest, aside from marriage. I always thought I'd hold on to my independence a little longer.

His fork clatters to the plate. "We've been together for a year and a half. When *will* you be ready?" His lip curls into a sneer that reminds me of his father.

How am I supposed to answer that? "Soon," I assure him.

He shoots me a glare as he cuts another bite. "I'm a catch, you know. If you don't want me, I'll find someone who does."

My chest deflates. I hate playing these games with him, but they've become a necessary part of our relationship. "Carter," I say, forcing his fingers between mine. "You don't need to do that. You know I'm yours."

"Do I?" He resists my hand, but I continue stroking his fingers until he softens. He sighs and meets my gaze. "Sometimes I get so scared I'm going to lose you."

"I know," I say. "But you really have nothing to worry about. I promise."

* * *

We head back to Carter's condo after dinner. He stayed aloof during the whole meal, and when I reach for his hand in the car, it remains limp and unresponsive. I entwine our fingers anyway, wanting him to see that I care, that I love him.

Our relationship has had its down moments, but whose hasn't? The Fitzgerald-Smythe family is newer money, meaning their fortune has only been around for a few decades. Carter assumes every insult directed at him and his family is because of this.

It starts raining before we arrive, a gushing fall deluge. Fortunately, the car park is underground, and we're still dry when we make it to his flat. Once inside, he yanks my bag from my hand and tosses it aside. Then he grabs my neck and drags me toward him. I come willingly, knowing it will be over much faster if I don't resist.

His kiss is hard, as is the hand he shoves up my dress. I will moisture to form between my legs. It's not enough, and he curses. "Why do you always have to make it so difficult?"

"I'm sorry," I whisper.

He clamps a hand around my wrist and drags me to the bedroom, where he sends me hurling onto the bed. "Take off your dress."

I do so without protest, trying to avoid breaking off any of the pearls. Once I've discarded it on the floor, he shoves me backward.

"You emasculated me tonight." He unzips his pants.

"I'm sorry," I say again.

"It's my duty to punish you for that."

I wish this was a turn-on, the way it is for many women. Instead, I want to cry, not climax.

"Turn over," he orders.

I obey, and he grabs my thighs, lifting me so only my torso is on the bed. Then he rams into me hard, sending my upper half scooting across the mattress. I'm not wet, and he did nothing to prepare me, so it burns with pain. I bite the duvet to keep from screaming.

He sets a relentless rhythm, pounding into me over and over. Finally, his breathing grows more ragged as he nears his peak. His release comes several seconds later. I breathe a sigh of relief into the pillow as his warm ejaculation fills me.

It's not always like this. We have good sex, too. But on nights when we fight, I'm not supposed to orgasm. If I do, the consequences become even worse. I'm never turned on when he's like this, so accidentally climaxing is the least of my concerns.

I remain face down on the bed while Carter pulls his pants back up. He walks out of the room and returns with a warm washcloth. His touch is gentle as he cleans off my thighs.

When he's done, he tugs me into his warm chest. I bury my face in that spot between his shoulder and neck. "I'm sorry," I murmur.

He strokes my bare back. "Shhh, it's okay."

I don't know if it's the culmination of everything that happened today or simply being in the arms of someone who loves me, but tears well up behind my eyes before I even realize what's happening. I clear my throat and blink several times to clear the moisture. "Seeing Alex really shook me up. I wasn't thinking clearly."

Carter's hand continues to draw lazy circles on my skin. "I know, babe. You're a good sister. Better than he deserves." He presses a kiss to the top of my head. "I love you."

I snuggle closer and inhale his Tom Ford scent, all sandalwood and vanilla. "I love you too."

It's true. I do love Carter. My hesitation over moving in together has nothing to do with him and everything to do with me. I want to make sure I'm ready before I give him an answer.

After pressing one more kiss to my head, he shifts me off his lap. "I'm going to the restroom. Why don't you stay the night?" He gestures toward the window. "Looks like the rain picked up."

I nod, because it will be easier than picking another fight. This way I won't have to bother with ordering a car, even if I'd prefer to sleep in my own bed.

He walks to the bathroom, his bare feet silent on the carpet. I grab the throw blanket on the end of the bed and wrap it around myself before falling backward into the pillows.

Carter's phone buzzes on the nightstand beside me, and I pick it up out of curiosity. It's locked, of course, and I don't have his passcode, but there is a notification on his home screen.

Victoria Reynolds sent a snap.

While I'm still holding the phone, a second notification pops up.

Victoria Reynolds sent a snap.

Victoria Reynolds is a boring bitch who climbs the ladder on other people's coattails. Her dad made a huge investment in Bitcoin back when it first launched, and their family's wealth quadrupled overnight, giving them coveted access to Wesbourne's high society. She talks too much and too loudly, always trying to draw the attention of everyone in the room. She's a selfish pig who would throw a child under the bus if it meant she'd become famous for it.

So what the fuck is she doing sending photos to my boyfriend?

There is only one kind of photo someone like Victoria sends to guys, which means the real question is, was Carter serious when he threatened to dump me for someone else?

* * *

We have sex again later, and this time I'm allowed to climax. It takes too long, and I can sense Carter getting frustrated, so I fake it. He orders breakfast for us, and we eat it in bed like we don't both have better things to do. When he heads to the gym for his daily workout, I order a car service to take me home.

Walking into my house is like breathing again after being underwater. The scent of the roses, the breeze floating through the windows, the comfort of all of my beautiful things. I give it all an admiring gaze, then pull out my phone and scroll until I find the contact.

The phone rings only once before a brisk female voice answers. "Elizabeth Gable speaking."

"Hello, Elizabeth," I say. "It's Lux Colombia-Clarke. I want to sell my house."

8

"Hey Brother" - Avicii

Slate

The gym is mostly empty this time of night, which works for me. The Junction doesn't have one of those fancy-ass gyms with TVs built into the treadmills and hot and cold plunges. We don't need pampering. A concrete basement with several heavy bags suspended from the ceiling and a few sets of weights suits us fine.

I fasten my gloves and get started. It feels good to release the day's tension into the bag. I try not to let Briar see my anxiety, but every time her name flashes on my caller ID, my entire body goes rigid.

I end my session with some lifting. There's no shower in the gym, but I only live a few blocks away. As I walk back, it starts raining, the cold drops refreshing on my heated skin. After showering and checking on Briar, I hop into my mum's old Fiat and drive to Laney's flat.

Laney moved out of the Junction after getting a job at the hospital. Nurses make just enough for her to be able to afford a one-bedroom flat twenty minutes from work.

She's still in her scrubs when she opens the door. They're covered in some stupid animated characters kids are obsessed with these days.

I wouldn't call Laney gorgeous, but she's attractive, with dark brown hair, curves, and a good smile.

"I'm gonna finish eating," she says, and disappears into the kitchen.

We don't usually spend much time outside the bedroom, and I've never gotten a good look at her living room. It's basic—sofa, TV, coffee table. The pair of matching cushions look like they came with the couch. No personal effects anywhere.

Laney isn't home much. She prefers to pick up as many shifts as she can. Her walls are empty except for a single color-coded calendar. This is one of the things I like about her—she's straightforward and asks for very little. With Laney, I always know what to expect.

I'm luckier than most guys. I've heard enough horror stories to know that the majority of women expect to be wooed with bullshit like flowers and chocolate. They call and text at all hours of the day and night, wondering where you are and if you're thinking about them.

I'm not saying I don't think a woman should be appreciated, but that's why I'm lucky to have Laney. She's happy with the gifts I bestow in the bedroom and doesn't ask for more than that. It's a give-and-take relationship that satisfies both of us. The minute that's no longer the case, we'll end it. When she's ready for someone who will take her out to dinner and help her choose baby names, she's free to go. Until then, she's a damn fine place to stick my cock after a long day.

She walks out of the kitchen. "Ready?"

I follow her into the bedroom and close the door.

She slides her hands up my chest, linking them behind my neck. "You seem tense."

I growl in agreement and drop my lips to hers.

She reaches for the button of my jeans, undoing it in no time, and tugs them down. I hiss when she grabs my dick, sliding her hand up and down. She swirls the bead of moisture around my tip, then gets to her knees.

I groan when she takes me in her mouth. My hands tangle in her hair as I rock into her. She sucks me deeper, using her hand to massage my balls. It's been close to a week since we've done this, and I'm coming quickly.

I pull myself from her mouth and yank her upright. We throw our clothes onto the floor in a matter of seconds. After slipping on a condom, I gently shove her back onto the bed and use my tongue to make sure she's ready. When she starts moaning, I replace it with my cock, thrusting in hard and fast.

When it's over, I roll off her and discard the condom on the floor. I'm too exhausted to get up yet, so I lie beside her in bed. We both stare at the ceiling, not touching, but not awkward.

Laney and I have been friends for years, since long before we came to this mutual agreement. At first she was worried it would ruin our friendship, but we're both too practical for that to happen. Neither of us has the time or desire for a genuine relationship, but finding someone new to hook up with every weekend is hard.

"You wanna talk about it?" she says.

I consider leaving—talking isn't something we do much of—but my muscles are already turning to jelly. "It's Briar."

Laney makes a sympathetic sound. She's known my family since she was little, was at both of my parents' funerals, and is well aware of Briar's health issues. "Did she have another episode?" She props herself up on one elbow so she can see me.

I shake my head. "She wasn't feeling well but claims she's fine."

"Did you take her in?"

"That never does any good." I didn't mean to snap, but boxing and sex haven't relieved as much tension as I hoped.

"It might," she suggests.

"It's been two and a half fucking years, Laney. They're only going to say the same thing." *There's not enough conclusive evidence for us to make a diagnosis.*

"All it takes is the right doctor."

I sigh and rub my hand over my face. "Do you know how many doctors she's already seen? How many tests they've done? They're all inconclusive, but they still give her a new prescription, which helps temporarily, then causes more side effects than she had before."

"I'm so sorry, Slate." Laney lays a hand on my stomach.

I tense at the contact but don't brush her away. "We always end up right back where we started. No one knows what's wrong with her."

"What specialists have you seen?"

"Rheumatologists, nephrologists, endocrinologists, immunologists." If you had told me three years ago that I'd be able to rattle off those words without a second thought, I would have told you there's no way in hell. Things change when your little sister gets sick.

"And no one was able to help?"

"They make a bunch of speculations, but what we hear most commonly is that Briar is a chronic complainer." My jaw threatens to snap from the strain I'm putting it under.

Laney jerks upright. "What?"

I exhale through my nose. "They think she's too worried about her health."

The last thing Briar wants is to be a burden on anyone. If she says she's in pain, I automatically double it in my head, because I know she's hiding at least that much from me. To suggest that she's simply concocting these things in her mind—

"Unbelievable," Laney mutters.

I roll out of bed and pull on my jeans. "That's our healthcare system for you." I tug my T-shirt over my head. "You know if a Silver Spoon walked in with the same symptoms, they'd work around the clock to figure out a diagnosis." I'd burn the whole system down if I could.

She walks me to the door in a satin robe. "Have you met with Dr. Clarke?"

I give her a warning look.

"Just—" She presses a hand against my chest. "He's a well-known neurologist. I switched floors a few weeks ago, and I've heard great things about him."

"There's nothing wrong with her head."

"He also studies the nervous system. What if he would be able to find something?"

I close my eyes and lean against the doorjamb. "Do you know how many times I've heard that? How many times I've wanted to hope that some new doctor would be able to fix her?"

"I know I'm only a nurse, but I do know how the body works. No one has sent you to him because they all think she's imagining her pain. What if Dr. Clarke was able to discover the actual problem? Wouldn't that be worth it?"

"Of course it would." I glare at her. "But I don't like getting her hopes up."

"He's very good. If he can't help you himself, I'm sure he can point you in the right direction."

I huff out a frustrated breath. "You really think this guy is that great?"

"I do." Laney pats my chest. "Just get an appointment. What can it hurt?"

Plenty. It can hurt plenty if Briar thinks this guy is the one and he turns out not to be. But Laney and I both know there is nothing in the world I won't try to help my sister.

9

"Lose Yourself" - Eminem

Slate

I don't tell Briar about Laney's suggestion. There's no use in getting her hopes up if I can't even get her an appointment. But Laney's a damn good nurse, and if she thinks this doctor can get some answers for my sister, a SWAT team won't be able to keep me away.

"Neurology department. How may I help you?"

I've been listening to stupid-ass elevator music for so long, I fumble the phone when someone finally speaks. "I'd like to make an appointment." My voice echoes through the empty warehouse as I pace back and forth.

"Okay," the receptionist says. "It is for yourself?"

"For my sister, Briar Lawson. B-R-I-A-R. I'm her legal guardian." I rattle off the rest of Briar's details in the correct format before the woman can even ask.

"And were you referred to our department by someone?" she says.

Shit. We'll probably need a doctor's referral to get in. "One of the nurses said Dr. Clarke might be able to help Briar."

There's a pause. No doubt the receptionist is wondering if she just wasted the last fifteen minutes getting Briar's info. "Can you tell me more about Miss Lawson's condition?"

I give her my well-practiced spiel. "She started experiencing symptoms several years ago. A lot of fatigue, some fevers. Her fingers and toes are always cold, and sometimes they get numb and swollen. She frequently has pain in her muscles and joints, to the point where she mostly stays home, in case the pain prevents walking."

My phone picks up the clacking of computer keys on the other end. After a few seconds, the woman says, "Okay, Mr. Lawson. Dr. Clarke is very busy. I can schedule you to see one of our other doctors—"

"It needs to be him."

She sighs. "In that case, I can't get you in until October twelfth."

"That's fine." The words fly out of my mouth. It's September twenty-fifth. We've waited two and a half years for answers. A few more weeks won't kill us.

"All right. I'll get that scheduled for you, and we'll see you next year."

I've already hung up when her words register.

Next year. October twelfth *next year.*

I redial immediately, but the stupid fucking system puts me at the back of the line again. I kick an empty metal barrel, and it goes skidding across the concrete. Tyler sticks his head out of one of the rooms we use as a makeshift office, but I wave him off.

Fifteen minutes later, I'm on the line with a different receptionist. I don't remember the name of the first one, so I can't ask to be transferred. After I've recited all of the same info, she tells me that there's nothing she can do.

"I'm sorry, Mr. Lawson. Without a doctor's referral, we can't get your sister in any sooner than next fall."

"That is utter bullshit."

She coughs. "I don't make the rules—"

"But you're happy to follow them." My trainers squeak against the concrete floor as I pace. "If my name was something different, like

Baldwin, I bet I'd be allowed to see the doctor then, wouldn't I?"

"I assure you, Mr. Lawson, we do not—"

"What if I offered to pay more? Money can buy anything, can't it? What's the going rate for a last-minute appointment with the good doctor, hmm?"

"I'm going to have to end the call if you—"

"That's fine. You're not helping anyway." I smash the End Call button with my thumb, but there's little satisfaction in it. I badly want to hurl the phone across the room, but then I'd need to buy a new one, which would mean less money to cover medical bills.

There's got to be something else I can do.

The woman said if I had a doctor's referral, she could get me in sooner. The only problem is I've burned all of the bridges with Briar's previous doctors. They were a bunch of asshat quacks, only wanting to sell her meds that did nothing but make her sicker.

I need a new doctor, and not one who treats Briar like she's so hungry for attention that she's making up diseases.

* * *

The hospital website kindly displays the names and photos of all of the doctors on staff. I scan them, looking for someone young enough to still be on the eager side. Attractiveness is a plus, but not a necessity.

Fate smiles on me for once and presents Emma Richardson, MD. She's in her early thirties, with shoulder-length blonde hair and a round face. Her Facebook profile reveals that she's recently divorced, no kids, and likes to party on the weekends—probably looking to get laid after that divorce.

Her most recent story is public and states that she's at the Green Elephant. This girl needs to learn a thing or two about online security. The Elephant isn't the seediest club in the city, but it's not one of those high-class ones either, with a name list and a handful of bouncers at the door, thank fuck.

The sky is clear, so I ride my bike to the bar. I've put in a little effort tonight, hoping to score points with the doctor. I'm still wearing black, but it's a button-up shirt instead of my usual T-shirt.

It takes me ten minutes and a single malt Scotch to spot Emma with some friends on the dance floor. She's wearing a hot pink dress that stops only two inches below her ass. This girl definitely wants action tonight.

A guy wearing a fucking floral-print shirt edges closer to her, but I have my sights set on my prey. He can go stick his cock in any other pussy in this place. Tonight Dr. Emma Richardson belongs to me.

She looks me up and down as I move in next to her. She smells good, which is a plus. Her blonde hair is damp against her forehead from dancing. A smile stretches across her pink lips, and she motions me closer.

I oblige, and she slides her arms around my neck. The music is too loud for talking, but we dance together through a few songs. She grinds against me—a nice touch, because it will make this whole thing easier.

When we're both panting, I lead her to the bar and buy her a drink. It's a little quieter over here, so we introduce ourselves.

"I'm Emma." She sips her cosmo and stares at me with lust-crazed eyes.

"Slate." I brush the back of my fingers along her bare arm. "What do you do, Emma?" I'm 99 percent certain this is my woman, but it never hurts to double-check.

"I'm a doctor," she says, in a tone that makes me think she chose that career because she liked the sound of those words. "What about you?"

"Corporate," I lie.

She gives me the "poor baby" look people love to bestow on those they believe to be in soulless jobs. I'll take that any day over the disgust that would have crossed her face if I had told her I'm a mechanic. Doctors may be willing to lower their standards for someone they think has a shot at becoming CEO someday, but they aren't going to sleep with someone working a blue-collar job, even if he owns the company.

We do that godawful thing where we stare into each other's eyes, pretending to know the deep-feelings bullshit the other person is trying to convey.

Emma's phone buzzes, breaking our "moment," and she pulls it out of her bag. Her cheeks blush as she taps out a reply. "My friends want to know if you're trustworthy."

I let my grin reach my eyes. "Considering the thoughts I've had about that dress of yours, probably not."

She blushes even further. The woman is practically putty in my hands already. She traces the tip of the sword peeking out of my left shirtsleeve. "My condo is only a few blocks from here."

* * *

Dr. Richardson lives in a modest flat in one of the downtown towers. I say modest, because compared to some of the places where I've crashed parties, this looks like the maid's quarters. But compared to my own house, or anything you'll find in the Junction, it's swanky as hell. No jaw-dropping views of the city or walls of windows, but a modern kitchen and new furniture.

And a cat.

How did I miss that she has a cat? It's gray with white paws, and it looks at me like I'm an intruder.

"You have a cat?" I'll have to find a way to salvage this.

Emma glances up at me from where she's smothering the thing with kisses. "You don't like cats?" She has that suspicious gleam in her eyes people get when they're questioning what is wrong with a person.

"I'm allergic."

Relief washes over her face, and she jumps up. "I keep allergy medicine in the kitchen, just in case."

Now that we've averted that crisis, it's time to get down to business. She leads me to the bedroom, dims the lights, and turns on soft jazz. Then we have the most vanilla sex of my life. I try to go down on her, but she tugs me back up.

It may be some of the worst sex I've ever had, but she sighs contently as she lies next to me. Normally I'd already have my pants back on, but I didn't come here for sex.

"Thanks for being a bright spot in an otherwise shitty day." I have no fucking clue where the words come from, but they have the desired effect.

Emma cranes her neck to peer up at me. "You wanna talk about it?"

I shake my head, not wanting to seem too eager. I tuck my arm around her shoulder and tug her close to my side. She scoots over without any hesitation.

This is almost too easy.

After a few more beats of silence, I heave out a sigh. "It's my sister."

Her fingers are still on my chest. "Your sister?"

"She's sick again, and I"—I insert a crack into my voice—"I can't get her an appointment until next fall."

She shifts onto her elbow. "An appointment where?"

"Neurologist," I say. "I tried seeing Dr. Clarke, but they told me without a doctor's referral, we have to wait over a year."

A frown puckers Emma's brow. "And you don't have a doctor?"

"They all think she's making it up."

I see the wheels turning in her head. She's trying to find a way to help. What is it with women and their insatiable need to fix everyone?

"Maybe I could write a referral. I'm not a—"

I shake my head, cutting her off. "I can't ask you to do that."

"I don't mind," she says. "After all, tonight was amazing, and I—"

Realization grips her face as the night flashes through her memory. It becomes obvious the moment she puts the pieces together.

Shit. I overplayed my hand.

"You used me." She jerks away from me and swings her legs over the bed. She wraps a blanket around herself before turning back to me. "Get out."

"Technically I didn't use you." I tug my pants back on. "But I would appreciate the referral."

"Get the fuck out of my house!"

I do as she asks because, while I may have played this wrong, I'm smart enough to realize when a ship has sailed.

At least I'm not any worse off than when I started.

10

"Gethsemane" - Sleep Token

Lux

On a scale from one to ten, how bad is a sister who leaves her brother in a house full of junkies? Pretty sure it's in the neighborhood of one hundred.

It's been four days since I walked out of that house. Four days since I've seen Alex. And each of those days I've done nothing but think about him. I don't even have a way of knowing if he's still alive.

Despite what some people think, I'm not a fool. I know I could ask Pierce, Rhett, and Heath to drag Alex out of there. But as soon as I do, he's only going to go back.

I need to eliminate the source of the problem: the Wolf. But until I discover who that is, I'm no closer to doing anything to save Alex than I was.

It's Tuesday, which means poker night, which means Rhett will be there, which means I might get some answers. Of the six of us, he's the one with the most connections to the drug world.

Walker and Heath are hosting for the first time tonight, at their Bates Motel–esque house. When I pull into the driveway, a literal shudder travels down my spine. It's decorated with disgusting cobwebs, dripping moss, and shrouded in a heavy fog that suffocates the whole place. The only thing missing is a serial killer on the front porch holding an ax.

As luck would have it, Rhett pulls into the driveway right behind me. I plant a kiss on his cheek once he gets out of his car, but before I can tell him I need to talk to him, Walker approaches us from the house. She's wearing her typical tweed uniform of short skirt and blazer.

"Pierce and Maeve are already here," she calls.

We exchange hugs and kisses before she leads us to the back of the house. I try to catch Rhett's eye, but Walker has her arm wrapped around me, and Rhett is texting as he walks. His blue long-sleeve shirt is so tight, his nipples show through it.

We walk onto the huge terrace, where a fire is blazing in a stone pit and candles flicker on the table. Steam rises from the hot tub on the other side.

"Dude." Rhett gives Heath a one-arm hug. "This place is creepy as fuck."

Maeve and I exchange kisses—she looks ravishing in a knit magenta dress from Caroline Spencer—before following Walker inside to gather drinks. I ask for the restroom, and while I'm in there, quickly type out a text to Rhett. *I need to talk to you privately tonight xx*

When I reenter the kitchen, Walker is holding a tray of smoldering neon-green cocktails. "Okay, we're doing this every week," I say.

"Why is your girlfriend trying to poison me?" Rhett asks Heath when we go back outside. I can't tell if he's read my text or not.

"Don't drink it until the dry ice is gone," Walker says. "It should only take a few minutes."

I set up the tripod I packed in my bag and attach my phone to it. "Everyone grab a drink!" I call out. We gather in front of the camera with our boiling cocktails. "To the best friends in the world!"

There are a few muttered grumbles about my incessant need for selfies, but it's not like any of them understand the need to satisfy 2.8 million followers. People expect something of me, and it's my job to deliver.

The camera flashes multiple times as Rhett tries to lick Maeve's cheek, Heath pretends to strangle Walker, and Pierce looks highly uncomfortable, which isn't surprising, given he's still wearing a suit.

When my camera roll is full of shots, we gather around the table. Walker has placed cashmere throws on the chairs. I wrap mine around my shoulders, then steal Pierce's for my legs. This white twill Chanel dress seemed like a good idea until I realized we were going to be sitting outside.

Rhett's sitting across from me, but when he catches me looking at him, he gives me a look of utter confusion, which then turns into idiocy as he mimes choking. I roll my eyes. Clearly he hasn't read my text yet.

I raise my fingers to my ear in the old fashioned phone sign, trying to be subtle about it in case anyone else is looking.

Rhett just stares. "What's wrong with your face, Lux?"

Everyone turns to look at me. I roll my eyes again and shake my head. This is never going to work.

We submit our first grievances, and Walker deals us in.

"Have you gone to see your dad yet, Heath?" Rhett asks.

Heath's dad is in prison for committing tax fraud. Since Heath himself was the one who turned his dad in, I'm going to assume the answer is no.

"I'm not visiting that asshole," he says. "Ever."

Just as I thought. "This cocktail is good." I direct the comment toward both Walker and Heath, since I'm not sure which one of them made it. "Is that . . . melon?"

"Mmm." Walker nods and sips her own drink. "It's the Midori."

I take another swallow, causing my armful of bracelets to slide toward my elbow. Beside me, Pierce hisses. His attention is focused on my wrist, where ugly black bands snake around the delicate skin.

"What the fuck is that from?" he asks under his breath.

I shove the gold bracelets back down to cover the bruises from Carter's ropes and tug the blanket closer around me. "Sometimes we get kinky," I whisper back.

Fortunately, the others are occupied in a discussion over the grievance Rhett submitted, but I doubt it will last long if Pierce keeps glaring at me like that.

"What?" I say in a sharp whisper.

He leans close. "You both get kinky, or *he* does?"

"Would you please let this go?"

"Not if he's hurting you."

"Nothing is against my will," I say. My mind fills with images of Carter tying me to the headboard three nights ago. It wasn't against my will. I never begged him to stop. Sure, I told him it hurt, but if I had truly wanted him to stop, I could have asked him to.

"Do you at least have a safe word?" Pierce asks. It's a miracle our whispered exchange hasn't drawn the attention of the others.

I glower at him. "Of course."

He settles back into his chair, content that my boyfriend isn't an abusive asshole.

Good thing I'm an excellent liar.

"Lux, is it true that Jojo Banks is going to be at your Gatsby party?" Maeve asks from across the table. She's burrowed beneath a camel-colored throw blanket, which offsets her blue-black hair beautifully.

"That's what her PA told me." The popstar RSVP'd this past weekend, driving the social value of this party even higher than it already was.

"When is the decorating crew coming? I might be able to help," she says.

"They're scheduled to arrive at nine." I scan the faces of my friends. "Now might be a good time to tell you this is likely the last party I'll be hosting."

"What's going on?" Walker straightens in her chair.

"Nothing." I wave a casual hand. "I'm selling. I met with the estate agent yesterday." Elizabeth Gable was confident I'd get multiple offers within a week. I told her I wasn't in a big hurry.

"Why?" Maeve's tone reeks of suspicion. "You love that house."

The blanket slides down my shoulders when I shrug, and I shift it back up. The temperature keeps dropping. "It's time for a change."

"Okay," Pierce says, fishing for the punchline. "Where are you moving to?"

"Carter asked me to move in with him." I grab my empty cocktail glass. "Anyone else need a refill?"

They all stare at me, varying shades of shock and disgust on their faces.

"What?" I say. "We've been together for a year and a half."

"Carter," Heath says. "The same wanker who nearly got my fist in his face for treating you the way he did at the beach house?"

I roll my eyes. "He was worked up that day. You caught him off guard."

"Doesn't he have a *condo*?" Rhett says.

"*You* have a condo, mate," Heath says.

Rhett's face colors. "Mine's at least in the fucking Dankirk Tower. His is like, down on Twenty-Eighth Street or something."

"So he has a condo," I say. "So what? He's not *poor*."

Rhett mumbles something under his breath I don't catch.

Maeve has been studying me this whole time. "Why doesn't Carter move in with you? Your house is much bigger and nicer."

I open my mouth to respond, but the words dry up on my tongue. I don't know the answer myself. "I think he would feel emasculated moving in with his girlfriend." When no one says anything, I turn to the guys. "Wouldn't you feel that way?"

Heath spreads his arms wide in answer. He's living with Walker in what was originally her house.

Rhett laughs. "If my girlfriend had a place like yours, I'd sell my condo immediately."

Pierce crosses his arms over his chest and stares at the table.

"It doesn't matter, okay?" I say. "I've already made up my mind. Now can we finish the game?"

One by one, they return their attention to the cards in their hands. Meanwhile, my thoughts run in a different direction altogether. Maybe the reason I can't get excited about moving in with Carter has little to do with my house and everything to do with Alex's situation being unresolved. If I can take care of that, I can throw myself fully into building a home with Carter, even if it is on Twenty-Eighth Street.

As if on cue, Rhett folds, then pulls his phone out. He must see my text, because he immediately looks up at me. Then, in the least subtle move possible, he clears his throat loudly and stands up. "I need to take a shit. It might be a while."

I close my eyes and rest my head against my fingertips. I have no idea if he's serious or not, so I give him at least five minutes before also excusing myself.

He's waiting for me in the kitchen. "What the fuck took so long?"

"You said you were going to the restroom. How was I supposed to know if you were serious or not?"

He opens the refrigerator and takes out a plate of half-eaten cheesecake. He begins pulling out drawers at random, shutting them so hard I'm surprised none of the oil paintings fall off the walls. I open the one next to me and hold out a fork.

Swiping it from me, he hops onto the marble counter, balancing the cake platter in one hand. "So what's the stealth mission? Are we planting a positive pregnancy test in Walker's bathroom? Or mixing up Pierce's tie collection?"

"There's no stealth mission. I was wondering if you've ever heard of the Wolf."

He pauses with his fork halfway through the cheesecake. "Who?"

"The Wolf. Apparently he's a well-known drug dealer?"

"I'm going to overlook the fact that out of all of our friends, you came to me for this information, and instead ask why you are interested in my connections to said drug dealer."

I smack his leg. "You know why I came to you. And I need to know because of Alex."

"Your brother."

"Last time I checked."

Rhett sucks on his teeth and presses the fork tines into his lower lip. "And if I said I knew the Wolf, what would you do with that information?"

"If I tell you, that makes you an accomplice. So let's pretend you don't need to know that part."

"Lux." His tone is more serious than I've ever heard it. "What's going on?" he says quietly.

I lean back against the counter and cross my ankles. "Alex isn't doing well. At all." I wiggle my heel-clad foot. "He's hooked on insidion."

Rhett doesn't react to this, just stares at the cheesecake in his lap. "He makes his own choices, Lux. You can't hold yourself responsible."

"I don't. I just—"

"You want to fix it though, right?" He sets the plate down. "You want to swoop in and save him from his own mistakes. You can't do that, okay? You can't put yourself in danger like that."

"Who says it's dangerous?"

Rhett shakes his head and hops off the counter. "The drug world is always dangerous."

"So you're not going to help me."

His eyes cut to mine as he slides the cake back into the fridge. "I can't help you. I don't know who the Wolf is."

I have no idea if he's lying or not, but it's obvious he's not going to tell me anything.

"Now, if you'll excuse me, I'm actually going to go take that shit." He winks and walks out of the kitchen.

I sag against the counter. Rhett was my last option. I don't know what else to do, aside from going back to that house of junkies and demanding someone take me to the Wolf. Maybe I should pose as one of them, strung out and needing another hit. Then I can take him down from the inside.

Or . . . maybe I need an inside man.

11

"I Knew You Were Trouble" - Taylor Swift

Slate

The pounding starts roughly three seconds into my beer. I've just gotten home, taken a cold one out of the fridge, and am starting to guzzle it when someone bangs on the door loudly enough to wake Mrs. Friedman from her nap three doors down.

I swing it open without bothering to check the peephole. I don't know who I expect to see—Mrs. Friedman herself maybe, wanting help tracking down her Chihuahua again, or the mailman with a package too big for the box. I know who I *don't* expect—Briar, because she's at the library, after convincing me she'll be fine and she has her phone; Tyler, because he never knocks, just comes right on in like he fucking lives here; and Lux Colombia-Clarke, because what the hell she would want, I don't know.

Looks like I'm about to find out.

She's standing on my porch, in a sleeveless white-and-pink-checkered dress that looks like something a sixties housewife would have worn to go shopping. Her blonde hair is pushed away from her face with a thick pink headband that gives me strong Grace Kelly vibes. Beneath her dress, a pair of tanned legs stretch on for an eternity, long enough that it would take delicious hours to map them thoroughly. They end in a pair of sharp white heels.

"Do you know who the Wolf is?" she blurts out.

I've never heard her talk before. Her face is plastered all over the city, the tabloids, and social media, but since I've never met her or watched any of her videos, I've had no voice to put with the face that's flitted in and out of my dreams ever since that day at Pop's.

The voice suits her. Slightly high-pitched and breathless, like life is too short for her to possibly say everything that's on her mind. It takes a second for the neurons in my brain to fire properly and register what she's said.

Do you know who the Wolf is?

I yank her inside the house and shut the door. Her skin feels cool beneath my fingers, and I instantly drop her arm.

Lux looks at me like I've assaulted her. "What the hell do you think you're doing?" She scrambles for the doorknob at her back, but her eyes don't leave my face.

"You can't go around saying things like that."

She blinks at me, those wide brown eyes framed by lashes so thick and luxurious, it's easy to see how she got her name. "I'll say whatever I want."

"Your funeral." What would she say if I suggested she do something with that mouth besides talk? I study her through narrowed eyes, relishing the way she squirms beneath my attention. My dreams are going to go fucking berserk tonight as I envision soiling her perfect image in my bed.

"Jonathan—"

"What did you say?" All thoughts of the bedroom flee as I glare at her.

"Do you prefer Jon?"

I darken my gaze even further. "I'd prefer it if you didn't talk at all."

"I don't know if that's supposed to be a terrible come-on or not, but I'm not interested." She punctuates this with a sniff, her nose in the air like a terrier. Her eyes flit down toward the tattoo sleeves on my arms.

I resist the urge to laugh, covering my mouth so she can't see my smile. "Your hair is different," I say.

"Excuse me?" Her hand flits to her head.

"Last time I saw you it was white. Now it's"—I lift a strand from her shoulder—"more like honey." I'm still trying to figure out which shade I prefer.

She couldn't look more disgusted if my hand were a live snake. This only increases my desire to ruffle her dainty feathers, see what kind of wild beast lurks beneath that immaculate exterior.

"I would appreciate it if you would stop touching me and answer the question," she snaps.

I snort. "Don't say that to anyone trying to mug you at the petrol station. They'll think you're begging for more."

Her nostrils flare, and I get another tiny glimpse of the fire inside her.

"Why are you asking about the Wolf?" I ask.

If she's surprised by my abrupt change of subject, she doesn't let it show, just tilts that perfect chin in the air and says, "I want to buy insidion."

This time I do laugh, abruptly and loudly, which only makes her look even more furious. "*You* want to buy insidion?"

"Is that so hard to believe?" She straightens herself, making her tits jut out even further.

"Frankly, yes." I gesture up and down the length of her body. "You're not the typical customer."

"I'm giving you the honor of helping someone who is light years out of your league."

"Honest *and* humble." I reach around her to grasp the doorknob. "You'll have to find someone else."

Lux backs up until she's flush against the door, trapping my hand behind her ass. Our faces hover inches apart, close enough that I can see flecks of gold in those dark eyes. The scent of roses tickles my nose.

Neither of us moves or says anything.

Several seconds pass, heavy and sluggish. I desperately want to palm that ass and squeeze, catch her little gasp of breath with my teeth. She inhales shallowly and says, "Please. I need your help."

I want to ask why it has to be me. Why, of all the doors she could have knocked on, she's here. Why the sight of her makes my blood pound faster than it ever has before. But that little "please" halts anything I'd normally do in its tracks.

"Tell me the truth, and I'll see what I can do."

Her eyes dart between mine, as if she's looking for something. "Fine," she says. "If you'll kindly remove your hand from my ass, I'll tell you."

I move slowly, allowing the tips of my fingers to graze her firm roundness. She stiffens but doesn't pull away. In spite of her bluster, I think she's all talk. Which is nice for me but could be devastating for her, depending on who is around to take advantage.

When I've extracted my hand from between her and the door, I step back and cross my arms. I'm still wearing the clothes I wore to the shop, and I hope she notices the grease stains on my jeans. Some of us work for a living. "Whenever you're ready, princess."

She clasps the tiny purse she's holding between both hands and seems to draw courage from some inner well. "My brother has recently become addicted to insidion."

When she stops, I motion for her to continue.

"I found out through some . . . *people* that the person supplying him is called the Wolf. No one seems to know who that is, though." She peers up at me through those thick lashes. "I was hoping you would."

I keep my hard gaze trained on her. "What if *I'm* the Wolf?"

She blinks twice, like she hadn't considered this. "Are you?"

I scowl and shake my head. Ridiculous woman. If she cares at all about her own well-being, she will leave the Junction immediately. "Let me give you some advice." I inch closer. "You can't go around asking people if they're the Wolf, if they know the Wolf, or if they have anything to do with the Wolf, okay? That guy's dangerous."

"So you *do* know him." Lux crosses her own arms over her chest, completely unfazed by my little spiel.

"Knowing *of* him is different than knowing him." Something occurs to me. "Why are you here anyway, asking me these bullshit questions?"

She smirks, actually *smirks*, like she has the upper hand. "I'm aware of your . . . extracurricular activities."

How she knows about that, I don't know—or feel particularly invested in finding out. Plenty of people know I deal on the side, including my own goddamn sister, it seems. "So what, you thought I'd lead you straight into the Wolf's den?"

"I assumed we would strike some sort of bargain, yes."

"And what do you plan to do if I lead you to him?"

She falters for the first time. "I'll figure that part out later."

The corners of my mouth twitch. The audacity of this girl. "No," I say firmly.

Those perfectly groomed brows furrow. "What do you mean, 'no'?"

"I don't know about where you're from, but around here, no means 'not at all.' You usually say it—"

"Shut your arrogant mouth," she snaps. Fire dances in those chocolate eyes. "Why won't you help me?"

I lean in and lower my voice until it drags over those sculpted cheekbones. "Why would I help an uppity bitch like you?"

Her chin juts out, and she clenches her jaw. "I can pay."

I scowl, putting distance between us once more. "I don't need your money."

As she glances around the room, I become aware of every water stain on the carpet and each frayed edge of my grandma's floral sofa.

"Could've fooled me," she says. "Or has business picked up at the Rebel Wrench again?"

A prickling sensation starts at the base of my spine and crawls up toward my neck.

"It did slow down around a year ago, didn't it?" She curls a manicured hand in front of her face, inspecting her bubblegum-pink nails.

"Get out." I don't know why she's here, but I no longer have any interest in finding out.

"Do you remember one sunny day in September," she says, a lilting quality to her voice, "you stole a parking spot in front of Cafe de Olla and then proceeded to wave your finger at me like the world's most arrogant asshole?"

I don't move a muscle.

"You picked the wrong person to mess with, Mr. Lawson." She drops her hand and meets my eye. "I know everything about you. And I have the power to make your life miserable."

"Is that supposed to make me want to help you?" I hiss.

"You didn't want my deal, so—"

"So you're going to threaten my business? Run me into the ground to show the world that Lux Colombia-Clarke always wins?"

"It worked, didn't it? I'm here. And you're considering my request."

I shake my head in disgust. "Is that what you Silver Spoons do up there in the Hills? Track people down so you can get revenge on them?"

She doesn't say anything, just stares at me coldly.

It shouldn't surprise me. Why wouldn't she use her power and wealth to bring down the little guys so she can watch them squirm like beetles flipped onto their backs? I thought—idiot that I am—that there was something different about Lux, something sweeter, more innocent. Proves what a pillock I am.

She's the classic femme fatale, captivating men before she makes them her victims. The pieces all click into place with startling precision. Rather than playing the seductive vixen, she takes on the role of innocent heiress, but her mission is the same.

"Why did you call me Jonathan?" I say.

She startles. Not completely above being riled, then. "Isn't that your name?"

I narrow my eyes, taking in that flawless skin, the small beauty mark on the right side of her face that she hasn't hidden with makeup. "That was my dad's name."

Her lips part in surprise, and a pink flush climbs her neck.

"So I guess you don't know everything about me, do you?"

She regains her composure quickly. "I know enough to be danger-ous."

"Yeah, I gathered that." I move closer, until she has to back up against the door to avoid touching me. "But don't forget that I'm dangerous too."

Her throat bobs as she swallows.

"I can make that sweet pussy of yours ache with need, until you're a dripping mess," I say into her ear. Her perfume finds a direct line to my groin. "I can force you to beg on your knees for my cock. I can wring you out until I am the only thing that could possibly satisfy you."

I gaze down at the long column of her tanned neck and wonder what it would look like branded by my teeth.

She swallows again before saying, "I can get your sister in to see my dad."

A slap would have felt less startling. I lean back so I can see her face. "Who's your dad?"

"Dr. Clarke." She lifts those doe eyes to me and blinks innocently. "Haven't you been trying to get an appointment for Briar?"

12

"Sweet but Psycho" - Ava Max

Lux

I knew I had him the minute his jaw went slack. A year ago, I assumed his sister would be his biggest weakness, but I didn't have the heart to go after a sick girl. Besides, *she* wasn't the one who stole my spot, and it's not her fault her brother's a jackass.

But that information couldn't have come in handier at a more appropriate time. I know I'm playing with fire, as evidenced by the rage he is barely able to keep from his face. I have indeed poked the bear, but the panther can take care of herself. And she's ready to play.

He has yet to respond to my offer, but before I can taunt him further, the door opens into my back. I let out an *oomph* as someone on the other side shouts, "Ohmygod, I'm so sorry!"

Jonath—damn it, I still don't know the prick's actual name—shoves me aside with a look of annoyance and swings the door open. A teenage girl in ripped jeans nearly falls inside, slamming into both of us. Her eyes grow wide as she takes me in.

"I am soooo sorry!" she exclaims again. "Are you okay?"

So this is the sister. She doesn't look sick, and the resemblance between them is impossible to ignore. She has the same thick chestnut

80

curls, and while his are pulled back into a half-up man bun, hers are dancing wildly around her face.

"I'm fine." I slide on the smile *Vogue* called "enchanting." "I'm Lux. You must be Briar? Your brother has been telling me all about you." I'd kiss her cheeks, but I'm afraid to get whatever sickness she has.

She cuts a glance at her brother before turning back to me. "Lux Colombia-Clarke is in my house. No freaking way!" A squeal pierces the air as she claps her hands together. "I follow you on Instagram, and that facial you did a few weeks ago—"

Her words halt abruptly as the jackass grabs her arm. "Briar. Out."

"But I—"

His face is stormy as he motions to a hallway. "Go."

She gives him a professional pout that has me silently applauding, but he is undaunted by those puppy dog eyes. Once she is safely out of earshot, he barks, "You and me. Outside. Now."

My heart jumps at the sharp command.

He points at a dark spot on the carpet near my feet. "Watch where you step. That's cat piss."

I do a little dance over the stain, which, in hindsight, must have looked downright stupid. We've been standing in the living room, which I'd call "Grandma chic for poor people." There are lots of plants around, which lends it a boho vibe, but it's obvious the furniture is older than I am.

I get a peek at the kitchen as we pass by on our way to the back door. A comment about the adorable vintage-style appliances in seafoam green hovers on the tip of my tongue, until I realize they are *literally* vintage. Some things get better with age. Appliances are not among them.

He holds the door for me—apparently he has *some* manners—and motions toward a bench that . . . swings. "Have a seat." His voice is gruff.

I stare at it. Several faded floral cushions that have long since lost their stuffing cover the slats. The whole thing sways gently in the breeze. It's suspended from some kind of rusty metal A-frame that looks sketch as hell.

"What?" he says.

I bite my lip and move toward the swing. If I want his cooperation, I'll have to put in some effort too.

"It's not flea-infested," he says. "Anymore."

My head spins around, and the horror in my chest must be visible on my face, because he throws his head back and laughs. It's a nice laugh, and he should use it more often, but not at my expense. I cross my arms over my chest and stare at him.

"Just sit, will you?" He grabs a white plastic chair and parks it in front of the swing. I will it to collapse beneath him, but it disappoints.

"Will this"—I gesture toward the swing—"hold me?" The way it moves back and forth does not give me hope.

"That's what you're scared of?" He mutters something under his breath. "Yes, it will hold you. You probably weigh less than my right leg."

I grab the seat with both hands and carefully lower myself onto it. After the initial adjustment, which sends my heart careening over a cliff, I realize he's right. It holds me up. I relax and settle against the back.

He's studying me, a quizzical expression on his face. "Have you never been on a swing before?"

I consider lying. I shake my head instead.

"Fuck my life," he grumbles under his breath. "What'd you do as a child?"

I observe the back garden. It's the size of my walk-in pantry, which is already smaller than I'd like. Other than the swing and a few plastic chairs, there's a barbecue pushed up against the house and garden beds tucked into every spare corner. I'm going to take a wild guess and assume those are his sister's.

He pulls a cigarette out of his pocket and lights it without asking if I mind if he smokes.

"Are you going to tell me your real name?" I say.

"You don't need to know my name. How did you know about Briar?" He takes a long drag on the cigarette.

I shake my head and smile. "A question for a question."

He rolls his eyes and mutters something that sounds a lot like *impossible women.* "Slate."

"If that's some kind of secret Junction curse word, may I remind you that I'm not from around here, so I don't know what the hell 'slate' means in regards to—"

"You talk too much."

I'm pleased by how little this stings, more like a tiny pinprick than a full-on blast to the gut—proof I'm doing better. "So I've been told." Many, many times.

"It's my name." He flicks ash onto the ground. "Slate."

Heat climbs my neck. "Oh." It suits him. Hard, cold, and unbending. The bike must have been his dad's. *A rookie mistake, Lux. Get it together.*

"Your turn," he reminds me.

I shrug. "I followed you to the hospital. Broke into the database looking for the name Lawson. Basic stuff."

There's an unreadable glint of something in his eyes. Admiration maybe? He blows out a plume of smoke.

"Must you do that?" I wave it away from my face.

"Is that your next question?"

"Is that yours?"

He shakes his head like he can't figure me out. His tongue skirts along his lower lip, and tingles erupt across my skin. Then he presses his hands into those muscular, jean-clad thighs and stands up. "I'm getting coffee. Want some?" He grinds the cigarette into the concrete with his foot, then bends to pick it up.

Now that the sun is setting, the air has started to cool. "Yes, please. With oat milk."

He stares at me for a few seconds, his expression unreadable, before retreating into the house.

I use the time to inspect the frame of the swing. I can't find any weak spots, but I don't know anything about metal or wood or any kind of building . . . things. The rust can't possibly be a good sign.

"You don't believe me, do you?"

Slate's voice startles me, and I fall back onto the swing with an ungraceful plop. He smirks as he hands me a cup of pale coffee. I glare at him.

Our fingers graze as I take it from him. There are several tattoos across his knuckles. My traitorous body immediately reminds me about the dirty things he whispered in my ear earlier. I cross my legs and squeeze my thighs together. "So." I blow on the hot coffee. "How should we do this?"

He settles back into the chair and leans forward, propping his arms on his thighs. "Let's get one thing straight," he says. "You will leave my sister out of this. She's not a pawn in your twisted little game."

I allow a spark to light my eyes, to let him know as much as he wishes he had control, we are on even footing. "And yet she's the reason you agreed to this, isn't she?"

I'm rewarded with the tightening of his jaw, visible in spite of the short beard covering it. "Here's how this is going to work. You will get my sister an appointment with your dad. Then *if* I learn something about the identity of the Wolf, I will let you know."

It's my turn to laugh. "I don't think so." I recline against the back of the swing, more comfortable with its shifting now, and cross my legs. His eyes track their movement, and a tiny fissure of something spreads across my belly. "My dad and I don't have a close relationship. He's a little too preoccupied with his new family to bother much with the old one."

Slate's eyebrows flicker downward.

"If I'm going to ask him for a favor this big, there will have to be something in it for me," I finish.

He dips his head. "Fine. I will do some digging and—"

"No. I want to go undercover."

A sharp bark of laughter punctures the cooling evening air. "This isn't a sting operation, princess."

I shoot him another glare. That sexy exterior is hiding some real assholery underneath. "If you aren't willing to help me, I will find someone who is. And your sister can continue being sick."

The laughter vanishes from his eyes. "I told you to leave her out of this." His voice is as steely as his name.

I curl my hands around the ceramic mug. It's covered in hand-painted yellow daisies with green stems. "What's wrong with her? With Briar?" I say, softening my voice.

He assesses me, like he's trying to decide if I'll use the information to hurt him further.

"She seems healthy," I add.

He leans back in his chair and runs a hand over his face. "No one can figure it out."

I don't press further. I rub my bare arms to ward off the chill that has wrapped itself around the garden now that the sun has sunk below the horizon. If I had known I'd be here this long, I would have brought a jacket. I'm not sure what I expected. That he would hand over the Wolf's address with a "good day to you"?

Slate pushes to his feet again and retreats inside without a word. Before I have time to process if that was my dismissal, he reappears with a crocheted blanket, which he drapes around my shoulders. The afghan is old but warm and smells faintly of something sweet, like vanilla.

"Thank you." I tug the ends tighter around me.

He merely grunts in response.

"So what's the plan?" I say. "Maybe you should explain how this whole drug-buying thing works. You're a dealer, but the Wolf is also a dealer. Do you have territories or something?"

"Do you answer your own questions often?" A touch of amusement glints in his eyes.

"Only when my conversation partner communicates in grunts and monosyllables."

A snort. Then he leans forward, making the plastic chair beneath him squeak. "You can't tell anyone what I'm about to tell you, okay?"

I humor him by nodding and sip my coffee.

"The Wolf is dangerous. He's the main supplier of insidion in the whole city. If his identity were revealed, the coppers would tear the entire operation apart. If he even knew we were having this conversation—" He glances to the side, as if checking to make sure no one is lurking behind the grill.

"Don't you see him when you're buying from him?" I ask.

"The guy's not stupid."

"Sounds complicated."

Slate quirks a brow. "It is."

"Wouldn't you feel better making your money the honest way?"

"You mean fixing cars for people like you?"

Our gazes meet, direct and chilled, across the pavement of the garden. "At least there you're helping people instead of destroying their lives," I shoot back.

"People make their own choices."

"Those choices are possible because of people like you." Alex's dilated pupils flash through my memory.

"You think I'm responsible for the world's problems?"

I lift my mug to my lips. "Some of them."

"My customers would just buy what they want from someone else."

I want to fight back, to tell him that mindsets like that are the reason my brother is currently tripping in a crack house with a bunch of strangers. But I need his help too badly. "If I can infiltrate that hierarchy, maybe he won't suspect someone like me."

"Why, 'cause you're a Silver Spoon?"

"A what?" That's the second time he's called me that.

"You were born with a silver spoon in your mouth."

I scowl at him. "You are clearly not without your own prejudices."

"Never said I was." He crosses his arms and leans back in his chair. The muscles in his upper arms strain at the edges of his T-shirt sleeves. A bit of tearing has already occurred in the soft fabric. My eyes ache to traverse the tattoos covering his skin. "So, what's your plan?"

I'm not really the planning type, unless it's a party. I always make better decisions in the moment, so until now, I had zero idea of the next step. But the idea comes to me in a sparkling flash. "I'm hosting a party this weekend. Maybe you can bring some of your colleagues?"

The edges of his mouth twitch behind the beard. "My colleagues?"

"You know what I mean."

"And what exactly would the purpose of this co-mingling be?" He pushes his tongue against the side of his cheek.

I drain the rest of my coffee. "We'll say that I want in. Maybe that I want to become a dealer. Whatever will put me in contact with the Wolf."

Slate lets out another snort, which I murder with a death glare. "Why would anyone believe you want to deal? You probably live in some mansion in the Hills. No one's going to buy that story."

"We'll say I have money issues. A bunch of debt. I don't know." I shift the blanket higher on my shoulders. "I think better on my feet."

"God help us all," he mutters.

"Do you have a better idea?"

He splays out his hands. "Not at all. It's your grave."

I roll my eyes. And they say women are dramatic. "The party is Gatsby-themed. Do you have something appropriate to wear?"

"I can figure it out."

"Do you even know who Gatsby is?"

His eyes narrow, and a thrill dashes up my spine. "I figured I'd just wear my 'I'm too good for this' face. That way I'll blend in."

I press my lips together and hold out my hand. "Give me your phone."

He lifts off the chair slightly to pull it from his back pocket, then passes it over without a word, his eyes never leaving mine. It's still warm, and I force myself to think about anything other than where it came from.

I enter my info and send a text to myself. "There's the address." I hand it back to him. "Don't bail."

We both get to our feet at the same time. "Wouldn't dream of it," Slate says, looking down at me.

"Great." My nipples are peaked from the cold night air.

"One more question," he says before I can pass through the sliding door and inside.

I turn to face him again, bracing myself for yet another remark about my fancy house or tight ass.

"What are you planning to do when you find the Wolf?"

Surprise kicks my heart. I don't have a plan. I assumed it would come to me when I met the bastard. But there's only ever been one option.

He waits.

"Kill him," I say.

13

"A Little Party Never Killed Nobody" - Fergie

Slate

I have no fucking clue what I'm doing here.

I adjust my black tie as Tyler pulls up in front of a huge white house framed with huge white pillars and two huge white bodyguards. We climb out, and Ty hands the keys of his Lambo—he doesn't have medical bills to pay—to the valet waiting curbside.

"Shit, they have fucking valet service." Nick whistles through his teeth as we stroll up to the front door. "Maybe we should case this joint tonight."

"No way, bro." Ty slings his arm around Nick's shoulders. "If Slate's right, this deal will be a whole lot sweeter."

I'm already regretting my decision to bring the two of them along, let alone show up myself, but those regrets are clouded by the thought of seeing Briar healthy again. If I have to dress like I walked out of a time machine in order to score my sister an appointment with Dr. Clarke, lead the way.

The two bouncers at the door give us hard stares, as if they can tell at first glance that our vests are polyester and that this tie feels like a noose.

"Name?" the one on the left asks.

"Slate Lawson." I motion to Ty and Nick. "And guests."

He scans his list, then without a word, opens the ten-foot-tall glass door, and we step inside.

The place *glitters*. There's no other word for it. Waiters pass in front of us carrying trays of martinis, a champagne tower is the focal point of the room, and an open bar is set up near another set of glass doors leading to the back garden, where a pool is visible.

A live jazz band plays tunes from the twenties, and a few couples are dancing. There are people everywhere, draped in fringe and fur. While our outfits wouldn't pass close inspection, we mesh well in a crowd this size.

I sip champagne and scan the room three times before I admit to myself that I'm looking for her. I can't allow my dick to distract me from my real purpose here, which is Briar. I'm about to give up the search when I spy Lux descending the stairs like a goddamn queen. She's wearing a tight dress with layers of fringe the same color as the champagne flowing throughout the room. A sequined headband cuts across the middle of her forehead.

"Hold up." Tyler stops beside me, his eyes also on Lux. "You didn't tell me this was *Lux Colombia-Clarke's* party."

"Didn't see how it was relevant."

"Holy shit, dude. How the fuck did you score an invitation to this thing?"

We've been to plenty of parties hosted by the rich before. Customers tend to line up out the doors. But there's rich—doctors and lawyers and shit, making their money on the backs of the average citizen—and then there's *rich*.

Ty finds his way into plenty of events, and Nick is learning the ropes from him, while I prefer to stick closer to home. But this level of extravagance is new for all of us.

Lux and I didn't discuss this part. I don't know what story she's selling to her friends, or if they even care, and I haven't had a chance to talk to her yet, so I guess I'm on my own.

"We had a one-night stand." I chug the rest of my champagne and exchange it for a full one from a passing tray.

"You"—Ty shoves a finger into my chest—"had a one-night stand"—he points to Lux across the room—"with that."

"Yep." I take a sip from my fresh drink.

He shakes his head. "I don't buy it. Not for a second."

"Why not?"

"No shade, mate, but she's not the type to go for all that hair." He chuckles as he waves his hand in front of my face. I did my best with it tonight, slicking it back into a bun, but there's a lot of it, and there's bound to be stray strands.

I level a glare at him. "What the fuck would you know about her type?"

He laughs again. "Have you seen her, man? She's a fucking snowflake. And you, my friend, are not snowflake material, no matter how good you are in bed." He pats my chest like he's consoling me.

"Guess I'll have to prove it." I stroll across the room toward Lux like it's the most natural thing in the world for a man like me to walk up to a woman like her.

She's talking to a small cluster of people, eyes wide with excitement and hands flailing as she tells a story. The exuberance pouring from her is contagious, and I find myself wanting to smile as I watch her.

I catch it just in time.

Her eyes rove toward me as I approach. Hesitation lurks in their depths, but she doesn't move away.

I lean down and whisper in her ear. "I told my friends we had a one-night stand, so act like you like me and want to get back into bed with me."

She stiffens at my words, but her smile doesn't slip. "In your dreams," she says under her breath, then turns to the group, who are staring at me like I'm a beast escaped from the zoo. "Everyone, this is Slate."

There are a few muttered replies before they all disperse.

"You sure know how to clear a room." Lux tilts her champagne glass back, and my eyes snap to her long, slender neck as she swallows, as if I'm Edward fucking Cullen.

"Not everyone can handle my charm," I say.

She takes in my outfit—white shirt, black jeans, gray vest, black tie—then says, "You managed to find something in your closet that isn't leather," with a smile made from sweet venom.

I drag a hand over my vest. "From my mum's funeral."

That shuts her up.

Tyler and Nick are watching us closely. "Showtime, baby." I place a hand on her waist and tug her toward me.

"What are you doing?" she hisses.

"They're watching." I lean in close. "Now throw your head back and laugh like I just said something hilarious."

She does, and that laugh sounds like Christmas morning. My hand curls around her tiny waist as if it belongs there. I suck in her scent as she brushes her body against mine.

All too soon, she pulls back, but she can't get far with my hand still on her. "If only you were actually funny," she says, and drains her champagne.

I take the empty glass from her hand. A waiter immediately appears with a full one. I give it to her, my other hand still secure around her. "My humor is too lowbrow for you to understand."

A real laugh trips out of her this time. "Listen, Rambo. We're going to take a selfie together, and then we split up until you're ready to introduce me to your dealer buddies."

I slide my hand along her back, letting my fingers graze her ass. She swallows tightly before leaning into me and snapping a picture with her phone.

She's still inspecting it when a guy who looks like he walked out of an Armani advert approaches. Three-piece beige suit, matching tie and pocket square, and a freaking walking stick. His hair is combed to the side with what was probably an entire bottle of pomade. He looks like a complete twat.

"Who's this?" he says to Lux, his eyes fastening on me like Velcro.

She glances at me as if she's already forgotten who she's standing next to. "This is Slate."

Before either of us have time for further introductions, he yanks her from my grasp. She yelps, and my heart freezes at the sound. He releases her once they're out of earshot, and I tell my body to relax.

I keep my eyes on them as they talk, and even though I can't hear what they're saying, it's obvious he is chewing her out. Her face is a mixture of remorse and shame. The fucking bastard rails on and on while she's nodding along like some kind of Stepford wife.

My phone vibrates in my pocket. It's a text from Laney. *I'm off at ten tonight. Wanna come over?*

I don't hesitate before replying. *Busy tonight i'll call later*

By the time I look up from my phone, Lux and the douchebag have disappeared.

* * *

The party passes the way these things do. No less than three people are shoved into the pool, someone makes a scene about the atrocious food, and more than one person has to be led out because they're too hammered to stand on their own two feet.

I'm sulking behind a plant that's taller than I am while Ty and Nick

93

pad their pockets with cash from the swanky clientele. They both came fully stocked. My eyes track Lux everywhere she goes. That tiny slip of a dress is the worst thing to happen to me tonight.

I should've left the minute Laney texted, bloody plan be damned.

A journalist is here doing a feature on our hostess for some bougie magazine. The photographer has been crawling all over the place like an insect, grabbing candids of guests who look anything but natural. I recognize at least six popstars and A-list actors in the crowd, but everyone's attention is on Lux. She's the queen of the hive, and they all know it.

I overhear several people talking about her being asked to chair some big charity gala that's coming up over the holidays. Apparently it's a big deal.

I'm starting to wonder what the hell I've gotten myself into.

The group of people gathered in front of me disperse, and a guy with his shirt unbuttoned to his navel walks over. The light from the chandelier glints off the multiple chains around his neck. I don't think he got the memo about the Gatsby theme.

His face stretches into a wide grin. "Hey, mate."

I don't tell him we're not mates or that he looks ridiculous, but keep my face expressionless. There's a reason Ty usually handles these gigs.

"You're the real party entertainment, right?" he says.

I suck on my teeth. "Depends on the kind of entertainment you're looking for."

His grin spreads even further. "A man of many trades."

"Outside," I say.

We take our transaction to the terrace. What kind of dealer would I be if I showed up to a party like this with empty pockets? The guy walks away with a tiny vial of white powder, and I get to go home with an extra ten grand to put into Briar's uni fund.

I light a cigarette and lean against the house, watching the people milling around the pool. I can't imagine having all of this and still choosing to get so wasted that you can't even enjoy it.

Someone joins me, and I nearly drop the cig when I see who it is.

"I need a break," Lux says, breathlessly.

I cock a brow and hand her the cigarette.

She takes a puff. "God, I wish this was weed."

"Sorry," I say. "Not my specialty." I stick the lipstick-marked end back into my mouth, thinking about her lips wrapping around it seconds ago.

"When do I get to meet them?"

I take one last puff, then grind it out with my heel. "Let's go."

This whole plan is as ridiculous as it is pointless, but if it proves to Lux that I'm trying, it gets me one step closer to that appointment with Dr. Clarke.

Tyler and Nick are in a hallway near the restroom, making a deal. If the gleam in their eyes is any indication, it's been a successful night. If Lux is offended that they're selling to her party guests, she hides it well.

After everyone else clears the hallway, I tell them about Lux's desire to become a dealer. As I expected, Ty laughs out loud.

"You're too pretty to be selling," he says.

She is not flattered. "I can hook you up with a bunch of new clients."

"Why do we need you when we can score invitations ourselves?" Ty flashes a wad of cash.

She rattles off the names of a dozen celebrities, asking if he's ever been to their parties.

Ty doesn't say anything.

Lux crosses her arms over her chest, further emphasizing her tits. "As I thought."

Tyler pulls me further down the hall, where the other two can't hear us. "I don't like this, mate. She's up to no good."

"Nah," I say. "She just needs the money."

"Bro, look around you. The girl is flush with dough."

"Look." I lean in close. "Just help me score this, okay? You and I both know she'll never make it if she sets foot in the Junction. But that doesn't mean I can't get a little something for my trouble."

Understanding lights up his eyes. "I got you, mate. Go get it." He slaps me on the arm before whooping his way down the hall.

I approach Lux, who is still waiting for me. With a slight incline of my head, I indicate the powder room door. She blinks several times before the deer-in-the-headlights look takes over. The girl is quick on her feet though, and the look is gone by the next blink.

She leads the way into the restroom. I close the door behind us, catching a glimpse of Ty's wink as I do so.

"What the fuck are we doing in here?" she hisses.

"They don't trust you," I say. "I needed to prove that this wasn't a setup."

"How is locking me in a bathroom with you supposed to accomplish that?"

"Do you want me to take the time to explain, or can you trust me on this?"

She looks like she wants to argue it further, but she backs down. "Are they listening outside?"

I close my eyes and inhale deeply. "Probably."

"I see." She straightens her spine and lets out a pathetic moan.

"Is that the sound you imagine you'd make if I was going down on you?"

She leans over the sink to fix her lipstick, sticking that ass into the air. "Men like to have their egos stroked, don't they?"

I wrap one arm around her tiny waist and yank her against me. A little gasp escapes her mouth. "If I wanted to make you feel good, the last thing you'd be thinking about is my ego, princess," I growl into her ear.

We have passed into dangerous territory. Too many options to get her out of this fucking dress are presenting themselves. Yank it up, yank it down, tear it at the side. All of them end with her tight ass exposed and me sinking into—

"Get your hands off of me." Her tone is icy.

Trapping her eyes in the mirror, I slowly release her. She recaps the lipstick and sticks it back in her bag.

"Who was the wanker?" I lean back against the wall and cross my arms.

Her gaze narrows, meeting mine in the mirror. "I don't know who you mean."

"He looked like he was going to shit a load when we took that photo together. Which you take way too many of, by the way."

She turns around with a hard laugh. "Do you even know what my job is? How hard it is to maintain this image the world has of me?" She zips the bag shut.

"What's wrong with being yourself?" I say quietly.

She scoffs. "Nothing, if 'yourself' is enough." She sets her bag on the vanity and props her hands on the marble edge. "And the guy was Carter. My boyfriend."

"You're *dating* that prick?"

"He's not a prick." She fiddles with a thin gold bracelet dangling from her arm.

I raise my brows. "Could've fooled me."

"He just gets jealous easily." She winds the chain absentmindedly, and it draws my attention to her wrists, where a different set of bracelets are fading into yellowish smudges.

"Did he give you those?" It's impossible to keep the steel from my tone as I gesture to her bruises.

She drops her gaze to her hand. "It was a one-year anniversary present." The gold sparkles as she touches it.

"That's not the one I meant."

Before she can respond, someone pounds on the door. "One second," she calls, then follows with a loud moan.

"How is this"—I wag my finger between us—"going to go down with him?" I should have thought about that sooner.

She lifts her shoulder and twirls a strand of hair around her finger. "I'll probably pay for it later—"

"You'll what?" I interrupt. "How will you 'pay for it'?"

She sighs. "Don't worry about it, okay? It's nothing I can't handle."

"Yeah, well maybe it's more than I can handle." I push off from the wall. "Why not leave him?"

"It's complicated." She toes a seam in the tile floor. "You wouldn't understand."

"Try me. I'm not as dumb as I look."

Her heeled foot halts in its path. "Just let it go, Slate." Then, with her eyes glued to mine, she moans loudly in a rising crescendo.

My dick throbs in my pants. Her acting ability is admirable.

"Let me know when you're ready for the real thing," I say as she rearranges her hair in the mirror.

She ignores me. Then, with her hand on the doorknob, she says, "We're done here," and walks out.

Tyler and Nick congratulate me on a job well done when I emerge from the restroom. Amid their slaps on the back, the only thing I can think about is that I should have taken Laney up on her offer. But it's after 2 a.m., and she's asleep already.

Which means I'm left with only an over-eager cock and visions of shredding Lux's dress for company.

14

"Rush" - The Score

Lux

The cleaners have done their job before I even get up. Which means only the most important part is left to do.

I settle on the sofa in the living room and start combing through the photos from last night. There are hundreds on my phone, and I can't post even a tenth of them. That's why curation is an art form.

After fifteen minutes, it's starting to grow tedious, and Slate's words come back to haunt me. Maybe I do take too many photos. But how can I make sure I get the perfect shot otherwise? That jackass doesn't know the first thing about life in the spotlight.

Since he's on my mind anyway, I give him a call. "Did it work?" I say when he answers.

There's a loud clatter on the other end, followed by a curse.

"Am I interrupting something?"

"Of course not. I was just sitting here, waiting for your call."

"Cute." I roll my eyes even though he can't see it. "So? Did it?"

"Did it what?"

"Did your colleagues buy our story?" I switch the call to Bluetooth and continue sorting through photos.

His snort is punctuated by a metallic click. "You realize this is a long game, right? One party isn't convincing anyone of shit."

"You can at least tell me if they thought I was legitimate."

"They thought you're a pampered princess who's getting bored and looking for a new toy."

I scowl at the selfie of the two of us. "Do they have any idea how hard I've worked for everything I have?"

The derisive smile on his face is easy to picture. "Maybe you can tell them your sob story next time."

"Bastard." I'm about to swipe to the next photo when something in the background makes me pause. I zoom in with two fingers. One of the guys Slate brought to the party is shoving a blue-and-white vase into his jacket. "Oh my god."

I get up to double-check the table in the foyer. Sure enough, the surface is empty. "One of your friends stole a Ming vase last night."

"What the fuck is a Ming vase?"

"You cannot be serious."

He grunts.

"Ming porcelain is rare and valuable. That vase was worth thousands!"

The sound of metal scraping metal comes through the line, and I wince. "I'm sure you can find another," he says.

"It's not like buying a black T-shirt. They're one of a kind. I happened to like that one."

"Sorry, princess. But if you only called to yell at me, I have work to do."

"Nice talking to you too." I end the call and toss the phone onto the cushion beside me. Why that man has the ability to crawl under my skin remains a mystery.

When he put his hands on me in the restroom last night, I felt . . . It's impossible to explain. *Alive*, perhaps. Safer than I've ever been, while also in the most dangerous situation of my life.

Fortunately, Carter did not get wind of our powder room rendezvous. It's not the kind of thing that would be easy to explain, and I don't want to hurt him.

My phone pings, and at first I think it might be Slate, apologizing for being a complete ass on the phone, but it's only my group chat with Maeve and Walker.

Walker: *Last night was amazing, L! x*

Me: *A blastttt!! xx*

Maeve: *You are the party queen, and we pay you homage.*

Me: *I accept your gratitude. Checks can be made payable to Her Majesty Lux Colombia-Clarke xx*

I consider telling them about my vase being stolen, but I hesitate. I don't want my friends getting involved in this, and when Maeve goes to bat for her friends, pity anyone who gets in her way. This is too important to bungle for the sake of gossip.

Maeve: *Who was the brooding guy staring at you all night?*

Me: *??*

Me: *Carter?*

I wouldn't call him brooding, but he does tend to sulk.

Walker: *I saw him too. Not Carter.*

Maeve: *Six-two, long hair, cheap vest. . .*

Oh god.

Me: *That was nobody.*

Maeve: *That was not a nobody stare.*

Walker: *He couldn't take his eyes off of you.*

I bite my lip. *Was* Slate watching me all night? And if so, why does the thought send a thrill racing along my spine?

Maeve: *And he is delicious.*

Me: *I'm happy with Carter, so he's all yours xx*

Maeve wouldn't be caught dead with a guy like Slate, which is why

I feel comfortable saying it. She's also wrong. If Slate was staring at me, it wasn't because he finds me fascinating. He's made it clear that I am the last person in the world he wants anything to do with. A great thought, because he is also the last person I could ever be interested in, even if I wasn't happy in my relationship.

Carter already knows everything there is to know about me, and even he finds me lacking. Why the fuck would someone with a chip on his shoulder about wealth ever think better of me?

* * *

I'm sliding the second tray of cookies into the oven when the doorbell rings. I open the camera app on my phone and blink in surprise at the sight of the figure on the other side of the door.

When I open it, Slate hands me a certain porcelain vase. I take it, and he shoves his hands into the pockets of his faded jeans but doesn't say anything. He keeps his eyes trained on mine.

Maeve's words keep circling my head. *Was* he staring at me?

Regardless of what he did or didn't do during the party, he is staring at me now. I'm wearing tiny denim cut-off shorts, which are mostly hidden by my oversized white sweater. I wasn't planning on seeing anyone tonight and can't even tug them down because of the vase in my hands.

"Do you own any colors besides black?" The words are out before I can stop them. As they echo in my head, it hits me that I've just admitted to noticing what he wears.

His lips twitch as he holds my gaze. Finally, he drops it to glance down at his shirt, which is molded to his broad torso, dipping into the valleys of his map of a chest. He pulls the fabric away, then lets it snap back. "I do,"—a wince—"but I didn't want you to get the wrong idea."

The hair on the back of my neck bristles. I'm on the verge of slamming the door in his face when he takes a step inside. I move backward to get out of his way, and in doing so, lose my balance on the waxed hardwood. Slate grabs me with both hands before the vase and I can crash to the floor.

He removes the urn from my grip and sets it in the correct spot on the foyer table.

"Thank you," I murmur as my timer begins beeping. "I need to grab that." I dart toward the kitchen, hoping he'll take the opportunity to see himself out.

A blush climbs my neck and settles on my face. It's not entirely from the open oven, either. There's something unsettling about the man, with his snug black T-shirt and denim-clad—

I yelp and fumble the tray of cookies. Slate has *not* shown himself out.

His lips quirk as I set the hot pan down. "Are you always this clumsy?" His tone is mocking.

"Are you always this annoying?" I use a spatula to transfer the cookies to a cooling rack.

He props a hip against the countertop. "Never pegged you as a baker."

"You don't know anything about me, so that tracks." I hesitate with the last cookie before holding it out to him. As much as he annoys me, I can't resist feeding people.

His eyes snag mine as he takes it, then immediately drops it. "Fuck. That's hot."

I smirk and take the pan to the sink. "Are you always this clumsy?" After retrieving a napkin for him, I lean back and watch him eat the cookie.

"You're not going to have one?" he says.

"I don't eat sugar."

"And yet you just baked two dozen cookies." He blows on the one in his hand.

My breath catches in my throat as my eyes latch onto those full lips.

"Makes perfect sense," he says.

"It's stress relieving. I usually give them to my housekeeper."

"I haven't had a monster cookie in six years."

"That's very specific." I grab a dish towel and wipe the crumbs from the counter.

"My mum used to bake."

I remember his comment at the party about her funeral. "What happened?"

Slate takes a huge bite, and I try to ignore the way his Adam's apple bobs as he swallows. "She started getting really bad migraines. Spent all day on the sofa, couldn't even heat a can of soup. A year later, she was gone." He flicks his wrist like he's not telling me one of the worst things that could happen to a person. "Brain tumor."

"I'm sorry." I place a hand on his arm, not sure when I moved closer to him. He's as warm as sunshine. "Is that why you're so scared about your sister?"

His muscles ripple beneath my fingers as he shifts his arm. "She's all I have left." He flicks his tongue to get a piece of chocolate at the corner of his mouth.

A tingling grows in my belly. I remove my palm from his arm, but the contact from his skin is imprinted there. I twist the dish towel between my hands to remove the sensation.

"These are really good," he says around the last bite. "Even better than my mum's."

"Take as many as you want," I tell him, working to regulate my tone. What is it about this man? I scrub at an imaginary spot on the counter.

"Only if you try one." His dark eyes are tracking my every move. I don't even need to look at him to feel them feeding on me.

"I told you. I don't eat sugar."

"One cookie isn't going to kill you."

"Is that what you tell yourself every time you light one of those cancer sticks?" Without meaning to, my eyes flick toward him to gauge his reaction.

His eyelids lower infinitesimally, snuffing out the spark. "I've been wondering when the lecture about my life choices would start."

"If you care about your sister so much, maybe you should try staying alive for her."

He snorts and takes another cookie from the rack. "I have no plans of living a long life. If the cigarettes don't do the job, there are plenty of other things that will."

The timer beeps again, and I remove the second batch from the oven. "Your optimism is nauseating."

"At least I'm not living in fear of sugar." He leans his elbows on the counter, then breaks off half the cookie and chews.

I glower at him and grab my own cookie from the rack. "Who said I'm scared?"

He watches as I take a small bite. It's good, but I set it down and use a napkin to wipe my fingers.

"A single nibble? That's it?"

I don't know what prompts me to do it—maybe that infuriatingly judgmental shake of his head or the smirk hiding in his eyes—but I pick up the cookie and shove the whole thing in my mouth. His eyebrows lift as I struggle to chew, but it goes down eventually.

I lift the back of my hand to my lips, mortified by my own actions. I haven't done something like that since I was fifteen. The powder room calls from down the hall. My feet beg to bolt in that direction, but Slate's presence keeps me frozen in place.

"You okay?" he says quietly, his face softening.

I reach for the water bottle on the counter, avoiding that heavy gaze. Drinking does little to ease the pain in my gut, but at least it gives me something to do.

His gaze grows even heavier. "I'm sorry," he says when I lower the bottle. "I shouldn't have taunted you like that."

I can't help but look at him. First returning the vase and now an apology? Concern is etched in the lines around his eyes. I don't know who this man truly is, but he isn't the guy I first thought he was. "I'm fine," I say.

"You've got a little—" He reaches out a hand, and before I can object, swipes the corner of my mouth with his thumb.

I've drunk half my bottle of water, but my throat is still dry. I need this man out of my house, but I can't find the words to ask him to go.

15

"Lips of an Angel" - Hinder

I feel bad about the cookie thing. I shouldn't have egged her on like that. It's obvious that she's as shocked by her own actions as I am.

I wipe my thumb on a napkin. It still tingles from the contact with her mouth. I flex it, but the sensation remains, as if she branded herself onto my skin.

Her eyes are wide with mortification, so I turn away to give her time to compose herself. I don't know what just happened, but I think it's safe to say I pushed her to a breaking point, and she's irritated by it.

"Excuse me," she murmurs, and flees the room.

I wander to the bank of windows overlooking the garden. Seconds later, I hear the unmistakable sound of retching coming from the restroom down the hall—the same one we were in last night.

Fuck. Whatever is going on in there, I am at least partially responsible.

I'm not stupid enough to think Lux wants my comfort, so I explore the kitchen while I wait for her to return. The place has transformed since last night. If I didn't know it was the same house, I wouldn't believe it.

An espresso machine is sitting on the counter next to the two wall ovens. There's a triple sink in the middle of the island, and there are not only hot and cold taps, but also one for boiling water. Who the fuck has an actual water-boiling appliance?

People who can afford not to wait.

The cupboards are pink. Briar would call them "salmon." It fits Lux's vibe, but I didn't expect her to actually use her kitchen, let alone be baking cookies in it when I showed up.

I should go before she comes back. I don't even know what the fuck I'm doing here, except that I can't stay away to save my life. She exerts some kind of magnetic charm I'm powerless to resist, regardless of how much she gets under my skin.

The bathroom door opens before I'm able to convince myself to leave. I lift my head as she enters the kitchen, and the sight of her face hits me like a blow. Her eyes are red, her face is blotchy, and her hair is disheveled. She does not meet my gaze.

"You okay?" I walk over to her, stopping a few feet away.

"I'm fine," she croaks, and reaches for her water bottle.

It takes me three seconds to realize that's not embarrassment on her face—it's shame. Deep, crippling shame. The kind that makes you want to shrivel up and die.

She stares at the cookies like she wants to murder them. I put a hand on each of her shoulders. She still refuses to look at me.

"Lux," I say quietly.

Her eyes shutter closed. I tug her into my arms. The action feels so instinctive I don't even know what I'm doing until she's nestled there, bringing the scent of roses and sugar cream with her.

I can't believe how delicate she feels, like a china figurine that will shatter from the slightest jostle. How often does she allow herself to be vulnerable in front of someone else? Because so far, the only side of her I've seen could take down an entire gang of bikers if they got in her way.

I'm tall enough that her head fits perfectly beneath my chin. I tuck it there and hold her close. Whatever demons are haunting her won't be getting access tonight.

It takes several minutes for her to relax in my arms, but I can feel it the second she does. It's like unspooling a breath you've been holding for far too long. She softens that tough facade and allows herself to be held.

"You don't always have to be strong," I say into her incredible-smelling hair. "Sometimes it's okay to let others be strong for you."

She doesn't say anything, but she doesn't pull away either. Finally, after a long time, she mumbles, "Thank you."

I hate to think that I may have played a part in whatever drove her over that edge. "Truce?" I lean back to look down at her.

Lux inclines her head. "Truce." Instead of relaxing back into my embrace, she drops her arms from around my waist, her steely facade back in place. "I think I should place an order for insidion."

I blink away my surprise and disappointment that I'm no longer holding her. "To sell?"

"I won't sell it, of course, but I want to let them know I'm serious about this whole thing." She takes a cookie from the tray and begins breaking off tiny pieces onto a napkin.

"I'll tell them I'm supplying you." I reach for another cookie as well, but mine goes into my mouth.

"It needs to be from someone other than you."

A short laugh breaks from my chest. "No way."

"I need to get info."

There is no explanation for the way my blood pressure is rising. "It's dangerous."

She brushes the crumbs from her fingers. "So give me a gun."

Actual tremors work their way through my hands at the thought of her needing a gun to protect herself. "Absolutely not." I try a different tactic. "They won't tell you anything anyway."

Her chin lifts in a mockingly haughty tilt. "You underestimate the power of a short skirt and high heels."

I've never understood the phrase "seeing red" until this moment. Contrary to her belief, I'm fully aware of the power of that lethal combo, especially after the outfit she wore last night. Especially after my sheets ended up twisted into a knot this morning.

My eyes dip down without permission to take in those long golden legs. They're a masterpiece, and I would pay good money to see them back in heels. The thought of another guy looking at them like that—

I step closer, until our chests are flush with each other again. I grasp her chin between my fingers, and the softness of her skin stirs a moan in my chest, which I keep suppressed. "I think you're the one who underestimates their power." My voice is nothing more than a rasp.

Her breath hitches in her throat with a jagged inhale. She sinks her teeth into that luscious lower lip, and it's that action that tips me over the edge.

I lower my head. Lux does nothing to meet me, but she doesn't pull back either. Our breaths mingle in the fraction of space between us. I stroke my calloused thumb over her chin, relishing her velvet skin beneath mine. God, what she'd feel like stretched out under me—

I drop my lips to hers, and then I'm flying to another realm of heaven. She's even sweeter than expected, and I'm spiraling into the ecstasy of her. She doesn't part her lips for me, but I don't mind, because even this small part of her is a fantasy too good to be true.

My hand glides along her jaw, seeking more of that buttery skin. I reach the back of her head, her face cradled in my palm, and toy with her luxurious hair. God, she's incredible. She tastes like peppermint, probably from brushing her teeth.

My other hand is clamped onto her waist, preventing her from bolting, although based on the gentle way she's offering herself up to me, I think it's an unnecessary precaution. I run my tongue along the seam of her lips, requesting that she open for me, no longer satisfied with the appetizer. I need the whole meal.

But before she can respond, a phone rings on the counter beside us. She jumps back as if I've singed her. Her eyes are frozen with horror, which sends a sucker punch to my abdomen.

I fucked up.

Her hand fumbles for the phone like she can't remember what you're supposed to do with such objects. She answers quietly. I consider leaving the room, but I'm not sure where else to go. She technically didn't even invite me into her house.

"Nooo." It comes out as a wail. I rush to grab her before she collapses onto the floor, but she manages to prop herself up on the counter. "No." A sob this time. "Please, god, no."

The phone drops from her hand. I help her into a chair near the window, then retrieve it. The call is still connected to "Mum."

"Hello?" I say. "Lux is . . ." Her face is buried in her hands. ". . . she's upset. Is there a message I can relay?"

"Where is Carter?" The woman on the other end sounds like the kind of posh that can only be cultivated through years of practice.

I scramble for some kind of explanation that will satisfy her. "I don't know. I was dropping something off at Lux's house when you called."

"She freaked out before I could even tell her everything. Tell her that her brother is fine. He overdosed, but he's in good hands at the hospital."

"Which—"

She ends the call before I can find out where he's at.

I set the phone on the counter and approach Lux. She doesn't remove her hands from her face, so I crouch down and rest a hand on her knee. "Hey," I say gently. "Your brother is okay."

She doesn't say anything, gives no indication she's heard me.

"I talked to your mum. He's at the hospital. Want me to drive you there?"

She lowers her hands at the speed of molasses. "Alex is okay?" Her face is as clear as ever. Whatever she was doing behind those hands, it wasn't crying.

I stand and offer my hand. Hers is cold. She leads the way to the garage, where that Ferrari Spyder sits like a trophy on a stand. She holds out a key ring. When I don't take it right away, she says, "You said you'd drive, right?"

She doesn't need to ask me twice. It's hard to decide which is better—driving one of the world's most beautiful cars or having one of the world's most beautiful women by my side.

We don't make conversation, except for Lux telling me which hospital to go to. It's obvious that her mind is on her family. When we pull up to the emergency entrance, I let the car idle and turn to her. "I'll park. You go on up."

I half expect a fiery retort about how she's not stupid enough to leave her car in my hands. But she simply nods and opens her door.

I park the car and am halfway to the red neon sign above the automatic doors when it hits me what I'm doing. I stop in the middle of the car park. What the fuck am I thinking? I can't go in there. I cannot afford to get tangled up in Lux's family drama, or any of her drama for that matter.

I tuck the car keys in the wheel well and have an Uber pick me up at a nearby petrol station. I left my bike at Lux's house, so I have them drop me off there. The night air helps to clear my head.

The last thing I need is to further complicate my life by letting Lux Colombia-Clarke into it.

* * *

I know something's wrong the second I turn onto our street. The lights are all on in the house, and Briar is meticulous about only lighting the room she's in.

My bike wobbles from my shoddy parking job as I bolt through the door. She isn't on the sofa or in her room. The bathroom door is closed, and I knock.

"Briar?"

A moan.

I shove the door open with my shoulder. She's crumpled near the toilet, her head resting on the fuzzy purple seat cover she insisted I buy. I scoop her up in my arms without bothering to find out what's wrong.

I'm on my way back to the hospital within two minutes, Briar safely buckled into the seat beside me. She's been unresponsive, aside from the occasional moan. Her head lolls to the side as I take the curves. It would be more comfortable for her if I slowed down, but doing so could cost her life—not a risk I'm willing to take.

My mum's rusty sedan eats up the miles much slower than my bike or the Ferrari. I curse the day Lux showed up on my doorstep. If it hadn't been for her, I would have been home tonight, and Briar would already be admitted to the hospital. I got so caught up in helping Lux with her family that it could very well cost me my own.

I throw the car into park and lift Briar from the seat. I'll come back out later to properly park it. The security guard pulls up a wheelchair when he sees us coming.

The admittance process is the same as always—way too tedious, too redundant, and too fucking long. Fortunately, by the time I'm allowed back to see her, her face has regained some of its color, and the pain has subsided.

I press a kiss to the top of her head, tell her to get some rest, and head out to park the car. I'm leaning against the back wall of the lift when it stops on the fourth floor. The doors open, and Lux steps inside before spotting me. They close behind her before she can change her mind.

"I thought you left," she says cooly to the instrument panel.

"I did." No use hiding it. I wouldn't be back here if it wasn't for Briar.

"I see." She remains at the front of the lift, while I lean back. No one would know that my mouth was on hers two hours ago. "I hope you didn't come back for me, because I—"

"I didn't."

"Are you here for your heart surgery, then? Maybe they'll give you a real one this time."

"My sister had another episode."

Lux whirls around, her face again awash with horror. "Is she—" Her hand clutches her slender neck.

"She's fine," I assure her. "They have her on pain meds."

The doors open before either of us can say more, and we step into the lobby. It feels awkward to leave her, but I'm not sure what more to say. She fumbles in her bag, which I take to be a dismissal, and I head for the doors at the other end of the room.

"Slate, wait," she calls. I turn back to see her pressing her phone to her ear. "Dad?" she says. "It's Lux."

Who has to introduce themselves to their own father?

"I have a favor to ask." A pause. "No, I don't need money. God," she mutters. Her cheeks bloom pink. "I have a friend who's sick. No one can figure out what's wrong with her, and I was hoping you'd agree to see her."

She ends the call a few seconds later and looks at me. "He said he'll have someone arrange an appointment."

My mouth has lost the ability to form words. I stare at her. How have I managed to be wrong on every count with this woman?

She inclines her head and slides her phone back into her designer bag. "That's what you wanted, right?"

I'm crippled by the need to kiss her, to show her what this means to me. I shove my hands into my pockets before they can do something I'll regret. "That wasn't our bargain."

Lux shrugs and licks her lips. I watch the action with an animalistic fascination.

"Sometimes the game changes," she says.

I was planning to cut ties with her, to say good riddance to this whole ridiculous plan, but here she goes again, upending everything and making me question the wisdom of my own decisions. How can I say goodbye when she's giving me exactly what I want?

"Thank you," I say. "That was nice of you."

"Anybody would have done it." She shifts her bag onto her shoulder and walks to the exit without looking back.

She's wrong. No Silver Spoon I've ever met would do what she did for a stranger. I'm not sure which disturbs me more—the fact that she's not at all what I expected, or the fact that I suddenly want to make her mine more than I want life itself.

16

"Nameless" - Stevie Howie

Lux

I chuck the lipstick into my bag with more force than necessary. Normally, I'd be excited about hitting a club with my friends—my *actual* friends, not the conniving wannabes—but I'm finding it difficult to muster enthusiasm for tonight.

It's bloody ridiculous. I have so much to be grateful for. Alex is out of the hospital, although he returned to the crack house the day after my mum brought him home. Carter made plans for us to go to Egypt this winter, and my bloody father texted to ask if we could grab dinner together next week.

Life is good. Life is great, actually.

So why am I snapping at everyone? Ms. Griffin got the brunt of it earlier today when I found a stray hair in the restroom.

I know what the problem is, but I'll be dead before I admit it out loud. As if taunting me, my phone chimes from my bag. I grabble for it with embarrassing speed.

It's been a week—a whole *week*—since I've heard from Slate. I got the guy's sister an appointment with a world-renowned neurologist. The least he could do is show a little gratitude. I'm not expecting him to serve the Wolf up on a platter, but would a little bit of communication hurt him?

My traitorous brain wonders if our kiss is haunting him the way it is me. It keeps reminding me that I've never been kissed like that before, and my chances of repeating it in the future are slim.

I fish my phone out and check the notification. Finally, thank fuck.

Slate: *It's on tonight 10pm old SaveSense car park*

I'm going to assume "it" is my buying drugs as a front to get information. Why he waited until two hours before to tell me is a topic for another day. Does the man not understand the concept of a schedule?

I send a quick group text to let everyone know I'm bailing on the club, then change into a different outfit. I can't imagine a sequined dress is appropriate attire for buying drugs in a dark alley, but there's little in my closet that is, so I settle for a leather miniskirt, black corset top, and knee-high black boots, then tuck my can of Mace into my purse. I need to learn how to use a gun. If this dealer wants to end me, I highly doubt pepper spray is going to stop him.

I text Slate back.

Me: *Would a little punctuation kill you?*

Slate: *It might*

Slate: *You sure you can play the role of dumb blonde*

Me: *It's not a role.*

* * *

It takes several tries to locate the old SaveSense car park. The GPS no longer recognizes it, so I have to circle the Junction until I spot the fading letters on the decrepit building. I could have called Slate for directions, but he already thinks I can't do this. No need to cement that belief.

A single blinking streetlamp lights up a small section of the car park, and I pull up near it. It won't do much to protect me, but it brings an ounce of comfort anyway. I've rented a basic sedan to avoid drawing any undue attention. A chill bites my skin as I get out of the car, and I'm already regretting not grabbing a jacket.

Crispy leaves skitter across the broken asphalt, making me jump at their scratching noises. Slate and I never discussed him coming with me. It doesn't make sense for him to, and I certainly don't need his help, but a dash of doubt is seasoning my conviction that this was a good idea.

No one else appears to be here yet, but I keep my eyes peeled for other vehicles. Slate never said where to wait, and the car park is large, so I can only hope the dealer finds me soon.

After I've been leaning against my door for what feels like an eternity, a low-slung black car pulls into the lot, muffler blaring.

Guess subtlety isn't on the menu tonight.

A man about my height gets out. As he walks through the glow of the barely working lamp, I catch a glimpse of greasy blonde hair. He's young, maybe only a year or two older than I am, wearing baggy jeans and a soccer jersey.

He swaggers as he walks and tilts his head to the side as he assesses me. The second his eyes take in my short skirt and tall boots, I know I made the right choice. His gaze lingers for far too long, but that just means it will be much easier to distract him into telling me everything he knows about the Wolf.

Should I introduce myself? What's the appropriate protocol? Why didn't I think to ask Slate any of these things?

A slow smile spreads across the man's face, dragging his upper lip into a sneer as he approaches. "You got cash?" His voice is a low drawl. A shiver scurries down my back.

I reach into my bag for the stack of bills I counted three times before coming here. It would be disastrous to underpay and have him track me down.

His look turns greedy as I tap the money against my palm. *Dumb blonde*, I remind myself. "I think this is the right amount." Self-doubt fills every crevice of my falsetto.

"I can count it for you." He reaches out a hand.

I hesitate before giving it to him, but I don't give a fuck if he hands over drugs. Information is my sole purpose for being here tonight.

He starts flipping through the cash, keeping one eye trained on my legs. I prop my arms on the bonnet of the car, letting my body fold backward like I'm simply stretching tight muscles. He fumbles the money and has to start over.

"Who's your supplier?" I say with as much nonchalance as possible, while my heart completes a triathlon in my chest. I wrap a strand of hair around my finger and keep my gaze on him.

The man's eyes shift up to stare at me, his greed as evident as his dilated pupils. "Same as everyone else."

"The . . . Fox or something?"

He grins indulgently, as if I'm a small child. "The Wolf."

"That's right." I snap my fingers like I should have remembered. "What's he like? Big, brooding guy in an office somewhere, right? I'll bet he collects Cuban cigars and *Playboy* posters."

The dealer smiles and shakes his head. *What a silly girl.* "I've never met him, but there are stories."

I straighten myself on the bonnet. "Stories?" I adopt the same eager look he has every time he glances below my face. "I love stories."

"I don't know much," he hedges, his voice lowered as if we're telling ghost stories around a bonfire, "but I've heard he runs his money through another business."

"Like money laundering?"

"They say it's like a restaurant or something."

Interesting. I expected something more white-collar, like a real estate conglomerate. "Which restaurant?" I say with extra excitement. "Maybe we can . . . pay him a little visit."

Fear replaces the cockiness on the man's face. "I don't know." It comes out in a rush. "It's just a rumor anyway." He shoves the stack of bills into his pocket and tosses something at me. "Hit me up again if you need more."

I fumble the small vial, and it falls to the ground. By the time I locate it with the torch of my phone, he's disappeared.

I'm sliding into my rental when an engine roar fills the car park. An orange McLaren drifts around the corner and stops opposite me.

I get back out of the car, wishing for the thousandth time I was wearing something warmer. "Carter? What are you doing here?" I'd be less surprised to see him on the moon than in the Junction.

He jumps out and stalks toward me. "I could ask you the same thing." The streetlamp brightens for a few seconds, illuminating his face, which is flushed with anger. He grabs my wrist and yanks me toward him. "What the fuck are you doing, Lux? Have you lost your fucking mind? You realize this is the Junction."

"It is?" I glance around with wide eyes, before tugging on my wrists. "Of course I knew that."

He tightens his grip. "Don't be coy with me."

I give up resisting. It will only hurt more and bruise worse. "How did you know where I was?"

His derisive laugh cuts through the night air. "You didn't think I'd be stupid enough to trust you, did you? I know you can't go two seconds without your fucking phone, so what better way to make sure my girlfriend is being faithful?"

Fear grips my heart in its claws and squeezes. How long has he been tracking me? Does he know Slate kissed me? That I didn't push him away?

I swallow the lump in my throat. If I can handle a seedy drug dealer, I can handle my own boyfriend. "Why would you think I was cheating on you?"

He clamps a hand on my neck and pulls me closer. "Don't lie to me, you scheming slut."

I brace myself for what's coming. The worst part is knowing I deserve all of it.

But before Carter can lay another hand on me, his head is knocked sideways with a sharp crack. I scream instinctively and duck. The assailant doesn't pay any attention to me. Instead, he pummels Carter into the pavement with his fists.

"Stop!" I screech.

At my plea, the guy in the black hoodie instantly halts his fist, which is halfway to Carter's already bloody mouth. His arm remains pulled back as he stares down at Carter's sobbing face.

"Please, man," he whimpers from beneath the stranger's body. "I'm sorry. I wasn't doing anything, I swear."

The fist lowers a fraction of an inch. "Do you consider laying a hand on a woman 'not doing anything'?"

That voice trickles into me, warming areas I didn't even know were cold.

Carter raises both hands. "I wasn't hurting her. She's my girlfriend." As if the two are mutually exclusive.

Slate pulls his arm back before letting it slam into Carter's face once more. "Not anymore, she isn't." Then he stands up and walks over to me. His hands cradle my face as he looks me over. "Are you hurt?"

I shake my head. "I'm fine. That really wasn't necessary." The cold has turned my skin numb, but I still shiver at his touch.

His nostrils flare. "He had his hands on you. Did you think I was going to sit back and watch?" He shrugs out of his leather jacket and drapes it over my shoulders.

I grab it with both hands to keep it from sliding off. It smells like him—worn leather, mint, and a faint whiff of tobacco. I curl into the residual warmth from his body, letting it thaw my bones.

Carter moans from the ground. Slate grasps my wrist and yanks off the anniversary bracelet. He tosses it onto Carter's chest. "Women aren't property or punching bags." To me he says, "Let's go."

He helps me into the passenger seat of the rental car. "Give me your phone," he orders.

I do so without hesitation. Objecting hasn't gotten me far in life.

After a few minutes, he hands it back. "There. Now that fucking loser can't track you anymore."

Carter still hasn't moved from the ground.

"Should we help him?" I say.

Slate looks at me like I've sprouted horns. "Are you fucking with me? After what he did to you?"

I slump back into my seat, and he starts the car. I'll deal with Carter later.

We drive in silence for a few minutes until I can't handle it anymore. "Why didn't you call? It's been a whole week."

Slate's eyes dart sideways before returning to the road. "I didn't realize regular communication was part of our bargain."

"You could have told me you were going to be there tonight."

"You thought I was going to let you meet that creep on your own?"

Knowing he was there all along—that I was never in any real danger—does strange things to my head. "I didn't need your help."

"Precisely why I stayed hidden."

"So you were just going to spy on me all night and then leave?"

His thumb taps the steering wheel. "What did you want me to do?"

I don't answer because I don't *have* an answer. I'm upset, but I can't even explain why.

"Exactly what look were you going for here?" Amusement lurks in his tone. His eyes are on my skirt, which has risen even higher now that I'm sitting.

I turn my attention out the window. "An effective one."

"And was it?" A pause. "Effective?"

"He told me the Wolf launders his money through a restaurant."

Slate huffs out a disinterested snort. "I hope that information was worth it."

"We'll see," I say.

"What the fuck was the wanker's problem?"

I don't have to ask if he means Carter. "He accused me of cheating."

"Fucking cocksucker."

I twirl a piece of hair around my fingers, keeping my eyes on the window. I don't trust myself to look anywhere else. "He's right though. I *did* cheat."

Silence swirls around the car as we both watch the city around us. An eddy of tension runs through the stillness, strong as an ocean current, sucking me in with its destructive strength.

"Feeling attracted to someone isn't cheating."

My head turns toward him of its own volition. His eyes are still fixed on the road, but when he senses my stare, he meets my gaze. His face is blank, like he's intentionally sheltering his thoughts.

I keep my voice steady, refusing to let him read my emotions. "Kissing them is."

17

"Over My Head (Cable Car)" - The Fray

Slate

This car is not big enough for the amount of tension emanating from my body. If Lux hadn't asked me to stop pounding that fucking asshat, he'd be an unrecognizable pulp right now.

When he called her a slut and grabbed her neck, it was over. I don't care if she feels guilty for that kiss in her kitchen. No man has the right to lay a hand on her and insult her like that.

My knuckles are white on the steering wheel, and I make a conscious effort to unclench my fingers. But as soon as my head fills with thoughts of what just went down, they're back to gripping it hard enough to leave grooves in the leather.

Beside me, Lux is quiet, staring out the window. I wish I knew what was going through her head, but something tells me it's about that motherfucking wanker, and I don't want to know what kind of sympathetic bullshit she feels toward him.

Her phone rings, and I see his name flash on the screen before she declines the call. When he tries again thirty seconds later, she turns the phone off.

I'm driving down her street when it occurs to me. "Does he have a key to your house?"

She slowly turns her head. "Who?"

"Your ex-boyfriend." I grind the words out.

Her expression drains away, leaving her looking peaked. "Yes."

"Fuck." I pass her driveway and turn back onto Twenty-Fifth Boulevard.

"What are you doing?"

"Give me a different address. I'm not leaving you alone in your house if that sod has access."

A long, heavy sigh escapes her mouth. "He wouldn't do anything."

"He left fucking marks on your neck, Lux." I might still kill the motherfucker.

"Plenty of people give hand necklaces."

A tremor shudders through my body at her flippancy. "You cannot compare that kind of abuse to stuff done between two consenting people."

"He just gets upset sometimes," she says quietly.

"Tell me you are not fucking defending him." I ram my fist against the steering wheel.

She startles, and I immediately regret it.

"I'm sorry." I reach for her hand and tuck it into mine. It's limp and cold. "Can I take you to your mum's house?"

Her shoulders lift an inch, then drop back down, as if it takes too much effort to keep them up. "Sure." She gives me the address but doesn't say another word as we wind up the curving driveway to the gaudiest mansion I've ever seen.

I park the car in the driveway. "Come on. I'll walk you in." She allows me to lead her up the front steps, but the distance between us feels a mile wide.

The woman who comes to the door looks like an older version of Lux, but lacks a certain grace that Lux has in bounds. "My god," she says. "It's midnight. I was already in bed."

"Sorry, Mum," Lux mumbles.

This woman is her mother? She looks more like an older sister, and she doesn't act like a concerned parent.

"Carter was mistreating her," I say. "I didn't feel comfortable leaving her at home tonight."

The woman's eyes take in my supermarket jeans and worn black T-shirt. "Who are you?"

"I—"

"He's a friend," Lux cuts in. "So is it okay? Can I stay here? Just for tonight."

Her mum cuts me another look before turning her attention on Lux. "You should work things out with Carter." She keeps her hand propped on the door. "He's a good guy."

"A good guy." A snarl erupts from my throat. "He was *hurting* her."

She doesn't bother looking my way again and directs her words at Lux. "Did you provoke him? No man can be expected to hold it together when he's being treated like a fool."

I grab Lux's hand. "We're leaving."

She follows me to the car, hand tucked inside mine, and climbs in while I hold the door. I slam it shut and turn back to the house, but her mum has already disappeared inside, not giving a single bloody fuck that her daughter was just abused by her boyfriend and is now in the care of a stranger.

I call Tyler as we drive back across the bridge and ask him to pick up my bike from the car park.

"Where are we going?" Lux asks, her voice half its usual size.

"Home."

"I thought you—"

"My home."

She doesn't say anything, and I never thought I'd wish so badly for her usual flood of words. I'm questioning whether I made the right move in interfering, in taking charge, in bringing her home. But it's done now, and there's not much I can do but take care of her.

Tyler pulls up on my bike at the same time we arrive. If he's wondering about Lux climbing out of the car, he—for once—has the decency not to say anything.

"Tyler, Lux. Lux, this is Ty."

"You were at my party," Lux says, and holds out her hand.

Ty shakes it, beaming at her recognition. "That party was dope."

She returns his smile, but even in the dark, it's obvious the wattage is significantly dimmed.

"See you later, mate." I slap him on the shoulder. "Thanks again." I wave at Chris, who is waiting on the street to give Tyler a ride home, before walking Lux to the front door.

Once we're inside, it occurs to me that I haven't thought through this scenario. I was so focused on getting Lux away from that motherfucker and that fuckup of a mother, I didn't stop to think about what I was going to do with her.

My house is a two-bedroom, which is fine, because there are only two of us living here. But the idiocy of my plan hits me as Lux looks around the living room.

"I'll take the sofa," I say.

Briar is already in bed, thank fuck, because I do not want to hear a word about me bringing a woman home, especially if that woman is Lux Colombia-Clarke.

I lead the way to my bedroom at the other end of the house. The only women who have ever been in here are Briar and my mum, and a strange discomfort spreads through me as Lux takes in the space. It's basic, with a bed and dresser filling most of it. The small window above the headboard lets in the light of the moon and the streetlamps.

She stands there in the pale moonlight, looking like a lost little girl, her arms wrapped tightly around her middle, my jacket still draped over her shoulders.

I pull one of my T-shirts from a drawer and hand it to her. "If you want to change," I add.

While Lux is in the restroom, I grab a fresh set of sheets from the hall closet and quickly strip the bed. By the time I hear the door opening, I've made it up with clean linens and turned back the comforter.

She walks into the room, and my heart drops down to my toes. My T-shirt barely covers her ass, leaving those long legs exposed and tantalizing. She's still clutching her midsection. "Thank you," she murmurs. "You didn't need to do all of this."

"I think I did." Our eyes meet across the small room. I want to cup her face in my hands and tell her that no one will ever hurt her again.

She drops my gaze and crawls into bed. It's only full-size, but it still dwarfs her. Her silky hair fans out across my pillow like spilled gold. I may never wash that pillowcase again.

"Good night," I say, and head for the door.

"Slate?"

I hesitate with my hand on the light switch, then turn back.

"Would you mind staying with me?" Her voice trembles.

Something catches in my chest. Stay with her? Until she falls asleep? Or for the entire night? Is there an option that won't drive me mad?

Lux props herself up on one elbow, her eyes large and doe-like. "I really don't want to be alone right now."

I don't know how the fuck I'm supposed to keep my hands to myself when she's hardly wearing anything and lying next to me in my fucking bed, but I'm not strong enough to say no when she's looking at me like that. I slip off my shoes and pad over to the bed, not even bothering to change.

She scoots back until she's near the wall, giving me room to slide between the sheets. I don't know if she can hear my heart thudding or not, but it's bloody loud. I'm trying to think of something—anything—other than her long, smooth limbs and gentle, sultry heat.

Her scent floats over to me like a quiet caress, flowers and vanilla and summer goodness. Silence envelops us, and I'm beginning to think I won't be getting any sleep tonight, lying here in this suffocating stillness, when she speaks.

"Thank you." It's as soft as the brush of a hand on a cheek.

I keep my gaze trained on the ceiling, not trusting myself to look at her. "You shouldn't need to be thanking me."

"But I am." Her hand searches around under the comforter. A bolt of heat races through my veins as I let her tuck it inside mine.

There is something frighteningly intimate about this. It doesn't matter that Lux and I barely know each other. There's an understanding here that no amount of inane facts can compete with.

"You've got some undeserving people in your life." That's putting it mildly, but I don't want to offend her.

Her sigh is full of things unsaid. "I've always managed to be both too much and not enough."

Those words hang in the air between us. My hand shakes around hers, anger coursing through me as thick and fast as water through a burst main. "Anyone who thinks that is a piece of shit."

A gentle squeeze of my hand is her only response.

"Promise me you won't go back to him," I grind out.

"I guess now I can keep my house."

I don't miss the way she changes the subject. "What are you talking about?"

"He wanted me to move in with him. I was going to sell."

"Fucking bollocks." I force my voice to remain calm. "Why did you stay with him? Was the sex really good or something?"

Her pulse thrums against my hand, strong and steady, not the flighty racing from a few minutes ago.

"To be honest, I dreaded the sex."

The bed creaks as I turn to look at her, waiting for her to finish. I can't keep my eyes away anymore, not after a statement like that. I need everything she's willing to give.

The pillow rustles as she moves her head so that we're staring at each other. Her eyes glitter in the faint light from the moon. "He often wouldn't let me—you know."

I draw my brows together. I *don't* know. "What?"

I can't tell if she blushes, but the way she lowers her eyelids tells me her neck is probably turning rosy. "Climax."

"He wouldn't let you *climax*? Ever?"

"Whenever he was upset."

The dark, smoldering anger in the pit of my stomach intensifies. "And how often was that?"

She bites her lip. "Maybe like once a week? I didn't keep track."

I want nothing more than to drop down on the bed, spread those incredible thighs, and give her the orgasm of her life. My tongue would teach her that not all men are jerks, and that her pussy deserves the same love and attention as anyone else's. Probably more.

Instead, I grip her hand a little tighter. "That fucker didn't deserve you."[1]

* * *

I wake to find Lux's head on my chest. Strands of her hair are Velcroed to my stubble. Her arm is flung across my middle as if she was afraid I might leave in the middle of the night. My morning wood is happy about this situation. I sincerely hope she doesn't catch sight of it when

---

[1] To read an alternate ending to this scene that DOESN'T end with Slate being a gentleman, visit jessicajude.com/queen-of-vengeance-bonus.

I get up—which I should do—but I'm the asshat who doesn't want to move the beautiful girl from his chest.

Sue me.

She stirs a few minutes later, a gorgeous pink stain blossoming on her cheeks when she realizes where she slept.

"Good morning." I'm unable to keep the corners of my mouth from quirking upward.

"Sorry," she mutters, and sits up. Her hair frees itself from my beard, and my fingers itch to reach out and smooth the golden strands down.

"Don't be. Sleep okay?"

She nods. I swing my legs over the side of the bed and head to the kitchen to give her some privacy.

Briar has coffee brewed when I get there but is blessedly out of sight. The last thing I need is my little sister snooping around where Lux is concerned.

Lux is back in her clothes from last night when I return to the bedroom, coffee in hand. "Thank you," she breathes, taking the cup. "You remembered the oat milk."

I don't correct her. She doesn't need to know everything.

"I should go," she says. "I've imposed on you long enough."

"I didn't mind." I rub a flaxen strand of her hair between my fingers. "Seriously."

She swallows and tugs her eyes away from mine. After a few more gulps of coffee, she heads for the front door, hardly giving me enough time to follow her with the keys to her rental car.

"Get your locks changed today," I remind her.

Sixty seconds later, she's gone, and I'm left with this aching hole in my heart that I don't know the fucking meaning of.

Briar has come out of her room and is leaning against the kitchen counter like a parent after curfew.

"What?" I cut her a sharp glance before tossing a pan on the stove.

She tilts her coffee cup to her mouth and looks at me over the rim. After a noisy slurp, she says, "So."

I shake my head and crack an egg into the skillet. "No."

"You bring a girl home for the first time, and you think I *won't* have questions?"

"It's not like that."

Her hands are buried in the sleeves of the oversized sweater she's wearing. It makes her look like a little girl. "Then what is it like?"

"I'm not having this discussion with you." I grab the salt and pepper and season my eggs generously.

"That's the second time she's been here, Slate. Shouldn't I get to know my brother's girlfriend?"

I snort and rest my hands on my hips. "Girls like that don't date guys like me."

"How do you know?"

"Fuck, Briar. Let it go." I shove my hand into my hair, which is still tousled from bed. "She would run far, far away if she knew even half of what I've done."

Briar refills both of our cups. "Not beyond redemption until you're dead."

"Okay, Socrates."

"You could invite her for dinner." She reaches into the cupboard for a plate.

I take it from her and flip my eggs onto it. "Why the fuck would I do that?"

"Because you're a nice guy." She grabs the hot sauce from the fridge and plunks it down in front of me. "And because you love your sister."

"That's debatable at the moment, you little shit."

She laughs and plants a loud kiss on my cheek. "We both know you will, so quit pretending otherwise."

"Don't you have a stupid TV show to watch or something?"

Her laughter follows her out of the room.

I settle myself at the kitchen table and dig into my breakfast. My thoughts drive the actions of my fingers, and before I know it, I'm scrolling through Lux's Instagram feed.

The photos are incredible. Shots of her with friends, at high-society events, on board a yacht, modeling bikinis, being interviewed, in magazine spreads, at parties, at clubs, at the fucking palace. In each of them she's flawless, a goddamn queen. Her skin glows, her hair shines, and her smile sparkles. She is the personification of beauty.

I glance around the room at the dated appliances and the cheap linoleum floor. We're so far from being in the same league, we're not even in the same universe.

"What are you doing?"

"Shit." I slam my phone down on the table as Briar skirts around it, a devilish smile on her lips.

"Just invite her," she sings.

18

"Uptown Girl" - Billy Joel

It looks like I'm throwing a dinner party.

I comb my hair back into a bun and run the trimmer over my beard. Somehow Briar always manages to weasel her way into my personal life, and soon her decisions become my decisions without any effort. Which is how I found myself calling Lux yesterday afternoon.

Surprise lingered in her voice when I told her I wanted to check on her. When I extended a dinner invitation for tonight, there was only silence, and I mentally cursed myself for hoping she'd accept.

"You can cook?" she said.

"I can order a pizza like the best of them."

She laughed at that—pure and clear music—and said she'd come, but only if I let her cook. It seems wrong, but if that's what the woman wants, who am I to refuse?

The knock on the door startles me, and I scramble to keep the trimmer from falling into the sink. I haven't even seen her yet, and she already has me dropping things.

Voices drift over from the living room, which means Briar has let Lux in and is currently interrogating her better than a police sergeant.

I swipe a quick hand over my stubble before heading toward my demise.

* * *

"What do you mean there's nothing to eat?" I walk over to the fridge and open it. "There's plenty of food in here."

"She means there's nothing here that wasn't bought by a bachelor," Briar calls from the living room.

Lux rises from where she's crouched, inspecting the contents of the small cupboard serving as a pantry. She's wearing an off-white jacket and matching shorts with big gold buttons, even though it's chilly tonight. Her hair is swept back into a ponytail, but several tendrils have escaped to frame her face. Her rose perfume is already scenting my entire house and fucking with my head.

"We need to go shopping," she announces.

Shopping wasn't part of the plan. In fact, if I had known it would be on the agenda tonight, I would have told Briar she could shove her dinner invitation.

"We'll order pizza," I tell her.

Briar says, "I'm tired of pizza" at the same time Lux says, "You have the palate of a child."

It looks like I'm throwing a dinner party *and* going grocery shopping. Fuck me now.

"Do you want to come along?" Lux asks Briar as the two of us walk to the front door.

"Nah, I'm good," the little traitor says from her position under a pile of blankets on the sofa. "You kids have fun, though."

I flip her off as I follow Lux out the door.

It takes us twenty minutes to reach a grocery store Lux deems "suitable." When we get inside, I understand.

135

"This isn't a grocery store. It's a food museum," I say. The scent of strawberries and flowers hits us as the automatic doors open, and inside we're surrounded by people wearing— "Is that a sweater made out of rope?"

Lux only narrows her eyes and grabs a cart. I have no choice but to follow her and try not to swallow my tongue when I spot the prices. She considers several different kinds of mangoes in the produce section, which cost more than a gallon of milk. Each.

She inspects a bag of kale while I make a gagging noise. Turning slowly, she appraises me before cocking a single brow. "The palate *and* the emotional intelligence of a child."

I end up pushing the cart—containing the kale—while she walks ahead, turning to drop things into the basket every once in a while. I can't complain, not with the sway of those hips in front of me and the way her ass pops into the air every time she bends over.

While she's browsing the cracker aisle, I pull a box off the shelf. "Look. Sawdust and cardboard."

She swipes it from my hand and returns it with a droll expression, but I catch a glint of amusement in her eyes. "Can you and Briar both eat gluten?" she asks.

I lean my arms on the buggy handle. "We're not rich enough for dietary restrictions."

"You're an imbecile." Lux yanks the cart forward, making me lose my balance.

I grin at her retreating back. Bickering with her has risen to the top of my list of favorite things to do.

** * **

I don't think our kitchen has ever seen this much action. Lux is a fucking powerhouse, chopping and blending and roasting like a chef at a hotel restaurant. I'd prefer to sit back with a beer and watch her work, but that woman is scary with a knife in her hands.

"Wash the cucumbers," she directs, using a nine-inch blade to indicate the vegetables in the sink. "Make sure to get all the dirt off."

"I assumed the dirt stayed. Isn't that why we paid extra?"

She bites the side of her lip and flips the chicken breast she's frying. Trying to make her smile is like a drug. Every time it becomes obvious she wants to laugh, a jolt of endorphins rushes through my bloodstream faster than a hit of cocaine.

I haven't done anything stronger than weed in years, and even that isn't something I partake in regularly. Other than cigs, it seems my strongest vice is standing in the kitchen with me, wearing an apron so big she had to wrap the strings around and tie them in the front.

"Do you have an oven mitt?" she asks.

I stare at her.

"What?" She turns back to the stove. "I don't know what it's like to be poor."

I toss the mitt at her. Now it's my turn to hide a smile. She's like a splash of cold water to the face. Half the time I don't know if she's serious or not.

Once the food is ready, the three of us gather around the table. Briar has changed into a dark green dress she only wears on special occasions. She gave us a wide berth while we were cooking, but now she is soaking up as much of Lux's glow as she can.

That makes two of us.

"What does a socialite do exactly?" Briar asks.

Lux looks like she's not sure if Briar is making fun of her or not, but my sister is as genuine as they come. I'm more than half-interested in the answer myself, but I hide it by taking a bite of the kale salad. Green stuff doesn't pass my lips very often, but this is really good.

The entire meal is phenomenal.

"Umm." Lux bites her lip in a way that makes my cock take a sudden interest. She's holding her phone twelve inches above her plate of food, which remains untouched as she snaps photo after photo. "I get invited to a lot of events. Sometimes I host charity galas." Her eyes flit to me, and she gives me a knowing look that feels startlingly intimate. "People like it when I take lots of pictures."

"You get paid to do those things?" Briar says.

I kick her softly under the table, but she ignores me.

Lux's face brightens to a beautiful shade of pink. "Not usually. Some of the events pay the chairperson, but I usually donate it to the cause of the evening." She fiddles with her phone for another few seconds, then tucks it away inside her little white purse.

"Kind of you," I murmur, and take a sip of beer.

Her color deepens even further. "Most people do."

"Are you hosting any upcoming events?" Briar's eyes are glued to Lux's face, waiting for any morsel she drops.

"I've been asked to co-chair a holiday gala, and if I make a good impression there, I'm hoping to be asked to chair the Humanitarian Aid Society gala in the spring. That's the big one."

"Wow." Briar's voice is breathless, and I understand why. My chest has been tight all night.

It's stupid. I know that much. But I can't stop thinking about how soft Lux's lips were and the way she melted into my arms like goddamn honey in the sun. Every person in the Junction becoming a millionaire is more likely than me getting a shot with her, but that doesn't keep my brain from envisioning it.

Her stretched out beneath me in bed, that golden hair fanned out around her face, me caressing her curves with my hands—

"You guys cooked. I'll do the dishes," Briar says.

I blink to clear the images from my mind. Lux glances at me and says, "I should go."

My heart kicks into triple drive, demanding I find a reason for her to stay. "We could talk outside. About . . . things."

She reads my meaning and nods. I grab a blanket for her from the sofa. Her legs will be frozen if she sits outside in those shorts.

We make our way to the back garden, and she settles into the swing without prompting. I move to get a chair, but she pats the space beside her.

"We can share the blanket," she says.

I give her two seconds to change her mind before joining her. The swing shifts with my weight, and she lays the blanket across my lap. I don't need a fucking afghan on my legs, but if it makes her happy, I won't say a word.

I grab a cigarette and lighter from my pocket out of habit. Lux's rose scent tickles my nose, reminding me who I'm with. I replace them without lighting up.

What the fuck is happening to me?

19

"Porch Swing Angel" - Muscadine Bloodline

Lux

"Will you teach me how to shoot?"

My question startles Slate. He's busy shoving his cigarette back into his pocket, but I can feel his eyes reading every inch of my profile. His gaze is a living thing, brushing against my skin like butterfly wings.

"Absolutely not."

I return his stare with a frown, jutting out my bottom lip. "Why not?"

"It's dangerous."

"It's more dangerous to be without a gun."

He drapes his arm over the back of the swing, not anywhere close to being around my shoulders, but the heat of him reaches me anyway. "You're not in danger when you're with me."

His words punch through every inhibition I have, a wrecking ball through a brick wall. He's right. I've never felt safer, and the sensation is so foreign, I find myself simultaneously wanting to scramble away and burrow deeper into his security.

Physically, I'm the safest I've ever been. Emotionally, I've never been in more danger.

We like danger, my heart murmurs. I shut her up with a dirty look. None of that. It's safer to change the subject. "How has Briar been?"

Slate's foot nudges the swing into motion. "Better. They changed her meds."

The relief that courses through me is unexplainable. I barely know the girl. "Have you made an appointment yet?"

"It's next month."

I nod repeatedly, because I'm not sure what else to say. An awkward tension hangs in the air like a tangible presence between us.

His thumb brushes the back of my bare neck. Goosebumps wash across my skin. I assume it is an accident until he does it again. His ocean-blue eyes are full of an emotion I can't read.

"Thank you again for that," he says.

It takes my brain a second to catch up. "It's not a big deal," I say. "I'm glad my dad agreed."

Slate shifts on the swing, causing it to sway again, and my body leans toward him as I try to regain my equilibrium. "How often do you see him?" he asks.

"A few times a year. More if we attend the same events."

There's a lengthy pause as Slate takes this in, long enough for me to wonder what he's thinking, if he's wondering how little value a person must have if their own father doesn't care to see them except on major holidays.

"His loss," he says as his thumb makes another feather-light swipe across my neck.

It's as if spun sugar is melting in my veins, leaving me breathless and dizzy as it sets my heart racing with its sweetness. I force a steadying breath into my lungs. "What about your dad? I know your mum died, but you've never talked about him."

"He died when I was eight."

"I'm sorry. I shouldn't have—"

"It's fine." His thumb skitters across my skin, and this time, his whole hand settles on my shoulder. The searing weight of it is delicious, and I imagine him on top of me, tracing the lines of my body.

I try to remember how to breathe. "What happened?"

"Officially? Heart attack. Unofficially? I think he overheard something he shouldn't have."

"Why?"

He's stroking lazy circles on my neck, and I wonder if he even realizes he's doing it. Meanwhile, I have to use every single brain cell I have to focus on what he's saying. "He had no history of heart trouble. He worked for this slumlord, a guy with a lot of properties here in the Junction. Several more of his employees died within a few years."

"Did you tell the police?"

Slate gives me a rueful smile. "If your address is in this part of town, the coppers don't care."

"Are you aware of the giant boulder on your shoulder?"

He runs his free hand over the stubble on his jaw—hiding a smile, no doubt—and uses the other to gently massage my neck muscles. "Don't tell me you'd like to make me your project."

I pretend to consider this. "Do you need 'project-ing'?"

His face twitches. "Sometimes I wonder if you hear yourself."

Trying to make him smile is becoming too addictive, which means it's time for another change of topic. "It's hard to believe Briar is sick," I say. "She looked so healthy tonight."

"It comes and goes. There's never any way to know when she'll have another episode."

I think about what it must be like, never knowing when the crippling pain will hit, if you'll be spending the night in your own bed or undergoing those atrocities at the hospital.

"Does your insurance at least cover her bills?" They must be astronomical by now.

He snorts and stares off into the distance. "Health insurance is for rich, healthy people."

"Excuse me?"

He gives me a sidelong glance. "You heard me."

"About that chip on your shoulder . . ."

His hand tightens slightly on my neck, then relaxes. "I haven't found a company yet that will take her on."

"That's ridiculous." I can't keep the incredulity out of my voice.

"Welcome to the Junction."

"You can't assume that everyone holds where you come from against you." My words are soft, floating in the night air. "I don't."

He drops his arm from the back of the swing and leans forward, elbows on his knees. I miss his warmth instantly. "It was in your eyes the day we met."

I picture it in my mind, feel the tension I carried as I walked up to his door, the shock when I was greeted with greasy jeans and hostility. I did judge him, despite the fact that I didn't know enough to form an accurate opinion. "I'm sorry." It's not enough, not nearly enough. My hand strokes his back, relishing the thick ropes of muscle beneath his T-shirt.

Slate looks over his shoulder at me, but his phone rings before he can say anything. He pulls it out of his pocket. "Shit. I gotta take this." He stands up in one fluid motion, sending the swing gently swaying.

This is a good time to use the restroom anyway. The scent of freshly brewed coffee greets me as I slip inside. Briar hangs a dish towel on the oven handle and turns to me with a smile.

"I made coffee if you want some."

"That sounds wonderful." I should go home, but there's something about the warmth of this place that makes my feet anything but eager to leave.

When I return from the bathroom, Briar has set two steaming mugs on the counter. "Thank you," I tell her. "I'm going to grab some oat milk for mine."

She gives me a funny look. I open the refrigerator and scan all of the shelves. There's only a questionable jug of cow's milk.

I shut the door and spin around. "I guess you're out?"

Briar's expression toggles between amused and confused. "*Oat milk?*"

I nod. "Slate put it in my coffee the last two times I was here." I flush when it occurs to me what I've just confessed to. I have no idea how much she knows.

Her mouth quirks in the same way her brother's does. "I've never seen oat milk here."

"Maybe you just missed it?"

"Yeah, maybe." She wipes at a spot on the counter with a cloth. "Or maybe he didn't tell you what he put in your coffee?"

It takes me three seconds to process this and arrive at the conclusion that it sounds exactly like something he would do.

"Slate Lawson," I yell, keeping my eyes on Briar.

She hides her smile in her shoulder, but the effect is the same.

"That imbecilic asshole," I mutter.

"You called?"

I turn to find him leaning against the doorframe, arms crossed over that expansive chest, smirk fully in place. Something travels through me at the blatant masculinity of him. "What the hell have you been putting in my coffee?"

20

"I Turn to You" - Melanie C

Lux

This petrol station is shady as fuck—giant cracks spreading across the concrete, weeds fighting their way to the surface. The tiny building looks like it predates my great-grandparents with its peeling paint and sagging roof, but the iron grates over the windows give me the most pause.

Two men keep circling the pumps like they're looking for something. Apprehension crawls up my spine and taps me on the shoulder, but I ignore it. Nothing bad has ever happened to me in the Junction.

I would never stop here under normal circumstances, but I've been using a car service the past few days. The last time I drove my car, I was too busy fuming to check the gauge.

My conversation with Slate three nights ago plays through my mind.

"Cow's milk? What if I was lactose intolerant, you jackass?"

"But you're not, are you? Just normal-people-food intolerant." The cocky way he'd leaned against the doorjamb colored my vision red.

Normal-people-food intolerant. As if requesting oat milk is a crime. Who the fuck doesn't have oat milk in their fridge?

And so I left. Without discussing our next plan for tracking down

145

the Wolf. Which, to be honest, we weren't doing anyway.

It was too distracting, sitting beside him, the warmth of him seeping through my clothes. His scent is captivating. Not expensive cologne, but something grittier, harder. Manlier.

My heart rate kicks up a notch at the thought of seeing him in a few minutes. I'm sure his assholery will be on full display, but there's no denying the quickening of my pulse whenever I'm in a room with him. It's like my body tracks his every move, more aware of him than of myself. Not something I'm proud of, but the body wants what the body wants. Maybe we should hook up and flush it out of our systems once and for all.

The pump clicks, and I slide the nozzle back into place. I'm about to open my door when a tiny whimper makes me pause. I incline my head to see around the pump.

A little girl is sitting on the curb, her face in her hands. She can't be more than four or five. I scan the area for an adult but don't see anyone. The two men have disappeared. I gingerly step over the stained concrete separating us and crouch down beside her.

"Hey, love." I place a hand on her shoulder. "What's wrong?"

She lifts her head to peer at me. "My ball." She points under the car in front of us. "I can't reach it."

Grabbing fistfuls of my white trousers to keep from mucking them on the ground, I crouch down even further to see under the vehicle. Sure enough, about an arm's length back, a pink ball sits, taunting me.

"Are you here with someone?" I ask.

She nods, sending her black coils bouncing. "Daddy's inside."

I would like to tell her daddy a few things about leaving a young child alone outside, but at least she's not abandoned. I take a deep breath and reach under the car, stretching my arm as far as it will go. My fingers graze the rubber, and the ball rolls out.

"You got it!" she squeals, dashing after it.

I smile at her and dust off my pants. Hopefully Ms. Griffin isn't intimidated by grease stains.

My fingers are gripping the door handle of my car when something hard slams into me from the side. I lurch back as my keys are ripped from my hand. "Hey!" I scream as someone runs around the other side of the Ferrari.

The man climbing into the driver's seat plants his foot on my stomach and shoves. The impact sends me reeling backward. The roar of my V12 engine fills the air as my head hits the concrete barrier between the pumps and everything goes black.

I don't know how much time passes before I come to. It takes a minute or two to blink away the dizziness and sit up. The little girl and her father are gone. No one has come out from the station to make sure I'm okay.

My head is throbbing, and I reach to touch the back of it. It's warm and sticky, and when I pull my hand back, it's covered in blood. Nausea surges at the sight. I pull myself up using the nearest rubbish bin and empty the contents of my stomach into it, then sink back down to the ground.

I can't even call anyone, because my phone is in my car. The station probably has one, but since I don't have a single number memorized, it won't do me any good. According to Slate, even the police don't pay attention to calls from the Junction.

I try to remember where his house is from here. I think I'm only a few blocks away. Using my hands, I carefully push myself into a standing position. My head hurts, but I don't think I have any major injuries.

I set off in what I hope is the right direction.

21

"Provider" - Sleep Token

Slate

Lux is late. Not exactly a crime, but she was supposed to be here thirty minutes ago. So where the fuck is she?

I part the living room curtains again, looking for any sign of her car. I'll be able to hear the engine from several blocks away, but that hasn't stopped me from checking every few minutes anyway. Briar's at the library, or she would be teasing me mercilessly about my pacing.

There's no sign of the Ferrari. I'm about to call her again when I spot a figure walking down the pavement. Pedestrians aren't unusual here, but ones dressed in all white are an anomaly. I'm out the door before my brain has even processed what I'm seeing.

She looks incredible as always, but even from a distance, it's obvious that something's wrong. I meet her on the sidewalk, and she falls into my arms when she spots me.

Then I notice the blood. A cold and penetrating fear grips me, stronger even than the times I've found Briar crumpled on the floor. I focus on getting Lux into the house, because my brain can only handle one thing at the moment, and her safety is my biggest priority.

Once we're inside, she explains what happened. I have to force myself to not react, to not bolt out the door to find those bastards myself and tear them apart, limb by limb.

I clean and disinfect the cut on the back of her head. It's not deep, and she begs me not to take her to the hospital. She doesn't seem to be struggling with dizziness, so I bandage it the best I can and help her to the restroom so she can shower.

As soon as I hear the water turn on, I call Tyler and give him the gist of it. "I need you to track down her car."

"I'm on it. And when I find them?"

I clench the hand that's not holding the phone into an even tighter fist. "Hold them for me."

Lux steps out of the restroom wearing one of my tees and a pair of Briar's denim cutoffs. Her own clothes are too blood-stained to be salvaged. My shirt is huge on her, but she's tied the hem into a knot above the shorts, leaving a strip of bare stomach peeking out.

My blood is pounding.

Her face is a cool mask, no trace of tears or rage or fear. Just cold apathy.

"Let's go," I say.

"Where?"

"The shooting range."

I lead her to the garage, where I march over to the locked cupboard on the far side and enter the combination. The doors swing open, and I shove the Walther PDP into the waistband of my jeans. I relock the cupboard and turn to find Lux gaping at me from the doorway.

No reaction to being robbed and assaulted, but shock at my gun collection. Unbelievable.

"What?" I motion for her to follow me outside.

"Why do you have a stockpile of guns?"

I swing a leg over my bike. "You really think I sell drugs and *don't* have protection?"

She stands there like she doesn't know who I am.

"Are you coming?" I say.

"On there?" She points to my bike.

I hold out my helmet. "Better put this on."

She approaches without another word, dons the helmet, and straddles the seat behind me. Tension blooms below my waist as she snuggles up close, wrapping her arms around my middle.

The drive to the shooting range would be more thrilling if I was less angry. With Lux's legs hugging my hips, there are a million fantasies I could fall into.

"You need to know how to protect yourself," I tell her when we're standing in front of the targets. "Self-defense is a must, but this will have to do until you can take classes."

Having a gun in her glove box wouldn't have stopped the carjackers, but I'm no longer comfortable knowing she has zero protection out there.

"You said you weren't going to teach me," Lux says when I move her into position, my hands on her graceful hips.

"I changed my mind." I wrap my arms around her, guiding her into a proper hold on the gun. "First, you need to learn how to stand. Spread your legs a little further apart."

I don't miss her sharp intake of breath as I nudge my leg between hers.

She feels so good in my arms, fitting against my body like a mold. It's rubbish, the thought, because we're the furthest thing from made for each other. But that doesn't mean I'm not going to soak up every minute with this woman in my arms, smelling like roses and making me wish, for the first time, that I had something other than this to offer.

"Your stance is important, because the kickback can be intense. Make sure your feet are firmly planted," I say softly.

Her hair brushes against my face, and it takes all of my concentration to not bury my nose in it and inhale deeply.

We've already covered the basics of loading the gun. Now she needs to learn how to aim and fire. I guide her hand lower. "Focus on the chest."

She braces herself, concentrating on the paper target downrange. I can't see her mouth, but I picture her biting her lip as she takes aim.

"Now pull the trigger."

She does, and the recoil sends her further back into my chest. We lower the gun together.

"Not too bad. How did it feel?" I release my hold on her.

She turns slowly, keeping the weapon pointed at the floor. "It was amazing. Powerful."

It was amazing and powerful, and it had nothing to do with the gun. Time to focus, I remind myself. "Let's try it again."

We do a few rounds together. When Lux feels comfortable trying on her own, I step back and let her do it. Her shots end up further from the target but aren't bad at all for a beginner. I tell her so, and she blushes with pride.

As she fires another round, I check my phone. There's a text waiting from Tyler.

Ty: *Located and detained*

Me: *Where*

Ty: *Warehouse*

Those assholes are going to regret the day they were born.

I drive Lux home on my bike. We didn't get a chance to discuss our next steps, but she's exhausted. Her crazy-ass plan for tracking down the Wolf can wait.

I walk her to her door to make sure that bastard she dated isn't lurking in the shadows. She inserts the key into the lock, then hesitates, turning back and biting that fucking lip. My insides lurch.

"Thanks for the ride." Her voice is soft, tentative. "Do you want to come inside? I can get some drinks . . ."

Fuck yes, I want to come inside. Any other night the answer would be yes, a thousand times yes. Unfortunately, there's a situation waiting on me back in the Junction.

"I'd love to." I run the back of my finger across her cheek, relishing the way her eyes fall closed at the sensation. "But there are some things I need to take care of."

She nods and swings the door open. "Good night, Slate."

Disappointment floods my veins as she disappears into the house. I hop back onto my bike and tear through the streets.

Beating those fuckers to a pulp is a better use of my pent-up frustration than whatever would have happened if I had accepted Lux's invitation. As the city lights glow around me, I plan each and every blow I will deliver once I arrive at the warehouse.

I will end their fucking lives if they ever step within thirty yards of her again.

22

"The Devil Wears Lace" - Steven Rodriguez

Lux

I tilt the wine glass to my mouth and empty the contents. Two glasses in, the tremors are finally starting to subside.

I turn on the tap and add more hot water to the tub, suds swirling around as the lather builds. Try as I might, it's still difficult to wash away the fear.

Is this the world Alex lives in, where people steal cars right out from under their owners' noses? Throw a woman to the ground and not bother to see if she's okay?

I let my body sink a little lower into the soapy water, wishing I could soak away the pain in my heart.

Slate was wonderful today, patching me up and teaching me to shoot, even giving me a gun that he told me to keep nearby at all times, especially if I'm in the Junction. In spite of my total ignorance concerning all things gun-related, he was patient and never once made me feel stupid. We even stopped to get me a new phone, because he refused to let me go home without one.

When he wrapped his arms around me, his breath tickling my neck, I came close to combustion. He makes me feel small in the best way possible, like nothing bad can possibly get through him to me. He might be the exact opposite of everything I want, but somehow I still want him, want him so much there's a physical ache in my chest because he's not here with me. I feel safe when I'm with him, seen and heard, like I'm more than arm candy.

I don't know what's going on between us, but there's enough curiosity churning through my veins to be dangerous. I move my hand between my legs and stroke my folds. If he hadn't declined my invitation to come inside tonight, maybe I wouldn't have to use my vibrator later.

A long, breathy exhale escapes as I reach for my breast, teasing the nipple while sliding my fingers deeper inside me. I let my head fall back against the porcelain rim of the tub, imagining Slate's hand urging me closer and closer to—

A chime sounds from downstairs, breaking my fantasy. I yank my hand out of the soapy water and reach for my new phone to check the camera.

Bloody hell. My fantasy in the flesh is standing on my back doorstep, hands in his pockets, hair loose and wild around his haggard face. Slate flicks his eyes side to side, then presses the bell again.

I scramble out of the tub, nearly slipping on the marble floor, and dry off as fast as I can. "I'm coming," I call through the camera's speaker while tugging his T-shirt from earlier over my head.

He's still at the door when I stumble through the kitchen and wrench it open. He's in the same clothes as before, but he looks one hundred times more delicious in those faded jeans. His eyes travel from my damp hair down to my bare legs and feet. Then he dangles a keyring from his finger.

I blink at it. Looking over his shoulder, I do my best to clear the remnants of my fantasy. "You got my car back?"

"Those fuckers won't touch you or it again. I made sure of that."

My heart picks up speed. "Did you kill them?"

He snorts, an amused smile playing at his lips. "I'm not a mob boss. Let's just say I taught them a lesson."

"Thank you." I grasp the door with one hand and accept the keys. "Do you want to come in now?" *Please say no, please say yes.*

His eyes grow several shades darker as he looks down at me. "That sounds dangerous."

Before I even realize what I'm doing, the words are tripping out of my mouth. "I thought you had a thing for danger."

Slate takes a step across the threshold, his attention riveted to me. "I do."

My heart jackhammers in my chest as he walks into my kitchen. I subtly suck in his scent as he passes me. *Delicious.*

The bottle of wine I opened earlier is still on the island, and I pour us each a glass—his for hospitality purposes, mine for courage.

When I hand him the drink, his eyes are on my legs, bare beneath his T-shirt. Our fingers brush against each other, and it's like touching a hot stove. I would've dropped the glass if he hadn't been holding it. His gaze collides with mine and grasps it for an eternity, wrapped in a few seconds. Then he tips the glass back and drains it in three gulps.

He sets it down and moves closer, close enough to brush the hair out of my face and tuck it behind my ear. "How are you feeling?"

On a scale of one to horny? Fifteen.

"Better." My voice wobbles. "I took a bath and—"

Something crosses his eyes. "Mmm." He leans in closer. "You smell good. You always smell good."

Heat creeps up my neck from his proximity and the wine I've had.

"Lux," he breathes out. His face is only millimeters from my neck, and the words brush against my skin, igniting it. "Is there a universe where this works?"

I arch my neck in response, my body acting of its own accord. "I hope so."

"That's the one I want to be in, then." He slips one hand around my waist and tugs my wine out of my grip with the other. After setting it down, he slides his fingers into my hair and tilts my head back. His lips find their way to my neck, traveling it inch by inch until my legs threaten to collapse beneath me. "What is it with this kitchen?" he purrs.

My breath comes out in shaky, halting gasps as his stubble scrapes against the skin of my neck and jaw. He nibbles his way to my lips, then takes my mouth like a man on a mission.

I surrender to his kiss, let him take everything he wants. He needs no further invitation. His tongue lashes against mine, demanding and unrelenting. It's unlike our first kiss, when I held back, not willing to go there with him. Now I want him to take everything, to make me his.

Slate buries his nose into my neck, inhaling deeply. "I didn't think I liked the smell of roses before, but I fucking want to eat you. In fact—" He leans down and tosses me over his shoulder. "That's exactly what I'm going to do."

A thrill chases my blood through my veins and pools in my belly. I'm pulsing with need as he lowers me onto the kitchen island.

His eyes grow hungry as he takes me in. "If I had known you weren't wearing anything under my T-shirt—" His calloused palms shove the fabric past my hips, leaving my naked lower half displayed on the countertop.

"Are you going to finish that sentence?" I ask as he kneads my thighs, his eyes focused on my core.

A low growl emits from his chest. "I'd have had you up here even sooner."

I gasp as he buries his face in the apex of my thighs. His hair is soft against the sensitive skin of my legs, a contrast to the sharp brush of his stubble.

"Spread those legs for me, baby," he commands, before wrenching them further apart himself. "Show me your feast." He drags me to the edge of the counter and tosses both of my ankles over his shoulders.

I hardly have time to prop myself up with my hands before his tongue strokes me, hot and slick. The cry that escapes my throat sounds foreign.

Using his hands, he splays me open, giving his mouth complete access. My head falls back, lolling aimlessly as he licks me and sucks me and annihilates me with his talented tongue.

"Open your eyes," he commands.

I do, meeting his gaze for a brief instant before he returns to torturing my clit with pleasure. Because of the angle, I have an unblocked view of everything he's doing to me. His tongue alternates between quick, pulsing flicks and longer, surging plunges. Heat floods my limbs and face as I watch him eat me out like a holiday meal.

When he drives a finger inside me, I arch into him. He chuckles and sucks harder.

My climax builds as he thrusts into me over and over. I scramble to find words, but my brain is a mash of jumbled sounds. Desperation clings to me like sweat after a workout. I need him more than I've ever needed anything.

"Slate," I manage to moan. "Please."

His answering moan is muffled by my pussy, which is swallowing him up.

Instead of slowing down, he picks up speed, adding a second finger to the first. They make a slurping sound as they move in and out of my body. His tongue grinds against my clit, then apologizes with gentle caresses.

A strangled cry is all the warning I have before my orgasm hits, a tsunami on his face. He continues his assault until I've finished, then gently removes his fingers and kisses my clit one last time.

My arms threaten to collapse from where they're still holding me up.

"Come here." He reaches for me, letting me fold myself over him instead.

I am wrecked.

He lifts me off the counter, and I wrap my legs around him. He carries me out of the kitchen, my head tucked into his shoulder. "Bedroom?"

I mumble directions. He finds it and carefully lowers me onto the bed. I open my eyes in time to see him strip his shirt over his head. Desire blooms as I take in his bare chest, those sculpted muscles, the rigid shoulders, the tattoos.

His eyes devour me, need pulsating in their depths. He pushes my shirt up, inhaling when he catches sight of my chest. "Fuck me, baby. You're beautiful."

Warmth spreads through me, even better than the post-orgasm flood of endorphins. I love the way he sees me when he looks at me, truly sees me and not the cardboard cutout I show the world.

His fingers stroke my nipple, teasing it into performing. "I can't wait to be inside you."

A shiver runs through me.

He smooths a palm over my bare abdomen. "I want you clamping around my cock the way you did around my fingers." He leans down to press a kiss to my neck.

I arch my back, so eager for him. My hands roam over his chest as he reaches down to undo his pants. I'm practically panting as I wait for him to get it out. When he does, sliding his hand up and down his length, I blink in surprise.

The man is huge. He must be at least ten inches long, and that's to say nothing of the thickness of him.

"Is it going to fit?" My voice breaks.

He chuckles, deep and dirty. "Am I the biggest you've ever had?"

That would be an understatement.

"Don't worry. I brought my own condoms." He fumbles in the pocket of his jeans for a foil square.

My tongue traces my lips as I watch him roll it on. My need is pulsing so hot and strong, I could come apart again just from watching him. "Was I a foregone conclusion, then?"

A gleam lights in his eyes when he catches me looking. "More like wishful thinking on my part. And I'll fit just fine, baby." He reaches his hand between my legs while keeping his eyes locked on mine. He groans when he slips it between my folds. "Still soaked."

Fisting his cock, he replaces his fingers, dragging it through my juices over and over until I'm writhing on the sheets.

"Slate, *please.*" Nothing but bare desperation.

"I love it when you beg," he says, then thrusts inside me without warning. "I'll give you every damn thing you want. All you have to do is ask."

He fills me so completely, stars flash at the edges of my vision. He gives me a few seconds to adjust to his size, then starts pounding into me with an intensity that threatens to make me black out. With each thrust, I slide up the bed, and he drags me back down.

I clench tightly around him, and he groans loudly. The scent of sex is strong, coupled with the leathery scent of him and the rose water on my linens. I register the silky texture beneath me, but it's drowned out by the weight of him over me and the pressure of him inside me.

A whimper slips past my lips. I'm already close, so close.

As if he senses it, he slows down. "Not yet, princess. I want to ride you longer."

My pussy clamps down in protest. I bury my nails into his back as he slides his cock in and out with painful slowness.

"Fuck." He drags the word out, and it hangs between us for two seconds before he picks up the pace, thrusting into me like the world will end any minute.

It takes no time at all for me to shatter. Slate continues his relentless thrusting as I soar, before joining me. He collapses on top of me, groaning into my neck through his pleasure.

"I've been dreaming about this since the day I saw you at Pop's." His voice is drugged. "You have no idea how good it feels to be inside you. It's like my dick found a tunnel to heaven."

My insides burst with warmth. How is it possible to feel like the most precious thing in the world just from being in someone's presence?

He rolls over and disposes of the condom, then tugs me to his side. Within seconds, deep breathing fills the room.

He's asleep.

I trace the lines on his chest and face, memorizing them. He doesn't stir. A jagged scar stretches across his chest from pec to pec. I want to ask him about it, but it will have to wait until he's awake.

I have no idea what any of this means. I gaze at the dark lashes fanning out on Slate's cheeks, his mouth parted in sleep, and I want to be his more than anything. He makes me feel alive, like I'm waking from a hundred-year-long sleep.

I have no idea how to fit this man into my life—if he even wants to be in it at all. Maybe for him this was nothing more than a one-time fling, as easily discarded as the condom we just used.

Maybe he doesn't know that I just gave him my heart along with my body.

23

"Villain for You" - LZ

Lux is sleeping, tucked in close beside me, her golden hair splayed across my chest like before. She looks like a fucking angel.

How can she not see that my darkness will snuff out her light?

I extract myself from her grip and climb out of bed. I have several text messages waiting for me.

Tyler: *Gage didn't show tonight. This was his third warning. What do you want to do?*

Laney: *I'm off at 11. Want me to pick up whipped cream?*

Briar: *Are you with Lux??? xx*

I don't have time to be screwing a Silver Spoon princess, for fuck's sake. I text them all back and go downstairs. I haven't slept with Laney in weeks, and after tonight, I can't imagine ever going back to her flat. Being with Lux versus Laney is like the difference between being awake and being asleep.

The lights are still on downstairs even though it's two in the morning. I stop in front of the glass doors leading to the back terrace and pool, but the only thing I can see is my own reflection.

I don't have a fucking clue what to make of any of this. Despite the condom in my pocket, I had no intention of sleeping with Lux tonight. I hoped, sure, but it was the distant kind of hope you get when you play the lottery, not actual belief that it would happen.

I'm not an idiot. I know I'm falling for her. But I also know I don't deserve her, not in any universe, under any circumstances. Not because I have low self-esteem but because it's a fact. If you were to tally up my life choices next to hers, no one in their right mind would say we belong together.

If she knew even half of what I've done, she'd kick me out of here faster than I could blow her a goodbye kiss.

What the fuck does she see in me? The quintessential "bad boy" she needs to get out of her system before settling down with some guy with a huge tech fortune? Maybe she enjoys flouting the system as much as I do.

Regardless of her reasoning, we both know that, at the end of the day, she'll go back to her high society friends, and I'll go back to the Junction, where I belong. She said she's light years out of her league, and she's right.

I still want to fight to make her mine forever.

24

"Vampire" - Olivia Rodrigo

Lux

He's still here.

It's the first thought I have when I open my eyes. The shower's running in the en suite bath. Sunlight drips through the drapes, reminding me that there's a world outside of our bubble.

Slate woke me during the night with gentle kisses, wordlessly asking if I wanted to go again. Like I would be able to turn this man down.

I'm sore in places I never knew existed. I've had generous lovers in the past, but Slate isn't just generous. It's like his entire mission is to make sure I feel as good as possible.

Not once did he criticize what I was doing. It's been a long time since someone accepted me so freely, without demanding anything in return or tearing me apart word by word, showing me how to be a better version of myself. I'm opening like a flower to him, letting him see the real me, and I'm terrified.

I don't know what that means for the future.

The restroom door opens, and Slate walks out, hair still damp. I quickly run a hand through my terrible bedhead and pop a mint from the bedside table into my mouth. I must look like an apocalypse survivor.

He grins at me, and my insides clench. Walking to the bed, he leans over me. "You're beautiful."

My heart reels. "Come back to bed?" I fold the duvet back.

He presses a kiss to my hairline. "I wish I could, but I'm already late for work."

It's easy to forget that we have real commitments out there. Jobs and obligations and disgusting responsibilities. "Okay." I succeed in keeping the disappointment from my voice.

He pulls back and considers me. "There's a poker game tonight. You could come with me."

I shift upright in bed. I need to be vertical to process this. "Explain."

He sits down beside my legs, resting one hand on my calf. The bed shifts with the addition of his weight. "I thought we could do a little recon. For your project."

My project. God, my vengeance plot has already slipped my mind. "They won't mind if I tag along?"

"Not if we make it obvious you're with me." Slate's eyes spark with sexy promise.

I quirk my mouth to the side. "And how would we do that?"

"You know, sitting on my lap, a few kisses here and there. Normal things."

"Normal things," I echo. My pulse skitters at the thought.

"Yeah. Normal." His smile crinkles his eyes. "Come early and we can practice."

My laugh borders on maniacal. "Okay."

He gets up and walks to the door, then pauses before leaving the room. "Wear something sexy."

***

I keep his words in mind as I dress for the evening. My heart rate is twice what it should be, and my palms are slick with sweat.

I'm surprising Slate with dinner. We can eat together like normal people, maybe even discuss what happens next—for us or for tracking down the Wolf. I don't even care. I just want to be with him, hear his voice, and get that cashmere feeling in my belly every time he's around.

The mee goreng mamak makes my car smell heavenly. I don't know if he likes Malaysian food—probably not, considering he has the tastebuds of a five-year-old—but he will after tasting this.

A storm is rolling in, thick black clouds moving across the sky like they're preparing for battle. I put the top up on my car. Even a quick shower will ruin the leather seats.

I have to park around the side of the Rebel Wrench. It feels like forever since the day I followed Slate here. I've done what I can to restore the shop's reputation, but it's going to take time to get it back to what it once was.

Grappling with the takeaway containers, I round the corner of the garage, then stop so abruptly, I struggle to keep my grip on the bag. Thunder cracks across the sky like it's weighing in on what I'm seeing.

Slate is standing outside, wearing his typical black T-shirt, jeans, and leather jacket. He looks so delicious, it's hard to believe he was in my bed only a few hours ago. It's even harder to believe when I examine the person with him.

She's slender, but not model material. Her brunette hair is pulled back into a no-nonsense ponytail that still manages to look hot. She's wearing jeans and a tight top that shows off a sliver of her stomach. She looks like the kind of girl Slate will eventually end up with.

Her hand is resting on his arm, and he doesn't seem bothered by this in the least. I'm too far away to hear anything, but they're standing too close to each other for their conversation to read as anything but intimate.

A giant boulder sinks to the pit of my stomach. For a few blissful hours, I thought I meant something more to him. But I've never been enough. I was his social experiment. *Let's see how the Silver Spoon is in bed.* When he told me to come over early tonight, he clearly had only one thing on his mind.

My mum is right. I'm an idiot. It's easy for men to break my heart, because I'm too dumb to see through their plays.

The sky splinters open, rain pelting every surface. Slate slips off his jacket and wraps it around the woman's shoulders. She rises on tiptoe and presses a kiss to his cheek before darting to her car. He slips back inside the shop without seeing me.

My hair and dress are soaked, but they hardly register. That's what happens when you discover how much of a fool you are.

I toss the takeaway in the trash on my way to the car.

25

"Hell of a Good Time" - Haiden Henderson

I stub out my third cigarette and check the time again. It's already eight o'clock, and Lux is still not here. I thought we agreed that she would come over early. I'd be lying if I said I haven't been imagining her in my arms all day.

Last night was a fucking dream. It would be difficult to recreate, but I am not above trying. She's all I've been able to think about. Her rose-and-vanilla scent, the softness of her skin against mine, her little intake of breath every time I touch her.

I pace the small patch of grass in front of the house. Maybe I should have offered to pick her up instead of her driving into the Junction again.

Fear seizes my chest in its claws. The last time she was late, those fuckers stole her car and assaulted her. What if something like that happened again? What if she's out there, bleeding and unable to get help?

I call her once more. This time she picks up.

"Hello?" Her tone is abrupt.

"Where are you?" I don't mean to sound so harsh, but why hasn't

"""

she answered until now?

"I'll be there soon." She hangs up.

I stare at the phone in my hand. What the fuck?

A minute later, that V12 roar echoes through the neighborhood. Lux pulls around the corner and comes to a stop in front of my house. Before I have a chance to get to her door, she climbs out and slams it behind her.

"You okay?" I hedge as she approaches.

Her cold expression doesn't change. "Fine," she snaps.

My eyes take in her outfit, although that word is too generous. Her dress is so tight the hollow of her belly button is visible. The white fabric ends at the tops of her thighs. I fully expect to see ass cheeks if she turns around.

"What the fuck are you wearing?"

She sweeps her eyes over her "dress." "Rachel West. New designer. You wouldn't know her."

I let out a low growl. "I said what, not who."

Her shrug is casual, like she has no idea how close to the edge she's pushing me. "You told me to wear something sexy."

"I didn't mean underwear," I retort. Now I'll have to keep an even closer eye on her than usual. I wouldn't put it past any of the guys to try something tonight, even if I'm sitting right there. Some of them have been high for years, and it affects their reasoning abilities.

"Sorry for not making sure it's okay with you, *Dad*." Ice glitters in Lux's voice and demeanor, but her eyes flash fire.

What the fuck is going on? I cross my arms and incline my head. "Did I do something?" I've been around enough women to know that it's usually the guy's fault.

"Of course not. What could you *possibly* have done?"

When I left her house this morning, she was sweet and vulnerable, nothing like the panther in front of me now. "We're not leaving until you tell me what's going on."

She stares down at her nails like she's bored. "I thought the game starts at eight thirty."

"Fuck the game."

She looks up. Her facade falters for half a second, and I see a flash of pain.

I cross the distance between us and tug her into my arms. "What's wrong, baby?" I murmur into her hair. It's a bad decision, because her scent goes straight to my dick. I want to ravish her.

She remains stiff and unyielding, an ice sculpture in my hands.

"Lux." I breathe her name directly into her neck. The tiny hairs on her skin prick up. I nuzzle the space behind her ear, something that caused her to moan last night. "Tell me what's wrong."

A battle seems to be raging inside her. Her body wants to relent, but her mind refuses. She pulls away and folds her arms over her chest. "Can I borrow your jacket? It's chilly out here."

I want to snap that she should've worn more clothing. "I don't have it right now. I'll see if Briar has something you can borrow."

"Where is it?" she asks, an even sharper edge to her voice.

Warning bells ring in my head. "A friend is borrowing it."

She nods in understanding. "Do your friends borrow your clothes often?"

"No." I drag the word out, scrambling to put the pieces together and figure out what the fuck she wants to know. I gave my jacket to Laney today when it started to rain, but—

Everything clicks into place. "Were you at the Rebel Wrench today?" I ask.

Surprise flashes in her eyes, but she blinks it away. "Why?"

"Just answer the question, baby."

"Don't call me that."

I follow my instincts. "Laney and I are just friends."

"And do you sleep with all your friends?"

Shit. Of course she picked up on that. I rub my hand along my jawline. "We have a friends-with-benefits relationship."

Lux tucks her lips inside her mouth and cuts her eyes to the side. "Were my 'benefits' not enough for you last night?"

I reach for her, but she pulls back. "Of course they were."

How the fuck did we end up here? This was supposed to be straightforward: lead her on a wild goose chase until she got Briar the appointment. I wasn't planning to hurt her, but I wouldn't have cared much if I had.

But now feelings and shit are getting involved.

What we had last night was good, great even. But it was never meant to last. I'm never going to be good enough for a girl like her anyway, so there's no use in trying. It's better this way.

"Let's go," I say.

We park Lux's car in the garage and drive my Fiat to the other side of the Junction. The game is being held at Suzy Q's, a dingy pub that reached its peak in the eighties and has been riding the wave down ever since.

Mikey, Rich, Todd, and Hector are already seated when we enter the small back room. There's no window, and the air is heavy with smoke from the lit cigars around the table. It's basically a fire waiting to happen.

Greetings ring out as we make our way to the table, but all eyes are focused on Lux. No surprise, since she looks like a fucking porn star tonight.

There are only five chairs out. Todd jumps up and smooths his short beard. "I'll grab another seat."

"That's okay," Lux purrs. "I'll just sit on Slate's lap. That's okay with you, right, babe?" She wraps her hand around my neck and scratches the back of my head with those long nails, a little more aggressively than necessary.

I swallow and pin her with a stare. "That's fine," I say coolly, and take a seat.

She drops her hand and perches her tight ass on my lap. There's no way that shimmying over my cock is accidental. I inhale through my nose and toss my ante into the pot.

The game starts, and Lux frequently asks questions of the guys while snapping her gum. Nothing obvious, thank fuck, just stupid shit like "What's the river?" and "What does it mean to fold?"

Mikey practically has drool dripping from his acne-scarred chin, and Hector leers at Lux, the buttons on his striped shirt straining over his gut. They know who she is, but based on the looks they keep throwing my way, they don't know what the fuck she's doing with me. I'd be confused too, if I didn't know I'm simply a means to an end with her.

Rich wins the hand. He runs his fingers through his greasy hair as he collects his winnings, and Lux bounces on my lap. "Can I play this round?"

I tighten my grip on her leg. This isn't what we agreed to.

Mikey tips over his own chair in his eagerness to grab a seat for her. "Here," he says, setting the chair next to mine. "We can help if you need it."

"Aw, that's so sweet of you," she croons.

Before I can react, she wraps her arms around my neck and plants her mouth on mine. She tastes like her spearmint gum and that particular sweetness that's all Lux. For a few short seconds, I forget about the fight we had earlier and the fact that she's bad news and focus on how good she tastes and how right she feels in my arms.

My hands grip her waist, fingers almost touching each other around its small circumference. She moans and ends the kiss, then leans into my neck and whispers, "Bring up the Wolf."

Sliding off my lap, she puts one final bit of pressure on my crotch. I stifle the growl that rises in my chest.

Mikey deals. Blood pounds in my head as Lux leans over to ask him if she has a good hand. Their heads touch as he bends over to consider her cards. She giggles at something he says.

I've had enough of this shit.

"Has anyone heard if the Wolf's network is down?" I keep my eyes focused on my cards.

Rich shifts in his chair. "Something happen?"

I scratch the back of my neck, then bring my hand down to rest on the back of Lux's chair. "Nah. Just heard people talking. Something about shipment delays."

We're all dealers. Some of us are better at it than others, but everyone here has a connection to the Wolf. If Lux wants information, this is the place to get it. But getting these guys to open up with what they know won't be easy. Everyone knows what happens to snitches.

"Who's the Wolf?" Lux twirls a strand of hair and studies her cards. She leans over to Mikey again. When no one responds, her eyes travel around the table. "Is he like . . . a bad guy or something?" She punctuates this with a hysteria-tinged laugh.

She's good, really good. I wonder if she's ever considered a career in acting.

Mikey, already wrapped around her pinkie finger, takes the bait. "The Wolf is our supplier. He supplies everyone in the Junction with insidion."

"What's his real name?" she presses.

I reach for her thigh under the table. *Careful.*

No one pulls a gun or gives her a suspicious look. She has thoroughly passed herself off as a dumb blonde from the Hills.

"Don't you tell your women anything, Slate?" Rich tosses another twenty into the pot.

Before I can respond, Mikey—Lux's personal tour guide, the fucking wanker—pipes up. "No one knows who the Wolf is."

"Ooh." Lux rubs her hands together, revealing her cards. "Like a mystery."

"This isn't Nancy Drew," Hector snaps. "The Wolf is dangerous."

She blinks at him. "How can he be dangerous if he's not even here?"

"Word could get back to him that we were having this discussion," Mikey says.

Lux wrinkles her nose. "But he won't find out unless someone in this room tells him, right?"

I increase the pressure of my hand, and she fumbles to remove my fingers from her thigh.

"I've always thought it was Ollie Saar," Todd says. He normally doesn't talk much, and I'm surprised he chose this moment and info to break his streak.

"Ollie?" Rich says. "No way."

"He's always driving new vehicles."

"Most of us are better dealers than you, mate." Hector slaps him on the back.

Todd's face sprints two shades past pink. "He's shifty and a hard hitter." His eyes flick to Lux like he's expecting her to bless him for this hypothesis.

Rich scoffs. "The Wolf is too smooth to be someone like Ollie. Personally," he says, jabbing a cigar into his mouth, "I've always thought it's someone younger, someone like Jasper Barnes."

Hector guffaws and slaps his thigh. "Jasper Barnes? You've got to be kidding me, mate."

"Rich is right," I say. "An old guy like Ollie wouldn't know how to do all the tech stuff. It has to be someone younger."

"Who do you think it is?" Hector asks the question, but they're all interested in my answer.

"No fucking clue." I throw a twenty into the pile to join Rich's. "I value my life too highly for those kinds of theories."

They continue their argument, voices rising as they provide reasons why someone could or couldn't be the Wolf. None of it is useful in the least.

I notice for the first time that Mikey is not engaging in this conversation. While Lux may have been distracting him earlier, her charms aren't having the same effect now. He keeps darting quick glances at the others, then shifting his eyes back to his cards.

The game ends an hour later, Lux and I both several hundred poorer than when we walked into the room. She climbs back onto my lap and tugs my mouth down to hers. I know what's coming this time and meet her enthusiasm with my own.

I feel her start of surprise at my aggression. That's what she gets for being a cocktease.

She ends the kiss abruptly.

"Hey," I say. "I was just getting into that."

She scans the empty room behind her. "Mikey knows something." She shimmies off my lap. "Come on. We need to catch him before he leaves."

I follow her from the room, trying unsuccessfully to ignore the feeling of her hand in mine.

When we step outside, Mikey is trying to start his forty-year-old car. The rain has started up again, a gentle shower this time rather than the downpour from earlier.

I slap my palms on the hood of his piece of shit, and he jumps in his seat. Lux and I round to the driver's side.

I bang on the window with my fist. "Open up, Mikey."

He opens the door, rain splashing in on the worn upholstery.

"What do you know about the Wolf?" Lux leans her head down to be heard over the patter of drops hitting metal.

Mikey shakes his head, messy hair flopping into his eyes. "I don't know anything."

I reach into the car and yank the keys from his hand.

"Hey," he yells.

"Tell us what you know, and I'll give them back." It's a pretty mild threat, but panic edges into his eyes anyway.

"I'm telling you, I don't know anything!"

"How about this." I prop my elbow against the roof of his car. I wish I had my jacket. Lux is shivering like crazy beside me. "Tell us what you know, and I *won't* let the Wolf know you were the one who told us."

"Fuck!" He grabs his hair with both hands and pounds his head against the steering wheel. When he's finally calmed down, he says, "I don't even know if it's legit. I just heard someone say he operates out of an old warehouse."

I push off the car. We came out here for this? "No shit. Everyone operates out of a warehouse around here. Is that all you know?"

His eyes flick to Lux before dropping back to his lap. "They also mentioned a street."

"Which street?" Lux says.

"Downing."

26

"Elastic Heart" - Sia

Lux

"What are we waiting for?" I thrum my fingers against the interior of the car door. "Let's go."

The vehicle smells like soap and something spicy, like cloves. Slate told me it belonged to his mum. Now it mostly sits in the garage unless he needs to take Briar somewhere.

He slowly raises his eyes from his phone to stare at me. "Straight away, Your Majesty."

I roll my eyes and angle my body toward the window. The rain is still coming down, casting everything in a wet blur.

The tension between us throbs. I'm still beating myself up for ever having slept with him in the first place. Guys like him are all the same. I should have recognized that from a mile away.

He turns onto his street, and I break our no-talking game to gape at him. "What are you doing?"

"Doing as you asked," he says, boredom thick in his voice.

"I didn't ask you to bring me here."

He stops in the driveway and cuts the engine. "You demanded we leave the car park. Where else am I supposed to take you?"

"Hello? Were you not there for the same conversation I was?"

He sighs like I exhaust him, which is ridiculous because he—this game we're playing—is tiring enough to put anyone to sleep. "What conversation was that?"

I search the ceiling for answers to this man's stupidity. "Mikey? The Wolf? *The warehouse on Downing Street?*"

A scoff. The man *scoffs* at me. "Why don't you just spell it out, Lux? Since I'm clearly too stupid to know what you want."

"I want to go to the warehouse."

Our gazes meet across the center console in his mum's beat-up car. Oxygen becomes scarce as we stare at each other. It feels *raw*, looking at him like this, more intimate than him going down on me or stripping our clothes off.

"No." It's quiet, hanging in the air between us.

I'm panting, drowning in the depths of his blue eyes. "What do you mean, no?"

"I'm not taking you to that warehouse." Slate's eyes stay on mine, a blow torch against the wall of ice I built to keep people like him away from the tender parts.

"Fine." I reach for the door.

His fingers clamp around my wrist before I can open it. "You're not going either."

I jerk out of his grasp. "In case you've forgotten, I'm on a mission to track down the guy responsible for my brother's addiction. If that means going to that warehouse, there isn't anything you can do to stop me."

"Why don't you paint a picture of what you think is going to happen?"

I inch away from the hard edge in his voice. "I don't—"

"You think you'll walk in, and he'll be sitting there, waiting for you to pull a gun and shoot him?"

"Of course not." When he puts it like that, I sound like a bloody idiot. "I thought we might be able to gain some information."

"Like an interrogation?" Slate shakes his head. "There's no way—"

"Like a stakeout."

He blinks once, twice. "Did you get that from a movie?"

"No," I say, and swallow. "Yes."

His laugh cuts through the viscous air. "Alright, Sherlock. We'll do a stakeout."

The edges of my heart soften the way makeup does when you apply cleanser, turning gooey and smudging until it becomes unrecognizable.

Slate drives us to Downing Street, which has more than one warehouse.

"How will we know which one?" I ask.

The entire area looks like it was once a shipping district or had something to do with heavy machinery. Many of the buildings have that distinct air of abandonment about them, all rusty doors and tall weeds.

"We won't." He pulls into a yard that was once gravel but is now nothing but dirt and loose pebbles. Today's rain has transformed it into a mud bath.

"Next time, we should bring blankets." I tuck my hands into the sleeves of the sweater I grabbed from my car before heading to the poker game.

Slate reaches into the back seat and retrieves a fuzzy blanket that smells like mothballs. "It's not the cleanest thing, but it should keep you warm." He tucks it around my legs.

"Thank you," I say softly, smoothing a hand over the nappy fabric.

We sit in silence for several minutes. The rain stops, making the quiet of the night even more pronounced. The Junction is insulated from the loud noises of downtown, so it feels like we're in a different world.

"What's the scar from?" I can still picture the thin white ridge stretching across his chest.

He shifts subtly in his seat, the only indication he's heard me. Eventually, he speaks. "Deal gone bad."

"Someone *cut* you because of a deal?"

He shrugs like it's old news. "A lot worse happens around here."

I know this in a hypothetical sense, but not in a realistic one. "Do things like that happen . . . often?"

When he turns to me, the corner of his mouth is tugged upward. "Worried about me?"

"Maybe."

He reaches for my hand, and I let him take it. His warmth seeps into my skin, which has grown cold in spite of the car's heating system. "It was a long time ago. I mostly stick to myself now."

"And Tyler," I add.

"And Tyler." Slate tucks my fist into both of his hands and blows warm air into the enclosure. With his lips so close, it takes restraint to keep myself from touching his perfect cupid's bow lips.

"Have you ever dated anyone?" The words are out before I can think to stop them. "Or is it always friends with benefits for you?" My stomach roils with bile.

His eyes flick up to mine, then drop back to our joined hands. "Once."

My curiosity surges. Only once? "Who was she?"

"Her name was Emily." He blows another puff of air onto my hands.

"You dated someone named *Emily*?" I sound biased and bratty, but the name is just so—

"What's wrong with that?"

"Nothing. It sounds so sweet and . . . *good*."

He reaches for my other hand, which I'm keeping under my thigh for warmth. "She was. That's why it didn't last."

Understanding trickles through the cracks in my heart. "How long ago?"

A breath of warm air. "Almost ten years."

"And you haven't dated anyone since then?"

"Between my family and the shop—"

"And dealing," I add helpfully.

He cuts me a wry glance. "And dealing, I don't have time for relationships."

I wrap my now-warm free hand around his. "Or maybe you think you don't deserve them."

Several beats pass. "What about you?"

"What about me?"

"Who was your first boyfriend?"

My breath comes out as a single huff, a small, mocking sigh at the tragedy that is my dating past. "Connor Mayfield."

"Sounds like a fucker."

"He was." I nod. "In more ways than one. I was twelve."

Slate's hands tighten around mine.

"He told me if I didn't have sex with him, he'd start dating Madison Farley."

"And?" A muscle jumps in his jaw.

"And what?"

"Did you?"

I shrug to show him that I'm fine, this is old news, that men manipulate women every day, and my story is nothing special. "Madison Farley was a skank. I couldn't let her steal my boyfriend."

His grip on my hand is so tight, I'm worried for my bones.

"Hey." I place a palm on his jaw. "It was twelve years ago. I'm fine."

"If I ever get my hands on that—"

Slate is cut off by the arrival of a white box truck pulling into the yard. Its sides advertise an alcohol delivery company I've seen at various events.

We're parked beside one of the warehouses, hidden by tall weeds and a rusty piece of equipment, which gives us a view of the yard without being visible ourselves.

The truck backs up to one of the warehouses on the other side of the yard. Several figures move out of the building, presumably to help unload whatever is in the back. Something tells me it's not alcohol.

Are we watching the Wolf's business unfold before our eyes? My heart races around my chest with the speed of a national champion horse. If we're spotted here—

One of the figures moves closer to speak to the driver of the truck. He looks vaguely familiar, and it isn't until he steps out of the shadows and into the light of the moon that I recognize him.

"Is that Tyler?" I whisper, even though there's no way our voices will carry that far.

"Looks like it," he says.

"Oh my god, Slate. Could he be the Wolf?"

His brow furrows with disbelief. "Absolutely not. He only deals on the side, like me. We mostly work together."

"Then what's he doing here?" I press. The more I think about it, the more sense it makes. Tyler's young, he's smooth and smart. He could run an empire like the Wolf's.

Slate shakes his head, attention back on the unloading. "He must have needed the extra money and offered to help unload. Guys do it all the time. Means nothing."

If someone accused my best friend of being a notorious drug dealer, I'd balk too. But just because Slate is convinced Tyler isn't the Wolf doesn't mean I am.

27

"Ludens" - Bring Me the Horizon

Lux

"Why would I do that?" Maeve says. It's Tuesday night poker at Pierce's flat, and she and Rhett are bickering like siblings, as per usual.

"For obvious reasons," he says.

She raises a razor-sharp brow. "And those are?"

Rhett leans back in his chair, arms crossed over his chest, Cheshire cat grin on his face. "Because I'm hot."

Heath snorts in amusement, Walker hides a smile behind her hand, but Maeve keeps her eyes trained on Rhett, her expression as blank as before. "You think I should pick your grievance because of your looks?" She's just won the game.

His grin grows wider, if that's even possible. "Fine, fine. You can do it for my skills in bed, but I'm warning you, it's a roller coaster."

It's a good thing there are no weapons in the room. Otherwise— judging by the look on Maeve's face—Rhett might find himself impaled on the other end of a fireplace poker.

"If I choose yours, will you stop talking?" she says.

He leans forward like he can't believe what he's hearing. "Yes, absolutely."

"I wasn't done."

The room stills. Even Heath quits fidgeting.

Rhett's grin is unflappable. "Do your best, May-eve."

She doesn't even flinch at the nickname, even though she's launched beer bottles at his head for using it before. A tiny tug at the corner of her mouth is the only indication she's not a statue.

"I'll choose yours if you stop talking," she says, "for the rest of the night."

Some of the amusement drains from Rhett's face, although he does his best to look unbothered. His eyes narrow as he takes her in. "Deal."

"Famous last word," Maeve says, finally breaking into a grin.

Rhett only glowers, probably already drowning in regret.

Maeve claps her hands and turns to the rest of us. "I choose Kieran Phillips. Any suggestions on a revenge scheme?"

Rhett told us when he submitted the grievance that Kieran had posed as a girl online, with the sole purpose of catfishing him and posting screenshots of their conversation, which included more than a handful of dick pics. Rhett's reputation has been mutilated enough recently. This latest scandal is only gasoline on the fire.

"What about setting him up with a prostitute?" Pierce suggests.

Rhett vehemently shakes his head.

Maeve stares at him. "That sounds like a great idea."

Rhett closes his eyes and sinks back into his chair. I give him a sympathetic smile. Maeve will put him out of his misery soon. She just likes to play with her food before she eats it.

While they plot to get Kieran caught with a hooker, my mind wanders. I haven't talked to Slate since we staked out that warehouse and saw Tyler unloading drugs from the truck. It's for the best, so why do I keep thinking about him? No one should feel this lonely while hanging with their best friends.

Even if Slate and I were something more—though *what*, god only knows—I can't see him being willing to fit into my life. And there's no way I'm going to turn a blind eye to his extracurricular activities or live in a house that's the size of my kitchen.

The chemistry between us is just that—chemistry. It doesn't have to mean anything else.

I try to imagine my friends' reactions if I brought Slate along to poker night the way he took me to his own game. Something tells me they'd be less welcoming than his buddies were.

My phone vibrates in my bag, yanking me out of that toxic spiral of thoughts. It's a text from Rhett.

Rhett: *1983 Porsche 944*

I try to make my face say "I don't know what the hell that means" without anyone else noticing.

He types rapidly on his phone, causing mine to buzz several seconds later.

Rhett: *Kieran. Suggest sabotaging his car*

I nod my agreement before turning to the rest of the table. "What if we did something to his car? I heard it's his baby."

Pierce turns that penetrating gaze on me. "What'd you have in mind? Egging? Keying?"

I can't look at Rhett without giving myself away. "Yeah, either one should work. Maybe both?"

Instantly my phone vibrates. When they're all preoccupied with the details, I read Rhett's latest text.

Rhett: *Not good enough*

I give him an exasperated huff.

Me: *I'm trying.*

Rhett: *We need a way to ruin it for good*

Me: *Suggestions???*

Rhett: *I don't know anything about cars*

I roll my eyes at the phone and stuff it back into my bag. Are all men this incompetent?

"I think we should ruin the car, do something to break it," I say, interrupting their discussion.

Heath's smile is lazy. "Like a wrecking ball?"

"I was thinking something mechanical," I say. "Destroy the engine or something so that he doesn't know it's ruined until he tries to drive it."

Rhett's approval sneaks over and wraps its arms around me like a hug.

"I don't know enough about engines to know what we could possibly do to it," Pierce says.

Beside him, Maeve snorts. "Do you know *anything* about engines?"

He shoots her a glare. "Did you have something specific in mind?" he says to me.

"Not really," I hedge. I can't give away Rhett's involvement in my suggestion, but I know less about cars than all of them put together. "It was just an idea."

Pierce sweeps his eyes around the table. "Heath?"

Heath raises his hands. "I can barely fill my bike with petrol, mate."

My bag vibrates again. I know it's Rhett, begging me to find a way, but the truth is, I'm out of options. I did my best. I offer him an apologetic look.

"If we can't find a way to ruin the engine, I think we're back to the egging idea," Maeve says.

Rhett's eyes bore into my head, but I refuse to meet his gaze.

I don't have any ideas. I type out the text, then stop before hitting send.

I do have another idea, even if it's one I'd rather not explore. Rhett is still focused on me with that eager-puppy attention that makes it impossible to say no to him. I sigh, erase the text, and instead type *You owe me.*

I clear my throat. "I know someone who can help us."

Five sets of eyes swing my way.

"The guy who owns the Rebel Wrench," I say. "Slate Lawson."

Walker's brow furrows in confusion. "How do you know him?"

"It's a long story. But I can call him if we want his help," I say.

Maeve's expression tells me this conversation is far, far from over. "Okay," she says. "Call your mystery man, and let's do some damage."

I retreat to the living room to call Slate, and because I know they're dying to discuss this bomb. It must be killing Rhett not to participate.

Slate answers on the first ring. At the sound of his voice, my traitorous heart leaps into the air and does a pirouette.

"I need your help," I say.

"What's wrong? What happened? Are you hurt?"

"Calm down." Something warm burrows its way into my heart. "I should have worded that differently. My friends and I need your help."

28

"We Are Young" - fun. ft. Janelle Monáe

Slate

She's sitting beside the road somewhere, abandoned because some fucker stole her car again.

She's battered and alone because that prick of a boyfriend came back to get revenge.

She's at the mercy of her mother, who isn't worthy of her existence, being berated and abused.

My mind is a devious devil.

The minute she says, "I need your help," it goes into overdrive, creating scenarios to fill in the gaps.

"What's wrong? What happened? Are you hurt?" I'm already grabbing my keys and heading for the door.

"Calm down." Her voice is hushed, like she's trying not to be overheard. "I should have worded that differently." There's a pause. "My friends and I need your help."

"What does that mean?" Her friends don't even know me.

"We need to sabotage a car?" Her voice rises at the end.

"You need to sabotage a car."

"Yeah." The word comes out in a rush. "None of us know much

about cars, and I thought maybe you could help."

I'm flattered that she thought of me when she's with her bloody friends, but—

"You realize I *fix* cars, not ruin them, right?"

"This situation calls for drastic measures."

"I'm listening." I slide the keyring onto my thumb and lean against the door.

Her sigh floats through the phone and tickles my ear. "There's this guy, Kieran Phillips, who did some pretty horrible things to Rhett. We're going to get revenge."

Is this what she does with her time?

"Slate?"

"I'm still here."

"So will you help us?"

"I doubt your friends are interested in my help."

"They are. I asked."

I huff out a breath. We both know I've already decided to do it—for reasons I refuse to acknowledge—but I won't hide the fact that I'm not happy about it. "I thought you were in trouble."

"I'm sorry." I picture her biting that damn lip. "I didn't mean to make you think that."

"Text me the address."

* * *

The next night, the address Lux sent takes me to a street of three-story townhouses with brick facades, polished doors, and pillared porticos. My Fiat looks as out of place as Lux did that day in Pop's.

They're all gathered around a hulking silver Grenadier. I lock my mental shields into place. There's no way I'm falling victim to whatever scheme they're about to spring.

Lux spots me and breaks away from the rest of them. She's wearing a long-sleeve beige jacket dress thing with buttons all down the front and tall boots. She looks incredible as always, her long hair swept away from her face and flowing down her back.

"Hey," she says when she's close enough to be heard. "Thanks for coming."

I want nothing more than to pull her into my arms and drag in a breath of that rose-scented air, but a tiny girl is watching me with evil eyes from the clusterfuck around the SUV. "Hey," I say quietly.

"Come on." Lux grabs my arm. "I'll introduce you."

She leads me back to the rest of them. I recognize a few of them from her party, but rich people all tend to look the same. The women drip with expensive jewels, and the men brandish their watches as if anyone gives a fuck how much they spent on something that only tells the fucking time.

I give them each a cursory nod, but they just stare at me like I'm an exotic animal at the zoo. The girl with black hair looks like she's plotting to kill me in my sleep. I give her a lazy grin in return. Let her try something.

"Okay, let's get started." A tall guy emanating CEO vibes claps his hands together like a scout leader. "Mr. Lawson, we appreciate your help with this. Lux, did you give him details on the car?"

Lux looks at him with incredulous eyes. "I don't know anything about the car." She's dropped my arm but is still standing close enough that her heat warms me.

Mr. CEO turns back to me. "The car is a 1983 Porsche 944. Any idea how we can ruin it?"

I hiss through my teeth. That baby is a classic. "Why the fuck would you want to ruin something like that?"

The guy's gaze flicks back to Lux, exasperated. "I thought you told him."

She angles her body toward me, shielding us from the rest of them, as though we have something worth protecting. "Please? You promised."

"That was before you told me what kind of car it was."

Her hand comes up to rest on my arm. "The guy deserves it, trust me."

"The car doesn't," I grumble. I focus on the guy in the rolled-up shirtsleeves. "If the screws on the side of the carburetor are adjusted, it'll inject enough fuel to idle the car but flood it out under throttle."

"And how do we adjust the screws?" he says.

I let out a deep sigh. "Take me to the car." Turning to Lux, I add under my breath, "You owe me."

They lead me to a townhouse several doors down, where the guy's girlfriend lives. The Porsche is sitting outside. Even though the clouds are hiding most of the light of the moon, its red coat gleams under the streetlamps. This thing has obviously been taken care of.

"I don't know if I can do this," I say to Lux when we reach the edge of the driveway.

She tugs on my hand. "For me?"

Her large brown eyes threaten to swallow me whole. I could drown in their depths and have no regrets.

"Just for you," I murmur into her ear.

As quietly as possible, I tinker with the carburetor's fuel to air ratio.

"There." I wipe my hands on my jeans. "He won't get very far before the thing breaks down." If I'm lucky, he'll bring it to the Rebel Wrench, and I'll be able to fix what I've broken.

"You sure it will work?" This comes from the guy in the polka-dot shirt. He's the only one of the group I've met before.

I shoot him a droll look. "Feel free to take a crack at it yourself."

"Nah, I trust you," he says with a huge grin. "Thanks, mate." He slaps me on the back.

We head back to our cars. I hang back, hoping Lux will join me, but she's caught up in conversation with the other two girls. Instead, Polka-Dot Shirt sidles up beside me.

"Hey," he says. "Good to see you again."

I know where this is going. "I don't have anything on me."

"Can we meet up tomorrow?"

His eyes are wild, and his hands are twitching. Do his friends know how high he is? "You should consider quitting, mate," I say. "That stuff is dangerous."

His smile grows bigger. "I know how to be careful." A three-second pause. "Tomorrow, then?"

Lux will kill me if she finds out I sold to her friend, not once, but twice. But if I don't supply him, he'll just find someone who will. At least this way I can control how much he gets. "Tomorrow," I say.

Lux is waiting for me at the Fiat. "Thank you for helping. Tell me how I can pay you back."

"Don't sweat it. I'm used to it."

Her spine straightens. "What does that mean?"

"Being used for my labor is nothing new."

The streetlamp catches the glint in her eyes. "Is that what you think?"

"Why would I think anything else?"

"Lux, you coming?" someone calls from the Grenadier.

Her eyes leave mine for a second as she considers this.

"I'll take her home," I call back.

Seconds later, the SUV roars out of the driveway and down the street, leaving Lux and me alone. I gesture toward my car. "Are you going to get in or are you waiting for me to open the door?"

She glares and yanks the door open. The slam reverberates through the night air as I round the Fiat to get into the driver's seat.

"I don't know why you're so upset," I say after starting the ignition. "We both know it's true."

Lux burns holes in my glovebox with her lethal stare. I want to point out that she has a tendency of sulking in my car, but I just merge into traffic.

"So what? You think I keep you around because of what you can do for me?" Her tone is so full of fire, I want to park the car and take her right here.

I laugh. "You just said you keep me around, like I'm your fucking pool boy. Maybe I'm not the one with the problem."

Her face is tinted blue from the glow of the car stereo. "I didn't mean it like that."

"Regardless, we both know I'm just your boy toy until someone better comes along."

"That's not true!" It comes out in a frenzied rush, her emotion peaking as she turns to look at me. "I don't think of you like that at all."

I pull onto her street. "Then what do you think of me as?"

She stays quiet as I park in her driveway. I cut the engine, intending to walk her to the door, but she makes no move to get out. "I don't know." Her voice barely breaks a whisper. "I keep asking myself that."

With my knuckle, I brush her arm through the sleeve of her dress. "You can't deny there's at least a little bit of truth in what I said."

Her throat bobs as she swallows. "Maybe." She drops her gaze to her lap.

I let my knuckle continue skimming the soft fabric of her dress. "Maybe I don't mind being kept around for what I can do for you."

Lux startles and looks at me, that gaze haunted and trapped but also intrigued. "What?"

I reach for her bottom lip with my thumb and tug it down. It's so full and luscious. I want it between my teeth. "A man doesn't forget coaxing those kinds of sounds out of a woman."

Her blush becomes a physical entity between us, combined with the heat of her arousal. "What are you going to do?" she whispers.

I move my other hand to cup the space between her legs. "You should ask what I'm *not* going to do. The list would be shorter."

She gasps, her eyes falling closed. I roll my thumb over her lip, loving how soft and wet it is. Her eyes fly open, and she grabs my hand in hers. She sucks my thumb into her mouth and clamps her lips around it.

"Fuck," I mutter as my dick strains at my jeans. I ditch the modesty that had me cupping her over her dress and move beneath the folds of fabric instead. She's even warmer now, sweating those sweet juices into my palm as she sucks my thumb like it's her mission in life.

29

"Burst into Flames" - Cavale

Lux

Slate's calloused fingers slip inside my panties, tugging aside the fabric like a stage curtain. He shudders when he finds me already wet for him. I drive my hips up, eager for him to take me roughly.

I've missed him so much.

He reaches across me for the seat lever. With a tug, it lurches back, allowing me to recline and give him better access. He takes it freely, removing his other hand from my mouth so he can slide it behind my back and scoot me further down the seat.

His fingers drive inside, seeking my core. I arch into his hand, already needing the release I know he can give me.

"Lux, baby," he murmurs. He tugs my dress up to my hips to get a full view of everything he's doing to me. Then, with excruciating slowness, he withdraws his fingers in order to lower my panties. I whimper at the loss of him.

Once they're off, I'm able to spread my legs even wider. He grasps both of my hips and opens me up. I prop both feet on the dash, spread wide like a hussy.

He leans across the center console and takes me with his mouth. I groan as his tongue makes long strokes along my seam.

This man is going to burn me alive.

I thrust my hips into his face, and he moans as he drives his tongue in deep. I splay my fingers into his soft, thick curls, urging him ever closer and deeper. He complies until I'm not sure how there's any space left he hasn't claimed yet, and then he manages to take it, too.

He pulls back, but only so he can minister more fully to my clit. He doesn't leave me wanting but moves his fingers back inside me to finish the job they started. He's using three of them now and fucking me hard. Every thrust jolts through my bones. I cry out at each one, but it's so good I will sob if he stops.

He thrusts again and curls his fingers to stroke me at the center of the fire he kindled. His tongue drags rough circles around and around my clit.

"Slate," I gasp after the last round. "Slate, I'm going to come."

He chuckles against my pussy. "Why do you think I'm buried inside you as deep as I can go? You'd better come for me, baby girl."

His words unlock something in me, and I climax in a full display of colors. Fireworks off the dock, confetti on New Years—they've got nothing on me and the way this man makes me feel.

Slate moans through my orgasm like it's as wonderful for him as it is for me. He uses his fingers until I'm nothing but shuddering spasms, my body drained of life.

When I've recovered from my mountain peak, I reach for his pants. "My turn."

His eyes smolder like smoke as I undo the button on his jeans and pull down the zipper. He scoots his seat back as far as it will go, giving me room to slide between him and the steering wheel.

The windows of the car are fogged up, providing a barrier between us and the outside world, even though anyone passing would know exactly what we're up to.

I shimmy into the space in front of him and free his cock from his pants. It takes me by surprise again. I swallow at the thought of putting the whole thing in my mouth. There's no way I'll be able to get it back very far.

He drives his fingers into my hair and tugs my face upward. "You're beautiful down there." His voice has a raspy quality to it, like he's barely holding it together.

I lick my lips and open my mouth wide. I tease the tip of him with my tongue, relishing the way he leans his head against the seat back and closes his eyes. Slowly I pull him into my mouth, sucking him deeper and deeper, until he's in my throat and I'm about to explode. He moans and uses his hands to slide my mouth up and down his shaft.

A harsh ringing fills the car. It's my stupid phone, buried in my bag. I ignore it and continue sucking him. His hips rock into me with rhythmic thrusts. I swirl my tongue around his tip, and he groans. "Baby, much more of that, and I'll blow."

I'd repeat his words back to him—*why do you think I'm pulling you as deep as you can go?*—but my mouth is too full for words.

The phone rings again. Slate opens his eyes and looks down at me, a question there. I shake my head, preoccupied with his dick.

This time he keeps his eyes open, watching me fuck him with my mouth. I can't even describe the expression there—something like awe.

My phone rings for the third time. He pulls back, lifting my head with his hands. "Maybe you should get that."

"It's fine." I reach for his cock. "We're not done here."

"Lux," he says softly. "Just see who it is."

I sigh and take my phone from him, frowning at the screen, still lit with the incoming call. "It's my mum."

He shifts upward in his seat. "Is that unusual?"

"For her to call me? Yeah."

"Answer it." He props himself up and tucks his cock back into his jeans with no small amount of effort. The thing is still huge and very hard.

I give it a longing look. "But—"

"Hey." He tucks my hair behind my ear. "We can finish afterwards. You should make sure it's not an emergency."

"It's always an emergency with my mum." She probably broke a nail and wants me to commiserate.

I wiggle out of the tight spot and back onto my seat. The ringing has stopped, so I dial her back.

"Lux, oh my god." Her voice is high—not unusual—and full of emotion—unusual.

"What's wrong?"

"It's Alex." The last syllable comes out on a sob.

My heart halts midbeat. "What happened?"

"He overdosed again."

No. No, no, no.

I let out a shaky breath. It's going to be okay. "I'm headed to the hospital," I tell her. I flick my eyes toward Slate, and he immediately starts the car.

"He's not at the hospital, love." My brain fixates on the fact that she called me *love*, something she hasn't done since I was five.

"What do you mean he's not at the hospital? They've released him already?"

The line is quiet for a few beats, long enough for the fear in my chest to morph into a huge monster.

"No, sweetie. He didn't make it."

The phone drops from my hand.

Slate's hand is warm on my leg. "What happened?" he asks softly.

"He's gone." The words sound hollow, because they are. There's nothing inside me anymore. I've been carved out like the stupid bloody jack-o'-lantern mocking me from my porch.

"Oh, baby." He tugs me into his arms. I let him because I don't have the strength to resist. He strokes my arm, my back, my hair. I don't feel any of it. "What do you want to do? You want me to take you somewhere?"

I shake my head and pull away from him. "I need to go by myself."

"Lux, you can't drive in this state."

"I'm fine." I open the car door and get out. I have to be fine, because falling apart is not an option.

Slate gets out of the car too, circling it before I make it to the wrought-iron gate. "Lux, listen to me. I'll drive if you tell me where to drop you."

I shake off his hand and open the gate. "I want to be alone."

He stops as if I've shocked him, and maybe I have, but I guess that's what happens when you stand too close to someone who's just been electrocuted. "If that's what you want."

I nod. "It is."

"Call me if you need me." He shoves his hands in his pockets.

"I will," I lie, and turn toward the house.

I won't call. Slate's world is the reason my brother is dead, and the universe is punishing me for playing with it. I was messing around with Slate while my brother lay dying.

Exactly what kind of sister does that make me?

* * *

It rains on the day of the funeral, because of course it does. The universe is working hard to convey its point. *If you hadn't been distracted by your stupid little fling, your brother would still be alive.*

Message received, bloody fucking universe.

I haven't seen or talked to Slate since that night in his car. He's texted a few times, even called once, to see how I'm doing, to see if there's anything he can do, but I ignored him.

What the fuck could he do? It's not like he can bring Alex back.

I give Maeve, Walker, and the guys tight smiles as they file in to sit beside me in the front pew of St. John's Cathedral. Walker squeezes my hand and tucks it into her own.

I don't move a muscle during the service. On my other side, my mum sits ramrod straight. There are no tissues, because we don't need any. Colombia girls don't cry.

Afterward, Rhett tugs me into his arms. "I know you're beating yourself up for what happened, but you're not responsible for his choices."

I force my lips into a small smile. "Thanks." It's the right thing to say.

Mourners file by, offering murmured condolences and clammy hand squeezes that leave me wanting to hurl into the bin in the ladies' room.

There's only one person who could offer me any shred of comfort, and I told him I didn't need him. That I didn't want him.

At the cemetery, Carter comes up to me. I brace myself, waiting for the inevitable barb about how Alex got what was coming to him.

Instead, he looks sad. "I'm really sorry, Lux." He reaches for my hand, which is hanging limply at my side.

My other hand clasps my umbrella even tighter. The rain is nothing more than a fine mist now, but the showers could start again at any time.

Carter's fingers are warm around mine, which have grown cold in the damp and chilly air. "I know how close the two of you were."

Not that close, I want to say. *Not if he could leave me like this.*

"I'm here for you, okay? I want you to know that. Whatever you need." He squeezes my hand more gently than he's ever done before. "I tried calling, but I think your phone was turned off?"

I don't tell him I blocked him after that night in the car park.

"I was a shit before. I was in a bad place, and I took it out on you. I will never be able to make up for it, but—" There's a long pause, punctuated by his loud swallow. "I want to try, if you'll let me."

I turn my head to make sure it's still Carter beside me. He never admits to being wrong.

"I've been miserable since you broke up with me. I know I wasn't always good to you, but it's not because I don't want to be. I can be a better man, the kind of man you deserve, if you'll let me."

I stare at him. Cold air seeps into my open mouth, but I can't find the words to answer him.

He takes my lack of rejection as encouragement to pull me into his arms. "What do you say, babe? Can we start again? Clean slate?"

He couldn't possibly know he's just said the name of the man my heart is keening for, but it's enough to break my trance.

"I appreciate your apology," I say, even though he never actually said he was sorry. I step out of his reach. "But I can't."

A flash of anger sparks in his eyes but quickly disappears. "If you change your mind, you know how to find me." Carter gives my hand one last squeeze before walking away.

I watch him retreat, but I won't change my mind. Burying my brother in the cold, hard ground has made one thing crystal clear.

Getting revenge deserves all of my focus.

30

"Dangerous" - Sleep Token

Slate

The funeral is massive. There are so many people in black holding umbrellas I can't tell which one is Lux at first. But that unmistakable hair and tilt of the chin eventually give her away.

The tall man with salt-and-pepper hair next to her is the famous Dr. Clarke. I recognize him from the staff photos on the hospital's website. Lux's mum stands on her other side, putting evident distance between herself and Lux's father.

The drizzle from earlier has slowed. I stick to the street, where no one will notice an old Fiat parked outside the pub. The cemetery is behind a black wrought-iron fence, giving the illusion of privacy, when in reality there's nothing private about a public cemetery.

People start filing away from the grave in twos and threes, whispering among themselves, and I imagine they're wondering how Dr. Clarke ended up with a son who made such poor choices.

My heart breaks for what Lux is going through.

She never called. I didn't expect her to, not after the way she practically pushed me back to the car that night. But that doesn't mean I wasn't hoping.

She holds her head high as she greets the last of the mourners. Ever the stoic one. I bet she hasn't shed a single tear yet.

Someone in a black trench coat that probably cost more than my car approaches her. When he takes her hand, I peer more closely at his profile.

Carter fucking Fitzgerald-Smythe.

What the bloody hell is that bugger doing here, and why isn't Lux sending him away? He tugs on their joined hands, and she goes into his arms. Willingly.

I cannot believe what I'm seeing. That fucker abused her in every way possible. And she fucking goes into his arms?

She pushed me away, but he gets a hug. I may not be the right guy for her, but *he* definitely isn't.

I shake my head and start the engine. I've had enough of this Silver Spoon bullshit. At the end of the day, it's always going to be about how much money is in your bank account and which side of the river you grew up on.

* * *

I'm cooking a dozen eggs on Friday night when someone knocks on the door. Briar is at Grandmum's for the weekend, so I'm fending for myself. She said it would be good for me to experience being a true bachelor. I told her to fuck off.

I open the door, spatula in hand, and my heart drops onto the vinyl floor.

Lux's face is calm, the picture of perfection. No one would know she buried her brother three days ago. But the signs are there if you know where to look. They're in the way the corners of her mouth aren't quite as high as usual. The way her makeup doesn't completely conceal the dark circles under her eyes. The way her eyelids droop, as if their weight is too much to hold up.

But the most remarkable difference is the fire in those eyes. I've seen her alive with anger before, even a thirst for vengeance, but this flame is different. Brighter. Deadlier.

"Hello," she says, like she's here to sell me an appliance. "Can I come in?"

"What do you want?" I keep my voice level and calm, even though there's a tornado spinning in my chest.

"I want to talk." A slight tilt of that pert chin.

"About what?" I lean against the doorframe, blocking the entrance with my body.

Her nostrils flare as her irritation blooms. "Slate, just let me in."

"Not until you tell me what you want."

"Something's burning."

I glance over my shoulder instinctively, and she uses the momentary distraction to push inside. The scent of charring eggs is too strong to ignore. I bolt to the kitchen and take them from the burner.

So much for dinner.

When I turn around, Lux is there, leaning against the refrigerator in a cream sweater and white trousers. She looks like luxury, completely out of place in this dinky kitchen with its plaid curtains and beat-up Formica countertop.

I prop my hands behind me on said countertop. "You didn't call."

"I was a little busy."

"Not too busy for Carter, though."

This takes her by surprise. She blinks and rears backward a fraction. "I don't know what you're talking about."

"I saw you with him. At the cemetery."

"Were you *spying* on me?"

"I was *worried* about you."

"That was unnecessary."

"Was it?" I push off of the counter. "I know what Alex meant to you. But when you found out, you pushed me away, and for what? For that prick's comfort?"

"You don't know anything." She delivers her iciest glare.

"I think I do. Have you cried yet? Hmm?" I brush a knuckle against her cheek. She shivers. "Have you told anyone how you're feeling? Or are you keeping it all bottled up inside like a good little girl?"

"Don't you dare," she hisses.

"Or what?" I taunt. "What are you going to do if I don't stop?"

She swallows loudly, and the image of her bending between my legs, mouth on my cock, flashes back to haunt me. God, I will never forget that as long as I live.

"I need to know if Tyler is the Wolf," she says.

It's my turn to blink in surprise. "I already told you he's not."

"You also said you don't know who the Wolf is, so technically, you don't know if it's Tyler or not."

I scrape the burnt eggs into the rubbish bin and turn back to the stove to start a fresh batch. "He's my best friend, Lux. Pretty sure I'd know if he was a notorious drug dealer."

"I think we've already established that you know far less than you think you do." She bumps my hip with her own, nudging me out of the way. She's already donned the apron again.

I cross my arms and lean back to watch her whip eggs in a bowl. "For the sake of the argument, what would you do if Tyler was the Wolf?"

She pours the eggs into the hot pan. "I already told you. Kill him."

I let out a single chuckle. "Yeah, okay."

The look she cuts me is fierce.

"I'm not going to let you kill my best friend, babe."

"He killed my brother."

"No, he didn't. Your brother made the decision to buy insidion himself."

Lux stirs the eggs with a vengeance that makes me glad they're not alive. She reaches for the salt and pepper on the shelf above the stove, and her sweater rides up several inches, revealing that buttery-smooth skin I would love nothing more than to lick. "The Wolf is ruining lives."

She straightens, and I drag my mind back to where it should be. "Tyler isn't the Wolf."

"All the same, I'd like to make sure."

"Is this your plan to work through your grief?"

Her shoulders bristle. "If I wanted a psych's opinion, I'd call my therapist."

"Save your two grand and talk to me." I place my hand on her shoulder, prepared for her to shake it off, but she doesn't. She feels fragile beneath my fingers, a bird easily crushed by the rest of the world.

She fiddles with her earring, then scoops the eggs out of the pan and onto a plate. They're fluffy and bright yellow. She sticks a fork into them and hands me the food. "Here you are."

"How did you do that?" I stare at the yellow clouds.

"They're just eggs."

I take the plate from her and set it back on the counter. Now that she's facing me, maybe I can have her full attention. "Lux."

She tenses when I put both hands on the sides of her face, preventing her from escaping me. Her pulse flutters in her throat. My eyes drop to her lips, which are absolutely tantalizing, but I force them back to her eyes.

"Do you have any idea how incredible you are?" I say.

A crease forms between her eyebrows. "Stop it."

"I mean it."

"Is this about the eggs?"

"No." I lean in to press my lips against her temple. Her breath catches on an inhale. "It's about everything."

"Please stop." Her voice has lost some of its bluster.

"I'm not going to stop." I brush the side of her nose with my own. She smells like a dream. "You go to bat for everyone but yourself. Why? Why can't you see that you're enough, exactly the way you are?"

Her jaw trembles, and just when I think she's on the verge of finally crying, she tucks all of her emotions away. "There's nothing wrong with trying to be better."

"There is if you think you need to in order to be loved."

"Who said anything about love?"

I slip my hand into her hair, my fingers stretching to take in as much of her as possible. "I did."

Her eyes meet mine, wide and tremulous. She looks terrified. I don't know how to reassure her, because I don't know what the bloody fuck I mean myself.

I lower my mouth to hers, the only thing I am sure of. She tastes sweet, like fresh peaches. She tastes the way coming home would if it had a flavor. I run my tongue along the seam of her lips, and she opens for me like a flower in the morning.

When I thrust it inside her mouth, she moans, tilting her head back to give me better access. I grasp the smooth pillar of her neck, keeping her locked in this position for me. I want her to trust me, to know that even if everyone else in the world abandons her, I won't.

I can't promise it—let's be realistic—but I want nothing more than to reassure her. And if that means making promises I'm not sure how I'll keep, then that's what I'll do.

"Lux," I breathe. She reaches for my mouth, dragging my head down by pulling on my neck. I happily comply, sucking her lip between mine and grazing it with my teeth.

She shudders, and I slide a hand up her sweater, beneath the soft fabric to even softer skin underneath. Her stomach is a hard, flat plane, but her breasts are ripe and lush. I take one in my hand, brushing my thumb across her nipple over the lace of her bra.

She moans into my mouth, and I eat it up, along with all of the other sounds she makes. I increase the speed of my thumb, flicking the nipple faster and faster. Her breathing picks up too.

Her nipple strains against the fabric, and I take pity on it, reaching for the strap of her bra. I yank it down, letting her breast spill out of the cup and into my waiting palm.

Her legs are trembling, so I back her up against the fridge, then lower my head to take that incredible mound into my mouth. Her peak is hard and ready for me. I suck on it gently, then harder, using my hand to massage the whole breast. She presses into me, the greedy little thing.

I smile against her. Nothing in this world can match the way she melts into my touch. I remove her sweater and bra, then sink to my knees, needing to be face to face with her goodness and needing to pay homage to her fine body.

Her breast dangles above me now. "Bring it to me, baby," I say, my hands gripping her hips.

She bends at the waist, dragging her breast over my face. I close my eyes as she dangles it back and forth over my mouth, my cheeks, my eyes. Then I open my mouth, and she drops it inside, earning herself a good, hard suck that sends her back against the fridge.

I chuckle, her breast still firmly tucked inside my mouth. Her eyes flutter open as she takes me in, sucking on her, and lust smolders in those dark depths. Slowly I release her, but only so I can scoop her up in my arms.

"As much as I'd love to take you right here in this kitchen, the bed will be much more comfortable."

When she's sprawled naked across my comforter, I make my way to my favorite part of her body. She's already drenched, and I've barely touched her yet. "God, it's like the biggest ego-boost ever, the way you saturate yourself for me."

She glows at this praise, arching her hips as I drag a finger through those fine juices. I chase my finger with my tongue, no longer able to resist the taste of her. I pin her to the bed with my hand as she bucks against me.

I settle myself between her legs, spreading them wide to get a good look at her. She's so fucking beautiful it makes my chest ache. Inside the confines of my jeans, my dick reminds me that it, too, is aching. I unzip my pants and get it out, then drag it through her moisture, mingling our pre-cum together.

She moans as I probe her entrance with my head. I don't have a condom on yet, but who said I can't play around first? I torment her clit with my cock, enjoying the way she writhes in blissful agony.

"Slate." She pants, opening her eyes into slits. "I need you. *Now*."

There isn't anything in the world I wouldn't do for this woman. "I'm coming," I reassure her. I grab a condom and roll it on. When I'm poised over her, ready to claim her and show her once and for all that she belongs to me, I pause. "I've never made love to anyone before."

Her brow crinkles. "You expect me to believe that?"

I reward her impertinence with a hard thrust, fully seating myself on the first go. She cries out, a ring of pleasure and surprise. I draw my hips back before surging forward again, making the headboard crash into the wall.

I lean down to whisper in her ear. "I never said I haven't had sex."

31

"Vigilante Shit" - Taylor Swift

Lux

I give Slate's sleeping form one last look. As a distraction technique, he is certainly effective. Last night was amazing, like every night with him is. But I can't let what I feel for him keep me from carrying out my plan. They are two separate entities that have no bearing on one another.

I run to my car, which is still parked outside. Whatever threats Slate issued must have worked. I don't think anyone has so much as looked at it since the day it was stolen. I cringe when the engine roars to life, but it can't be helped.

Fortunately, I dropped a pin at the warehouse several weeks ago. I suspected even then that Slate would never take me back.

It's as if he thinks I'm some hothouse flower who needs to be sheltered and protected from the big, bad world. He doesn't know that I'm fully capable of taking care of myself. My mum may not have been the best role model, but she taught me how to get what you want when you're a woman.

And what I want is the Wolf dead.

Tyler is my best lead. If he's not the Wolf, he knows who is. I'm sure of it. This whole secrecy thing is nothing but a front. It's impossible that no one in the drug world knows who is supplying them, and my money's on Tyler. It doesn't matter that he's Slate's best friend.

Seeing Alex lying in that casket, his body cold with death, honed my purpose to a razor blade. The Wolf is going down.

My GPS directs me back to the old warehouse Slate and I staked out. It isn't abandoned this time. A truck similar to the one we saw that night is sitting near the loading dock.

Perfect.

Slate claimed that Tyler was only there to make extra cash, but if he is the Wolf, as I suspect, he's going to be here every night.

My car will attract attention no matter what, so I don't bother hiding it this time. It's dangerous pulling right up to the front of the building like this, but my security is in the glovebox.

As I approach, the men unloading the truck stop and watch me. My hands tremble on the steering wheel, but I manage to park. I lean over to retrieve the weapon Slate gave me. Let's hope I remember how to use it.

Confidence is key, I remind myself as I climb out of the car, handgun tucked securely in my waistband under my sweater. The eyes of the men cling to me as I walk over. I twirl a strand of hair and put on my best Barbie doll face.

"Hello," I call when I'm a car length away. "I'm looking for Tyler."

A beefier guy steps closer to me, sending a trickle of sweat down my back. *Stay calm, stay calm.*

"What do you want with Tyler?" He reminds me of one of those fat sausages hanging from the ceiling of the artisan butcher's shop I visit occasionally when I'm throwing a party. Thick neck, thick arms, thick body. Even his voice is thick.

"That's between me and him," I say as nonchalantly as is possible when my heart is speeding around a racetrack. "Where is he?"

"We'll tell you after we pat you down." A leer drags the corner of the man's mouth upward. "Can't have any weapons around here, you know."

I narrow my eyes, no need for acting skills now. "If you lay one finger on me, I will have the entire Wesbourne City Police Department descend on your asses so fast, you won't even have time to hitch up your pants." My eyes flick down toward his sagging jeans. "Which I highly recommend you do."

His face turns crimson. Without removing his eyes from mine, he calls to the others, "Take her to Tyler."

A grim satisfaction steals over me when I hear those words. If I had any doubt about Tyler's identity as the Wolf before, it disappears. He wouldn't have an entire squad of security guards if he didn't have something to hide.

When I get inside, the warehouse is dark and chilly. Rows of boxes sit against the wall, stacked taller than my head. I imagine all the vials of insidion inside, like a little army ready to destroy lives.

The man guiding me stops on the other side of the cavernous room. The door there has been propped open, leading outside. I wipe my sweaty palms on my trousers. If this is where I die, at least it was for a good cause.

"Yo, Ty," the guy calls.

Tyler emerges in the doorway, phone pressed against his ear with one hand, cigarette in another. He shifts his focus from the man to me.

"Lady wants to talk to you." The guy juts his chin at me. "You good?"

Tyler stares at me for a few more seconds. "Yeah, mate. All good." He disconnects the call and sticks the phone in his pocket.

The man walks away, leaving Tyler and me alone. If I thought my heart was racing before, I'm not sure what to call its current speed, but I think it puts me at risk of a heart attack.

"What's up, *Lux*?" He puts an emphasis on my name that feels mocking, then takes another drag of his cigarette.

"Can we talk?" I say, forcing my voice not to wobble.

He steps backward through the door, which is my invitation to follow, I suppose. We're in a gravel yard similar to the one out front, full of discarded junk. I scan the shadows for glowing eyes, but it's hard to see anything.

Tyler leans back, propping one foot against the metal wall. He studies me through narrowed eyes as he puffs on his cigarette. "If you're here to proposition me, I should tell you I don't cross swords with—"

"Ew." I screw up my face. "No."

He grins and drops the cigarette to the ground, grinding it out with his shoe. He's wearing black jeans, a gray T-shirt, and dark boots, the perfect outfit for blending in out here. Meanwhile, I'm like a walking target in my all-white outfit.

"What can I do for you?"

The cold metal of the gun presses against my tailbone, reminding me of why I'm here. I won't be fast enough to pull it while he's watching, so I need a distraction. I should have thought this through.

I fumble for my phone in the pocket of my pants. "I was wondering . . ." It falls to the gravel. "Shit."

Before I can pick it up, he bends over and snatches it, giving me the perfect opportunity. I yank the gun from my waistband and point it at him.

He straightens slowly, giving the weapon a weighty glance before raising both hands, my phone still clutched in one of them. "What the fuck?" he mutters softly. "Are you a cop or something?"

My hands shake around the gun. I'm trying to hold it the way they do in the movies, but no one tells you how uncomfortable that position gets after twenty seconds. "No, I'm not a cop."

Tyler's expression slackens with relief. "Then put that down and tell me what you want."

"I'm not a cop, which is unfortunate for you," I say. "Because I have no qualms about killing you in cold blood."

His mouth drops open, and I have to applaud his acting skills. There's no way he hasn't imagined someone doing this exact thing once they discover who he is.

I take a deep breath. *Just pull the trigger.* Just pull the damn trigger.

I've played this scene out thousands of times, even if he hasn't. I'm finally here, finally on the brink of getting revenge for Alex. All I need to do is pull the bloody trigger.

It's too far away. My finger doesn't have the strength necessary to pull it back. On top of that, my hands are shaking like crazy now, meaning I have a better chance of hitting the side of the building than Tyler.

But I have to do this. I have to kill him. If I don't, he's only going to take thousands more lives.

"Put the gun down, Lux."

32

"Fix You" - Coldplay

Slate

Lux is outside the door, feet braced in the gravel the way I taught her, arms held out at a ninety-degree angle, both hands clutching the gun. She looks like an angel in that white outfit, set off against the night sky—if death masqueraded as an angel.

Even from here I can see her trembling. She's nervous as fuck, and she should be, pointing that gun at Tyler's fucking head like she's a cop in a bad TV show.

I take another step closer to the door, slowly so I don't startle her, but she doesn't see anything but the man at the end of her gun. *My* gun.

Goddamnit. "Put the gun down, Lux." My voice is firm and steady, the opposite of my heart. I think she feels something for me, but she may have been playing me this whole time.

If I'm not careful, this whole thing could blow up in our faces.

She wavers, lowering the Walther several inches as she whips her head to the side. Her beautiful face looks less surprised than I expected, given how quietly she tried to slip out of the house thirty minutes ago.

It was the click of the door that woke me up, and at first it didn't register. But the minute I gained enough clarity to remember that Lux was supposed to be in bed beside me and no longer was, I was out the door in a heartbeat, jerking my pants on as I ran to my bike in the garage.

"Lux," I say again. "Drop the gun, babe."

She raises it again, and it's now pointing directly at Tyler's chest. She hasn't had enough target practice to be able to hit something accurately from a distance, but Ty is only five feet from her. Hitting him isn't a guarantee, but I don't like the odds.

I step outside, and the gravel crunches beneath my shoes. I grabbed the first pair I could reach, which happened to be the greasy boots I wear to the shop every day. There was no time for socks, so my ankles burn where the insides are chafing against them.

"You have no proof that Tyler is the Wolf." I say it as much for her sake as to give Ty context for why he's currently facing the muzzle of my Walther PDP.

Lux's jaw clenches, and she repositions her hands on the gun. Good. She's getting tired of holding it up. "You have no proof that he isn't," she says, eyes still locked on Tyler, whose gaze I can feel flicker between me and her.

"And you're willing to go to prison for killing a guy you're not even sure supplied your brother?"

Her gaze swings toward me, making her hands drop a few inches unwittingly.

"Come on, babe." I gesture around us. "Everyone saw you come in tonight. It won't be hard to figure out who fired the shot."

The frown lines between her eyes deepen, and she turns back to Tyler. "Tell me who the Wolf is."

His eyes flit to mine, begging me to do something about this crazy-ass woman holding him at gunpoint. "I-I don't know," he stammers.

"Bullshit." She wiggles the weapon, and I tense. She really has watched a lot of cop shows. "Tell me what you know."

"I don't know anything," Tyler says. "Swear to god."

Disappointment tugs at her face. Did she think he was going to stand there and fess up to being the Wolf?

She doesn't belong here. She belongs somewhere far, far away, where the stench of street crime doesn't cling to you like dog shit on the bottom of your shoe.

"Lux, give me the gun." I'm done waiting, done trying to reason with her. I need to get her out of here. I step forward, tug it from her hands, and wrap an arm around her waist.

Tyler lets out a big sigh. Did he actually think I was going to let her shoot him? I jerk my head toward the door, and he tosses Lux's phone at me before retreating into the warehouse, already pulling out another cigarette. The guy will probably go through an entire pack tonight.

I wouldn't mind one myself.

Lux collapses into me, her body shaking with nerves. "Hey," I murmur. "It's okay." I wrap both arms around her so I can turn the gun's safety on, then slip it into my waistband.

With the weapon properly handled, I give her my full attention. She tucks her face into my chest, and I stroke her back.

God, was she really going to pull that trigger? I knew she was upset about her brother, but drawing a gun on someone takes guts. Nerves of steel. She's strong, but even I never expected this.

I followed her from the house, but I didn't know which way she'd gone. She could have headed home, but why leave without saying anything and in the middle of the night? I tried calling, but she didn't answer. I drove around the Junction, looking for signs that she'd gone out to grab a late-night snack or drink, but didn't see her car anywhere.

That's when it hit me. Her obsession with tracking down the Wolf, her stone-cold gaze when she told me she'd kill him if she ever found him.

I headed to the warehouse we staked out that night, because I knew how hung up she'd been on it. It didn't take long to put the pieces together after that.

Her shuddering subsides. I draw lazy circles on her back, suddenly aware that she's not wearing anything but a lightweight sweater on this chilly night. "Here." I move to take off my jacket, but she clings to me, arms wrapped securely around my waist.

I'm not going to pry her off of me, not when she feels this damn good, so I let her burrow herself into my chest and wrap my arms tighter around her to provide at least a little warmth.

Maybe I shouldn't be so quick to console the woman who pulled a gun on my best friend, but I know why she did it. Hell, I'm supposed to be the one helping her. Instead, I've been dragging my feet on this whole thing, not wanting to lead her into danger, but not willing to let her go either.

"Babe, you know you don't have to hide your tears from me." I lower my head so the words brush the shell of her ear.

She turns so her voice isn't muffled by my chest. "What tears?"

I lean back to take her in. She's right. There isn't a streak on her face.

I've never seen her cry. Not when she was mugged at the petrol station, not when her brother overdosed the first time, not when he died, not now.

I move my hands to her cheeks and thrust my fingers back into her hair. "You don't have to pretend to be okay with me. You know that, right?"

She stares at me placidly, like she's not sure what I'm trying to say. "I'm fine."

"You just tried to kill someone."

She lets her shoulders rise and fall. "I'm fine," she says again.

"Lux." I smooth a hand over her face. "When's the last time you cried?"

I expect her to say after Alex died, when she was alone.

"When I was a kid." Her voice is so nonchalant, I have to double-check she's not bluffing.

She's serious.

"That's not healthy," I say. "Everyone needs to cry sometimes."

She gives me an impish look. "When's the last time you cried?"

I don't need to think about it. "Two years ago. I thought I was going to lose Briar."

Her eyes flutter as she takes this in, then she lifts her chin. "My mother taught me to conceal my emotions."

Her fucking mother. It's such a boarding school response. Conceal your emotions, my ass. "I hope I'm not the first one to tell you this, but your mum is a terrible person."

Lux lets out a humorless laugh. "No one needs to tell me that."

I catch the tiniest changes in her expression—the way her eyes flick from object to object, the twitch of her nose, the way her brows drag downward a millimeter.

"She used to lock me in my room for crying."

The admission rings out in the still night. My arms tense around her instinctively. "How old were you?" I say quietly.

She shakes her head. "I don't know. Two or three maybe when she started. Maybe even younger, I don't remember back that far. By the time I was five or so, I figured out that if I wanted to avoid being locked in there, I needed to keep my tears to myself." She lifts that beautiful face up to me. "So I did. I locked them up and she quit locking me up."

My heart drops like a bullet. "She locked you in your room for *crying?*"

"Yep. Said a lady doesn't show emotion."

"For the love of god." If I ever come face-to-face with that bitch again, she's going to wish she had locked herself up instead. I pull Lux close, pressing against the back of her head. She snuggles into me, warm and fragile in my hands.

"You don't need to hide anything from me," I say. "I'll never punish you for showing emotion."

She nods in understanding, her face lost in my T-shirt. We stay like that for a long time.

Minutes, maybe even an hour later, I discover that my shirt is wet.

33

"arms" - Christina Perri

Lux

"I've never gone to anything like that," I say into the phone. "What do I wear?"

"I'm guessing you don't own a flannel?" Slate's voice is doing a poor job concealing his smirk.

"I refuse to dignify that with a response." I pull out a vintage pink Dior dress with the cutest pockets and gold buttons, but it's probably unsuitable for this event. "What is a potluck anyway?"

"Everyone brings a dish to share."

"Even me?"

"Even you."

Now I need to decide what to wear *and* what to bring. I hang the dress back up. "Do they have food sensitivities or allergies? Are they mostly vegetarian—"

"Lux."

"—or vegan or—"

"*Lux.*"

I stop speaking.

"Bring whatever you want. It'll be fine."

I've never attended an event that didn't require an invitation or have a dress code. I blow out a puff of air, making the wisps of hair around my face float away. "Thanks for nothing," I mutter, and pull a denim miniskirt from my closet.

Slate's laugh is still echoing in my ear when he hangs up.

* * *

It's the perfect autumn night. Brisk, like walking into an air-conditioned art museum on a hot day. Leaves swirl downward from the trees in vivid shades of red, gold, and orange. Smoke hangs in the air like a fog, and stars peek out through the curtain of the sky.

Slate surprised me with his invitation to the Junction's annual potluck. No clue why he wants me to come. He even picks me up, his Fiat fresh from the car wash. It feels suspiciously like a date.

I've never been to Junction Park—the origin of the neighborhood's name—but I can't imagine it looks like this every day of the year. People mill over the grassy lawn like insects. The twinkle lights strung between the trees look like stars dropped to earth. Laughter and chatter combine to make a heartwarming melody.

A warm ache grows in my chest.

"Ready to meet some people?" Slate asks. He carries my heirloom tomato tart over to one of the many tables heaped with casserole dishes and disposable pie pans. I follow two steps behind.

"Oh, Slate!" a woman with a head full of white curls croons as he hands her my dish. "Tell me you didn't make this." Her grin is punctuated by missing teeth. She looks like Betty White.

"You know I love you too much for that, Benita." He leans down and presses a kiss to her papery cheek. "Actually, my—" He turns toward me with an outstretched arm, suddenly unsure how to introduce me. "Lux made it."

221

"Hello, dear." The old woman reaches for my hand, clasping it between her two crepey ones. She has a surprising amount of strength for her age. "Better hold on to this one," she murmurs to me with a wink.

Slate takes my arm with a last kiss for Benita.

"She's positively smitten with you," I say as we walk toward the lawn.

He inhales deeply, inflating his chest. "I carry a certain charm ladies find irresistible."

I let out a sharp laugh. "Keep telling yourself that, Romeo."

His grin creates a hazy bubble around me, locking me inside a space and time where a breath of air becomes impossible. What is happening to me? He twines our fingers together. My pulse skitters at his touch. I should be used to it by now, but I'm not.

I'm not sure I ever will be.

We only take a few steps before we're stopped by a man wearing a black-and-white flannel—it seems like everyone's wearing them tonight. All jokes aside, Slate was right. I wouldn't stand out like Barbie at a truck stop if I owned something plaid.

Slate drops my hand, and I tuck it into my pocket, hoping no one noticed. He evidently doesn't want to be seen holding hands with me, which is fine, but I make a note to act like we're platonic friends. After giving the man a firm handshake and clap on the back, he reaches back toward me as they chat. It takes three seconds for me to understand that he's reaching for my hand. I tuck it back into his calloused warmth. My heart twirls around my chest like a ballerina.

The man walks away to attend to a toddler screaming at him from the playground. Slate turns to me. "You okay?" he asks.

I nod and offer him a weak smile. How do I tell him I feel like an outsider?

"You're cold." He nods at my arms, which are wrapped around my middle.

Before I can explain that it has as much to do with insecurity as the chill in the air, he slips his black hoodie over his head, then tugs it over mine. Eyes watch us from all sides as he scoops my hair up and pulls it out from inside the sweatshirt.

Goosebumps spray across my skin where his fingers brush the back of my neck. He doesn't remove his hands, just slides them until he's cupping my jaw. Then, with the eyes of the entire neighborhood on us, he lowers his lips to mine, branding me as his own in front of dozens of witnesses.

I'm instantly swept away into the kiss. This man has the ability to make the whole world disappear. He makes me forget my own name. He keeps the kiss chaste, but my skin heats all the same. His thumbs sweep across my cheeks, and I cling to his bent elbows, wishing we could leave.

When he breaks away several seconds later, my face carries the heat of a thousand suns. His smile is only for me, pouring out of his eyes and into mine. I want to drown in it.

He's forgiven me for holding a gun on his best friend. Is it too much to hope that maybe whatever this is can last?

The weight of the eyes around us pops our little bubble. I clear my throat and scoot back an inch. "People are watching," I say.

"Since when do you not like an audience?" Slate's invisible grin bleeds into his voice.

I swat at his arm. "Not children," I hiss.

A small girl with blonde ponytails is scrutinizing us from the edge of the playground. He follows my gaze, and a lazy smile jerks up the left side of his mouth. "Come on."

He grabs my hand and leads me to her. Her name is Bridget, and she's the daughter of one of his employees.

"I'm going to marry Slate," she informs me when he introduces us, with a glare I wouldn't have thought a seven-year-old capable of.

"Oh." It comes out in a laugh. "Be sure to invite me to your wedding. I'll take lots of photos."

She looks at me like she's trying to deduce if I'm telling the truth or not.

Slate tugs on one of her ponytails, making her head bob to the side. "Be nice to Lux. She doesn't know anybody here, and she could use some friends."

Bridget keeps her arms folded over her chest, but her frown softens. Her eyes spark with the realization that she has an advantage over the new girl.

More people approach us, and Slate introduces me. He's switched our hands so he doesn't need to let go of me every time he greets someone. The place where our skin is fused together holds much more of my focus than any of the people we meet.

It attracts more than a few inquisitive glances as well.

We make our way through the crowd. Everyone wants to talk to Slate. At first I think it's because they want to scope out the interloper in their midst, but they don't pay much attention to me. They discuss a million different things—their children, their jobs, their pets, their homes, their dreams.

Slate engages with all of it. He knows the names of everyone's kids and dogs. He knows where they live and offers to help them fix broken shutters or repair holes in their roofs. He gives advice on jobs that are paying better than others, employers who are willing to hire in spite of a felony record.

Several people attempt to make conversation with me, but it doesn't take them long to figure out that I'm from the Hills and don't have anything to add about supermarket deals or the latest cuts at the factory or the surge in school bullying that's been going on. If they're wondering what Slate is doing with me, they're not alone.

I smile at the woman currently prattling on about the sundress she's wearing, her frizzy red hair swept back into a purple-and-yellow bandana. She purchased the dress at a secondhand store, and my heart soars at finding a shared connection over our love for vintage treasures, until she tells me the generic brand and how much she paid for it.

Nothing in common after all.

How could I think for a second that Slate and I could have a future together? I can't live like this, pretending to care that the price of petrol is finally coming down or that some guy was arrested for beating someone up in broad daylight.

The woman in the sundress doesn't clock my lack of interest. "He was trying to protect his girlfriend, but the cops didn't care about that. He threw the first punch, and they carted him off to jail."

I offer a sympathetic murmur, while inside I'm wondering how that could possibly be true.

"Last week, Lena Jenson was found squatting in the old Kitzpatrick place with her children. They threw her out, even though they had nowhere to go. Not since her jackass of a husband kicked her out."

I blink at the woman, again doubting the validity of her story. "What about homeless shelters?"

She lifts an overplucked red brow. "Homeless shelters? Her daughter was molested at one of them while Lena was tending to her sick baby."

My chest lurches.

The lady shakes her head, her messy bun swaying gently. "Those places are more dangerous than the streets."

Slate tugs on my hand, and I offer the woman a sad smile before turning to him, her words still echoing through my mind. "I need to go talk to some people," he says. "Will you be okay by yourself for a second?" He draws me closer, until our chests brush against each other.

My nipples spring to life. I tilt my face up to his. "I am an independent woman. I'll be fine," I say, even though my palms are growing sweaty. Put me in a room full of supermodels, and I'm fine. But these people are looking at me like I'm an alien, and not the good kind.

"Okay." He drops a kiss on my lips. "I'll be back soon, and then we'll get some food."

Slate vanishes into the crowd, and I'm left standing by myself. I raise my hand to my nose and sniff the cuff of his hoodie. God, he smells divine. I know what all of this means. I'm not always the dumb blonde I pretend to be. I'm falling for him.

Which is the stupidest thing I could possibly do.

When I cried for the first time in twenty years the other night, I realized how hot the water I'm standing in is. For a man to be able to coax tears from me—

Someone grabs me from behind. I yelp and turn to find Briar standing there, a giant grin on her face.

"You scared me!" I say, hand on my heart.

She only laughs and loops her arm through mine. "I thought my brother was going to hog you all night."

"I didn't realize you were here." Briar and I haven't spent much time together, but there's something about her that makes me lower my guard. She's so real and genuine. "Are you feeling okay?"

She leads me toward the food tables. "Pretty good today." She hands me a plate, then drops my arm to load her own with an array of food.

I scan the tables for something wholesome. There are crocks of what might be chicken swimming in so much sauce it's hard to tell, vegetables bathed in cream, and desserts piled high with fluffy whipped topping.

"Are there any salads?" I ask Briar quietly.

She gives the table a quick scan. "Doesn't look like it. But this sweet potato casserole is to die for. Here." She plants a large dollop in the center of my plate.

By the time her plate is heaped full, mine contains the orange casserole and a few celery sticks. Briar shakes her head when she sees it. "Take mine," she says. Before I can object, she thrusts her plate into my hands and takes mine back to the food line.

Several minutes later, she joins me on a park bench, our plates looking identical now. Piles of questionable casseroles and unidentified meats touch each other. There's so much cheese sauce covering one particular glob that it's running into everything else.

I blink at the atrocity. "How am I supposed to take a photo of this? It's the least aesthetic plate I've ever held."

Briar throws her head back and laughs. "Don't you ever eat for the sake of eating?" Her cheeks are tinged with pink from the cool air, and her eyes sparkle with a bubbling joy the world hasn't managed to stamp out yet. She seems fine tonight, but I've never actually seen her look sick.

I work up the nerve to taste the least horrendous-looking thing on my plate—a deviled egg, which is surprisingly good. It gives me the confidence to nibble at a couple more dishes. We eat in silence for a few moments, until I can't stay quiet any longer.

"I heard some things tonight."

She flicks her gaze my way, a chicken leg held up to her mouth.

I tell her about the stories, the things these people have had to stoop to in order to survive. "Is it really that bad?" I ask.

She shrugs and licks her fingers off, one by one. "I mean, a lot of it, yeah. Some people obviously make bad choices, and that's why they end up where they do, but for others . . ." She scrunches up the napkin in her hand, and her nose mimics the gesture. "It's not always black-and-white, you know?"

I *don't* know, but maybe I'm beginning to see. Slate's been forced to make similar decisions to care for his family.

My eyes search for him in the crowd, my heart already missing his steady presence next to me. When I finally spot him, he's deep in conversation. It takes me a few seconds to realize he's talking to Tyler. No wonder he left me behind. Nothing like being held at gunpoint to kill the mood.

"I've never seen him act like this." Briar's voice startles me, and I quickly look back down at my plate.

"Who?"

She nudges my arm, evidently not fooled. "Slate."

"Oh." I swallow the bite of creamed corn on my spoon, hoping it will wash down the lump in my throat as well. It only confirms my dislike of corn.

"Did you know he quit smoking?"

I choke on the bite. After I'm finished coughing, I turn to her. "He what?"

She nods and swirls her fork through a dessert that probably contains at least five hundred calories. "I haven't seen him with a cigarette in two weeks."

I process this while chewing my food more slowly. "And that is relevant how?"

"Didn't you ask him to quit?"

I blink at her. Where did she get an idea like that? "No," I say, dragging the word out. "I only made it clear that it's a dreadful habit."

Briar smirks and licks off her fork.

"That's not the same thing," I say defensively.

"It's not," she agrees. "It's even better."

I'm still processing this when Slate joins us. He gives the plate in my lap a pointed glance. I've barely made a dent in it. "I see you found food without me." He bends down and captures my lips with his.

"Gross," Briar mutters from beside me. She wanders off, taking her plate with her.

"You scared off my only friend," I say when he breaks off the kiss.

"I'll scare everyone away if it means I can have you to myself," he murmurs.

Heat flames in my cheeks. I hope the people near us can't hear. Slate snatches a brownie from my plate and demolishes it in two bites.

"Please help yourself," I deadpan.

"Don't worry. I will." His eyes hold a dirty promise.

My stomach dips. "You're practically a celebrity around here." I scoot my plate toward him. I'll explode if I eat another bite.

He snorts and shovels a forkful into his mouth. "Hardly."

"Every single person here thinks you hung the moon."

He sets the plate down on the grass, then kneels in front of me and places his hands on my thighs. "Does that include you?"

My mouth goes dry as I stare into those bottomless eyes, the same ones that can make me feel the full range of human emotion. "I—" What do I say? The truth is that I can't imagine my life with him.

But I can't imagine it without him either.

We're trapped in the in-between, with no hope of ever finding our way out.

The warmth of Slate's hands seeps into my tights-clad legs. He's inches away from my core, where I know he can make me forget that anyone exists in the universe but the two of us.

"Do you want to get out of here?" His voice is a low rumble that causes my clit to start pulsing. "I'm ready for dessert."

34

"Speakers" - Sam Hunt

Slate

It's a stupid question. I can smell Lux's arousal from my position in front of her legs. But on the off chance that she's sick of me, I ask anyway.

Her eyes heat, and my dick pulses inside my jeans. That's going to get uncomfortable soon.

"Come on." I help her to her feet. There's no way we'll escape this crowd by leaving through the main entrance. I'll get stopped a million times before we make it to the car.

I scan the car park on the other side of the lawn. Tyler's old truck is over there, the whole lot enveloped in shadows.

"I have an idea," I say, and tug her through the back of the gathering.

She comes willingly, already trusting me far more than I deserve. "Where are we going?" she whispers when our feet crunch against the gravel of the car park.

"Right here." I pull her to a stop at the back of Tyler's truck, no longer able to keep from touching her. She's so soft and warm, and my hands eat her up like she's my last meal.

Lux melts against me, and I cradle her head in my hands, lifting her face to mine. Her lips are cool but pliable. I ravish them with my own mouth until she's moaning and gasping for breath.

I let her come up for air, then resume my advances. Using my tongue, I explore every centimeter of her mouth, claiming it all as my territory, because it is. She moans when I slide a hand under the sweatshirt she's wearing, brushing against bare skin.

Every time I caught a glimpse of her wearing my hoodie earlier, I wanted to take her right then and there. The fact that she paraded around in *my* clothes, holding *my* hand, is enough to make me hard for a whole fucking week.

I am so thoroughly fucked.

I make quick work of the tiny scrap of bra she's wearing. She whimpers when I begin flicking her nipple. She knows what's coming.

"Slate," she moans. "Please, I need more."

We can't go to my house, because I don't know when Briar will be home. And Lux lives on the other side of the city. No way either of us will last that long.

"Are you growing damp between your thighs?" I give her a wolfish smile. There's nothing in the world better than knowing this woman is wet for me.

"Damp?" she pants. "Try drenched."

I growl in her ear. "I'm going to eat that pussy until it's dripping." She lets out a gasping breath as I close my teeth over her ear and push her against the side of the truck. Thank god Ty didn't bring the Lambo tonight.

I move my other hand under Lux's skirt. "This skirt has been taunting me all night." I move to her panties, but I'm blocked. "What the—" A little more groping reveals an extra layer of fabric separating me from my destination.

She lets out a soft laugh. "I'm wearing tights."

I groan against her neck. "Why do you torture me like this?"

"They unsnap."

I lift my head and look down at her with a cocked brow.

"Just try it," she says, head tilted back, eyes closed.

I fumble around beneath her skirt, letting go of her breast in order to use two hands down there. Then I find the small snaps along the seam of her crotch. I undo them with a quick flick of my hands, and an entire flap of her tights opens up.

A laugh trips out of my mouth as I make contact with . . . not silk panties, but warm pussy.

"I thought you deserved a reward if you made it through," she says breathlessly.

I stroke her between her folds, causing her back to arch and her mouth to part on a gasp. "Good girl."

She's as wet as she promised, and it takes everything within me not to take her against the side of the truck. But anyone could walk by, and I'm not about to share the sight of her bliss.

"Hold on for one second," I tell her as I slide my fingers out.

She whimpers in protest while I open the passenger door of the truck and search the back seat. I find a ratty blanket that's probably older than Ty's grandpa and smells like a combination of urine and wet dog. I grab it anyway.

"What's that for?" she asks, growing lucid again.

"You'll see," I say, and jump into the truck bed. I spread the blanket out over the cold metal. It's not fancy, but at least it will protect her from the cold.

Once that's done, I reach down a hand to help her up. Lux takes it and steps onto the truck's bumper, scanning the setup with questions in her eyes. Her sex hormones win out, because she steps over the tailgate.

I lay her back onto the blanket. The night has grown chilly, so I'm going to leave her clothes on. "These tights are genius," I say, reaching for her again.

She bucks as my fingers make contact with her tight bundle of nerves. I lower my head beneath her skirt to preserve as much warmth as possible and take her in my mouth.

She tastes fucking delicious, dripping all over me like a leaky faucet. Her hands grip my hair, and she holds on as I fuck her senseless with my tongue. When she's a sopping, writhing mess, I pull out and wipe my mouth. There's no way to hide my grin.

"Slate, *please*. I need you inside of me," she whispers.

I stifle the groan rising in my chest and pull a condom from my pocket. "God, it cripples me when you need my cock like you need oxygen."

I lift her skirt in order to see her landing strip, directing me where to go. Shoving her legs further apart, I slide inside her with a gentle thrust.

It's not as gentle as I thought, because it sends her scooting across the truck bed. She bumps her head against the metal side.

"Shit, baby. I'm so sorry." I crumple on top of her.

"It's fine. I'm fine," she says. "Please don't stop."

I press a kiss to her head and lift back onto my hands. I slide my cock out, then drive it home again, being more careful this time.

Her eyes flutter closed. "Look at me, baby," I murmur. I want to see what this is doing to her.

She obeys, those dark eyes opening and dragging me down into their depths.

Her pussy is hot and tight around me, the perfect antidote to the cold night air. She clenches tightly, and I have to focus on her eyes so I don't spill my load right there.

There's a noise at the front of the truck. Lux's eyes grow wide. *What is that?* she mouths.

I lift my head and look through the back window. "Fuck," I mutter, and sink back down. "Tyler's coming."

Questions flit across her eyes, but she's too afraid of being caught to make a sound. Instead, she keeps her gaze focused on me. She's trusting me to take care of her.

Tyler opens the driver's door and climbs in. Fuck me now. He's leaving.

The engine starts, and the truck backs out of the car park. Lux's eyes have taken on a horrified glow. "What is happening?" she hisses.

"Looks like Tyler's going home."

"I thought this was your truck!"

"I don't have a truck." I give her what I hope is an apologetic smile, but I'm pretty sure it comes out sheepish. "On the plus side, I've never had sex in a moving vehicle before, so . . ."

Her fingers tangle in my T-shirt. "Me neither." She tugs me back down.

I'm still inside her, so I punctuate the movement with another thrust. Cold air whips around us as we travel down the streets of the Junction. Every time we take a corner, I brace myself to keep Lux from rolling around the truck bed.

She giggles when Ty brakes extra hard, almost sending me into the cab. I growl and seal my mouth over hers. I'll teach her not to laugh at me.

I sink into her again and again, making her forget about the truck and about Tyler being inches away from us. She tightens around me, her orgasm waiting in the shadows to erupt. When it finally does, it's so strong it takes me with it.

After we're both done, I lie on top of her and shower her neck with kisses. We'll wait until Tyler goes inside before climbing out and walking to my house a few blocks away. "You're so incredible," I murmur.

I don't know how it happened. One minute I hated everything about

Silver Spoons and their lives in the Hills. The next I'm finding myself in love with one of them.

How is it possible to love someone who represents everything you hate?

35

"End of Me" - A Day to Remember

Lux

"Some bitch spilled her wine all over my vintage Valentino at Gemma Rothenhall's party Saturday night." I toss a chip into the pile in the center of the poker table. My opening grievance won't be chosen, which is why I didn't bother tracking down the girl's name.

Maeve hisses through her teeth. She understands the pain of wine-stained couture. "How's the planning for the holiday gala coming along?"

I stall by sipping tonight's cocktail, a lavender-infused Bee's Knees. "Great." I inject enthusiasm into my voice and smile.

The truth is, I've hardly been focusing on the gala, thanks to a certain man who keeps distracting me. I need to tighten my focus if I am to stand a chance of pulling off the best event this city has ever seen.

Rhett submits his grievance—someone left a nasty comment on his latest TikTok music video—then turns to me. "Where's your boy toy tonight?"

I scowl at him and rotate my glass on the green baize. "I don't have one, you moron."

He grins, completely undeterred. "Man-whore, then."

I flip him off and take another sip of the drink, which seems to be getting stronger. Something occurs to me. I turn back to Rhett. "Why are you asking?"

He shifts in his seat, splaying his hands on his knees. "No reason."

I've known Rhett Cole for ten years. He's always been a terrible liar. "Tell me, or I'll key your car."

His eyes widen. "You wouldn't dare."

I reach into my bag and pull out my keys.

"Shit, Lux." He leans forward, probably so the others don't overhear. They're ensconced in a conversation about something that went down at Maeve's family's foundation.

"Fine, I'll tell you, but only if you promise not to get mad," he says.

"You don't have any bargaining power."

"Fuck." He closes his eyes and winces. "He's sold to me a couple of times, and I'm running low."

"Sold to you?" I blink at him. "What, like oxy?"

He looks at me, pupils dilated to an alarming size. How have I overlooked this? "I've already got an oxy supplier."

My jaw grows tighter as I stare at Rhett. "What did he sell you?"

But he doesn't need to say it. It's written all over his face.

"You're on *insidion*?" I keep my voice low so the others can't hear, but it comes out as a hiss.

"I don't take much," he says. It's a cheap reassurance.

"When?" I demand. "When did he sell to you?" I can't believe Slate would do that after what happened to Alex.

Rhett rubs his bare, tattooed arm. It's thirty degrees outside, and he's wearing a T-shirt. God, I should've noticed the signs. "At your party."

The Gatsby party. That was right after I met Slate. Relief surges through my chest.

"And the night we screwed up Keiran's Porsche."

Nausea chases the relief and threads its way through my organs, threatening to make me hurl the contents of my stomach across the table. The night with the Porsche was only a few weeks ago. Slate and I were already . . . whatever we are.

Rhett's face twists. He's either in withdrawal or feeling guilty. Maybe both.

I stand up. "I need to go."

Maeve looks up. "You can't go. We haven't even started the game."

"I'm not feeling well." I sling my bag over my shoulder. It's not a lie. I will probably have to stop beside the road to be sick.

Walker's face grows concerned. "Should we call a car?"

I shake my head. "I'll be fine. I just need to get home." Even though home is the last place I intend to go.

They let me leave, and I make it to my car in the underground garage without throwing up. The further I get from Rhett and his disgusting revelations, the clearer my head becomes.

Slate was using me to sell to my friends. That's obvious now. I was a means to an end. I may have started our relationship with the same intention, using him to bring down the Wolf, but at least I was upfront about it.

And it had nothing to do with why I stayed.

* * *

The lights are on inside when I pull up in front of Slate's house. Briar might be home, and this isn't a conversation I want her to overhear.

I call him. My traitorous heart skips a beat when he answers.

"Hey. I thought you had something with your friends tonight."

"I bailed."

There's a smile in his voice. "Missed me, did you?"

"Are you home?" I ask.

"I will be in a few minutes." The sound of his bike engine flares in the background.

"Good." I disconnect the call and slump back in my seat. Confronting Slate is not how I intended to spend my evening, but I'm not going to ignore what Rhett said either. If Slate is selling to my friends, we are over.

Pain bleeds from my heart at the thought.

We don't have a future together, that much has always been obvious, but that hasn't kept me from dreaming of possibilities. He makes me feel more than I knew I was capable of. When I'm with him, the world glows more brightly. At least now I know it was all a mirage.

His motorbike roars around the corner, and he pulls to a stop in the driveway. He removes his helmet, shaking out that head of hair I love to run my fingers through, and I have a flashback to the first time I saw him outside the salon.

My thighs tingle in anticipation, even though they won't be touched tonight.

He opens the passenger door of my car and slides into the seat. He reaches for me, sealing his lips over mine before I have a chance to pull back. His strong hand holds me captive as his mouth tells me how much he's missed me.

It would be so easy to melt, to say it doesn't matter. If I confront him about this, everything will be over for us. If I stay quiet, he might take me into the backseat and do unspeakable things to me. It's no secret which my body would prefer.

But my heart taps me on the shoulder and reminds me of what I stand to lose if I continue this charade. I've already lost Alex. I can't lose my friends, too.

I break off the kiss, then scoot closer to the door so Slate can't reach me as easily. His brow furrows, but he doesn't try to bring me back.

"Rhett told me." I throw the words at him like a dagger.

His mouth tightens. "Told you what?"

"That you've been selling to him."

The expression drains from his face. Probably the color too, but it's too dark to see that. He stretches out his hand. "Lux—"

"Don't you dare 'Lux' me."

"He approached me at your party. We weren't anything to each other at that point, so I didn't see what the harm was."

My nostrils flare as I suck in a breath. "But that wasn't the only time, was it?"

He opens his mouth to respond but thinks better of it.

"You sold to my friends!"

He slumps against the seat like a deflated balloon. "I'm sorry." It comes out hushed.

"*Sorry* doesn't undo Rhett's addiction. How could you?"

He shakes his head and runs a hand through his hair. "I told you. I wasn't in love with you yet."

He stops, and we stare at each other. He's alluded to it, but neither of us has said it yet, and he chose this moment to speak the words.

"No one who truly loved me would sell my friends the same drug that killed my brother."

"Baby, I'm sorry."

"I—" My phone rings, cutting off my words. I dig it out of my purse, expecting it to be one of the gang letting me know who we're getting revenge on, but it's a number I don't have in my contacts. "Hello?"

There's a crackle on the other end, then a male voice says, "Is this Lux?"

"It might be. Who's this?"

"If you're Alex's sister, then I have something you may want."

My heart bleeds at the sound of his name. I sit up straighter in my seat, avoiding Slate's gaze. "I am. What is it?"

"A carton of things he left."

I restart my car. "Where?"

He gives me the address, and I quickly type it into my GPS.

"I'll be there in five minutes." I end the call, then turn to Slate. "I need to go."

He looks at the map on my screen and doesn't get out of the car. "You're not going over there by yourself."

I let out a cackle. "You're mistaken if you think you have any say over what I do."

"I know where that is. You're not going there alone." He leans his broad body against the door like he's settling in.

I sigh and tap my fingers on the steering wheel. "Get out of the damn car, Slate." When he doesn't budge, I put the car into gear. "Fine."

We drive in silence. He doesn't ask what we're going to do, and I don't offer any information. As far as I'm concerned, he can play bodyguard if he wants, but as soon as I drop him back at home, we are done.

We arrive at the same house where I found Alex. That feels like a lifetime ago. Fortunately, the guy who called me meets us on the porch. I'm not sure I'd survive another trip into that hellhole.

He hands me a cardboard box. The flaps are open, showcasing a variety of items inside. He gives Slate a wary look, then retreats back inside without another word.

Slate takes the box from me and carries it to the car. "I'll drive," he says.

I sit in the passenger seat with the carton on my lap. There's an array of clothing and junk inside. It has taken this entire time for it register—this is Alex's stuff, the last of his things I'll ever hold.

I lift an old T-shirt to my nose and inhale. Somewhere through the thick cloud of smoke and weed, I get a faint whiff of my brother. I keep my face buried in the soft fabric.

Eventually I set it aside to rummage through the rest of the contents.

There's nothing of much interest, but it doesn't matter. These were the things Alex cared enough about to take with him.

There's a picture of our family, from back when Alex and I were little, before our parents' marriage imploded. And at the bottom, a small silver flip phone, the kind people used twenty years ago.

I power it on. He must have bought it after selling his smartphone for drug money. The list of contacts is short and must be where his friends found my number. I scroll through the names he thought important enough to store.

The last entry makes my blood turn to ice.

Wolf.

If there was ever any doubt in my mind before, it has disappeared. Right here, in pixelated proof, is the evidence I need that Alex had connections to the Wolf.

My hands tremble as I stare at the name. Despite the cold outside, I am hot with rage. Without another thought, I smash down the call button.

The ringing starts, and at first I attribute the echo to a glitch in the old phone. I sift through the box on my lap once more, looking for a second phone.

There's nothing there. The ringing isn't coming from the box, nor is it coming from Slate's phone in the cupholder.

It's coming from his pants pocket.

36

"Liar" - Jelly Roll

Lux

"Pull over." My voice sounds hollow. The buzzing in my ears makes it hard to concentrate.

The ache in my chest makes it hard to breathe.

"Lux—"

"Don't."

Slate turns to look at me, but I keep my eyes focused on the road ahead. The ringing has stopped, the silver phone still clutched in my hand like a lifeline.

"I can explain," he says.

"Pull the fucking car over!"

He brings it to a halt in front of a small decrepit house, the light of a television shining through the curtains in the front room. I climb out of the car, leaving the carton of Alex's things behind me on the seat.

I march around to the driver's side. Slate is still standing there, holding the door open like he's a fucking gentleman. But when I approach, he doesn't move out of the way.

"Move," I say with as much venom as I can muster.

"Baby, listen to me."

I slap him across the face. The resounding crack cuts through the ringing in my ears. "Don't you ever call me that again."

He rubs a hand across his jaw, but he doesn't move from the open car door. "Do you want to hear what I have to say?"

"I don't ever want to hear another word from you again."

He has the audacity to look hurt. Him—*hurt*. As if he wasn't playing me this entire time, pretending to help me, when all along—

"I hate you!" I slam both hands against his chest, but it's rock solid, and he barely sways. "I hate you more than I ever thought possible."

"Fine. I deserve that." He grabs both of my wrists. "But can you let me explain before you walk out of my life for good?"

"There is not a single explanation that would make this okay." I yank on the restraints, but he won't let go.

"I never would have sold to him if I'd known he was your brother." Slate tugs me closer.

"You mean the way you didn't sell to Rhett because he's my friend?" My words shock him enough that I'm able to free my wrists. I stagger backward, catching myself on the side of the car.

"They're going to buy from someone. I may as well get a cut. How else am I supposed to pay for Briar's medical bills?"

"Oh gee, I don't know. Maybe something that doesn't involve *killing people?*"

Slate shakes his head as if I'm being unreasonable.

I was right all along. This was never going to work, for all of the typical reasons of social and economic differences, but also because I will never be able to trust him. If he lied to me about something this important, when can I trust him to tell me the truth?

I should have seen it coming. The clues were there all along. The late nights, the way everyone knows him, his business expertise. The way he kept steering me away from my goal.

"You're the Wolf." The words come out exhausted, like they just climbed their way out of my belly. "Of course you are."

"It's not like it sounds."

I laugh as the sky cracks open and rain starts to fall, drenching us both within seconds. "Really? So you're *not* the most notorious drug dealer in the city?"

He doesn't say anything, which is more than enough of an answer.

"That's what I thought," I say.

"Can we get back in the car and talk? Please?" Slate's hair is already stuck to his forehead and dripping into his eyes. He's still the most beautiful man I've ever seen.

"I'm never going anywhere with you again."

"Lux, come on. You can't just walk away. Not after everything."

"You mean after you lied to me and killed my brother? After you got my best friend addicted to the same drug, all so you could make a buck?"

"It wasn't like that."

"You pretended to help me while covering up who you are," I scream through the rain.

"You wanted to kill the Wolf, right?" His eyebrows drag low over his eyes as he fumbles in his waistband. He shoves his gun at me. "Do it then."

I back away instinctively, the metal of the car cold through my clothes as it brushes my side.

"Take the gun, Lux. Shoot me."

I raise my eyes from the weapon to him. He stares right back at me, daring me to do it.

"You'd be doing me a favor," he says.

My head shakes of its own accord, a reflex response at being asked to do something foolish.

Slate reaches for my hand, wraps it around the gun, and shoves it against his chest. "Pull the trigger, baby."

Standing this close to him is dangerous. His orbit is pulling at me, trying to drag me back into it. "Why should I?"

"Because I don't want to live in a universe where you aren't mine."

My eyes burn, and the back of my throat feels like it's on fire. "Stop it." I pull my hand from his iron grip. The gun clatters to the pavement.

"I am madly in love with you, Lux Colombia-Clarke." He cradles my face in his hands, the way he does every time he kisses me. "I know I don't deserve you, but it doesn't change the fact that I would sell my soul if you would just forgive me."

I take a step backward, pulling my face from his hands. "You should have thought about that before you killed my brother."

37

"I Hate Everything About You" - Three Days Grace

Lux

Rain slashes against my windshield as I make my way back through the city. It isn't until I'm pulling into my driveway that I realize the dampness on my face isn't from the rain but from tears.

Slate unlocked something in me the day he told me to cry. I'm not sure I'll ever stop.

Locking up my emotions has always prevented me from getting hurt. But everything was different with him. He made me feel things I've never felt before, things I'll never feel again. How can I ever give my heart to another man when he's still clutching it so tightly?

Once I'm home, I draw myself a bath. It's warm, but my body screams when I lower myself into it, still icy from the rain. I ignore the protests from my cold skin and sink beneath the surface.

Within seconds, my body adjusts to the change in temperature. If I'm lucky, maybe my heart will too. Given enough time, it will close up the Slate-shaped hole in its center and keep beating.

I shouldn't be surprised. My dating record is full of stories like this. I attract men who care more about their shoe collections than they do about me.

Slate is no different from the rest of them. Ready to use me to get what he's after, then discard me as soon as he has what he wants.

I've always thought this was a reflection on me, proof I'm not worthy of a man's undying affection. That I don't deserve it. But maybe the problem isn't me. Maybe the problem is them.

Maybe I'm enough, and *they* don't deserve *me*.

* * *

The shooting range is empty the next morning. I fumbled my way through my Pilates session and brunch with Haven Global Aid before coming here. I even managed to record a quick video for my followers without my voice wobbling, highlighting the smoothie I picked up to support a new shop opening before giving it to a homeless woman on the street.

But as soon as I step inside the doors of the range, calm washes over my body, halting the trembling in my bones. Here I can let out all of the frustration trapped in my cells.

I stand in the lane, gun cocked and aimed at the target. My mind replaces the bullseye with Slate's face. That sharp jawline, those steely eyes, the stubbly beard. His thick hair pulled away from his face into a bun.

The weapon wavers in my hand, and I jerk it back up. I can't falter now. If I'm going to carry out my mission, I need to be able to look into his face and pull the trigger.

I was such a coward last night. He handed me the perfect opportunity to avenge Alex, and I fumbled it. Pressing that gun against his chest, imagining him gone from this world—it broke something inside me.

But I need to put that part back together, because this is the endgame.

Slate isn't going to quit dealing insidion. The only way to end this is to end him.

The more I try to force my hand to stop trembling, the stronger the shakes grow. No one in their right mind would entrust someone in my state with a firearm, but fortunately, nobody is watching. I lift my arms again, focusing on the target, but the weight is so much heavier than it used to be. I gulp back a sob and lower the gun.

I can't do it.

That bastard fucked with my head *and* my heart. Both are refusing to cooperate. Putting a bullet through his heart will put one through mine as well.

Any doubt about my feelings for him have dissipated. Maybe this isn't love, but it's a hell of a lot closer than anything I've experienced before.

I turn the safety on and stick the gun back into my bag. This clearly isn't going to work.

I imagine calling the police, giving them their biggest lead of the year, telling them I know the identity of the Wolf. I imagine the look on Slate's face when they show up at his door with handcuffs, reading him his rights as they snap them on his wrists. I imagine the horror on Briar's face when she comes out of her room and sees them, watches them lead her brother away for what will be a very long stint in prison.

It's this last one that trips me up. If I take him away, what will happen to Briar? Who will protect her? Who will take her to the hospital when she has another episode? Who will advocate for her with all of the doctors?

No matter how angry I am, no matter how badly I want to destroy Slate, I can't do that to her. Or to him, if I'm being honest. Apparently, love isn't a switch you can flip on and off. He is making me so angry I can hardly breathe, but that doesn't change the fact that he's the oxygen for my soul.

But just because I can't ruin him doesn't mean I can't hurt him.

* * *

Ten missed calls. Two voicemails. Fucked as I am, I listen to both of them.

"Lux, I want to explain." There's a long pause, then Slate's voice starts again, thick with emotion. "This has been my life for as long as I can remember. It wasn't my first choice, but when the opportunity came up, I was trying to find a way to pay for my mum's medical bills. Then Briar got sick, too. It's—shit—I know it's fucked up. I know *I'm* fucked up. I've never pretended to be otherwise." His sigh is long and loud.

"You make me want to do better, to *be* better. I love you, Lux. With all of my goddamn heart. I've never felt this way before. I know I don't deserve you, even without all of the shit I've done, but I want to try harder, to be better. Please—" A long beep sounds as he's cut off.

I wipe the tears from my face and play the next voicemail.

"I'm not stupid enough to think I have a shot with you, not after everything. Probably not even before."

A beat of silence hangs in the air. I picture him scrunching his fist in his hair, the way he does when he's frustrated.

"If there is anything I can do to win you back, I'll do it. But I know that's not likely. I just want you to know this had nothing to do with you. That if I'd known you before, I—" His voice breaks. "I'd really like to have this conversation in person. Can you please call me back? I love you."

"Fuck!" I scream, and throw my phone across the room. It hits a potted plant on the coffee table, knocking it to the floor and spilling dirt everywhere. I expected Slate to beg me not to turn him in, but it's like that thought never even occurred to him.

I flop onto the sofa. This isn't going to work. If I give him space in my head, he's only going to take advantage of it. Which means I'll be stuck with an aching heart forever.

I need to end this here and now.

My computer fires up, and I hack the hospital's database within seconds, faster than the last time I did it when I was hunting for dirt on Slate. If I stop to think about what I'm doing, my conscience will get the best of me, so it's important to leave my mind out of this. To get in and do what needs to be done.

I find the file easily enough. Not too many people with the name Lawson, and only one who's seen my dad. A quick perusal gives me the basics of the format they use, and a short Canva session later, I can't even tell the difference myself. I'd say I did a pretty good job.

Beside me, my phone chirps. I rescued it from the floor earlier, but I should have silenced it as well. I ignore it and send the file to the printer. When it's done, I scan it to make sure I got everything right.

It's perfect. I seal it inside an envelope and put a stamp in the corner, Queen Celia's face staring back at me, questioning my actions. I flip the letter upside down. I don't need her judgment.

My phone trills again, and I pick it up without thinking.

Slate: *please call me*

Slate: *you have no idea how sorry i am*

I growl and change his name in my contacts.

Brother-Killer: *baby please give me another chance*

I'll give him another chance at life, but only because I'm too weak to pull the trigger, not because he deserves it. Any other chances are not happening.

My phone rings in my hand, and I consider throwing it across the room again. I should block his number, but I can't do it. Not yet.

I'm about to slam it down on the desk again when I catch sight of the name. Not Slate.

I clear the aggression from my tone before answering. "Hello, Miranda."

"Lux!" Her high-pitched voice grates on what's left of my nerves. "I'm calling about the gala. Do you have a minute?"

I've been so focused on Slate that I've put the event preparations on the back burner for far too long. Despite her annoyingly cheerful voice, Miranda has been great about picking up the slack while I fuck around and get my heart broken.

We're co-chairing this thing, and it's time I stepped up. "Yes, absolutely. What if we met over lunch? I have some ideas I want to run by you."

"Oh." She sounds surprised. "That would be lovely."

We set up a lunch date, and when I hang up, my heart feels lighter. Maybe this is exactly what I need to get my mind off of the fucked-up state of my heart.

And if there's anything I know how to do, it's throw a party.

38

"can u see me in the dark?" - Halestorm and I Prevail

"DeShawn Cohen is asking for another batch." Tyler looks at me like he expects an answer.

"That douchebag hasn't paid for the last two he got." I shove another box on top of the stack.

"Said he was helping his grandma or some shit like that."

"Right," I mutter, and slap my palm against the cardboard. The small cartons look like an Amazon delivery, but they're full of something much deadlier.

"So what should I tell him?" Ty has his eyes glued to his phone.

"Take him out." I straighten the last stack.

"Take him out," he repeats.

"You heard me, Ty. A guy like that will bring this whole thing down."

He rubs his shaved head. "Man, you haven't given me an order like that in a long time."

I spin around and march up to him, backing him flush against the wall. "Then it's about time I did, don't you think?"

"Okay, okay." He raises his hands to get me to back off. I do, but only a little. "What is up with you, mate?"

"Just handle Cohen, okay?"

"You not getting laid? Is that it?" Tyler grins like a fucking cat.

I don't respond, just pull my phone out for the millionth time. I know there won't be any missed calls or texts, but I can't help checking.

"What about Lux, man? She seemed really into you. A little crazy maybe—"

I lunge for him, pinning him to the wall with an arm under his chin. "Don't ever mention her name again."

His eyes bulge out of their sockets. "Chill, mate." He wraps his fingers around my arm. I ease up the pressure. "I won't."

I release him and stalk to the other side of the warehouse.

"What the fuck? You can't pin your man up against a wall like that." Tyler's eyes dig into my back. "Yo, Slate!"

I ignore him and keep walking. If I don't, I'll do something much worse.

The air is a cold slap to the face when I get outside. It's perfect. I need a good slap. I've been out of control lately, and it needs to stop.

I pull a cigarette from the carton and light it. The nicotine brings instant calm. I lean against the wall of the warehouse, watching Tyler's truck start up and roar away into the night. He's off to handle Cohen, before that fucker brings the whole operation down.

I don't need a five-hundred-an-hour shrink to tell me what's wrong. It's obvious that Lux's leaving fucked me up.

She thinks I'm a fuckup, and she's right. I'll never be good enough for her, so why bother trying? If I show her what she narrowly avoided, she can live her life with the knowledge that she was right.

It doesn't stop the ache though, that hole in the middle of my body that won't stop throbbing with pain, the way your toe does after you stub it.

I didn't expect it to hurt like this. We both knew all along it wasn't going to work out, so why does it feel like my arm's been cut off and the rest of my body is still searching for it?

I miss the way she laughs, throws her head back and blesses the world with that incredible sound. I miss the way she sucks in her breath when I touch her, that little gasp that lets me know I'm doing something right. I miss the way her eyes light up when she's teasing me, that tiny glint of mischief in her otherwise pageant queen exterior.

I miss her the way you miss a soul mate.

Too bad such a thing doesn't exist.

* * *

I don't go home after the garage tonight. Instead I work late, then head straight to the warehouse to handle the new shipment. After that, I hit the gym for a quick session and don't get in until two in the morning. Briar has too many questions, so I avoid the house unless she's sleeping.

The mail is still on the table where she sorted through it earlier. She left a stack of bills for me to handle—more every month—but my eyes are drawn to an open envelope, a sheet of paper sitting next to it.

The hospital's logo and info is at the top. It looks similar to the bills they love to shower us with. But instead of a bunch of charges, it's a letter.

I sink into the chair and read it.

Dear Miss Lawson and guardian,

We are writing to inform you of the test results of your recent evaluation with Dr. Clarke. After extensive testing, it appears that you are suffering from an autoimmune disease known as giant cell myocarditis. GCM is very rare, and it is likely you will eventually need a heart transplant.

At this time, there is no known cure for giant cell myocarditis. We are prepared to walk beside you every step of the way. Dr. Clarke is putting together a plan to manage your symptoms. While the fatality rate is higher than we'd like to see, Dr. Clarke is confident you still have many years ahead of you.

The letter continues with empty platitudes. I let the paper fall onto the table. My head drops into my hands.

Will likely need a heart transplant.

Confident you still have many years ahead of you.

It's like the universe has decided to fuck me over once and for all. Losing my dad, my mum, and the woman I love isn't enough. I'm going to lose my sister, too.

"Fuck!" I yell, and slam my chair into the wall. Too late, I remember that Briar is in bed.

I stalk outside to the back patio. The moon is full tonight, lighting up the garden with an unearthly glow. I light another cigarette. Quitting was the stupidest thing I ever did. I started up again the night Lux left me.

I still can't believe it all fell apart so neatly. It wasn't like a bomb being dropped, debris and chaos scattering citywide. This was such a clean, neat mess, so quietly contained to the street. By the next morning, the rain had washed away all traces that we'd ever been there, no one the wiser that she'd driven off with my heart in her palm.

I'm a fucking idiot for getting involved with a Silver Spoon in the first place. Now the universe has decided to punish me.

A fucking heart transplant.

I don't need to be an expert on medical statistics to know those don't usually end well. It'll buy Briar some time, but it's not like a kidney or liver transplant. Hearts aren't meant to be shared from body to body. She could get lucky, sure. But with me as her brother, it's unlikely.

Besides, the hospital probably cherry-picks the hearts of athletes for patients who can afford to make large donations and sing their praises. Briar will probably end up with the heart of a man who smoked a pack a day.

I flick ash from the cig in my hand. Fitting.

It's a bad idea. I know it is, but I still find myself pressing the phone icon next to Lux's name.

She won't answer. She hasn't answered for the past week. I haven't spoken to her since the night she drove off, leaving me on the pavement in the rain.

But I've heard her voice. It's not enough, it could never be enough, but it's like an addiction all the same. Her charming voicemail, that voice she uses for the rest of the world. It's nothing like the smoky, sultry one she spoke in when we were together, but it's better than nothing.

So until she blocks my number altogether, I'm going to keep calling for my fix.

"Hello, this is Lux," she sings. "I'm obviously busy, but if it's super-duper important, you can leave a message. Or text me, because phone calls are overrated. If I think it's important enough to call you back, I might."

It used to make me simultaneously roll my eyes and smile. Now, I do neither. When the beep sounds, I clear my throat. "It's me. Listen, I know you don't want to hear from me, but I need to talk to you. You know the tests your dad ran on Briar? They came back. And it's not good."

I take a shaky breath and run my hand through my hair. "She has some giant cell disease. They said she'll eventually need a heart transplant, and that the fatality rates are pretty high."

My voice breaks. I squeeze the bridge of my nose. "Anyway, I thought you'd want to know."

I end the call. Lux doesn't want to know. She doesn't care about Briar. The whole thing was a hoax, a little social experiment to see how the other half lives.

She could be turning me in right now, telling the coppers she knows who the Wolf is. But if she was going to do that, they would have showed up on my doorstep days ago.

She's probably dating someone new already. A woman like that doesn't stay available for long. It's better to stay off social media. If she posts pictures of a new guy, or worse, that fucking wanker Carter, I can't guarantee I won't drive across the city and tear his head from his shoulders.

I don't want to think about her with someone else, but I do it anyway to punish myself for ever letting things get this far.

When I'm at the garage doing payroll the next day, I let the images come.

Her going down on him with a smile on her face.

Her screaming as he makes her climax.

The two of them going at it so hard the bed knocks into the wall.

My phone rings on the desk, scattering the images. When I glimpse the name, my heart skips a single beat, and then I answer.

"Is everything okay?" I don't need to mention her name for him to know what I'm asking.

"Of course," he says. "Why wouldn't it be?"

"Why the fuck are you calling me, Rhett?" I keep my voice low, getting up to close my office door.

There's a maniacal tone in his voice. "Look, mate, I'm completely out. I thought maybe Lux would bring you to poker night, but—"

"We're not together anymore."

"Oh." There's a pause. "Well, listen, I can come to you. Just tell me where to meet."

I pinch my eyebrows together with my fingers. "I can't."

"You can't what?"

"I can't sell to you any more."

Another apprehensive chuckle. "Why not? I can pay, don't worry."

"You need help, mate." I spin a pencil between my fingers. "Rehab or something."

"I don't need fucking rehab. I need another vial."

I clench the pencil so hard it snaps in half. "Do you have any fucking clue how this stuff will ruin your life?" I don't even *take* insidion, and it managed to screw me over epically.

"I'm not asking for a life coach, mate. I just need another hit."

I toss the remains of the pencil into the trash. "Then you'll have to get it from someone besides me. Because I'm not selling you anything."

He's still cursing me when I hang up. I toss the phone onto my desk with a spin. Heart transplants cost money. *Lots* of money. And I just lost a client who could have funded a good portion of it. One who's mad enough to drag my name through the mud with everyone he knows.

It won't do any good. It won't win her back. She won't even find out about it. I don't stand to gain a single thing by refusing to sell to him.

So why the fuck did I do it?

39

"Northern Lights" - Teddy Swims

Slate

I'm cooking eggs when Briar walks into the kitchen wearing a robe that is at least three sizes too big for her.

"What are you doing up?" I turn back to my skillet.

She reaches for a mug in the cupboard. "I heard you get up and wanted to make sure you remembered our appointment today."

"What appointment?"

She sighs and pours herself some coffee. "It's on the calendar."

"I didn't see it." One of my eggs breaks when I flip it. "Shit." Over twenty years of cooking eggs. I should be better at it by now.

"Because you didn't look." She stares at me over the rim of her mug as she sips the hot liquid. I don't need to look at her to feel that stare. "You haven't looked at much of anything recently."

"Not true."

"Oh yeah? Did you notice my lip ring then? Or my new tattoo?"

I swivel toward her, the egg sliding from the spatula and onto the floor.

She grins and takes another sip of coffee. "See? You haven't looked at me in weeks."

"If you got a tattoo, we're going to have other issues on our hands." I toss the egg in the bin.

"Relax. I just wanted your attention."

"You have it," I snap. "Now what do you want?"

"What's going on, Slate?" Briar sets her cup down and crosses her arms. "I know you've been avoiding me. You haven't brought Lux around for weeks. What I don't know is why."

"You don't need to know why." I crack another egg in the pan to replace the ruined one. "Want one?" I ask her.

She shakes her head, looking tiny in Mum's old robe. "Why won't you talk to me?"

"Because it's none of your business." Because I don't want her knowing what a fuckup I am or thinking that Lux was right in dumping me. It's one thing for a Silver Spoon to think that. It's another for my sister to.

"Right." Briar braces her hands on the counter. "So you're coming to the hospital this morning?"

I frown at her. "Hospital?"

"My god, Slate. I just told you I had an appointment."

"You didn't tell me what it was for."

"I don't know what it's for. Dr. Clarke's office called yesterday and asked if we could come in."

My mind whirls. If the doctor's office is calling, it has to be about the letter they sent. Which can't be good. Does she need a transplant already? Did they see something else that needs to be conveyed in person?

"Stop freaking out," Briar says, placing a hand on my arm. "It's going to be okay."

This is so typical of her. She is dying as we stand here, but *she's* telling *me* it's going to be okay.

"I'm not freaking out," I say, and slide the last egg onto my plate.

We haven't discussed the doctor's findings. I was avoiding her because of the Lux situation, but after reading the letter, I didn't even want to see Briar. Didn't want to be reminded that I will lose her too, someday soon.

If I don't look at her, maybe I can convince myself that everything is normal, that nothing has changed.

"We need to be at the doctor's office at ten," she says before heading back to her room, coffee in hand.

Looks like I won't be able to bury my head in the sand after all.

* * *

Dr. Clarke's office looks like a movie set. Highly polished mahogany desk, framed diplomas and certificates, rows and rows of books with matching spines. It smells expensive, like his secretary walked around spritzing some overpriced shit before we came in. Or maybe Silver Spoons just ooze luxury scents from their pores.

"Briar. Good to see you again," the doctor says, shaking her hand. He extends his hand to me. "Mr. Lawson. Please have a seat."

Briar and I sit in the two chairs he indicates on the other side of his desk. The doctor and I have never met, because I don't go with Briar into the exam rooms, just sit in the waiting room for an eternity while they perform all manner of tests on her.

Dr. Clarke has a head full of graying hair, but it's thick and there's no receding hairline in sight. He has Lux's high cheekbones and the same dark brown eyes.

The ache in my chest intensifies.

"I called you in to discuss the results of the tests we ran." He steeples his fingers on the desk and peers at us over his reading glasses. "I'm pleased to tell you that it's good news."

My suspicion flares. How could a potential heart transplant be *good* news? Unless he's thinking about padding the hospital's pockets with our hard-earned money.

He opens the file on his otherwise empty desk and scans it. "I'm diagnosing you with MCTD, or mixed connective tissue disease. Are you familiar with it?"

Briar shakes her head, and I knit my brow. That doesn't sound like the one he mentioned in the letter.

"I'm sorry, how is this good news?" I ask.

"I'm getting there." Dr. Clarke's lips lift in a shadow of a smile as he turns to Briar. "MCTD is an autoimmune disorder. In autoimmune disorders, your immune system, which is responsible for fighting off disease and keeping you healthy, mistakes healthy cells as foreign ones and attacks them.

"MCTD is an autoimmune disorder, but more specifically, it's a connective tissue disease. That means it attacks the fibers that provide the framework and support for your body, which is why you've had so much pain and muscle spasms.

"MCTD can present the signs and symptoms of a variety of other disorders, primarily lupus, scleroderma, and polymyositis. I believe this is why your previous doctors had such a hard time diagnosing you. Your symptoms matched with many other diseases. We call this an 'overlap disease.'"

"You mentioned good news?" I interrupt.

"Yes," he says. "The good news is that, while my team works with many autoimmune disorders, MCTD is a specialty of ours. We've developed a treatment for it that has seen a 97 percent success rate in the past three years."

He drones on about what we can expect going forward—carefully avoiding any mention of price—but my brain is still tripping over everything he's said. Briar sits beside me, nodding at everything, soaking it up like a sponge.

"Sorry to interrupt again, Doctor, but I'm confused." I pull the envelope the hospital sent last week from my jacket. "In here you diagnosed Briar with"—I search for the name—"giant cell myocarditis. You said she'll need a heart transplant and that the prognosis isn't exactly favorable."

He removes his glasses and lets them dangle from his fingers. "I don't know what you're talking about." He extends a hand. "May I?"

I hand him the letter, then sit back as he reads it. Briar shifts in her seat and offers me a shaky smile. God, has she always tried so hard to hold it together for my sake? I reach for her hand and squeeze it.

Dr. Clarke clears his throat and sets the letter on his desk. "This is very confusing."

"Care to explain?" I say.

He splays his fingers, eyes still on the letter. "I wish I could, but—" He shakes his head and looks up at us. "This letter is fake."

"What?" I say. "What does that mean?"

"Mr. Lawson, we never—and I mean *never*—send a patient's diagnosis, whether it's good news or bad, by mail. We always schedule a consultation with them to discuss possible options."

Possible moneymakers, you mean. "So why did we receive this, then?"

"I wish I knew the answer to that."

"It's stamped with the hospital's info at the top."

"Yes, I see that. And it's done very well." The doctor's voice has taken on a musing quality as he looks at the page. "Whoever did this must be good with computers." His eyes flick up toward us. "And bear a huge grudge in order to do this to you."

He continues discussing the treatment with Briar, but my eyes are drawn to the photos behind his desk. There's one of Lux from at least ten years ago. She looks younger, but I would recognize that smile and those eyes anywhere.

The ache in my chest grows. There's only one person in the world with not only the skillset to do this, but the motivation as well.

She couldn't pull the trigger, but in some ways I wish she would have. It would have sucked for Briar to lose me, but she could have stayed with Grandmum until she's legally an adult in a few months. Dying would have been preferable to knowing Lux hates me enough to go after my sister. She didn't hurt Briar physically, but to make both of us think her time on earth was going to be severely shortened? That's harsh.

In her mind, it probably made sense. I went after her brother, so she went after my sister.

It's so fucked up.

We end the consultation and walk back to the car in silence. When we're on our way home, Briar finally speaks.

"Are you going to talk about it now?"

"What?"

"Come on, Slate. I'm not a child anymore. You can tell me what's going on."

I keep my eyes on the road. "I don't know what you're talking about."

"Right." She crosses her arms. "You have no idea why I received a falsified diagnosis. You have no idea who is capable of doing something like that or who would want to. You're completely unaware of everything going on around you, is that it?"

"Don't be ridiculous."

She laughs sharply. "I'm the one being ridiculous? If you'd get your head out of your ass long enough to look around, you'd see that you're the idiot."

Silence falls in the car and lasts for several minutes, an eerie quiet that's only amplified by the muffled traffic passing us.

"What are you saying?" I ask.

Briar's whole body turns as she looks at me. "I'm saying go after her."

I flick a frown her way. "Who?"

"Oh. Em. Gee." She flounces back into her seat with a teenage flourish. "You are the biggest plonker I know."

"Gee, thanks." I rub a hand across my eyes, already exhausted, and it's not even noon yet. "How would going after Lux help anything?"

"She's the one who did this, right?"

"How could you possibly know that?"

"I know more than you think. And I saw the look on your face in the office when you figured it out."

I snort. "Cocky bastard."

She grins. "She obviously still cares about you if she'd go to these lengths to hurt you."

"I think you missed the point of 'caring about someone.' You go out of your way to do nice things for them, not sabotage them."

"Yeah, but the opposite of love isn't hate. It's indifference. If she didn't care, she would have walked away without a backward glance." Briar holds up her pointer finger. "But she didn't."

I shake my head. "Okay, Aristotle. What do you suggest?"

She squeals with glee and tucks her legs underneath her on the seat, shifting into an animated position. "You need to prove to her that you deserve her."

One of my brows inches upward. "The whole world knows I don't. Next idea."

"Mm-mm." She shakes her head. "I mean it, Slate. You have to fight for her. The best way to do that is to become the man she deserves."

I stare at this girl who I swear was still wearing braces and pigtails yesterday. "What did you have in mind?"

40

"Haunted" - Taylor Swift

Lux

"It looks amazing." Miranda scans the ballroom of the Carlton, wonder in her eyes.

"Love, it looks fucking fabulous." I swoop up the last vase of amaryllis in my arms and deposit it on one of the round tables.

"You're right." Her face gleams like the dance floor in the center of the room. "It is."

We've spent the last several weeks putting the last-minute touches on the Rosewood Research Foundation's Holiday Gala. Everything from the decor to the caterers to the DJ has been chosen with excruciating deliberation. Now I just need the evening to go smoothly.

"They'd be crazy not to ask you to chair the Humanitarian Aid Gala," Miranda says, adjusting a place card.

It's the big one, the highlight of any socialite's career. The entire royal family attends, and chairing it would be an honor I would not take lightly. But that doesn't mean they'll ask me.

"You'd think so, but the selection committee can be bitches."

"I hear you, babe. But you got this." She pats my shoulder. "I'm going to freshen up."

I glance around the room one last time after she leaves. It belongs on the pages of *Elysian Living*. I snap several dozen more photos, even though my phone gallery already holds over two hundred pictures from tonight.

The grand entrance is flanked by towering fir trees, their branches frosted in shimmering white and twinkling with fairy lights, as if kissed by a winter frost. A plush crimson carpet leads into the hall, edged with garlands of holly and golden ribbons that seem to beckon the guests into a world of holiday enchantment.

The large domed ceiling is adorned with white lilies and evergreen boughs. The centerpiece of the room, beneath the dome, is a towering Christmas tree, dressed in ornaments of crystal and gold, cascading strands of pearls, and with a radiant star at its peak. Each table holds a gold candelabra—the only sources of light in the room—sweet-scented pine boughs, and glittering strands of faux diamonds.

The air itself carries a sense of festive indulgence, with hints of spiced cinnamon, mulled wine, and the fresh, clean scent of evergreens mingling to create an atmosphere that's as luxurious as it is inviting.

Miranda's right. If the selection committee doesn't ask me to chair the spring gala, they're idiots.

I follow her to the powder room to check my face and dress one last time before guests start arriving. I'm wearing Fritz Herman tonight, an up-and-coming designer who took my breath away when he showed me the dress he'd designed with me in mind. It's the color of champagne and made entirely of feathers that rise up to cup my breasts. The train swoops away from me in a dramatic flow, a cascade of feathers rippling across the floor. I assured Fritz that I would become a lifelong client after this masterpiece.

I swipe on another layer of rosy-mauve lipstick. My favorite makeup artist came to the Carlton to do my face, and it still looks perfect. There isn't a single other thing I can do to present a better image to the selection committee.

If they don't choose me based on what they see tonight, I have failed at life.

* * *

I sip my champagne, careful to only let a tiny drop pass my lips. I'm limiting myself to one glass for the entire evening. I can't let alcohol make me hazy, not when I'm expected to be on my best behavior.

A hand brushes my arm, and I instinctively turn. Carter is standing beside me, his crisp black tux and white bow tie putting him at the height of gentlemen's fashion.

"Hello," I say. "You look great."

"God, so do you." He takes me in from head to toe. "That dress is incredible."

"Isn't it?" I brush my hand across the soft feathers. "I feel like a goddess."

His hand lingers on the small of my back. "You look like a goddess." His voice is soft and gentle, the way it used to be. "I've been thinking about you."

I let my eyes drift sideways to him. "Why?"

"I know how close you and Alex were. I thought about reaching out, but I wanted to give you space."

I tilt my head to fully take him in, opting not to tell him I blocked his number. "That's sweet of you."

Carter's face splits apart in a grin. "I can be sweet. You should remember that."

"I do." I nod and lower my gaze back to the drink in my hands. Tiny bubbles rise to the surface, only to pop once they reach oxygen.

Geraldine Jacobs approaches, her gray-blue eyes twinkling as she takes us in. "You two are such a lovely couple. Will we be hearing wedding bells soon?" She tucks a strand from her sleek brown bob behind her ear and tilts her champagne flute to her mouth.

My face heats, and Carter dodges the question with a quip that I don't register but that causes her to laugh. Geraldine is on the gala's selection committee. I need to make a good impression.

"You look absolutely stunning," I tell her. "Who are you wearing?"

She spends the next few minutes telling me about her dress. When she walks away, I give myself a mental pat on the back. That went better than expected.

Carter's thumb strokes tiny circles across my bare skin. "So? How are you?"

I take a deep breath before answering. "I'm good. Really good."

"That's my girl," he murmurs. The pressure of his thumb increases. "Always bouncing back."

A small lump forms in my throat. I'm not his girl, not anymore, but I could be, couldn't I? "I try," I say, the lump distorting my words.

He doesn't seem to notice. "To be honest, you're the only thing I've been thinking about. Things got bad there for a bit, but you know I love you. I've always loved you. I made some shitty decisions, but that's not who I am."

There's a pause, like he's waiting for me to say something. I give him a small, forced smile.

"You know that, right, babe?"

The lump in my throat grows larger. I nod and take a gulp of champagne before remembering my decision to pace myself. "Yeah," I say. "I know that."

"That's why I love you, Lux." He moves closer, sliding his hand across my back to cradle my hip. "You always see the best in people."

Do I? A trickle of unease runs down my spine. Is seeing the best in people the reason I always fall for the wrong ones?

"I was thinking we should try the new sushi bar opening next weekend. What do you think?"

I consider saying yes. Geraldine was right. We do look good together. You'd have to be blind not to see it. Walking through the gala with Carter Fitzgerald-Smythe on my arm would only boost my chances with the selection committee.

So why the hesitation in my heart, then? "I don't think it's a good idea." I slip out of his grip before he can tighten it. "Thank you, though. I appreciate the invitation."

His jaw tightens, but then he releases it. "I'm going to fight for you, Lux. You're it for me."

"Please don't." I shake my head. I can think of few things worse than Carter fighting for me, not because it would be an ugly sight, but because I wouldn't last long.

He leans close, his tone growing more rigid. "Is this because of that bastard who jumped me in the car park?"

"I don't know what you're talking about," I say without thinking. *Is it about Slate?*

"Don't fuck with me, Lux." Warning drips from his words. It's all the reminder I need.

"I didn't break up with you for anyone else." Slate may have helped me see the situation for what it was, but I didn't leave Carter for him. "I did it for myself."

His mouth hangs open as I walk away. I hope he takes my words to heart and decides not to fight this, but I'd better prepare myself all the same.

I find our gang hanging out next to the pillars of the north entrance. "Where's Rhett?" I say when I'm close enough to be heard.

Maeve looks at me like I've just asked for reindeer to deliver the gifts. "You don't know?"

My heart skips a beat in its rush to catch up. "Know what?" I glance at Walker, Heath, and Pierce, but they look as surprised as Maeve.

"He's at Fairhaven," Maeve says quietly, her eyes darting around the room.

"He's in *rehab?*" I keep my voice just above a whisper.

Pierce nods. "He wasn't doing well."

"How long has he been gone?" I say. "And why didn't anyone tell me?"

"A week," Maeve says. "I assumed he'd told you."

I shake my head. "He didn't." I've been so busy with this gala that I didn't even know what was happening with one of my best friends. "How long will he be gone?"

"Three months."

I swallow and nod. All the more reason to land the spring gala. Things will be too weird without Rhett around. I'm going to need one hell of a distraction.

Walker grabs my arm as I'm heading back to the center of the party. "Hey," she says when I stop to look at her. "Are you okay?"

Why does everyone keep asking me that? "I mean, I've been better, but haven't we all?"

She doesn't smile. "You don't look like yourself."

My hand automatically flies to my hair. "What's wrong? Is it the contour palette? She wanted to use a new combo, and I said—"

"No, it's not that. You aren't"—her shoulders lift and drop again as she searches for the right word—"*glowing* anymore."

I drop my hand to my heart. "God, Walk. You could have just said this color isn't working for me."

"I'm sorry." Her brows pull together apologetically. "I don't mean it as an insult. I want to make sure you're okay."

"I'm fine." Or I will be once I check my face in the powder room and book a consultation with a color specialist.

Before I can do either, one of the security guards approaches. I take a deep breath to brace myself for whatever situation needs to be handled.

"Sorry to interrupt, ma'am," he says, glancing between Walker and me. "But there's someone in the lobby asking to see you."

I purse my lips at his towering frame. The only people who would have a reason to see me are all here in the ballroom, stuffing their faces with lobster tail or dancing away their champagne fog. "Who is it?"

He winces. "I didn't get a name. I can go back and do that."

I shake my head. "Don't worry about it. I'll see what they want." I give Walker's hand a final squeeze and follow the guard to the entrance.

It's probably a reporter wanting access to the party. The security personnel should have been informed to deny access to any members of the press who aren't on the list of exclusive attendees. One more fire to put out as gala chairwoman.

It takes me a second to spot who I'm supposed to be seeing. He looks so out of place with his hands shoved in the pockets of his jeans that at first I mistake him for a hotel guest. But as soon as my eyes lift to Slate's face, the edges of my vision start to blur.

My feet continue walking, even past the point of recognition, like the communication lines between my brain and limbs are down, like my body is fully intent on getting what it wants, even if it's at odds with what my head knows is best.

I remember the way he smells, the way it feels to be in his arms, the taste of his lips on mine. I remember what it felt like to be his, to feel safe and protected for the first time in my life. I also remember what it felt like to discover it was all a mirage.

I jerk on the reins controlling my feet, stopping them short before I can do something completely insane.

What is he doing here?

How dare he look so good?

What made him think he could crash my party like this?

The questions ping through my head like rapid-fire bullets, which only makes me think of the shooting range and the gun and the fact that I held one to his chest and considered pulling the trigger.

"Lux." It's part anguished groan, part desperate plea.

I can't do anything but stare at him, my heart in my throat. I lift my hand to my neck, like that will hold back the avalanche of emotions threatening to bury me.

"Can we talk?" The tendrils of his voice reach across the space to brush against my skin, coaxing me to give in to him.

I can't speak. I can't move. I certainly can't talk to him—not here, not anywhere.

As soon as he takes a step toward me, my frozen body springs into action. I hold up my hand, halting him in his tracks.

A drop of moisture lands on the figurative hand still clamped around my throat. Tears are streaming from my eyes, and I didn't even know it.

Slate looks like he's in pain. *Good. That's what we want*, my head reminds me.

My heart wants to curl up in his embrace.

"Baby, I'm so sorry," he whispers.

The security guard has retreated and is now standing by the door, having assured himself this man poses no threat to the party.

He didn't inquire about the threat to my heart.

"Please go." My voice is clogged with moisture, and I clear it before saying it again. "I need you to go."

Slate takes another step closer, but I retreat the same distance, maintaining the space between us. "You're crying," he says.

"Nothing that will kill me."

"I want to make up for what I did. To explain."

I offer him a humorless smile. "You assume I'm interested in anything you have to say."

"I'm going to fight for this. For us." He pulls a hand from his pocket and runs it through his hair, which isn't pulled back into a bun for once. It hangs in thick curls around his face.

It's so similar to what Carter said an hour ago that I want to laugh. "Don't bother," I say. "You'll never win."

His eyes turn the color of a storm at sea. My core heats because it's a bloody traitor.

"Tell me what I need to do to make it up to you."

This time I'm the one to step closer. I don't have the nerve to push my finger into his chest, afraid the mere touch of him will make my will crumble. Instead, I keep a healthy distance between us but force myself to meet his stormy gaze.

"You can't make it up to me. The only thing I want is for you to leave me alone," I say as my heart shatters into a million pieces. Again. Who knew hearts could break so easily?

"You don't mean that." Slate shakes his head, despair bleeding into his voice.

"I do," I whisper.

He doesn't move, so I turn and head for the ladies' room. There's no way my makeup has survived this travesty.

I don't turn back as I walk, but I can feel his eyes on me the whole way. Is he regretting what he did or assuring himself he didn't have a choice? Is he imagining taking this dress off before being slammed with the reality that it will never happen?

The powder room is blessedly empty. I do the best I can with my makeup, but my desire to make a good impression disappeared the second I saw Slate in the lobby.

How is it possible to still feel like this after a month apart? I hardly experienced any pain when I broke up with Carter, and we were together for a year and a half.

Maybe that's what happens when you give someone your heart and they refuse to give it back.

41

"I Refuse" - Five Finger Death Punch ft. Maria Brink

Three Months Later

Lux

"He's going to hate that." Maeve stares up at the banner Heath and Walker have strung across their front porch, the words "Welcome Home, Rhett" written on it in large red letters.

I nudge her shoulder. "You know he'll love it."

She sighs and crosses her arms. "You're right. I'm the one who hates it." She walks through the front door without knocking. "Please direct me to the alcohol."

I stay outside, looking at the sign and the balloons attached to the posts of the porch. Rhett's been in rehab for three months, but Pierce is picking him up right now. To say I'm nervous to see him again would be an understatement.

Walker sticks her head out the front door. "You coming inside?"

"Just getting some vitamin D," I say, and follow her into the house. "It's cramping my style to be so pale."

"You spent last month in Barbados," she deadpans as we walk into the kitchen. "You're practically the color of fried fish."

I gasp and look down at my bronze arms. While I did get sun in the tropics, my tan has since faded. "Not all of us are blessed with a complexion that doesn't need the sun," I point out. "It's not on brand for me to be anything less than bronze."

"You and your brand," she mutters, handing me a cocktail the color of the sun.

"What are we drinking?" I take a sip from the glass. It tastes orange-y with a hint of champagne.

"Don't tell Heath, but they're practically mimosas," Walker whispers, casting a glance at Heath and Maeve engrossed in conversation on the other side of the kitchen island. "He thinks he was creative."

"Perfect." I drain the contents of my glass and hand it back. "Means we can drink more."

It's Tuesday, our usual poker night, but since Rhett's been gone, our games have been hit-or-miss. That, combined with a ridiculous amount of broken-hearted sulking and grief, was what drove me to the Caribbean coast. I needed something to get my mind off the way my life is falling apart.

I've lost Alex and Slate and nearly lost Rhett. The only good thing that's happened was being asked to host the Humanitarian Aid Spring Gala. With that to divert my attention for the next two months, I may survive after all.

I visited the cemetery this morning for the first time since the funeral. It was much more cathartic than expected. I let go of some of my guilt around my brother's choices. We all make our own decisions. Alex's may not make sense to me, but that doesn't make them my problem to solve.

There's a knock at the front door, then Pierce's voice echoes through the foyer. "We're here!"

The four of us in the kitchen exchange looks before moving to greet him and Rhett. Tonight we're skipping the poker game in favor of celebrating Rhett's return. I'm not sure how we'll stay busy. This already feels awkward as fuck.

I'm the last to enter the foyer, so I witness Rhett's homecoming from afar. When he's wrapped everyone else in an awkward hug, he turns to me.

I should say something, but my mouth is dry. All I can think is that I wish Alex could have had the same chance Rhett did. That it's not fair that he's here, healthy and whole, while Alex is cold in the ground.

"Lux." That full-mouth grin is there, the one I know so well I've even dreamed of it a few times since he's been gone. Rhett opens his arms, and everyone's watching, so I don't have a choice. I let him tug me close, the scent of his familiar cologne giving me a comfort I don't deserve.

I pull back after a few seconds, but he doesn't let go. He stares down at me with a slight frown. "You okay?" he whispers.

I nod. "Of course. Just happy you're home."

He releases me, and we all head to the back terrace, where the caterers have spread the table with our meal. The sun is sinking below the horizon, taking the day's warmth with it, but Heath has a smokeless fire going nearby.

"Oh my god," Rhett says when he spots the lamb chops with fig jam and mint pesto. "You have no idea how often I dreamed of eating something besides cardboard."

We take our seats and start filling our plates.

"How are you feeling, mate?" Heath asks Rhett as he serves fresh cocktails.

"Pretty good, actually." Rhett leans back in his chair. "Rehab's definitely not for the faint of heart, but I feel loads better."

I'm surprised to hear him say so. Rhett usually downplays anything that won't label him as a rebel. Either this is a new leaf he's turning over, or he's found a way to spin rehab to his advantage.

"Did they make you write shit?" Heath says.

Rhett chuckles. "Oh, yeah. We had 'daily journaling time.' It was fucked as shit, so I wrote songs instead. Filled a whole notebook."

Walker passes the honey-glazed carrots. "Are you going to record any of them?"

Rhett takes a bite and swallows before answering. "That's the plan. I've been letting my music slide, but the past three months gave me clarity on my future."

I can't do anything but stare at him. When he catches me looking, he tosses me a wink and washes his food down with water. He hasn't touched the cocktail in front of him. I lower my gaze to my plate and push my salad around with my fork.

Silence falls over our group, a rarity for us. This is almost as awkward as when Walker came back six months ago. There's a giant fucking elephant in the room, and none of us have the nerve to confront it.

"So tell me what's been happening while I was gone." Rhett directs this question at Maeve while shoveling food in his mouth faster than I can chew. It's like he hasn't eaten the entire time he's been gone.

Maeve fills him in on the latest gossip and news, with everyone else chiming in every now and then to correct or embellish her stories. By the time she's done, the atmosphere feels close to normal.

As if sensing my discomfort, Rhett turns to me. "Did Slate tell you he came to see me?"

I lift my eyes to his face to see if he's joking. What is he thinking, bringing up Slate of all people? Did he forget who sold to him in the first place?

"Who's Slate?" Maeve asks, looking between the two of us.

"Lux's friend, the mechanic," Rhett supplies. "He helped us with the Porsche, remember?"

Maeve quirks a brow. Insignificant people don't take up space in her brain. "Why was he coming to visit you? I thought he was a drug dealer."

"Not anymore. He came to see me once a week."

Walker shifts beside me. Across the table, Pierce's gaze drops to his glass. As far as I know, the rest of them only visited Rhett a few times. I never had the strength to go even once.

"Once a week?" Maeve repeats. "Why?"

She's only saying what we're all thinking. Everyone's gaze fixes on Rhett, who looks suddenly bombarded. "Uh, because we're friends?"

The calm from a few minutes ago dissipates. Their thoughts are all as clear as glass. *If this guy—whom none of us really knows—went to visit Rhett once a week, where does that leave the rest of us on the friend scale?*

My brain is still tripping over something else. "He's no longer dealing?" I say.

Rhett's eyes meet mine, letting me know he understands what I'm asking. "He quit a while back, right before I went in, I think."

My lips part in surprise. I don't know where to file this new information. Slate gave up dealing? "You're sure he didn't just say that?"

Rhett laughs and unwraps a toothpick. "Pretty sure. He's the one that convinced me to get help in the first place."

A slight breeze could knock me over. Good thing it's a still night. "I'm sorry, he *what*?"

Rhett sticks the toothpick in his mouth. "He talked me into rehab, then drove me there and checked me in himself."

Did the rest of them know about this? Their faces are as blank as mine feels.

"That explains a few things," Pierce mutters.

I thought I was the only one confused by Rhett's sudden enrollment in rehab and subsequent three-month disappearance.

Rhett doesn't need to say the rest.

Slate was an actual friend.

He was there for me when I needed him most.

He's more than a drug dealer.

I don't want to confront that truth. I'd give my entire vintage Chanel collection to go back in time and erase this knowledge from my brain.

It's been three months since that night at the holiday gala, when I told him the only thing I wanted was to never see him again. He had already taken Rhett to rehab at that point, convinced him to get help, and saved him. The opportunity Alex never had.

Maybe he didn't do any of it for me.

Maybe he genuinely felt bad for selling to Rhett and wanted to help him.

Maybe he decided to be someone his sister can be proud of.

But none of it changes the fact that he did it. He gave up dealing, and he checked Rhett into rehab without telling me any of it. He could have used it that night to show me that he'd changed. Instead he revealed nothing, choosing to honor my request to never speak to me again.

What the hell am I supposed to do with that?

42

"Damn Regret" - The Red Jumpsuit Apparatus

Two Months Later

Lux

Looks like my idiot father is cheating again, and in broad daylight. Could the guy be any more stupid?

"If it helps, your mum is still prettier than all the others since her," Walker says. "Including that one."

He hasn't spotted me yet, ensconced in his corner booth with a girl who looks like she's barely five years older than me. Her tan legs snake out from beneath her skirt to rub against his under the table.

I push my plate away. There's no way I'm getting another bite down.

"We know that skank is only after one thing." Maeve spears a bite of her salmon. "And we're exceptional at taking down skanks."

I let out a deep exhale. "I can't afford to get mixed up in a scandal. The gala is only a week away."

"Your precious gala," Maeve mutters. "Some things are more important."

I give her an unamused look. "It's the biggest event of my career."

Maeve shakes her head and sets down her fork. "You're a socialite.

That's not a career."

"Excuse me?" I toss my napkin onto the table. "What are you saying, Maeve?"

"Girls," Walker warns. "Not here."

She's right. There are more than a few interested eyes pointed in our direction. Incidentally, none of them are my father's.

"Fine," I say. "Let's take a selfie." I tug my phone from my bag. "I need content for my non-job." I cut Maeve a look as I move to the other side of the table.

She tosses her hair over her shoulder and smiles into the camera. We press our faces together and put on the best bloody show we can, Maeve's midnight-black hair and Walker's auburn waves framing my blonde head in the center. I've taken at least a dozen shots when the camera cuts out, replaced by an incoming call.

"Who is Briar?" Maeve asks.

I fumble for the call button as I stand up. Why is Briar calling me? "Hello?"

"Lux." The smile in her voice travels through the phone.

"Is everything okay?" I keep my voice low as I make my way back to my seat. I can only think of one reason she'd be contacting me, and it's not something I want to dwell on. "Are *you* okay?" Guilt coats my tongue with a metallic taste.

"I'm great! How are you?" I can practically feel her sunshine.

"I'm good . . ." I flick my eyes toward Maeve and Walker, neither of whom is doing anything to mask their interest in my conversation.

"I haven't seen you in a long time, so this is probably unexpected," Briar says. "But I have a huge favor to ask you."

Here it comes. The setup for the disappointment I'm going to have to give her. Because there's no way I'm doing a favor for Slate's little sister, regardless of how much I might owe it to her.

"I'm graduating in a week, and I really need a dress," she continues.

"I'm not sure I have anything that would fit you." Briar's small, but she's at least six inches shorter than me.

"Oh, no," she says quickly. "I'd never ask to borrow something. I was wondering if you'd go with me to find one."

"Oh." I sit back, doing my best to take in this new information. "You want me to go shopping with you?"

Maeve and Walker give each other a look before returning their attention to me.

"You're the most fashionable person I know," Briar says. "It would mean the world to me if you'd help me pick something out."

"I—" How do I let her down gently? "I don't think—"

Walker's mouth drops open, and she gestures something I can't understand.

"Please?" Briar says. "I know it's a huge favor, and I'm sorry it's so last minute. I wasn't even sure I would be able to attend, especially when I was falsely diagnosed with giant cell myocarditis."

And there it is. She knows it was me.

"I suppose I could make time for one shopping trip," I say. "As long as—" I can't do it. I cannot say his name out loud.

"He won't be around, I swear," she says. "He won't even know you're taking me."

I sigh into the phone. "Okay."

Briar squeals, and after we arrange a time for me to pick her up, I end the call and turn to the vampires sitting at the table with me.

"Let's have it," Maeve says.

"The check? Oh, that's so sweet of you." I drain the rest of my wine.

"Spill," Walker says.

I roll my eyes and set my goblet back down. "That was the sister. She wants me to take her shopping."

"*The* sister?"

A nod.

"Oh my god."

Yep.

One night, after way too much Beluga, I told Maeve and Walker the entire story of Slate's and my ill-fated relationship, his betrayal, and my subsequent sabotage of his mental state with Briar's fake diagnosis.

"Are you going to see him?" Walker asks.

"She said he wouldn't even find out, so please pray that is the case." I'm not sure my cells can handle being in his vicinity without spontaneously combusting. Driving to his house will be bad enough.

* * *

Briar is waiting for me on her front steps when I pull up. She bounds to the car, not unlike a golden retriever. "Oh my god, your car is amazing." She buckles the seatbelt, then runs a hand over the leather detailing on the door.

"Where are we going?" I shudder as we drive past the petrol station where I was mugged. The same iron grates are over the windows, but the lot is empty of cars.

She gives me directions to the first store. It's less than five minutes away—outside the Junction, but barely. The white paint on the cinder block walls is faded and peeling in places. The metal roof was once red but has now faded to a disgusting shade of mauve. The sign over the entrance reads "Dress for Less."

Garbage greets me when I get out of the car, blown up against the curb by the wind. I avoid a piece of chewing gum stuck to the pavement as I climb out. Briar is already waiting for me outside the store.

I lean against the open car door. "Is there another place we can go instead?"

Her brow wrinkles. "Um, yeah, I think so." She walks back to the car and climbs inside.

"Sorry," I say. "That place gives me the creeps."

The next one isn't much better. The dresses all look like something from a supermarket overstock ten years ago. Briar tries a few on, but I can't stomach the idea of her buying any of them. There are *deodorant stains* on several of the armpits.

Back in the car, I turn to her. "Are you open to going downtown?" So far, we've stayed on the south side of the river, where the neighborhoods are sketchy and the prices low.

She wrinkles her nose in a wince. "I don't have a very big budget."

I wave my hand and start the ignition. "Don't worry about the money."

We go to my favorite vintage shop first. Fortunately, they don't put prices on the clothes, because Briar would never have agreed to try on the Vera Wang minidress if she'd known how much it costs.

She walks out of the dressing room, and I gasp. Gone are her jeans and sad little T-shirt. The dress hits her midthigh, and the magenta color sets off her complexion like an Instagram filter. Thin straps hold it up on her dainty shoulders.

At my excitement, she turns to the mirror on the wall. Her entire face beams as she takes in her own reflection.

"This is more like it," I murmur. "Now try these." I hand her the rest of the dresses I scooped up while she was changing.

Her eyes bulge as she takes in the stack. "I could just get this one."

"Nonsense. Half the fun of shopping is trying things on," I say.

She dutifully returns to the dressing room, coming out after each dress to get my opinion. Two hours later, we have a definite winner: a sleek navy-blue sheath that is channeling Audrey Hepburn, whom we discover we have a shared love of.

"*Roman Holiday* was her best," Briar says after changing back into her jeans.

"I will always be partial to *Tiffany's*." I lead the way to the door.

"Wait." She grabs my arm. "I need to pay."

I push open the door of the shop. "I already did."

She struggles to keep up with my long steps. "What do you mean, you already did?"

I toss her a grin over my shoulder. "I paid while you were changing. Honestly, love, it was nothing."

"I'm sure it wasn't nothing," she says, breaking into a jog. "I can't let you do that."

"Too late. Besides," I say, slowing my stride, "I think I owe it to you, right?"

She doesn't say anything, but the understanding gleam in her eyes tells me more than words ever could.

We make our way down the pavement, but instead of turning toward the car park, I lead her to the next street over.

"Where are we going?" she says.

I loop my arm through hers. "I just discovered the magic of shopping for a little sister. And I'm not ready to call it a day."

Her look is full of trepidation. "Do I even want to know?"

"Probably not." We sail into another vintage boutique I visit at least once a week. You can't find the treasures if you don't shop often.

"Lux," Antony calls from behind the counter, his dark hair slicked to one side. "I have a few pieces you're going to love."

"You're a sweetheart, Antony, but I'm not shopping for myself today." I place my hands on Briar's shoulders and propel her toward the counter. "This is Briar."

Antony bows low over her hand and places a kiss on the back of it, turning her cheeks the color of her popsicle-pink T-shirt. "It is always a pleasure to meet such a beautiful woman."

I snap my fingers at him. "Enough. Show us what you have that she might like."

As he retreats to the back, Briar looks at me, wonder in her eyes. "I want to be you when I grow up," she says breathlessly.

I laugh and brush my hand against a cowhide bag on display. "Be careful what you wish for. It's not as glamorous as it seems."

"Really?" she says, with the sincerity of a five-year-old. "Sure seems all glamor and glitz."

"Even socialites have hearts," I say quietly, and set the purse back. "And glass ones shatter easily."

She pulls a pair of sunglasses off the rack and tries them on. "He hurt you, didn't he?"

I hide my surprise behind a pair of shades of my own. "I've experienced worse."

"He told me a little. About how he lied to you."

"It's in the past," I say, sliding the glasses back on the rack.

Briar touches my arm. "For what it's worth, I was hoping the two of you would work out."

I give her a grateful smile. "I'm the first woman he's brought home. The others will be even better."

It's true, but that doesn't make it less painful to think about. It's been five months since I saw him at the gala, but there isn't a single day that I don't think about him. Half the time I'm cursing him, but still. The thoughts are there, and they're painful.

"How could they be better than you?" She motions to my outfit, a black-and-white-checkered skirt and jacket set with a cropped white shirt and black string tie. "You're a fashion icon."

"Just because I look good on the outside doesn't mean I'm good on the inside."

She shakes her head and thumbs through the spring jackets Antony has on display. "I don't believe that."

"I'm sure you also didn't want to believe that I could send that letter, right?"

Her hand stops on a floral Chanel with incredible beadwork, but she doesn't turn to me. "I'm sure you had your reasons."

I let out a disbelieving scoff. "You're determined to see the best in people, aren't you?" Something Carter accused *me* of recently. When she doesn't answer, I continue. "It was never about you. I hope you know that."

"I assumed," Briar says softly.

"I wanted to hurt him the way he hurt me. I know how much he cares about you, and it was the only thing I could think of to get back at him for what he did."

She looks at me over her shoulder. "He messed up, but he's a good guy."

"I know," I whisper. I drop her gaze, no longer able to look into those eyes, so similar to his. "I'm sorry for all of it, okay? I know that doesn't make it better, but I hope you can accept my apology."

"Of course I do." She turns and throws her arms around me as Antony returns from the back.

"Okay, ladies. I have some treasures that will make your hearts melt."

* * *

It's not until I pull up in front of her house that I regret buying so many things for Briar. I got carried away, intent on dressing her in much better clothes than she's used to wearing, and didn't stop to consider that I'll now need to help her carry the bags into the house.

I don't see the motorbike in the driveway, but that doesn't mean Slate hasn't parked it in the garage. The lights are off, but he could be taking a nap on the sofa. He could be wondering what the hell I'm doing chauffeuring his sister around town.

How rude would it be to leave her and the bags on the pavement and drive off?

Too rude for me to sleep tonight.

We each grab an armload of shopping bags from the boot and walk toward the house. If Slate is inside, I plan to dump them and run before he gets a good look at me. Let Briar explain what we were doing.

The front door is still locked—a good sign—and Briar has to set her load down to fish out her key. I scan the street behind us.

"He's not here," she says, and pushes the door open.

"I was admiring the flowers."

I follow her to her room and deposit the bags on her bed. The space is small but bright with a yellow floral bedspread and pillow shams. The walls are painted pale green and decorated with photos.

"Did you take those?" I ask, pointing to a collage of landscapes.

She nods. "I love photography."

"They're excellent."

"Thanks." Her smile is sweet and a little embarrassed. "And thank you for today. You really didn't need to get all of these things." She waves a hand over the pile of designer bags.

"I wanted to."

"I'll never be able to explain them to Slate." She opens her closet door. "He'll shit a load if he finds out."

I exhale and retreat from the room. "On that note, I should be going."

"Wait a second," Briar calls from the closet, her voice muffled. "I have something for you."

The seconds tick by, me standing in her doorway, unable to see or hear her, wondering how soon her brother will be coming home from work.

"Briar," I call. "Everything okay?"

"Yeah, I'm having trouble finding it."

I don't know how it happens, whether my feet separate themselves from the rest of my nervous system and grow a mind of their own, but I end up at the threshold of Slate's room. The same room where he made me fall apart more than once, then put me back together more fully than he found me.

I'm hit with his scent, that masculine leather I'll never be able to smell without remembering him. I step inside, knowing it's a bad idea, but no longer able to resist the pull he has over me.

The room is much the same as it was the last time I was in here, neat and minimal, with a glass of water on the nightstand and a discarded pair of socks beside the laundry hamper. There's a photo stuck in the mirror frame, and I walk closer to see it better.

A sharp pang rips through my heart when I recognize the selfie I took with his phone one night while he was grabbing us a postcoital snack. It's over six months old. Why does he still have it up?

I reach for the desk chair to steady myself, and my fingers close over soft fabric. It's my pink cashmere sweater. I must have left it here the last time I wore it. Why it's still hanging over the back of his chair is less easily explained.

"Lux?" Briar's voice floats down the hall, snapping me out of my trance.

"Coming!" I call, and dart out of Slate's bedroom before I have even more explaining to do. "Sorry, I needed to use the restroom."

Her eyes narrow a tiny fraction, and then she thrusts a thick envelope into my hands. "I wanted to invite you to the ceremony."

"What ceremony?" I tear the envelope open and pull out a creamy-white invitation.

You're invited to celebrate Briar Lawson's high school graduation.

"I didn't tell Slate, but you can still come. He doesn't need to know."

"This is so sweet, Briar. I'd love to come." I scan the rest of the invitation, and my eyes land on the date. "Oh, no."

Her eyes grow wide. "What's wrong?"

"Damn. This is the same day as the Humanitarian Aid Society Gala. I'm the chairwoman, so I kind of have to be there." I hand the invitation back with a deflated spirit. "I appreciate you inviting me, though. It means the world to me. Especially after . . . everything."

She offers me a sad smile in return. "Keep it. In case your plans change."

I tuck it into my bag and don't tell her that the chances of that happening are slimmer than cows flying, or whatever the saying is. "Thanks for a wonderful day." I press a kiss to her cheek.

Her face blooms with color. "Thank *you*. I really wish things could be different."

"Me too." I pull open the front door and look over my shoulder one last time. "Me too."

43

"Power Over Me" - Dermot Kennedy

Something weird happened a few days ago. I walked into my bedroom and was met with the scent of roses. My mind immediately tripped over itself, my eyes landing on Lux's photo stuck on the mirror.

It was like she'd been there, which was stupid, of course, but the scent lingered in my memory long after I left my bedroom. Roses will haunt me for the rest of my life. I'll have to stay out of florist shops, which shouldn't be too much of an inconvenience, considering I have no one to buy flowers for.

That was the plan, until it occurred to me that I should get Briar flowers in celebration of her graduation tonight. Now my car smells like a fucking floral emporium, the bouquet of white and pink roses carefully wrapped in brown paper and lying on the back seat.

I finish lathering my face, then run the straight razor over my cheek. It's been a while since I've given much thought to my appearance, but tonight is special. Tonight needs to be perfect.

There's a knock on the doorjamb, and I turn to find my sister leaning against it, watching me. I almost nick myself when I see her dress.

"Where did you get that?" I ask, turning back to my reflection.

"Online."

"It looks expensive."

She shrugs. "I got a good deal."

I roll my eyes and run the blade over my chin. "Excited about tonight?"

Out of the corner of my eye, I see her playing with the fabric of her dress, which I'm still not convinced she's telling the truth about. "Sure."

"What's wrong?" I rinse the lather from the razor. "Nervous?"

"Not really."

"Then what?"

"Is this going to be our life, then?"

I lower my hand and stare at her. "What do you mean?"

"This." She gestures around the bathroom like that clears things up. "Us pretending that everything is fine, just going about our lives like nothing has changed."

"Everything *is* fine."

"Right." She crosses her arms. "Then why have you been moping around like a lovesick teenager for the past six months?"

A laugh escapes my mouth. "I think you're getting me mixed up with someone at school."

"Funny. Ever since Lux, you've been a miserable bastard to live with."

I ignore the pang her name sends through my heart. "I'm just swamped at work."

"Is that why you haven't been to see Laney all this time?"

I shoot Briar a look. "Laney has a boyfriend." News that should have disappointed me, but only brought relief when I found out.

"How about why you're avoiding me like the plague?" Her eyes challenge me to deny it.

I can't. Because she's right. I have been avoiding her for months

295

now, afraid we'd end up having this exact conversation. I toss the razor into the sink with a clatter. "Listen to me." I prop a hand on the doorframe and lean down so she doesn't miss a word. "I buy you everything you need. I plan on throwing you the best bloody graduation party the Junction has ever seen. Sometimes you have to take what you get."

Her eyes blaze back at me, not intimidated in the least. "I don't want any of that."

I blink incredulously. "Fine. I'll cancel tonight." Never mind the fact that I spent thousands on all of the details.

"Good. I don't want a party anyway."

"God, Briar." I pick up the straight razor and resume shaving. "Glad you're not hard to please."

"You know what I want?" She taps her fingers on her arm.

"I have a feeling I'm about to find out," I mutter, and make a neat swipe across my jawline. The stubble I've been sporting for years disappears beneath the blade.

"I want you to get your head out of your ass and go after Lux."

My hand falters enough to nick the skin near my lip. "And I want a million bucks, but you can't have everything."

"Why do you refuse to fight for her?"

"I *did* fight. She wants nothing to do with me."

"I don't believe that."

I snort and meet Briar's eyes in the mirror over the sink. "And why is that?"

"You have to promise not to get mad." She gnaws on her lip, looking nervous for the first time in this whole conversation.

Dread blossoms in my stomach. "Dear god."

"She took me shopping. And we talked."

My hand stills, eyes still trained on hers in the reflection. "Tell me you're joking."

"I'm not. She bought me this dress. She bought me a closet full of clothes."

"What the fuck were you thinking?" My nostrils flare as I inhale.

Briar's eyes don't carry even a shred of remorse. "I wanted her help. And I wanted to see how she felt about you."

"Un-fucking-believable." I drop my sister's gaze and finish shaving my face. My head is spinning with all of her bloody revelations. I'm terrified that next she'll tell me she's dating a prick whose pants don't cover his ass.

"She felt bad about what she did."

"As she should." I turn on the tap, letting the water warm up.

"I think she still has feelings for you."

I cast her a glare before ducking to rinse the lather from my face. "I don't care if she's the bloody queen of Wesbourne."

"I caught her in your bedroom."

My hands freeze on my face.

"She tried to pretend she was just using the restroom, but I saw her coming out of your room."

I towel off without a word. So I *wasn't* imagining the roses. I already know Lux's perfume lingers for weeks. I slept on the sofa just to get away from it.

"She said she wishes things were different."

My hair has dried from my shower, and I pull half of it back into my usual bun, leaving the rest to hang around my shoulders.

"Slate, say something."

"Trust me, you don't want to hear what I have to say."

Briar sighs, looking like a deflated balloon. "I *really* like her."

I drop my facade for a second. "Yeah, me too."

"Then go after her." She places a hand on my arm. "Just once more. For me."

I close my eyes, but we both know I'll do it. Because I've never been able to deny a woman I love anything. "I'll think about it."

* * *

The graduation ceremony is a miserable excuse for an evening. I shift on the hard metal folding chair and adjust my collar. Again. My suit is too tight, thanks to spending more hours at the gym over the past six months.

This is what my life would consist of if Lux and I were to try something long-term. That would, of course, require her to listen to me for more than thirty seconds. Which is as likely to happen as me break-dancing across this auditorium.

When it's Briar's turn to cross the stage and accept her diploma, I cheer louder than anyone has all night. She comes to find me afterward, a glow lighting her eyes and cheeks. She holds her diploma out in front of her like a diamond. In the Junction, it kind of is. Less than half of the kids make it to this day.

"Congrats, kiddo," I say, tucking her beneath my arm.

"Hey, careful." She pulls away from me. "You'll mess up my hair."

"You ready for your party?"

We drive to the hotel ballroom I've rented for the event. It's not even half as fancy as the one where Lux hosted her event last winter, but it's pretty damn nice for people like us.

Briar gasps as she walks into the room and sees the handiwork of the party planner I hired online. Balloons and streamers hang from the ceiling, and a large bouquet of flowers sits in the middle of the food table.

It all kind of looks like a child's birthday party, but she seems genuinely pleased. "It's amazing, Slate. Truly."

I snort. "Glad I didn't cancel after all?"

She gives me a sheepish smile and goes to admire the three-tier pink cake on a cloth-covered table.

Guests start arriving, and the DJ plays some new music all the kids are into these days. Briar gets pulled onto the dance floor by a tall kid in glasses. I shoot him a warning glare, but truthfully, I'm glad to see her so happy.

This day wasn't always a certainty.

The treatments she's been taking have been working. She hasn't had an episode in months. I have Lux to thank for that.

Briar grabs my hand, nearly spilling my drink. "Do you know what would make this so much better?" she says over the music.

I shake my head and take a sip of beer before she can ruin her dress with it.

"If Lux was here." Her voice is loud in my ear.

"Give it a rest, Briar."

"Tonight is the perfect night for you to make a grand gesture." She shakes my arm.

"Did someone spike the punch? You're acting ridiculous."

"This is what I want for my graduation present."

"I already gave you your present." The four-year-old Toyota Camry is sitting in the car park as we speak.

She pouts, and we both know I've lost. "She's hosting the Humanitarian Aid Society Gala tonight at the Museum of Art. It's a big deal."

"The perfect reason for me *not* to show up."

"If you show up, you'll prove that you'll do anything for her, even walk into an uncomfortable situation."

"You read too many romance novels."

She grins sweetly and presses a kiss to my smooth cheek. "You know I'm right."

"'Insane' is the word I had in mind."

"Good luck!" she calls on her way back to the dance floor. "And don't worry about me. I'll catch a ride home with Andrea."

Women. They think they rule the world.

That's why we can't let them know they're right.

The air has cooled off since the sun went down. I slide into the driver's side of the Camry and rest my head on the steering wheel. What the fuck am I thinking? Am I actually going to walk into that Silver Spoon party and demand that Lux talk to me? I already tried that once, and she threw me out. Why in the world would this time be any different?

I start the engine and back out of the car park. Briar thinks Lux will appreciate the grand gesture, but she sure as hell didn't appreciate it the first time. I think about her dancing with some other bloke, and my fist tightens on the wheel. For all I know she's seeing someone else by now, although I'm sure Briar would have pried that information out of her.

Does she still think about me the way I think about her? Lying awake at night, imagining her head on my chest, the silky-soft feel of her hair against my beard? Does she ever reach for her phone to tell me something, then remember that we're no longer speaking?

This is why I don't do relationships. They get bloody fucked up, and then the rest of your life is this big, soggy mess.

The thing is, when they're working, they're great. Really fucking great.

Briar's right. Lux and I deserve another chance. What we had was special. It wasn't your run-of-the-mill fling. It had deep roots that could have sprouted into something if given enough time.

Time is the one thing we didn't have. But if she'll listen to me, maybe I can get her to see that we can try this again.

If she refuses to see me, I'll sit outside her house until she calls the police on me. I'm not giving up again, not without one more chance. She owes me that after what she did to Briar and me.

I pull up to the curb a few blocks from the museum to avoid the valets. I can park my own fucking car, thanks. There aren't many people outside. Most are probably inside stuffing their faces full of caviar and whatever else rich people eat.

The doormen will be a problem, though. They'll have a guest list and make a big to-do about looking for my name, even though I'm not even dressed in a tux. This too-tight suit came from the mall.

"Hello," I say, adjusting my lapels as I approach the two guys at the door. "I'm here to deliver a message."

"We can do that for you, sir." The man on the left looks me up and down, his own suit several sizes too small, but for different reasons.

"I was told this one needed to be hand delivered by me."

"Are you on the guest list?"

"I think we both know the answer to that."

"I'm afraid we can't let you in without a formal invitation."

"It's a very important message," I say. "If you could just let me speak to the chairwoman—"

"I'm sorry, sir. You'll need to wait here." The two men exchange looks, then the one on the right goes inside.

I stare down the remaining bodyguard, but he ignores me. My heart is pounding like a mallet in my chest, my palms slick with sweat at the thought of seeing Lux again. Footsteps sound on the other side of the glass, and my heart rate kicks into higher gear. When the bodyguard finally appears, it's with a brunette woman.

"Yes?" she says when she sees me.

"I need to speak with Lux Colombia-Clarke," I say once I find my voice again.

"I'm afraid that's not possible." She glances at the guards with irritation.

"What do you mean it's not possible?" I step closer, sizing up the two men. If I play this right, I can take them down with minimal effort. They're big, but they've both had too much booze and donuts over the years to be able to move very quickly.

The woman slips back inside, leaving me no closer to seeing Lux than I was. She stops to talk to another woman, who looks through the glass for her own glimpse of the circus that's about to go down.

"Okay, gentlemen." I inch closer to the doors. "We can either play this the easy way or the hard way. I'll let you decide."

They don't move a single muscle in their faces, just continue staring straight ahead.

"The hard way, then. Okay." I pull back and let my fist connect with the first guy's jaw. The other one grabs me from behind, but he's too slow to pin me down. I shift away and throw a punch into his soft gut.

A small *oomph* pops out of his mouth like a champagne cork. The other guard slams his fist into my face, sending my head backward and a spray of blood from my mouth. It hurts like hell, but before I can retaliate, a shrill female voice cuts through the night air.

"What in god's name is going on?"

We all stop midpunch and look at her. She's tiny and wearing a giant gown of cascading bloodred roses. Her jet-black hair is pulled away from her face into a low bun, several tendrils escaping to frame her face.

It isn't until her eyes connect with mine that I recognize her.

"Unhand this man," she tells the two bodyguards, who are still stunned speechless by her arrival. "I know him."

44

"I Can Do It With a Broken Heart" - Taylor Swift

Lux

It's amazing how three months of working on the highlight of your career, the project of your dreams, can feel as flat as cheap champagne.

The gala is perfect, the guests are happy—if you can trust the smiles—and I couldn't have done a better job if I'd had a year to plan it. My phone is loaded with photos, enough Instagram content for weeks to come. So what the heck is the problem?

I drag my mind back to the conversation around me. I'm in the middle of a group of socialites discussing the latest Chanel drop. Apparently, it caused quite a stir. I haven't even seen it yet, which is saying something.

I exchange my empty champagne flute for another and pretend to be listening to Crissy Andrews extol the virtues of timeless pieces and the horror of watching brands whore themselves out to trends. It all feels as meaningless as fuck. I'm numb, cold to the touch, and I don't have a damn clue what to do about it.

I excuse myself from the group—one can only listen to Crissy's screeching voice for so long. As I pass, people stop to tell me how wonderful the party is and what a fantastic job I've done as chairwoman.

Normally I'd bask in the praise, but tonight I have to force the smile onto my face. When I reach the ladies' room, I realize the problem.

Now that the gala has arrived and I've achieved the biggest milestone of my career as a socialite, my life feels over. What else is there to strive for when I've already reached the highest mark?

I suppose I could aim to become the party planner for the palace, but that holds less appeal than the idea of trying to finagle my huge dress into a restroom stall.

Life isn't supposed to feel this empty. What's the point of going on if there's nothing waiting for you?

Unexpectedly, my conversation with Briar last week floats back to haunt me. It's done that more times than I'd like to admit. I successfully pushed Slate out of my mind while I planned the gala, the event effectively filling my thoughts to overflowing. But now that it's done, my brain is like a magnet for every random, stray thought out there, ready to torment me.

According to Briar, Slate is miserable too, which he deserves to be, that son of a bitch. But god, why does that thought not bring comfort?

Is he miserable because he lost me? Or because I made him feel like he failed at something? Was I just another accomplishment to congratulate himself on, up until the minute I slipped away?

Or did he actually care?

Because if he did, isn't that worth fighting for?

Until Slate, I didn't know it was possible for someone's absence to destroy your appetite or your desire to get up in the morning. I didn't know they could scrape out a pit in the bottom of your stomach that gnaws at your insides, reminding you of the hell you're in every second.

Isn't the possibility of getting rid of those feelings, of feeling alive again, worth pursuing?

He's probably given up on speaking to me. It's been six months since he showed up at the holiday gala. It's taken me months to wash away the guilt that clung to me like an ill-fitting dress after I told him I never wanted to talk to him again.

When I walked back into the foyer after fixing my makeup that night, part of me hoped he'd still be there, still be waiting, ready to fight once more. I told myself that if he was, this time I'd listen. I'd reward his persistence with five minutes of my time.

And we both knew if I'd given him five minutes, he would have used them to win me over. Which was why I resisted so strongly.

But now I'm beginning to regret driving him away. Would he have come with me tonight? Worn a tux and greeted guests with me? It's too difficult to imagine.

I don't know where Slate fits into my life, but I'm never going to figure it out staring at myself in the mirror of the ladies' room. I grab my bag and head outside to the valet stand. Somewhere in the recesses of my car, I still have Briar's invitation. I didn't have the heart to throw it away, even though I knew I wouldn't be able to attend.

After the valet brings my car around, I search the back seat until I find it, crumpled but still readable. The location is some hotel I've never heard of before, and the party started hours ago. It's likely over by now, but I have to try.

I send a text to Miranda, who is helping me co-chair again, telling her I had to leave because of an emergency. The gala will be over in a matter of hours anyway, and it's nothing she can't handle.

It isn't until I'm driving over the bridge that it occurs to me how out of place my dress will be at a graduation party. It's a form-fitting strapless pale pink gown with 3D floral detailing throughout, another Fritz Herman masterpiece. But I couldn't care less.

The only thing that matters is getting to Slate and telling him I'm ready to listen. I hope I haven't wasted my last chance.

What if he's there with *her*, the girl he gave his jacket to outside the Rebel Wrench? My stomach churns at the thought, and I swallow back the taste of bile. There's no way he hasn't been dating—or having sex, in his case—since our breakup. I'll have to take my chances.

Because all of it is worth it if it gets rid of this empty feeling inside me.

45

"Ordinary" - Alex Warren

Lux

The room is empty except for a couple of teens taking down the atrocious pink and purple balloons. A few sad streamers fall down with them.

"Excuse me," I say. "Is this a graduation party?" Maybe I got the room number wrong. It looks more like a birthday party for a five-year-old.

The guy popping balloons looks up at me. "Was. It's over now." He gives the room an exaggerated glance. "Obviously."

"Thank you." I leave before he can give my dress any further curious stares.

Damn it. I smack the steering wheel. While my aim was to see Slate, I also wanted to surprise Briar by showing up.

I pull out of the car park and wind my way through the streets of the Junction, which were familiar less than a year ago. Now they remind me of how foolish this whole thing is.

There are lights on inside the house, which is a good sign. I was afraid they'd both be in bed already, and everything would've been for nothing.

I knock quietly on the door. My pulse is thrumming so strongly it's rattling my hands. I shake them out, hoping it will calm my nerves.

What am I going to say when he opens the door? Will he shut it in my face? (I deserve that.) Will he be upset that I showed up so late? (I deserve that, too.) Will he—

The door opens. Briar is standing on the other side wearing flannel pajamas. She takes in my huge gown, and a giant grin spreads across her face.

"Lux!" She throws her arms around my neck, not caring that she's crumpling my one-of-a-kind dress.

To be honest, I couldn't care less either. I hug her back. "I went to the hotel, but the party was over. I'm sorry I missed it."

She laughs. "I would've missed it myself if I could have. It was pretty awful."

"I didn't bring a present. This was kind of a last-minute decision."

"Are you kidding? You bought me an incredible dress and an entire wardrobe. That's more than enough."

I smile, glad I can make at least one person happy. "Is . . ." I try to grab on to the words, but they float away like leaves in the wind. "I was wondering if . . ."

"He's not here."

"Oh." I lower my gaze and clear my throat. "That's fine. I just thought I'd, you know, say hi if he was." God, he's probably at that woman's house.

"He went to find you, actually."

I jerk my head back up. "What?"

"He went to the gala to talk to you. Didn't you see him?"

"No." He came to a gala *again* after the way I treated him last time?

She rolls her shoulders. "He probably chickened out at the last minute."

"Okay." It doesn't explain where he is, but that's what I get for doing too little too late. I turn to go, but she stops me.

"Do you want me to tell him you were here?"

I stare at her for a few seconds, her face freshly washed of makeup. She looks like an innocent child even though she's only a few years younger than I am. It feels like a century. "That's okay," I say. "It's probably best to let things lie."

I offer her a sad wave as I walk back to my car. Is this going to be the story of my life from now on? Lux Colombia-Clarke, coming in late to everything.

We never should have ventured to combine our two worlds. If we had been satisfied keeping things the way they were, I wouldn't be driving home with an ache in my chest the size of the ocean.

* * *

The garage door shuts behind me. I sit in the car for a few moments, imagining the past hour in my head if I had done things differently. If I had stayed at the gala, would Slate have found me? If I had left there earlier, would he still have been at Briar's party?

It doesn't matter. What does matter is that fate intervened, saving me from a lifetime of heartache. It might not feel like it now, but this pain would have magnified if Slate and I had attempted some sort of reconciliation, only to be slapped in the face with reality when we ventured into the real world.

Better to rip the plaster off now rather than later.

I trudge up to the back path to the house. The solar lamps in the garden blink on as I approach, highlighting the pool and patio, where dead leaves are still gathered into piles in the corners like grieving widows. Maybe I should put this place on the market after all. It's too big for one person.

I fish for my key in my bag. It's lost at the bottom, and my fingers close around it as I register the figure on the stairs. I scream instinctively and back up, my feet tripping over the brick pavement.

The figure stands, and I see now that it's a man, but his face is still in shadow.

"Don't move," I say. "I'm calling the police." It sounds better in the movies. My voice is too weak and wobbly to bear much threat.

"Lux."

At the sound of his voice, my fingers freeze around my phone. A sinking whoosh echoes through my midsection, taking my stomach with it. "What are you doing here?" I whisper.

Slate walks down the steps, but I can't move away. I can't do anything. It's like my feet have grown roots, right through the bricks and into the ground.

"I needed to see you," he says, stopping when he's only an arm's length away.

We're sharing the same air space, something I didn't think would ever happen again. No matter how many times I've dreamed of this moment, nothing could have prepared me for the feeling of being this close to him. The way my body wants to hurl itself at his chest, be wrapped in those arms. It's downright ridiculous.

I clear my throat. "Okay."

"Really?" His voice is gruff, like it hasn't been used in ages.

"Sure." I shift my bag higher on my shoulder. "Nice outfit."

Slate smooths a hand over his crumpled mess of a cheap suit. "Thanks." If he was wearing a tie before, he's ditched it. The top three or four buttons of his white shirt are undone, leaving more than enough bare skin to be dangerous to my pulse.

I look away.

"Can we go inside or . . ." He jerks a thumb over his shoulder at the house.

"Here's fine." If we cross that threshold, all bets are off. Better to stay outside, where the chilly breeze can cool my cheeks.

"Okay." He runs a hand through his hair, which is a tangled mess. How long was he sitting out here? "I went to the gala."

"I heard."

"Your friend told you?"

I scrunch my nose. "Briar told me."

Now it's his turn to look confused. "When did you talk to Briar?"

I swallow the lump growing like a weed in my throat. "When I went to your house."

"My house."

"I went to the graduation party first, but it was already shut down," I say, as if that explains anything.

Slate takes another step closer. "And what were you doing at either of those places?"

My teeth sink into my lower lip. "Looking for you." It comes out in a rush of air.

He walks until the toes of his shoes meet mine. With his thumb, he pries my lip from my teeth. "Why?"

I inhale, but it's shaky, preventing me from getting enough oxygen to my brain to formulate an answer.

"I'm sorry," he says. It's such a simple statement, and he's apologized a million times before tonight, but for some reason, this time it makes me want to break apart. "I'm sorry for everything, for all of it. The drugs, your brother, lying to you. God, Lux. You have no idea how often I've cursed the day I was born."

"Not the day you met me?"

"God no." His thumb strokes my cheek. "That was the best day of my life."

A tiny whimper escapes my mouth, causing his eyes to drop to my lips. "You checked Rhett into rehab."

He inclines his head. "I did."

"Did you do that for me?"

A brief pause. "Maybe a little. But it was the right thing to do. He needed help."

I rest my hands on his chest. His heart beats beneath them, strong and steady. "Thank you," I whisper.

Slate nuzzles my jaw with his nose, sending goosebumps racing down my arms. "I'd do anything for you."

I struggle to grab on to a thought—any thought—that isn't a vision of him taking me inside and doing "anything" for me. "You quit selling?"

"Yes."

Hearing it confirmed does things to my heart. "I'm sorry about Briar. It was an awful thing to do."

He carefully bites my earlobe, flicking it with his tongue. "I deserved it. She didn't, but I did."

"You realize this will never work." I let out a shaky gasp as his teeth press into my neck. "Your world and mine."

He straightens until I can see his eyes again, the garden lights reflecting in their dark depths. "I thought so too, until I realized you've become my whole world."

I melt into him, let him lower his lips to mine for a kiss that is both incredible and torturous in its simplicity.

"You're going to regret every second you weren't in my arms," he murmurs.

"I already do."

"You're going to never want to leave them again."

"I already don't."

"You're going to be mine by the end of the night."

"I already am."

46

"Fire Up The Night" - New Medicine

Slate

I slow the bike as I near the Rebel Wrench. A familiar white car is approaching from the opposite direction. I toss its driver a grin as we both enter the car park at the same time, then I pull into the open spot near the front door with practiced ease.

The squeal of brakes sounds behind me, followed by Lux's enraged cursing. "You bloody fucking bastard," she yells. "You knew I was going to park there!"

I drop the kickstand on my bike and dismount. Then I turn and walk toward her car, unable to resist grinning from ear to ear.

She looks mad enough to spit nails.

"Good morning, princess." I lean into the convertible for a kiss, but she takes off again, leaving me in a cloud of dust and fumes. The laugh that echoes from my chest feels good. In fact, I can't remember ever feeling this good.

Lux parks on the other side of the building. I wait for her at the front door. When she marches toward me, the heels of her tall white boots hitting the pavement like gunshots, I duck into the shop. I hear my name being yelled as the door swings shut behind me, drowning out the rest of her voice.

Lux is meeting me at the garage to discuss our upcoming renovation plans. Business has been steadily increasing, and it's time to expand. I closed on the empty building next door two weeks ago, which will allow us to double our current space.

With her eye for design, I know she'll be able to make the Rebel Wrench *the* place to take your car. Unfortunately, it looks like she'll need some cool-off time before we can start discussing blueprints.

She bursts through my office door, glare firmly etched onto that beautiful face.

I smile at her with faux surprise. "Hey, babe. What took so long?"

She stalks over to my desk and crosses her arms. "I cannot believe you."

"What did I do now?" I tilt backward in my chair, stretching my arms overhead.

"Don't you *dare* patronize me." She presses down on my armrests, jerking me upright.

I encircle her wrists with my fingers. "What are you going to do about it?"

"Nothing that would please you," she snaps.

"I don't think that's true," I purr into her ear.

Her resistance melts a fraction, but she quickly recovers. She tries to yank her hands away from me, but I don't let go. Instead, I tug her onto my lap in one dexterous move.

With her ass firmly on my thighs, I'll be able to wear her down in no time. She squirms for a few seconds, until she realizes my cock is growing beneath her. It flared to life the minute I spotted the tiny little skirt she's wearing.

My fingers are still wrapped around her wrists, but I move both of them to the same hand and slide my free palm up her thigh. "I thought we talked about you wearing stuff like this to the shop."

Her glare has softened into that of an injured kitten. "You don't get to tell me what to wear."

"Is that right?"

She pauses for a few seconds, searching for the correct answer. "Yes," she whispers.

"Hmm." I pretend to consider. "Wrong answer."

Her breath snags in her throat. "Oh."

I've reached her silk panties now, and I brush against them with my knuckles. She rewards me with a tiny gasp. "I'd say you've been a very naughty girl."

Her eyes and mouth both widen. She bites down on her lip, and my dick pulses against my pants.

I slip one finger under the hem of her panties, running it back and forth as her breathing gets heavier. "Naughty girls need to be punished, you know."

"Yeah," she rasps.

Before she can say anything else, I release her hands and flip her over my knees. A startled gasp flies from her throat, but she doesn't say a word. I position her across my legs so she won't fall off. She hangs over both sides of my lap like a rag doll.

Slowly, like I have all the time in the world, I flip her skirt up over her back, revealing her tight, plump ass inside its silk thong. I groan and slide my hand across it, wanting to go as fast as possible, but forcing myself to move slow.

She whimpers as I slide a finger beneath the string of her thong, letting my knuckle graze the seam of her cheeks. They clench around my finger, and I can't resist wedging it in an inch. She clamps around it with the ferocity of a tiger.

I chuckle deeply. "Good girl. But you still need to be punished for wearing this skirt." I rub my palm in circles over her ass, then draw my hand back and release it again with a smack against her pale skin.

Her cry is soft and weak, born mostly from surprise, rather than pain. The white flesh of her ass turns a mottled pink. I caress it with my palm before bringing it back down for another smack. This time her cry is ringed with desperation.

"Shhh." I lower my lips to her ass, kissing the sting away. "You're being a good girl." I suck on my finger for a few seconds, then navigate it around her thong to find her back entrance. She moans as I press inside.

She is so tight I could probably come just from having my hands inside her. I gently pull my finger from her ass and spread her legs apart. Then I land one more smack, making sure to hit her pussy square-on.

Her cry this time is loud. I haul her upward so she's slumped against my shoulder, then I resume the work my fingers began.

Her pussy is drenched, soaking through her panties and into my jeans. Good. Now I can walk around with a reminder of her all day. I slide three fingers through her juices as she writhes on my lap.

"Hold still, baby," I murmur. I have one arm wrapped around her to keep her on my lap while the other finds her clit and strokes.

"Slate," she moans.

"I've got you." I push one finger deep inside her. She's so hot and so tight that I immediately add the second and third. The sucking sound they make as they move in and out is the equivalent of an angelic choir.

She quivers as I stroke her walls, a ball of nerves in my arms. Seconds later, she breaks, crying into my shoulder as the climax tears through her. My fingers pump into her hard as she rides it out.

When she's done, I remove my hand, wet with her arousal, and help her to her feet. We don't go far. I clear the center of my desk, then bend her over the surface. Her skirt has fallen down, but I am only too happy to lift it back up.

I don't even bother removing the thong. It feels raunchy and hot to fuck her while we're both still fully clothed, in my office with the door unlocked, but I'll need to be quick.

Fortunately, we stopped using condoms after both testing negative. She's been on birth control since she was twelve—something I refuse to think about without a punching bag nearby.

I open my pants, and my dick springs free. I fist it, then tug the strap of her thong to the side. She moans when my fingers slip inside. I want to tease her all day, but one of the guys could come looking for me any minute.

She's still so slick, ready for me to take her and fill her up.

So I do. Hard and fast. She grunts and shifts against the desk, but her feet stay firmly planted. I pull back out and use my now-lubricated cock to taunt her anal opening. She pushes back into me. There's no way she's ready to take all of me, but I press in half an inch.

She grinds against me, and I almost spill my load. I glide to her pussy and drive inside, deep. Her cry is music to my ears. I pound into her again and again, reaching around to torment her clit.

Every time I pull back out, I lose stamina, staying buried a little more, until we both break at the same time. She squeezes so tightly around my cock, my vision blurs. I collapse on top of her, breathless. "You're incredible," I say into her hair.

After a few minutes, her panting slows. "How incredible?" she asks.

I sense the trap she's laying for me, but I'm too fucked to care. "I'll give you anything in the world." I don't have the means to do so, but I'll sell every organ in my body if I have to.

She tightens around me once more. "I want my own parking spot."

<h1 style="text-align:center">47</h1>

"Here's to Us" - Halestorm

Lux

"Would you relax?" Slate looks at me from the driver's seat. "It'll be fine."

I shift in my seat again. "You don't know that."

He reaches over and clasps my knotted hands. "Then we'll cut out early."

"That's not allowed."

He throws his head back and laughs. "Your friends don't scare me."

My lips part in surprise. "I'm sorry, have you *met* Maeve?"

"Is that the little black-haired vixen?"

"She'll chop you up and eat you for breakfast."

We pull into the underground garage.

"I'm pretty sure I can handle her." He parks the car, then lifts my hands to his lips. "Trust me, okay? I'm actually very charming."

This makes me smile. "Not a word I would use to describe you."

"No?" He gets out and comes around the car to open my door. "Is it the long hair?"

"I think it's the surly attitude." I stand on tiptoes and press a kiss to his lips. "But I like both."

318

"Good thing." He slides both hands up my neck to my face, then leans me back against the car and takes my mouth in his. "Because you're mine."

My pulse spikes, and for a minute, there's only us in this garage, the rest of the world melted away. But then my phone jangles from my bag. Slate pulls back but doesn't let go of my face.

"That's probably Maeve, wondering where I am," I say.

"Let her," he says, and drops another kiss onto my lips. Then he releases me, because while he's more than willing to forget his own phone, he knows I can't rest if there's an unread message on mine.

Maeve: *Where are you?*

I show him the screen, and he rolls his eyes.

"When's the last time that woman got laid?"

We step onto the elevator, which moves faster than it ever has before, but that may be due to Slate's relentless kissing and groping. By some miracle, no one else joins us on our way to the twenty-second floor. When we reach the door of Pierce's flat, Slate's hand is still possessively clutching my middle.

"You might want to tamp down the PDA," I say.

"Why?" He nuzzles my neck from behind.

"My friends can be a little . . . judgmental."

"I thought we covered this. I am charm itself."

The problem isn't with Slate himself, per se, although that presents its own set of issues. It's that none of us bring significant others to poker night. *Ever.*

"Wait, you've never brought a guy to these games?" he says when I tell him this.

I shake my head and press the door buzzer. "Never." I dated Carter for a year and a half, and he never had more than a few conversations with my friends.

I wipe my sweaty palm on my dress right before Slate scoops it up in his. "But they know I'm coming, right?" he says as the door swings open.

Pierce grins at me, but then his eyes alight on Slate standing behind me. Then on our joined hands. Then back on me. By the time they meet mine again, the smile has slipped from his face. "Lux," he says, then steps back as Maeve barrels her way to the front door in a scarlet dress with a plunging neck.

"Finally," she says when she sees me. "We've been waiting for— Oh." She stops short when she sees Slate. Her eyes flick between the two of us, trying to determine why I've brought him.

"This is Slate," I tell them. "My boyfriend." We're still navigating the joining-of-two-worlds thing. So far, the only person who knows we're together is Briar. And now my friends.

I tug Slate past their gaping mouths and toward the game room. Walker and Heath are arguing like an old couple about whether they should put up wallpaper in the bathroom. Rhett has his feet propped on the table, toothpick dangling from his mouth as he scrolls on his phone. All three of them look up, then do a double take when they see Slate.

"I told you lot I might be bringing a guest," I say defensively as Pierce and Maeve follow us into the room.

"I thought you were referring to vodka." Rhett clambers to his feet and circles around the table to slap Slate on the back. "Good to see you, mate."

It's the most enthusiastic welcome anyone has given so far, but I didn't expect anything else.

Someone grabs another chair, and we start the game. We're playing five card draw, one of my least favorite poker variations. Things are as awkward as I expected, although I have to give Heath and Walker credit for trying to engage Slate in conversation. He doesn't win any favors by being good at poker, but fortunately only Pierce really cares about that.

Rhett has been unusually quiet tonight. I've tried to catch his eye several times, but every time I do, he just shoots me a small smile and looks back down at his cards.

We're nearing the end of the game. Walker has already folded, but Pierce and Slate are eyeing each other in a way that makes it evident neither of them has any intention of going down easily.

When Pierce begins another round of bidding, I fold. My cards aren't any good, and the way these two are betting, I don't stand a shot of winning anyway. I scoot closer to Slate so I can see what he's holding. Ace, queen, king, joker, and a jack. Holy shit. No wonder he's bidding like a crazy person.

Slate reaches for my leg under the table, letting his hand travel up the length of my thigh until he reaches the hem of my dress. I squirm, but his touch is possessive and insistent. Everyone else is too distracted to notice, thank god.

Maeve submits her masseuse for using the wrong oil and causing a rash, and Rhett throws his latest hookup into the pot for leaking a picture of him going down on her. But when the bidding reaches Slate, no one is prepared.

He shoves all of his chips into the center of the table with his free hand. "Carter Fitzgerald-Smythe."

I jerk my head around to see his face, leaning back as I do so.

He simply tightens his fingers on my leg and stares at Pierce.

"What for?" Pierce asks. There might be a question mark in his tone, but it also holds a note of quiet threat, not directed at Slate or me, but at my ex-boyfriend. I can see on Pierce's face that he dreads his suspicions being confirmed.

Slate's jaw flexes, and his grip on my thigh increases slightly. I wonder if it will bear the mark of his fingers tomorrow and if he's even aware he's doing it. "He abused Lux."

Maeve's mouth falls open, Walker lets out a small gasp, and Rhett scoots his chair back. "What?"

"Slate," I whisper. He could have asked me before submitting my ex-boyfriend for a revenge plot.

He glances at me. "He deserves it," he whispers back.

I blink because he's right. Carter is a fucking asshole. I'm embarrassed to not have seen it earlier, but my therapist says that's common for abuse victims.

As if he can read my thoughts, Slate eases up his grip and rubs my leg gently. "Let me do this for you," he murmurs. I give him a tiny nod, and he turns back to the rest of them. "He was physically, emotionally, and sexually abusive."

Every single one of them looks ready to tear Carter apart limb-by-limb.

"I asked you about those bruises," Pierce growls, looking at me.

I wince. He did, but at the time, I was still under the impression that everything Carter was doing to me was nothing less than I deserved.

"What's important," Slate says, "is that he can't hurt her anymore."

Maeve tosses her cards onto the table. "I'm in. Let's take that son-of-a-bitch down."

Pierce eyes Slate with a look that's less aggressive now than it had been. "What did you have in mind?" he asks.

Slate tosses me a quick glance before resting both arms on the table. "I have enough evidence we can plant to convince the authorities he's the most notorious drug dealer in the city."

* * *

If Slate's submission of Carter and subsequent revenge plot have done anything to warm my friends up to the idea of a new member joining our group, they would never explicitly say so. But if their posture and manner of speaking are any indication, I'd say he's won his way in fair and square.

We've spent the last hour hashing out the details for planting evidence that Carter is the Wolf. It's a brilliant plan, one that will not only prevent Slate from being hauled off to prison himself, but will put Carter exactly where he belongs.

Things are wrapping up when Rhett clears his throat and leans back in his chair. "I'm going on tour."

"Tour?" I say.

"That's fantastic, mate." Heath reaches across the table to bump fists with him.

"Yeah." Rhett smiles, but it doesn't reach his eyes. He fiddles with his cocktail glass, twisting it around on the tabletop. The toothpick in his mouth twitches up and down.

He signed with a record label last week, but a tour? That's huge.

Congratulations pile in. He soaks it all up, but he's fidgeting a lot more than usual. Something is definitely wrong.

Maeve doesn't look particularly pleased with this news. "How long will you be gone?"

"Six weeks."

She's calculating what this will do to our group, how our dynamic will change with the addition of Slate and the loss of Rhett.

"It's not forever," Rhett assures her.

She doesn't need to say what she's thinking. It won't be the same. When his tour is over, who knows how things will have changed? Is this the end of poker nights as we know them?

"What do we think about the Princess Royal's fiancé?" Heath asks in an uncharacteristic gush of words. Rhett shoots him an appreciative glance.

Maeve launches into a tirade against Princess Beatrice's choice. Rhett's face shows no sign of remorse over his ex-girlfriend moving on. Rehab really has changed him. He excuses himself to the kitchen for a refill. I squeeze Slate's hand and move to follow him.

Rhett's pouring whiskey into a shot glass when I get there.

"Hey." I lean against the counter and watch him. "Everything okay?"

He tosses the shot back and wipes his mouth. "Why wouldn't it be?"

"You didn't seem as thrilled about the tour as I would have expected."

He's wearing a large Hawaiian shirt and a pair of loose white jeans. But even with his cool exterior, I can tell there's something he's not telling me. "I'm excited."

"Rhett." I place a hand on his arm, causing him to finally meet my eyes. "Isn't this everything you've ever wanted?" For as long as I've known him, he hasn't shut up about making it big in the music world the way his dad did.

"Of course it is." He spins the shot glass on the wooden countertop. "It's just—" He shoves his hand into his hair instead of finishing his sentence.

"Just what?"

His eyes flit to mine, then he drops his gaze again. "I'm scared."

I can't help the way my mouth drops open. "You're scared," I echo. I haven't seen Rhett scared. *Ever.* Not even when he was nearly arrested.

"I've been clean for four months."

"And you think the tour will mess with that?"

"Do you know what it's like out there?"

"Not really." But I can form a pretty vivid picture. "But that doesn't mean you have to be a part of it, does it?"

He shakes his head. "The pressure—it's intense."

The pieces are starting to click into place. Rhett has never been able to handle not being liked. Going on tour means saying no to the one thing that could determine his acceptance.

"What if you took someone with you?" I say. "To help?"

"Help with what?"

"To, like, help you say no?"

"What, like a handler?"

"Sort of." I shrug. "Someone to remind you of why you're clean in the first place."

He looks up from the speck he's scratching on the counter. "I don't need a babysitter."

I roll my eyes. "My god, Rhett. That's not what I was suggesting. Just a mate to stand beside you."

"I don't know. People will get suspicious. The record label can't find out about the rehab."

I lick my lips. It makes sense, but at the cost of potentially going back to addiction? An idea blossoms. "What if your handler was a girl?"

"You mean so I could bang her instead of shooting up?"

I cool my expression. "Of course not. But what if you let people think you were dating? As a way to explain her presence."

The corner of his mouth lifts into a mild sneer. "A fake relationship." The idea settles itself into his mind like a dog before a nap.

"Exactly."

"That could be . . . fun." His eyes have taken on a particularly devious sparkle.

Oh god, what have I started? "If you can find someone for the job," I add.

A cocky smile lights up his face. "I already have the perfect person in mind."

* * *

To read an alternate ending to the one bed scene from Lux's POV, visit jessicajude.com/queen-of-vengeance-bonus for a spicy bonus chapter.

Keep reading for an exclusive chapter of the next book in the Hand of Revenge series!

Excerpt from Book 3

Do all men take this long to shit? Standing outside the bathroom, the only room in the whole flat with a door, I knock. "You're going to be late," I call through the thin wood.

Nate mutters something incomprehensible.

I move into the kitchen and pop open the ibuprofen bottle, then shake a few into my hand and toss them back. I'm washing them down with tap water when he finally emerges, forty-five minutes after retreating inside. I bite my tongue before a passive-aggressive "finally" can slip out.

He slings his deployment bag over his shoulder, eyes on the phone in his hand. "Guess this is it, then."

"I guess so." I edge around the kitchen counter.

He looks good in his uniform, almost exactly like he did when we first met a few years ago. Tall, close-cropped brown hair, blue eyes that promise the world. Over his shoulder I spot our wedding photo, taken on the steps of the courthouse. Just two fools who thought love could conquer all.

As if reminding me, a stab of pain shoots through my mouth. "Before you go—" I say.

He glances up from the screen, trying to mask his irritation, but I catch a glimpse of it behind that cool veneer.

"This toothache is getting worse. Is there enough in the bank to cover a dentist visit?"

He blinks twice, then lets out a mocking chuckle. "You have a job.

Two, actually."

My lips part in surprise, an old instinct that hasn't fully worn off yet. I swallow the bile I feel rising in my throat. "I work for a nonprofit. It doesn't exactly pay well."

He slips his phone into his pocket and shifts his bag higher on his shoulder. "And whose choice is that?"

"Nate," I say as he heads for the front door.

He stops with his hand on the knob but doesn't turn around.

"It'll probably just be a few hundred," I add.

His fingers turn white as they clench the gaudy brass handle. "Yeah, well I don't have a few hundred."

I cross my arms over my chest, unable to help myself. "Don't tell me the last paycheck is already gone."

Finally, he turns, but only to glare at me. "That's my money, okay?" He points a finger at my chest. "I work hard for it. I don't just play around on social media all day." The corner of his mouth rises in a sneer. "If you want money to see the dentist, maybe you should get a real job."

I should be used to the pain of his words by now, but it still manages to catch me off guard as it slams into me. Squeezing my arms tighter around my midsection, I fill my voice with ice. "My work is important."

"Yeah, making a bunch of losers feel better about themselves."

"When did you become such an asshole?"

He narrows his eyes and pretends to think about this. "Maybe around the time I married you."

I clench my jaw tightly, stifling the tears that badly want to spring up. He's right, and we both know it. Neither of us was like this before. The last three years have been hellish, tolerable only when he's on tour. Which he has been most of the time, fortunately.

"I'm sorry, babe." Dropping his pack onto the floor, he strides toward me. His long legs eat up the space in two steps. He pulls me into his arms and, not caring that I'm still stiff as a board, just tucks my head beneath his chin. "That was shit of me to say."

Something melts inside me, draining away the animosity. For just a second, I allow myself to imagine the old Nate, the one I fell in love with at twenty-one. Back when I was a stupid girl who decided to get married because she thought she'd found someone who wanted the same things from life as her.

I sniff the rough fabric of his uniform where it's scratching my cheek. We met when he was on leave, started writing letters like we were in a Nicholas Sparks movie, and visited the courthouse the next time he was home, without having spent any real time together.

There's something intoxicating about young love. It convinces you that you're the only two people in the world to ever have experienced these emotions, that no one could possibly have felt the way you do before now, because if they had, how would they ever have gotten anything done?

I lean away from him, letting my hands run along his arms before dropping them at my sides. "Take care." My words are soft, but they are sincere. As much as I don't enjoy living with my husband, I don't want anything to happen to him.

"I will." He straightens his shoulders, his hand hesitating in the air as if he plans to tuck my hair behind my ear. At the last second, he brings it back down. "You too."

Pain bleeds through me. How did we end up here? I can still smell the bath salts he used to add to the bubble baths he drew for me. I can still feel his hands on my shoulders, rubbing out the tight knots after I'd worked a twelve-hour shift on the hotline.

He lifts his bag and slings it back over his shoulder. "Guess I'll see you when I see you."

"Yeah," I croak. "Be safe."

I can't remember the last time we said "I love you" to each other. The phrase fell out of our vocabulary the same way you fall out of a boat.

Nate opens the door and walks out, tossing me a quick glance before disappearing.

I pause in the doorway, listening to his footsteps on the stairs leading down to the car park. Should I have gone with him? Seen him off at the base? That's what a real military wife would do, isn't it? But it's been a long time since I felt like a wife and not a prisoner in a jail cell of my own making.

I move toward the 1950s dresser I thrifted soon after we moved in. The attached mirror is cracked right through the center, making my reflection look like something from a fun house.

I inherited my tight black curls from my Black dad and my turned-up nose from my Polish mum. My brown skin is a mix of both of them, along with my love of books—hence the teetering stacks throughout the room.

My jewelry box, a gift from my grandma, is sitting on top of the scratched surface. Twisting the ring on my left hand several times, I take a deep breath, tug it off, and tuck it into the box with the other trinkets. The old friendship bracelet I made at summer camp still lives there, tattered and faded after all these years, but I can't seem to toss it out. Nate accuses me of being sentimental as though it's a crime against humanity.

Opening the top drawer of the dresser, I pull out an oversized Pink Floyd tee. Before I close it again, I lift up the stack of shirts. It's still there—the crisp manilla envelope holding my freedom. I extract it and peek inside. "From the Desk of the Court of Family Affairs" parades across the top of the page. Nate's and my names are listed beneath it, along with the date of our impromptu wedding.

My phone blares from the kitchen counter, and I shove the documents back into the envelope before returning it to the bottom of the drawer. It's time to leave for work, and I'm not even dressed yet. Signing divorce papers will have to come later.

* * *

I dash up the stairs to the suite I've worked in for the past five years. You would think after all this time I would remember about the loose rubber strip at the top, but it trips me for the millionth time.

During my second year at university, in the evenings after my classes, I started volunteering at Restore Hope Initiative's crisis hotline. Nearly two years ago, they offered me an internship position, and I accepted, much to Nate's disapproval. I create content for our social media accounts that promotes mental health and addiction awareness, with the added purpose of trying to catch the eye of potential donors.

It's definitely not what I saw myself doing when I first started at uni. I was going to be a teacher like both of my parents. It was an easy way to make them happy, and I knew I would have no trouble getting a job at a local school. Teachers are harder to hold on to than wet fish. But after a few weeks working the hotline, I knew I had found my calling. I switched my major to communications and haven't looked back since.

I skid to a halt in front of the administrator's door and adjust my beanie. There's an unidentifiable smudge on my combat boots that I probably got on the train. I wipe it off with my palm, then straighten.

Sondra looks up from her desk when I rap on the doorjamb. "Hey, girl." She waves a hand. "Come on in."

I know I'm lucky when it comes to bosses. Sondra is the best.

"Sorry I'm late. Nate left this morning."

She tucks a loose strand of blond hair into a ponytail that's already messy, despite it only being eight in the morning. She blames her regularly disheveled state on her two kids running her ragged before they head for school. "For a second there, I thought you meant for good."

I exhale a tiny puff of air through my nose.

"I'm sorry," she says. "I just don't see why you're still married to that jerk."

Nausea swirls in my belly, churning the contents around until I can feel my breakfast rising. I tamp it down and force my lips into a smile. "It's complicated."

Sondra removes her reading glasses and holds them out to the side as if asking "And?"

"I loved him. Once."

Gnawing on the end of the earpiece, she lifts a single brow.

I sigh. "I need the housing stipend. And the health insurance." I hate admitting this out loud, especially to my boss, who is already fully aware of how little I make working here.

She closes her eyes. "I know your paycheck isn't large, but if that scumbag wouldn't gamble it all away—"

"I know," I rush to assure her. "The papers are drawn up."

She tosses her glasses onto the desk. "It's about time."

"They're just not filed yet."

"Then get your ass in gear and get it done."

I take a deep breath and release it. "I will. Soon. I need to open a personal checking account first."

"Saylor." She blinks at me. "You haven't done that yet?"

"I didn't have enough until now." The bank requires a thousand dollars to open one. It's taken me four months of selling my old clothes and things around the flat to save it up. "I'm going over there on my lunch break."

I used to have my own account. But when we got married, Nate told me his credit score was shit. Bad enough that none of the local banks would let him open one. I agreed to add his name to mine, giving him access to both the money in it and my good standing with the bank. I lost control of it—and the money—soon after.

"That man will bring you down if you don't get out," Sondra says.

"You don't think it's cruel to file for divorce while he's on tour?"

She cocks her brow again.

"What if something happened to him because of it?" I add.

"Let me tell you something." She steeples her hands in front of her. "You are not responsible for that man. You're not responsible for anyone but yourself."

I fiddle with a string hanging from my distressed denim shorts. This feels a lot like a lecture from my parents.

"Just because he doesn't respect you, doesn't mean you shouldn't respect yourself," Sondra says.

Raising my head enough to meet her eyes, I nod. I know she's right. I also know she'll kick my ass if I don't do something about it. "I'll file the papers."

***King of Obsession* coming November 2025! Pre-order today and get your copy on November 4th!**

* * *

If you're in a reading slump after that or just want more of the same, you might want to try the *Queen of Wesbourne* trilogy, starting with *Thrones We Steal*, or the first book in this series, *Ace of Betrayal*, if you haven't read Heath and Walker's story yet.

Join Jessica Jude's email list to be notified when new books launch and to receive more exclusive bonus content. Visit <u>JessicaJude.com/ Newsletter</u> to sign up.

Acknowledgments

To Jesus, with whom I've never been too much or not enough, and who loves to remind me I'm the perfect amount.

To the love of my life, Curtis, for believing in me, for being the first to read my stories, for being willing to sell the hypothetical farm that you'd much rather keep, in order to fund this crazy dream of mine—I'll never stop loving you.

To my family, who say they're proud of me all the time and whom I definitely do not deserve and will recklessly love forever.

To Melinda, for not only being the world's best sister but also the best PA I could have asked for. So excited to take this adventure with you at my side! Love you to the moon and back.

To Jenny dePierre, my incredible editor, who sprinkles magic fairy dust all over my words and makes them sing. Don't ever leave me.

To Haya in Designs for making a gorgeous cover I still can't get over. To Rumaisa and Rachel, you're both so incredibly talented. Thank you for bringing Lux and Slate to life. I'll cherish your artwork forever.

To my incredible Facebook group moderators: Madeline Hovey, Macy Holt, Andriana Callahan, Althea Gutierrez, Heidi Lauper, Kimberley Knott, and Sarah Whymer. I don't know what I'd do without you!

To Jensen Sly for helping with sensitivity issues and warnings. Your feedback is invaluable! And to Kelly Renee, Catherine, and Emma Williams for catching several doors ajar.

To Isabella Romine for teaching me more about cars than I could have dreamed. Chapter 28 is for you, babe.

To my Swiftie Squad, who will never let me down when I need the perfect Taylor song and basically told me to include the entire *Reputation* album in the playlist:

- "I Did Something Bad" – Kennedy Ridgeway, Ang Labuda, Charlena Jaclyn Doral, Bella, Kris West, Alana Tomlin Denton, Gurmeher kaur, Pages with Pearl, Chante, Nisma Basheer, and Brittany Crum.
- "Vigilante Shit" – Jackie Gill, Arbin pajiyar, Janell, Maddie, Amber Coughlin, Leanne Alex, Kayleigh Hyder, Bridget Flannagan, Danielle Assadourian, and Sheesha.
- "Look What You Made Me Do" (an honorable mention since it's already on Ace of Betrayal's playlist) – Harley Peterson, Sophie Spataro, JennJa, Emilee Decker, Stacy Durbin, Taylor O'Brien, Morgan Kearney, Angela Green-Carter, Cyenne Cross, Alesha, Gina, Danielle Agnello, Renee Thomason, Bethany Boyd, Nadine Le Blanc, Jenny's Book Corner, and Hannah Hawthorne.
- "I Knew You Were Trouble" – Maddy Van Damme, Stacey Niedzwiecki, Iris Wallace, Elizabeth Rudloff, Gracie Williams, and Casey DeMoss.
- "Bad Blood" – Grace Dringenburg, Kelsey Messmer, Elizabeth Kaiser, Courtney Wood, Jennifer Lucas, Alexis DeCorby, Naomi K., Soundcheck, Alex Watkins, Rhea Lal, and Cathyvon.
- "I Can Do It With a Broken Heart" – Kaitlyn Haraphongse, Meg Pinho, Ashley Merwin, Kaitlyn Miller, and Rebecca Parkin.
- And to the rest of the Taylor-loving squad: Brandy Frank, Sumaiya Tharif, Haydlee Jefferson, Cortnie Taylor, Kylie Lacy, Taylor Johnson, Randi Lynn, Ali Willos, Meaghan, Stace, Lya Riley, Melanie Beard, Kimberley Jane, Paola Castillo, Billie Bee, Mariana Miller, Krystal-Ann Gilmore, Maddi, Holley Lentner, Tara Baas,

Brittany Wingler, Jamie-Leigh wood, Brynley Kinane, Chelsea MacRae, Sanne Unicorn, and Moa Isaksson.

To the babes who understood that "Face Down" by The Red Jumpsuit Apparatus was the only appropriate song choice for Lux and Carter: Julie Persinger, Thaiyah Sharell, Danyele Henson, Valissa, Taylor Lawson, Victoria Franklin, **A**lbum, Laquita Agwiak, and Faith Hadcock.

To those who submitted some absolutely perfect songs for the book: Laine Taffs, Kayla Gonzalez, Caileigh (@thrillandthrone), Natascha Høvsgaard, Jamie Reynolds, Megan Thorn, Jamie Houlton, Leslie Hutchings, Ashley, Mackenzie Alexander, and Alicia Hudson.

Another honorable mention for those who suggested "Poker Face" by Lady Gaga–a perfect fit, but it's already in *Ace of Betrayal* and I'm OCD like that: Irais, Aimee Burath, Angela Jenkins, and Sheena S.

To the Sleep Token fanclub, thank you for introducing me: Emma Errickson, **Y**ell, Hillary Van Petten, Amy Lowe, Heidi, Emily Abrams Lockett, Kenzie Payne, Nadine Sturgill, K Marks, Carolyn Firth, Elisa Estrada, Ariel Bullock, Kerri Mrozinski, Bianca Hinton, and Zoe Escott.

To the Guardians of Grammar and the Plothole Police, for helping me put out the cleanest manuscript possible: Emma Reed, Allison Malin, Haley Johnson, Kitty, Alisha Perez, Meggan, Keeley Warters, Phoebe M.C., Savannah Luppino, Katie, Angela Jenkins, Jessica Taylor, Krystal Gabbert, Brittany Molebash, Samantha F, Katie Bessire, Sara Roub, Afton Freed, Leah Taylor, **L**yrics, Laura Monaghan, Michaella King, Chelsea Judge, Jess Dizon, Samantha Dávila, Mica V, Kassandra Q, Sharon Reed, Krisie Stocker, Emily Hall, Geisol Torres, Alana Hodges, Sumaiya Tharif, Miya H., Cheyenne Pawlowski, Grace Aston, Danielle odlum, Nicole Parish, Shellie D., Alexis Ford, Marcella Loza, and Sam Nicole.

To my scene queens for helping me figure out which ones are

gold: Chelsea Heron, Carley Brummell, Alexus Silva, Emily Garkow, Ashley Dalley, Cassie Petty, Kayla Bautista, Ky Weigh, Meg Mo, Kassie McElfresh, Sami, Makayla Rae McCutcheon, Emily Jones, Caitlin Isley, Vanessa Ortiz, Rachel Cavanah, Virginia, Olivia Adams, Chantel Donegan, Lily Carvell, Julia Spaller, Nicole Singh, Sydney Baker, Sondra Macias, Kat Carlile, Christiana Camacho, Angelica Rodriguez, Alicia, Ashley Sunderland, Onstage, Molly Binfield, and Bethany Gibbs.

To the quotation nation for hitting me with all of your favorite lines from the book: Macy Fleetwood, Wendy Kern, Jeanine Rohde, Alexis R Biddie, Demi Heinrich, Lara Gerson, Jessica Oberembt, Cass Gesinghaus, Shyanne P, Milica, and Lena Kozlova.

To everyone who introduced me to new music, you're officially hired as my personal DJs: Carmen Gonser, Madi Walters, Abby, Ashley, Katie, Nini, Bailey, Jemma Cavanagh, Riley Provo-Scott, Isabel, Maxi, Taylor Rowland, Fiona Cole, Britt, Victoria Breen, Sarah Cotterman, Annette Evans, Jeanette, Ashley Trusty, Linsey Langenberg, Roadie, Hailey Jackson, Jorie L., Sairen, Brandt Stuart AKA Fizzin Fly Girl, Bernice Gresham, Mackenzie Alexander, and Morgan DeGruchy O'Connor.

To my entire ARC squad, of whom there are far too many of you to name individually, for believing in this book and these characters and for launching them into the world with so much love and gusto.

And to everyone who has taken a chance on this story, thank you for helping my dreams come true. Eight-year-old Jessica still can't believe it.

Also by Jessica Jude

Hand of Revenge Series
Ace of Betrayal
King of Obsession (coming November 2025)

They're rich. They're reckless. They're out for revenge.
A group of wealthy Gen Zers plays poker to determine the victims of
their weekly revenge plots. What they don't bargain on? Falling in
love with the people who could destroy them.

Queen of Wesbourne Trilogy
Thrones We Steal
Castles We Storm
Crowns We Save

Magnolia Parks meets The Princess Diaries in this angsty, slow burn
trilogy that will take you on an emotional roller coaster and leave you
completely wrecked.
They want me to marry him. I know he's gorgeous and charming and
his voice makes your body sing. I know he's the bloody crown prince.
I know you think I'm crazy for hesitating. But you don't know him
like I do. You don't know what he did.

About the Author

Jessica Jude loves nothing better than sending her characters on an emotional roller coaster of love, angst, and drama, but in reality her life is very ordinary, drama-free, and probably boring to anyone watching. (Which would be weird. And creepy.)

She married her high school sweetheart at nineteen. Being an author is a dream she's had since she was six years old and wrote her first book, which was ten pages long, about a girl named Mary getting lost in the woods. (It was never published, but good news: Mary was eventually rescued.) When she's not writing, she's reading, reading about writing, or eating ice cream. In another life, she would live in England in a sprawling manor house with hidden passages and secret stairways, but for now, she's content with her old brick farmhouse in the Midwestern United States.

Still a fan? Here are some ways you can ~~stalk~~ stay connected!

JessicaJude.com/newsletter

Instagram @JessicaJudeBooks

Threads @JessicaJudeBooks

TikTok @JessicaJudeBooks

Discussion Questions

1. What do you think drove Slate to make the decisions he did? Was he justified in doing so?
2. How do you feel about Lux's response to Slate's revelation?
3. Do you agree that not every choice is black or white? Why or why not?
4. Do you think Lux's rage over her brother was justified? Why or why not?
5. What did you think about the relationships depicted in the book?
6. How did you feel about the theme of revenge in this book?
7. Contrast Lux's disdain for those she dubs beneath her with her loyalty toward her brother and friends.
8. What scene in Queen of Vengeance made the biggest emotional impact on you and why?
9. What quote or moment haunts you?

Want the rest of the book club kit? Visit jessicajude.com/bonuses to download a full kit to share with your club, as well as the rest of the bonuses for this book.